W

1. **This book may be kept three weeks. It is to be returned on / before the last date stamped below.**
2. **A fine of 20p will be charged for every week or part of week a book is overdue.**

CRESCENDO

CRESCENDO

MARY McCARTHY

POOLBEG

Published 1998 by
Poolbeg Press Ltd,
123 Baldoyle Industrial Estate,
Dublin 13, Ireland

© Mary McCarthy 1998

The moral right of the author has been asserted.

The Arts Council
An Chomhairle Ealaíon

A catalogue record for this book is available from the British Library.

ISBN 1 85371 857 2

Cover photography by Attard
Cover design by Poolbeg Group Services Ltd
Set by Poolbeg Group Services Ltd in Garamond 10/13.5
Printed and bound in Great Britain by
Cox & Wyman Ltd, Reading, Berkshire.

Note on the Author

Mary McCarthy is a secondary teacher in Dublin. Her first novel, the best-selling *Remember Me,* was published by Poolbeg in 1996. This was followed by *And No Bird Sang* in 1997. *Crescendo* is her third novel.

Also by Mary McCarthy

Remember Me
And No Bird Sang

Published by Poolbeg

Acknowledgements

As usual, I am indebted to many people who gave freely of their time and expertise to answer my questions and offer advice.

I would like to thank the following:

John Doyle, Marie Moran, Maeve O'Reilly, Orla Strumble, my friends in school from the Music Department (Nuala, Marie and Fran) and the German Department (Susan and Nuala).

My family, friends and colleagues who supported and encouraged me through the bad times and good – particularly Dara Mac who ran up and down the stairs morning, noon and night – bringing me the vital cups of coffee!

A special word of thanks must go to Pauline Gildea, who painstakingly and enthusiastically read the script and offered invaluable advice.

This book is dedicated with love and gratitude to the memory of Kate Cruise O'Brien, editor and friend.
I miss Kate dearly.

CRESCENDO

Prelude

The dream was always the same.

Alone in the locked room, she stood at the window, staring forlornly out at the pitch-dark garden. The bare trees stretched their branches eerily up to a starless sky. She was afraid.

Trapped.

A silver candelabra on the baby grand housed four milky-white candles which shimmered in the autumn darkness. Trance-like, she approached the piano stool.

The music book on the stand was waiting for her. A gentle breeze blew the pages mysteriously, magically, lifting and turning them. The book fell open at Mozart's "Fantasia in D Minor", her favourite piece.

Kismet, she told herself, and began to play.

In the candlelight, her fingers glided masterfully over the ivory and ebony keys. The opening *arpeggios* sang out roundly, smoothly. Outside it began to rain.

The key creaked in the lock.

She heard the footsteps behind her but she didn't stop playing. Nothing could stop her and nothing could stop what was about to happen.

The short semiquavers of the *Adagio* lulled her momentarily. The music was alive, it flowed, poured, pulsated through her veins. Higher and higher she soared. The rain got heavier and dashed against the glass of the window-panes, some of it splashed into the room and soaked the curtains and the wooden sill.

His shadow loomed on the wall in front of her.

"Michelle!" he whispered. "Michelle!"

The shadow grew longer, larger. The wind grew stronger, wilder, and the storm swelled outside.

"Michelle!"

She shuddered as he crept up behind her. The curtains flapped and the candles flickered out, plunging her into blackness. His cold hands closed around her throat.

The dream was always the same and it haunted her for years.

One

Michelle Bolger made herself comfortable in the taxi as the driver took charge of her luggage. She was excited. Weeks of planning, organising, last-minute arrangements . . . at last she was here.

Vienna.

She took off her white jacket. The day was hot, very hot. But overcast. Pity the sun wasn't shining – grey days were for Ireland, not Austria.

The taximan got in and turned to her. *"Wohin möchten Sie gehen?"*

Oh dear.

"Sprechen Sie Englisch?" she asked hopefully.

"Nein." He shook his head politely. *"Es tut mir leid."*

Michelle enunciated each syllable slowly as she showed him the page of her diary where she'd scribbled down the address.

A smile of recognition. "Ah, Weihburggasse."

"Yes." Michelle nodded. "Weihburggasse."

He started the car, pulled out without indicating and bullied his way into the line of heavy traffic leaving the airport. They crawled along until they reached the motorway and then the driver put the boot down.

She could have been leaving any airport – Dublin, London, Paris – any city in Europe or the States. Roads to the left and the right, above and below, criss-crossed the landscape. However much they helped to speed up travel, motorways were all the same, functional and boring.

The taxi-driver accelerated again and switched on the radio. Good, a Strauss waltz or a Mozart concerto to put her in the mood. Maybe a motet from the Vienna Boys' Choir? Not a bit of it! "It's Such a Perfect Day"! Michelle had to smile. He must have put on an English station for her benefit.

She stared out of the passenger window and watched the broad expanse of fields with their nondescript, factory-like buildings and grey-black smoke billowing up to join the gathering clouds. Lanes of cars, buses and lorries whizzed alongside, honking horns. The driver swerved to avoid a motorbike and cursed under his breath. You didn't have to be bilingual to hazard a guess at what he'd said.

It was stifling in the car despite the air-conditioning, but she didn't have enough German to ask the driver to open a window. All she'd practised was "Please" and "Thank you", "I'd like to book a table" and "Could you tell me where the post office is?"

Soon they were on the outer ring road of the city.

"Schottenring," the driver shouted back to her.

He drove down a wide boulevard clustered with tall, graceful buildings, some very ornate with cornices and sharp angles, others plain and simpler in design. This is what Ken had been telling her about yesterday – all the different types of architecture side by side, a mishmash of all ages and styles . . .

"I'd love to be able to go with you, Mich, but the hotel's jam-packed at the moment. There's no chance of my getting away."

"August's one of your busiest months, Ken. I didn't expect you to come."

He stroked her shoulder. She was warm, glowing from their recent lovemaking. Sex with Ken was always good but when they knew they were going to be separated, it took on a kind of urgency. They'd spend hours in bed before he went away on a business trip, trying to make up for the time they'd lose.

"I'm going to miss you like hell," he said.

"I'll miss you, too."

"No, you won't. You'll be dashing around like a mad thing. There's so much to see, Mich."

"I've made a list of what I'm going to do. I've only three days' sightseeing before the classes begin."

"Don't miss the Kunsthistorisches, the collection's terrific. Holbein, Van Dyck, Rubens, Vermeer – "

"I don't know, Ken, when we went to Paris last

summer we didn't get to see a quarter of the paintings in the Louvre. I won't have that much time."

She squirmed with pleasure as he lightly brushed her nipples with the tips of his fingers. "Anyhow, I'm not an art buff like you and Beth."

"Well, I still think the gallery's worth a visit." He stretched out to the bedside table and handed her a half-drunk glass of wine.

"Ugh, this is warm," she protested.

He laughed and took the glass from her. "No sense wasting it." He dipped a finger in the wine and lovingly smeared her breasts. Then he bent his head and licked her slowly.

She moaned softly as his hand travelled down over her tummy. She opened her legs wider . . .

"Votivkirche," the driver announced, pointing to a magnificent gothic church. Before she'd time to see it properly, he pointed again. "Rathaus." She hunched down in the seat to get a better view of the parliament building.

"Universität. Justizpalast. Burgtheater."

They were gone in the blink of an eye.

She'd have to come back here and take a stroll around tomorrow morning, bright and early, in the sunshine. Some of the buildings looked quite melancholy, but perhaps it was because it was such a dull afternoon.

Tuesdays were definitely grey. And this one was

greyer than most. It was just her luck that she'd planned her walking tour of the Innere Stadt for this evening. Tomorrow, no doubt, the sun would be splitting the stones. Wednesdays were bright orange, Thursdays blue, Fridays yellow, Saturdays black.

Did other people do that, have colours for the days of the week? Michelle had always seen Sundays as red, Mondays white but Tuesdays were grey – she didn't like grey.

The taximan continued to point out buildings and monuments as they flew by. He chattered on, gesticulating and laughing every now and again. She hadn't a clue what he was talking about but she made polite sounds which seemed to gratify him. Michelle suspected that this grand tour was taking them a good bit out of their way, but she didn't mind. It was a nice introduction to Vienna.

They arrived in the city centre and he drove slowly up the busy Kärtnerstrasse, to allow Michelle the opportunity to gaze out at the expensive-looking shops with their colourful window displays, the pretty cafés and restaurants.

It was a very elegant city.

They passed the majestic Staatsoper and Michelle resolved to come back to Vienna when the opera season began again. She'd persuade Ken to take a long weekend off work. She'd give her eye-teeth to go to a performance of *Don Giovanni* or *The Marriage of Figaro*.

Minutes later the driver turned right into Weihburggasse.

This was to be her base for the next ten days and Michelle was thrilled that it was so central. She was right in the heart of the city, it'd be like staying in the Shelbourne at home.

She got out of the taxi and inhaled deeply. Coffee – that's what she smelled. It wasn't unlike the smell of the hops from the Guinness Brewery.

The Albany Hotel was tall and grey-stoned, sandwiched between other four-storey buildings of the same type, not quite as stylish as the Shelbourne. The glass entrance-door was wide and welcoming with potted ferns on each side. The taximan carried her luggage up the steps, tipped his cap and beamed when she refused to take the change from her fare.

The receptionist checked the register. "Yes, Ms Bolger. You're in room twenty on the second floor." He handed her a key. "I'll get someone to bring up your luggage."

"No, there's no need. I've only one suitcase and this briefcase. I'll manage."

"Sure?"

He had big brown eyes and a lovely smile.

"Absolutely."

"You're Irish? I know you'll probably laugh at this, but my grandmother's Irish. My father's mother. She's from Kerry, somewhere near Killarney, I think."

"A lot of Americans have Irish ancestors," Michelle said amiably.

"My name's Geoff McCabe. I'm working here for the

summer. I'm studying hotel management back in Boston."

Ken always told her that any man who was involved in the hotel business was by nature a good egg! This Geoff was certainly friendly.

"You're staying for ten days?"

"That's right, I'm here for master-classes," she told him.

Another big grin. "You're a musician?"

"I teach piano," she said, smiling back. His smile was infectious.

"I envy you. Music must be a great life if you've the talent. I took up the trombone when I was a kid. I was useless but they wanted trombones for the school band so I joined up. My dad said that was a good move since I was full of hot air!"

Michelle laughed. "I'm not starting my classes till Saturday but I came over early. I'd like to see as much of Vienna as I can."

"These will help you." He picked up some brochures from the counter. "A few of the composers' museums. Schubert, Hadyn, Beethoven – I guess they're what you'll want to see?"

"Mmh, especially the Figarohaus – I adore Mozart."

"Ah, you're in luck." He handed her another leaflet. "It's in Domgasse, only a five-minute walk from here. Most of the places you'll want to visit are in or around the Innere Stadt. The best way to see Vienna is on foot."

"That's what my boyfriend says," Michelle replied.

9

"Ken's a great one for walking. Last year we took his daughter, Beth, to Paris. We spent hours in the Louvre but a morning of studying the paintings was quite enough for me. I left them to it and went shopping – they're both big into art."

"The Kunsthistorisches is fabulous," he said.

"So Ken told me but I don't think I'll have time. What about the Belvedere Palace? There's a gallery there, isn't there?"

"Two, one in the upper palace and the other in the lower. The two palaces are linked by gardens you can walk through. You'll like the gardens. Are you interested in modern art?"

"Not really," Michelle confessed.

"Well then, your best bet is to visit the lower palace – that's where they house the eighteenth-century baroque. And there's the medieval collection in the Orangerie."

"Is the palace far from here?"

"No, you get the subway at Karlsplatz and then streetcar D. The transport here is very good."

"It might take me a while to get my bearings," Michelle said. "I don't know how I'm going to fare on my own. I usually have Ken to rely on – he likes organising."

"You'll be OK, it's a compact city," he assured her. "You couldn't get lost if you tried."

"You don't know me!"

"Take this map – it's very detailed. If you start with St Stephen's Cathedral – see it there in the middle just beside my finger. Hey, you must have spotted it from the taxi."

"I caught a glimpse of the roof, the coloured tiles are – "

"Aren't they spectacular? You could spend an hour just looking up at the roof. But, like I say, if you start from there, it's easy to plan your routes. You should take a trip up to the observation platform on top. You'll get a super view of the whole city . . . that's if it doesn't rain, of course."

"Please! Don't even mention rain! I've just come from Ireland!"

"Well, we've had some very hot weather for the past week and here that's often followed by a downpour. The weather in Vienna's a bit unpredictable."

Her room was big and bright: blue carpet and curtains, blue-and-white matching duvet and pillow-cases. She plonked her suitcase on the bed and went to have a good look around. Large bathroom with toilet, bidet, shower and large white bath; white towels and a fluffy white bathrobe on the back of the door; pale blue tiles on the floor and around the bath. On the shelf by the sink were all sorts of toiletries: shampoo, shower gel, a shower cap, tissues, body lotion, even paper slippers!

Back to the bedroom. Michelle opened up the huge built-in wardrobe – plenty of space for her clothes, an upper shelf for her suitcase and extra blankets on the lower shelf. No need for them in this heat.

There was a small television on a trolley in a corner, a coffee table with a bowl of fruit, a small sofa covered in the same material as the curtains and a minibar.

The hotel was deluxe, expensive, plush – a luxury Michelle could never have afforded on her salary. Ken had insisted on paying for her stay here.

She walked over to the floor-to-ceiling window and opened the top wider to let in more air. She looked out on the street. Directly opposite were another large hotel, a cake shop and what looked like a pharmacy.

So, here she was at last, ensconced in her hotel room in Vienna. She glanced at her watch. Seven-thirty. She was tired but excited after her day's travelling – a plane to Heathrow, two hours of a wait and then the long flight here. She'd have a soak in a perfumed bubble bath, wrap herself in the bathrobe and rest for an hour.

The remote control beside her bed, a brandy from the minibar and her diary out to plan her three days of sightseeing and self-indulgent living before her classes began.

She'd eat in the hotel tonight and have a quick stroll in the Inner Stadt to familiarise herself with the place – start her exploration of the city in the morning.

Two

Wednesday morning was not bright orange – it was a murky grey! Michelle sat at a table by the window in the sixth-floor café of the glass-and-marble Haas-Haas shopping centre. She would have had a perfect view of the western façade of St Stephen's Cathedral, had it not been for the torrential rain. Viennese rain is hard, cutting, vengeful – as she'd just found out. She'd spent the morning nipping in and out of the expensive shops in the Kärntnerstrasse, pricing jewellery, admiring the leather goods and porcelain and browsing in bookshops. She'd invested in an umbrella – her only purchase.

She smiled at the girl who came to take her order.

"Einen Kaffee, ohne Milch, bitte . . . und ein Stück Sachertorte."

Coffee and chocolate cake. Sinful. The waitress had the good grace not to smile at her shaky attempt at speaking guide-book German.

She wouldn't let the rain spoil her morning. For the first time in ages she was a free agent, could come and go as she wanted, visit the museums and churches and walk the beautiful cobbled streets – maybe take in a concert or two.

She took out her Berlitz Pocket Guide to Vienna and began to read the chapter on Stephansdom. She knew this marked her out as the typical tourist but what did she care? She was on holiday and she could do whatever she pleased.

The waitress came back with her order and Michelle gave her a cheerful smile and a large tip.

Where to, this afternoon?

She'd start as everyone did with a visit to the cathedral. She stirred a spoonful of sugar into her coffee and tasted the chocolate cake. It was rich, a bit too heavy for her liking – definitely nothing to write home about. It didn't look as nice as the ones she'd seen in the cake shops this morning, not the epicurean delight she'd imagined, but then, she'd heard that you had to go to the Hotel Sacher for the real thing.

Back to the map.

She traced the streets with a finger – it was only a short distance up the Rotenturmstrasse and then a leisurely stroll by the outdoor cafés in Lugeck square, over to the Fleischmarkt.

She wanted to drop into the Griechenbeisl for her next coffee – walk in the footsteps of Wagner, Beethoven and her beloved Mozart. And, of course, she had to visit the Figarohaus museum in Domgasse. Would she have time for all this in one afternoon?

She was wearing her flat, sensible shoes, thanks to Ken. He'd warned her to bring an umbrella and she'd laughed at him.

She wasn't laughing now! She was drenched to the bone. She wiggled her bottom on the chair. Her summer dress was sodden, sticking to her.

To think that only yesterday afternoon she was in Ken's arms in her house in Whitehall discussing all the sights she had to see, and now here she was in a café in the Stock-im-Eisen-Platz – actually sitting here sipping coffee, opposite the cathedral. A day later but a world away.

Ken.

She never thought she'd find anyone like him – passionate, kind, attentive. He was such a warm person, the first man she'd met who didn't think the world revolved around him. Bringing up his daughter on his own wasn't easy and –

"Excuse me." A plump middle-aged woman looked down at her. "You're Michelle Bolger, aren't you?"

Michelle was taken aback. "Yes. That's right."

"I hope I'm not disturbing you."

"Em – "

"It was my husband who spotted you." She pointed towards a corner table where a tall, grey-haired, bespectacled man gave a little wave. "He thought he recognised you and I said, 'Oh I don't think so. You haven't seen her in years and people change.' But I was wrong."

"I'm sorry – "

"Oh, silly me! I forgot to introduce myself. I'm Ruth James. You only met me once or twice before – it's my husband, Gordon, you knew."

Gordon James. Gordon James?

"You remember . . . the organist in St Augustine's?"

Michelle stood up and shook hands. "Of course, I'm terribly sorry, Mrs James. It's just that it's been so long and when you're away from home you don't – "

"Oh, I know, I know. Who'd have thought we'd meet up like this in Vienna of all places and after such a long time? Gordon's often spoken about you over the years and how talented you were. His best student ever, that's how he describes you."

Michelle cleared her throat.

"Please come over to our table and join us, Michelle."

So much for being alone.

Michelle had no wish to renew an old acquaintanceship but she couldn't be rude. She took up her handbag and followed, a smile planted on her face.

"Michelle Bolger!" Gordon James got to his feet and grasped her hand. Then, to her consternation, he kissed it ostentatiously. "I *knew* it was you, Michelle. Didn't I tell you, Ruth? I said it was Michelle. Sit down, sit down, please. My, how elegant you look."

Hardly, she thought, with her wet hair plastered to her head and the end of her red dress soaked and creased.

He pulled out the seat next to his for her. "Doesn't she look wonderful, Ruth? I'd have recognised you anywhere – the same golden hair."

Michelle blushed.

"I can still see you sitting up at the organ playing the . . . let me see now, the *'Ave Verum'*. You had a lovely light touch. That's the mistake a lot of organists make you see – too heavy and plodding but you – "

"Would you like some tea, Michelle?" his wife interrupted, sensing her embarrassment. "Or coffee, perhaps?"

"No, thanks. I've just had a coffee."

Her former organ teacher had aged very well. His rimless glasses suited him, gave him a distinguished air. He was still handsome. Ruth James looked years older than her husband but Michelle reckoned they were both in their early fifties.

"So, what brings *you* to Vienna?" Gordon James asked as his wife poured more tea. "Are you sure you won't have something?"

"No, thanks all the same. I'm here on holiday – well, a sort of a holiday. I'm combining business with pleasure."

"Business?" Ruth James was surprised. "You've gone into business?"

"No, no, I didn't mean it that way. I'm here to observe the master-classes."

"Oh?" Gordon James leaned forward, eagerly. "Are you still teaching piano, then? I heard that's what you were doing." His eyes grew narrower and his lips twitched slightly.

"Oh, yes, I'm teaching – part-time in the music school, and I take private pupils at home. I play organ for the church ceremonies, believe it or not, in St Malachy's."

"Good, good. So, you're here on a musical adventure, is that it? No better place, Vienna. Which classes will you be attending?"

"Professor Karl Harrach – he has a great reputation."

"Indeed. Yes, indeed. We saw him play last year in the Musikverein with the Viennese Philharmonic. Mozart's his speciality – your favourite, if I remember correctly?"

"Yes, that's right. You've certainly got a good memory, Mr James."

"None of that, none of that, you make me feel ancient. Call me Gordon. So, when do you start?"

"On Saturday morning."

"And you're free until then? Splendid. We could show you around. We know this city like the back of our hands – we spend a lot of time here with Ruth's brother."

How could he afford to do that? Vienna was expensive.

"It's really beautiful in spring," Gordon said. "That's my favourite season, but it's lovely at this time too. We'd be happy to show you around."

"Oh no, Gordon, I'm sure you're far too busy – "

"Not at all, Michelle," Ruth said. "We'd be delighted."

What now? She nodded and fiddled with the strap of her handbag.

Ruth James took her cue.

"I think maybe Michelle would prefer to see Vienna at her own pace, Gordon."

"No, it's just – "

"Say no more." He winked at her. "Perfectly understandable. No doubt you're here with friends and – "

"No, actually."

"Oh? Well, why don't we meet up for dinner tomorrow night? Is that OK with you, Ruth?"

"Of course." She patted Michelle's arm. "Leave you in peace for a day or two to explore. You're right, you know, much better to tour around on your own."

"To be honest, I'd prefer it."

"Myself and Ruth are staying with her brother, Cyril – "

"Yes, he's manager of a hotel. We come over a lot, as Gordon said. Cyril's employer is an Austrian, from Salzburg originally – a lovely man. They put us up free gratis and for nothing! We're lucky."

"Cyril likes to have his family stay with him," Gordon interrupted. "He misses Ireland, I think."

Free accommodation – that explained their frequent visits.

"We're literally around the corner, Michelle, in Grashofgasse," Ruth James went on. "A grand old building in a quiet cul-de-sac."

"I didn't think anywhere around Stephensplatz would

be quiet!" Michelle laughed. "I'm in a hotel near here, too. The Albany."

"In Weihburggasse? Yes, that's a beautiful building – eighteenth century, isn't it?"

"Nineteenth, I'm reliably informed."

Ken rarely got his facts wrong.

"There's a lovely reception area with old-world furniture, you know the sort of thing. My room's comfortable and the staff are very friendly, obliging."

"Well, I always maintain you get what you pay for," Ruth said. "What if we pick you up there tomorrow night at about eight?"

"Perfect. I can meet you in the foyer."

"You know, Ruth, we could drive out to Grinzing. Michelle would love it." He turned to her. "You can't miss a visit to the *heurigen*."

"Oh, great. I'd intended to go there on the tram tomorrow."

"No, no," Ruth insisted, "much better fun at night. The village is so quaint, we'll have a little walk around first."

"I heard the wine's very deceptive," Michelle said.

"Mmh," Ruth James agreed. "You can say that again. The first wines of the season are strong."

"A good kick in a wine – nothing like it!" Gordon James smacked his lips together . . . just as he used to do, she suddenly remembered. He had peculiar little habits, always fidgeting, patting your knee, whistling.

"But we'll let *you* be the judge of the wine tomorrow

night, Michelle." He stood up. "Don't let us delay you any longer."

Michelle shook hands. "Great to meet you both again. Until tomorrow evening at eight, then."

She left the café and took the lift down to the ground floor. A crowd, sheltering from the downpour, huddled in the doorway. Pulling her jacket collar up around her neck, she opened her umbrella and stepped out into the rain.

Michelle walked slowly around the cathedral, gazing at the statues and sculptures. Ah, there it was: the pulpit carved by Anton Pilgram. Augustine, Gregory, Ambrose, Jerome – the fathers of the Church – positioned at the top of the stairs, looked down in all their glory. The faces were brilliantly carved, the expressions haughty and proud. The staircase wound its way down and there, underneath, was the statue of the sculptor himself looking out of a window. Cheeky!

Michelle was jostled out of the way by a small woman in a headscarf. Japanese. They were everywhere. Why did they travel together in such large groups? She edged away as they milled around the pulpit, blabbering and jabbering and getting excited.

Time to move on.

Michelle had a cup of coffee in the Griechenbeisl, the oldest tavern in Vienna. It was packed with tourists escaping from the rain, so she finished her drink quickly and left. Umbrella up, she walked over to the corner of the Grashofgasse. Then she spotted it – the Basiliskenhaus. Standing there in front of it, Michelle shuddered. The thing was quite grotesque. She'd just stepped right back to the Middle Ages. She stared at the ugly features of the basilisk, half-rooster, half-lizard. She looked it up in her Berlitz. The superstition was that it had polluted the drinking-water by breathing its foul fumes. Michelle could well believe it. It looked positively poisonous.

Right next door was a pretty house with small latticed windows, the former home of Schumann. She might call in there later if she'd time.

She hummed to herself as she ambled along, up the Bäckerstrasse full of restaurants and cafés with brightly-coloured awnings. The tables and chair were stacked outside, the rain depriving them of their usual customers.

Not knowing the scene, Michelle decided it would be safer to book a table for dinner that evening. She called into Oswald und Kalb.

A waiter came over. *"Guten Tag."*

"Ich würde mögen einen Tisch bestellen, bitte." There, she was quite proud of herself.

"Kein Problem, um wieviel Uhr?"

Right, now to count up to nine in her head. *"Um neun Uhr, bitte."*

"Und für wieviele Leute?"

We will what?

This was too complicated for her. *"Sprechen Sie Englisch?"*

He shook his head politely. *"Ein Moment, bitte."*

He called to another waiter, who hurried over. "Yes? You'd like a table, madam?"

"Not for now," Michelle explained. "I'd like to book a table for tonight."

"Follow me, please."

He led the way over to a large, oak sideboard which served as a desk. He took up a leather-bound book marked *Reservierung*.

"What time, madam?"

"Around nine?"

"Yes, OK. How many people?"

"Oh," Michelle faltered, "just myself."

If he thought it odd, his expression didn't change.

"Very good, madam." He bowed slightly. "Nine o'clock."

Michelle left the restaurant, crossed the street and went into a beautiful ivy-covered Renaissance courtyard. She sat for a few moments and closed her eyes. It was so peaceful – the only sound to disturb the silence was the pitter-patter of the rain on the cobbled stones.

Fancy bumping into Gordon James and his wife like that. She hadn't seen him for years. When had he left St Augustine's? The year before her Leaving Cert, wasn't it? Yeah, the year her father died. Michelle didn't want to think about her father's death. It depressed her.

A sudden heart attack on his way home from work. An ambulance whisked him to the Mater Hospital but he was dead on arrival.

No, she didn't want to think about it. Didn't want to go back over those years when she'd had to look after her mother and younger brother, Declan. A sixteen-year-old girl with the responsibilities of an adult. Her mother had become totally dependent on her . . .

But Gordon James? He'd left his position as organist some time before that. When exactly was it? The details were vague in her mind. At fifteen or sixteen she hadn't questioned things all that much, too busy living her life; study, concerts, practice, music lessons, local discos. The fact that her organ teacher had left hadn't really bothered her. Now, looking back, it *did* seem rather sudden. One Thursday afternoon Michelle was on her way out to her organ lesson as usual . . .

"Oh, I forget to tell you," her mother said casually, looking up from her ironing. "You don't have to go today, Michelle, he's gone."

"Who's gone?"

Her mother neatly folded Declan's shirt. "Mr James. He's left the parish. Father Dempsey's employed a new organist. A woman, I hear."

"Mr James has left? Why?"

Her mother shrugged. "Who knows? He's a musician, isn't he? They're very unreliable."

. . . Michelle was amused by her mother's dismissive attitude to musicians. Unreliable? Michelle had thought him eccentric but definitely not unreliable.

She remembered those lessons in the church. Gordon James was often nervy, agitated, would fly off the handle at the least thing. Of course he was a musical genius, you had to make allowances. And the wife, Ruth. Hadn't she been a singer? Maybe he was offered a better-paid job somewhere else? Granted, he was temperamental but most of the time he was kind, fatherly to her in many ways, encouraging. Her mother had never liked him . . . but then her mother had funny ideas about people.

It was very odd bumping into him again. What about tomorrow night? Now, she wasn't in the humour for it at all. Ah, to hell! The damage was done and it would only be for a few hours. Enough sitting around. She wanted to visit the Figarohaus before they closed at four-thirty.

Thankfully, there were very few in the Mozart museum. The rain dripped from the leaky roof down to the courtyard as Michelle climbed the bare stairs and strolled through the once-ornate rooms. She glanced up at the ceiling – more intricate sculpting. The craftsmen of those times took such care, such time with their work.

She scrutinised the preserved pieces of manuscript in glass cases. Wasn't it fabulous to be here looking at the pages, the words, the notes that Mozart had actually written in his own hand? Unbelievable. She picked up a headset and listened. *The Jupiter Symphony.*

She got back to the hotel just after five.

"Ms Bolger." The receptionist smiled a huge smile. It was the American student she'd been chatting to last night. "Did you have a good time?"

"Brilliant, Geoff! The cathderal's marvellous – I could have spent the day there." She folded her umbrella and held it upright to avoid wetting the plush green carpet. "I'm like a kid in a toyshop – want to see and enjoy everything. By the way, thanks a million for that map, it's so detailed even *I* couldn't lose my way!"

"Another big day planned for tomorrow?"

"Absolutely. Oh, my key, thank you."

She made for the stairs but he called her back.

He handed her a long, brown envelope. "A letter – I think it's for you."

"For me?"

"Yes, there's no name or room number on the envelope. He said it was for the Irish lady and since you're the only Irish guest here at the moment – it must be for you. It was delivered by hand."

"Oh?"

"I've just come on duty. Josef took it earlier this afternoon. You could ask him about it in the morning."

"Thanks. And thanks for all your help."

Michelle got to her room, took off her wet shoes and

dress and sank down on the bed. In a few minutes she'd run a hot bath. She took the letter from her handbag. Who could this be from? Must be Gordon James or his wife. Nobody else knew she was here. Probably cancelling tomorrow night – not that she minded one way or the other.

She tore open the envelope and lay back on the puffed-up pillows. The page was pleated over and over. Intriguing. She unfolded it layer by layer. Two scrawled lines in the middle of the page.

Did you enjoy the Figarohaus? I like you in red. Do your knickers match?

Three

"Hi. How *are* you, love?"

Michelle, snug in her warm bathrobe, cradled the receiver to her ear. "Hi, Ken. Good to hear your voice."

"How's it going, Mich? I didn't think I'd catch you at this hour but then I remembered you like a hot bath after a day's running around so I took my chances of finding you in your room."

"You were right. Oh, Ken, Vienna's out of this world – just as you described. I spent the day walking, my feet are killing me."

"*I'*d change places!"

"I still can't believe I'm here! The buildings, the streets, the cafés, the atmosphere. Mind you, the rain's something else! Now I know what they mean when they talk about the soft Irish weather. It's literally coming down in sheets here and it's been at it all day."

"Don't say I didn't warn you! Anyhow, you're having a good time, that's the main thing. What did you see today? I suppose you went to the Figarohaus?"

"Naturally. I spent over an hour there. The guy at the information desk was selling tickets for a concert in another of the houses Mozart lived in – somewhere off the Singerstrasse. The programme looked good so I bought a ticket for Friday evening."

Did you enjoy the Figarohaus.

Who had seen her there? Who?

She cast her mind back. Three or four Japanese, a couple of French and a young English-speaking couple she gathered were from Australia. But she hadn't spoken to any of them. Hadn't spoken to anyone except the guide and he'd been very friendly. Think, Michelle, think. What had she said to him? Had she told him she was from Ireland? Yes, yes, she had . . . he'd *asked* her where she was from . . . she'd told him where she was staying –

"Sorry, Mich, hang on a sec. No, Paul, room ten, I told you. Yes, I did. Where's Clare, let *her* handle it. All right, all right, I'll come in a minute. Mich, are you there? Sorry about that, this place is bedlam this evening."

" . . . What?"

"I was just saying this place is like a madhouse at the moment."

"Oh . . . right."

"Mich? You OK? You sound a bit vague."

"No, no, I'm fine. Tired, that's all."

"Are you going out again tonight?"

"Just for an hour or two. I've booked a table in a restaurant in the Bäckerstrasse. It looked nice when I called in and it was recommended in the Berlitz. Styrian food."

"I'll be thinking of you. *I'm* working late. We've bus-loads of American tourists."

"Over here it's the Japanese!" She laughed.

"What's your room like? I want to be able to picture you in it."

"It's great, Ken. Spacious for a single room. The usual *en suite*, telly and minibar . . . and wardrobe and dressing-table, of course."

"Not a graphic description, Mich!"

"OK. The curtains are blue and they co-ordinate with the blue-and-white duvet cover and – "

"Mich!"

"The sheets are pristine white and starched – "

"And I wish I could be with you between them! I miss you, Mich."

"I miss you, too."

"You're not lonely, are you?"

"No, you were right, I haven't the time to be. Oh, I almost forgot, I bumped into an Irish couple earlier today and you'll never guess. He was the organist who taught me years ago. Imagine, meeting him like that out of the blue after all these years and in Vienna of all places! He and his wife have asked me out to dinner tomorrow evening."

"Your former teacher? That's a surprise. Well, I'm glad you'll have some company."

"Mmh."

She wasn't all that pushed about company. Mind you . . . her eyes fell again on the note on the bedside table.

Would she tell Ken about it?

No, it was someone's idea of a practical joke. Silly in the extreme. And prurient. A childish prank, one of the waiters carrying out a dare. The chambermaid in on it, no doubt.

"I'll have to go, Mich. Some mix-up in the lounge. The head barman's out sick and the rest of that crew couldn't organise a piss-up in a brewery!"

"Right, good to talk to you. I'll phone you tomorrow night. Are you working?"

"Yes." He groaned. "And the next night and the next."

"How's Beth?"

"Staying over at a friend's house, or so she says. Carmel Richardson. You met her at that Christmas party."

"The one living in Stillorgan? She's a nice girl."

"Mmh, I hate to say this but I'm relieved Beth's gone away for the night – she's in foul humour lately, moping around the house."

"What about the part-time work in the hotel? Did you suggest it to her?"

He sighed. "She wouldn't consider it even though she's fed up – told me hotel work wasn't her scene."

"It's a pity her art classes are over. Still, she'll be back in school in a few weeks, Ken."

"Yeah, and then it'll be moans about homework and teachers. She'll find it hard after Transition Year. She's been warned that Fifth Year will be difficult."

"They all find that," Michelle said. "My pupils are the same. They sail through the Junior Cert and think they're wonderful and then comes the shock. But she'll be fine, Beth's a clever girl."

"I know that, sometimes she's a bit too clever for her own good. She's getting very quick with the smart answers."

Michelle smiled. Ken had forgotten what it was like to be young.

"She's hanging around the house every night, deafening the neighbours with her so-called music. Then she watches that bloody MTV till the early hours. If I say anything to her, she accuses me of neglecting her, of not taking an interest, of 'not being there' for her. Jesus, when I *do* take an interest she says I'm interfering!"

"Well, as we say in the school, at that age they're very well balanced."

"Balanced?" he echoed derisively.

"Yeah." Michelle laughed. "A chip on each shoulder."

"Too true," he agreed. "I'm up to my eyes in the job. She doesn't realise I'd be far happier staying in at night and being there for her, as she calls it. Her real problem is that she misses Mark."

"Mark's due home soon, isn't he?"

"That's a mixed blessing, Mich. It's not that I don't like him . . . but I think he's far too old for her."

"Beth's sixteen, Ken. A nineteen-year-old isn't too old for her. Girls mature much quicker than boys. I think Mark's great."

"You always had a soft spot for him. I still think he's not right for her. I mean, he's in college and all . . . drinking and carousing and God knows what. Drugs? Aren't they all at it nowadays? That bloody cannabis or E."

"Will you stop worrying, Ken? Beth's got her head screwed on."

"But she's bored all the time and that can lead to anything."

"Being bored is par for the course at sixteen, Ken. It wouldn't be cool to be anything else."

"She wouldn't be bored if she'd taken that summer job I offered her. Wants a decent social life, that's the latest. A social life, I ask you! If I had spoken to my parents like that I'd have got a clip around the ear-hole."

"Ken Leavy, will you listen to yourself? Next you'll me telling me you used to brush your teeth with soot! Beth's like any other girl of her age. I've put enough of them through my hands to know."

"Teaching them isn't the same as rearing them, Mich."

"Sometimes, it can be worse. Look, just be grateful that Beth has found herself a nice fella, OK?"

"She expects me to fork out for her social life. We'd another argument last night about a rave. I told her I didn't want her to go but then she was on to the friends and they called for her. What could I do?"

"It's hard, I know, but if you lay down the law too much, she'll rebel."

"In a way I wish Mark *was* back. She left the house last night in a miniskirt – practically up to her neck. She's asking for trouble."

"Come on, Ken, there's no pleasing you tonight. Beth dresses like all the girls of her age dress. The skirts were *much* shorter in your day!"

"Maybe. . . I just feel as if I'm losing the little bit of control I had."

She could hear the tension in his voice. "Maybe you should be more firm. I could try – "

"Fine, Paul, fine. I'm coming. Sorry, I *have* to go, Mich. And sorry for dumping on you tonight."

"You're not. If you can't let off steam now and again – "

"No, I shouldn't be unloading on you like this. I've had a lousy day and . . . "

"And what?"

" . . . It doesn't matter. It'll wait till you get back. Forget I said anything. Oh, I called over to your mother this morning and brought her to Crazy Prices to do her weekly shopping."

"Ken, you shouldn't have, I – "

"It was no hassle. So, Mich, I hope you're having a ball. Enjoy yourself, you deserve it. I'll talk to you tomorrow."

"OK. Mind yourself. Bye, Ken."

She'd have liked to have had a longer chat, tell him all about the rest of her day, how she'd loved the cathedral and the Fleischmarkt and about her plans to visit the Belvedere.

She was being selfish. Ken was addled. There was something else on his mind, she was sure of it. He didn't usually overreact like this.

Should she step in? Have a word with Beth? The girl would probably tell her to mind her own business. It was a tricky situation and she didn't want to make matters worse.

She picked up the crumpled page again. A scribble. Spidery handwriting. Huge circular dots on the I's. That was supposed to mean something but she was damned if she could remember what.

Do your knickers match?

What kind of a lunatic would write that?

Who *was* he?

There had to be a logical explanation. Someone had seen her at the Mozart museum, taken some kind of a fancy to her – or else decided a woman alone was easy prey.

That was it.

Maybe it *was* the guide she'd spoken to. She tried to call up a picture of his face but she couldn't. Michelle had never been good at faces . . . not too good with names, either, but she had a good ear and her perception was largely based on sounds.

Long after a conversation Michelle could never recall what the other person was wearing, or what day of the week it was or sometimes even where the conversation took place. But she always remembered *what* was said, who said it and the tone of voice.

The guide whose face she couldn't visualise – now his voice came back to her, low and gutteral. He was from Rohrau, he'd said, the birthplace of Haydn. He'd advised her to visit the restored farmhouse with its thatched roof, recommended the concerts there. He'd been friendly, informative.

She'd told him about the master-classes, that she was Irish and she'd told him where she was staying. Said how handy, how central it was and he'd agreed with her – he'd been all ears. Very interested . . .

Too interested?

What kind of an idiot was she? That was her problem, Ken always said. She was too trusting.

"You'll have to learn to be more cautious, Mich."

Maybe she would.

She screwed the note into a ball and threw it into the waste basket in disgust. She resisted the impulse to phone her mother, although she knew she was in for a lecture the next day. Her mother couldn't sleep when she hadn't heard from Michelle. She'd imagine all sorts of disasters – plane crashes, food poisoning, being whipped off to the white slave trade. You name it – her mother worried about it . . .

"I like to hear from you every day, Michelle – to know you're all right. I'm running short of my blood pressure tablets, could you collect them for me? Why didn't you ring? A phone call's not too much to ask for, is it? Declan always phones."

Bully for Declan!

Ken was very good to have brought her mother shopping today. Hopefully she wouldn't take advantage of his kindness while Michelle was away. Granted, her mother was in her sixties and she was living alone but it wasn't as if she had a serious medical condition. She was manipulative.

Maybe she should phone and tell her mother that there was some weirdo hanging around? That might give her something genuine to worry about.

Scolding herself for the thought, she opened the wardrobe. What to wear this evening? Her cream-coloured skirt and black top – they looked well. She'd tie back her hair, put on make-up and go off and enjoy herself.

* * *

The restaurant was packed – it was a good thing she'd made a reservation. The guidebook hadn't lied, this place was obviously very popular. Trying not to look self-conscious on her own, Michelle had a good look around: the room was large, with nooks and crannies, plain decor, wooden tables and chairs, no tablecloths.

The maître d' led her to a table near the kitchen where waiters, dressed in formal black-and-white, dashed to and fro, skilfully performing balancing acts with loaded trays.

Two women, deep in conversation, sat at the table.

"All right?" The headwaiter smiled at her and when

she didn't object, he handed her a menu. "Would you like something . . . to drink, madam? An . . . apéritif?" He spoke English haltingly but well. Tinge of an American accent. "Might I suggest a Kir?"

"Thank you," she said.

She didn't like the idea of sharing a table but it seemed to be the way things worked here. Most of the tables were long and wide and sat six or eight comfortably. She hung her black blazer on the back of her seat and sat down. The women gave her a cursory glance and continued their conversation.

Michelle opened the menu. Underneath each dish was the English translation so at least she could leave the Berlitz in her bag. *Weiner Schnitzel* – she didn't like veal and, judging from what the women in front of her were eating, the portions were huge. It was a toss-up between the *Backhendl* – roast chicken, coated with egg and breadcrumbs like the veal – or *Tafelspitz* – boiled beef in vinegar.

The waiter brought over her Kir. "Have you decided, madam?"

"Yes." She pointed to the beef on the menu.

"Good choice. We serve it with *Kren* and *Schnittlauch*. He noted her confused expression. "Horseradish and chive sauces, madam. Excellent."

"And vegetables?" Michelle asked.

"Potatoes, boiled with the beef."

Some kind of a stew?

"Fine. And could you recommend a wine?"

"Our house red is very good, particularly with the beef."

"Thank you. A half bottle, if you have it."

"I'll bring you a carafe, madam."

Michelle had brought a book with her to read because she wasn't used to eating alone in restaurants and she was slightly uncomfortable.

She was halfway through chapter one of Anita Brookner's *Brief Lives* when the waiter came back with the wine. He poured a glass for her and she took a sip – it was quite dry.

A youngish, dark-haired man approached the table. He pointed to the empty chair beside her.

"Excusez moi, madame. Ça ne vous dérange pas, si je m'assieds ici?"

French and classy with it.

"Pas du tout, monsieur."

She didn't smile. She'd be polite but not encouraging. Although it might be nice to brush up her French, she didn't want to engage in conversation with yet another stranger. She took a quick look at him and went back to her book. Black hair, biggish nose, tanned. There – she was getting a bit better at this. She could train herself to be more attentive to detail, couldn't she?

Had *he* been in the Figarohaus this afternoon? She hadn't a clue whether he had been or not. Ah, cop yourself on, Michelle, she told herself. He's an innocent tourist out for the evening, just like yourself.

The waiter arrived back with her meal.

"Enjoy!" he said and beamed at her.

Yes, she *would* enjoy her meal, she decided. She'd banish all thoughts of scribbled notes and over-friendly guides and lunatics leaving messages in hotels.

The beef was almost rare!

Michelle loved her meat well done and it had never occurred to her that *boiled* meat could be underdone. But she was starving. She smeared a piece of beef with the horseradish sauce and put it in her mouth without looking at it. Mmh, it was nice, actually.

"Vous êtes Anglaise?" the Frenchman asked her.

"Non, Irlandaise," she informed him coolly.

She picked up her book again and he got the message. It was difficult to read and eat at the same time but she wanted to avoid any further attempts on his part to initiate conversation.

By the time the waiter arrived back with his *Wiener Schnitzel*, the Frenchman was chatting and laughing with the Danish girls opposite. Michelle was relieved and peeved at the same time. He hadn't tried very hard, had he? Was she losing her touch with men?

For dessert she ordered a *Palatschinken*, a Hungarian dish – pancakes filled with jam.

She pretended to read but she was earwigging on the conversation at the table. The Frenchman's name was Luc and he was telling them all about his native village near Chamonix. He liked Vienna, he said, apart from the rain. He'd spent the day at Neusiedler, a beautiful lake and a birdwatcher's paradise. Michelle smiled to herself. He liked birdwatching all right but of a different variety!

Her dessert was delicious. She finished her wine and called to the waiter. It was time to head back to the hotel.

"My bill, please."

"It's already been paid, madam."

"I'm sorry?"

"Your bill has been, how you say . . . settled."

"I don't understand!"

"The gentleman at table six near the window – he paid for your meal not ten minutes ago."

Michelle jumped up and craned her neck in the direction the waiter was pointing.

"The gentleman left, madam. He assured me it would be all right – that he was a friend of yours."

Michelle nodded and sat down again.

What the hell was going on?

The Bäckerstrasse was deserted and it was only eleven o'clock. Viennese night life wasn't like Dublin – people went out and came home earlier. She fastened the buttons on her blazer and put up her umbrella. The rain was still pelting down. Luckily it was only a five-minute walk to her hotel. She hurried down the street and turned left onto the Rotenturmstrasse.

She thought of the bustling crowds here this afternoon . . . now there was only a handful out walking. She was nervous as she hurried along. Who had paid for her dinner? And why?

She reached Stephensplatz. There were more people strolling here and the lights from the restaurants and coffee houses provided welcome cheer.

She was on the Kärtnerstrasse when she heard footsteps behind her. She quickened her step, not daring to look around. But the footsteps grew quicker, too. Her heart started to race.

She was being followed.

She gripped the umbrella tightly and broke into a run. Her rubber-soled shoes squelched on the wet pavement as she rushed on past the Singerstrasse and finally reached her turn. Left into the Weihburggasse and now only a few more yards to run.

The footsteps were coming, faster and faster.

Heart thumping, she reached the steps of the hotel, dashed up, pushed the heavy entrance door and panted her way in.

"*Guten Abend*, Ms Bolger."

Geoff! She felt like hugging him.

She *had* to see who was after her. She hurried back to the entrance, pushed the door open and looked up and down the street.

No one . . . but she distinctly heard the pounding of running feet.

And laughter.

Four

Michelle slept fitfully, tossing and turning, half-waking at regular intervals during the night and then drifting back into troubled sleep. The sheet wound itself around her hot, sticky body. Despite the open window, the air in the room was heavy. Oppressive.

The rain beating against the windowpanes finally woke her at six-thirty. She'd a crick in her neck.

Groggily, she reached for the glass of spring water on the bedside table and gulped down the tepid drink. She was parched. She'd never be able to go back to sleep now, so she might as well get up and make an early start. It would give her more time for Schönbrunn palace.

She went over to the window, drew back a curtain and peeped out. The rain came down relentlessly, plopping on the roof of the hotel annexe, running in rivulets along the gutter to the drain-pipe where it surged downwards.

Bloody marvellous.

A cool shower would revive her flagging spirits. She padded on bare feet into the tiled bathroom and adjusted the taps until she got just the right temperature. The water pressure was very good – not many guests up and showering at this hour of the morning, she guessed. She lathered her body in bath gel and the water gushed down her back in sand-blasting fashion. She washed and rinsed her hair, squinting as the sudsy water streamed down her forehead, nose and cheeks, stinging her eyes.

She sat at the dressing-table and cleansed her face with tissues and the cream which promised eternal youth, but Michelle didn't believe in miracles. Her eyes felt gritty; she reached for the Optrex. Two drops in each eye – that was a bit better. She threw the used tissue into the wastepaper basket. There it was – the crumpled-up letter.

She sighed aloud and the sound in the silent room seemed to mock her. All right, this was probably meant as a joke but she didn't find it amusing. She was angry. Someone was out to get at her – to make her, at the very least, uncomfortable. He'd had the gall to pay for her dinner last night. And the footsteps following her back to the hotel?

This was harassment.

She should go to the police. And say what? That she was being pursued? What evidence did she have? Well, there was the note, for one thing. She retrieved the letter from the bin, straightened it out and put it in a drawer.

Witnesses?

The head waiter in the restaurant – he'd remember

whoever had paid for her meal. Or would he? It wasn't a crime to pay for someone else's meal, was it? Maybe not, but it was certainly an invasion of privacy.

The restaurant had been packed last night. If what Ken had told her about the hotel business was anything to judge by, the maître d' would be used to seeing and hearing all sorts of goings-on – clandestine affairs, marital tiffs, business partners' rows.

Geoff downstairs. He'd vouch for her – assure the police that she wasn't a crack-pot. But he didn't know her, did he? Two or three polite conversations hardly constituted a lifelong friendship. And she didn't want to drag Geoff into this.

She was making a mountain out of a mole-hill . . . No, she hadn't asked for this. She was a tourist here, minding her own business, not interfering with anyone. She had a right to privacy, a right to go about her business without being targeted or bullied or frightened.

She'd call into the police station on her way to the underground station this morning and make an official complaint.

That would be difficult enough to do in Ireland. How would she explain it to a German policeman? No matter how good his English might be . . .

And what could the police do?

Tell her to ignore it? Advise her not to go out on her own at night? What if they thought she was responsible, had brought it on herself – that somehow she'd given off the wrong vibes?

No, she wouldn't report it. Most likely, it would all pass.

She dressed in navy-blue leggings and a white T-shirt. After breakfast, she'd go and buy a raincoat with a hood. She didn't want to be dragging the umbrella around all day.

Transport in Vienna was superb, Michelle was beginning to find out. The U-Bahn network was tiny in comparison to the Paris Métro or the London underground, but it was fast, clean and efficient. The trains arrived every three or four minutes and it was only about a thirty-minute journey to the palace, according to Geoff. She headed in the direction of the U4 line.

Michelle managed to find a seat, although the train was packed. Dripping umbrellas, damp bodies and wet shopping bags and cases covered the floor. Out with the Pocket Guide again. She'd read as much information as she could take in before she got there.

A young, dark-skinned man in an anorak sat beside her, his thigh rubbing up against hers – a bit too close for comfort. Michelle, her eyes still glued to her Berlitz, edged away.

A woman, sitting opposite, upbraided a toddler who was crawling backwards and forwards under the seat after a plastic rabbit, annoying the old man in the next seat. The child stuck out her tongue at the man and the mother smacked her on the legs. A loud howl and then a wail of protest.

Michelle had managed to buy a rainproof jacket which covered her upper body but not her legs. Now, the wet leggings clung to her and her left leg began to itch like hell. It seemed like an eternity until the train pulled into the underground station at Schönbrunn.

The avenue up to the palace was about a mile long with no shelter! Michelle trundled along in the pelting rain, blinkered by her hood. On a fine day, this would be a beautiful place for a ramble and a look at the trees and the flowers but she had to struggle on, keeping her head down. She abandoned her original idea of visiting the gardens first – it was far too wet.

To the right of the entrance was the Schlosstheater where the summer chamber operas were performed. On a notice, Michelle saw that there was one scheduled for later this afternoon, but she wouldn't have time to stay for it. Gordon and Ruth James were to pick her up at eight.

The entrance hall with its tiled floors, tall stone columns and elaborate ceiling was enormous. There was a book and souvenir shop on the left, booths and information desks dotted around and a cloakroom on the right, for the wet coats and umbrellas.

She paid her entrance fee.

"Englisch?" the lady at the desk asked.

"No, Irish."

The lady smiled and handed her a set of headphones playing a taped, English-speaking, guided tour of the rooms of the castle.

The interior of the palace was exquisitely decorated but had a warm, friendly atmosphere. From the windows upstairs, Michelle looked out on the beautifully landscaped park and saw the Gloriette – a neo-classical colonnade perched on the top of a hill. What a shame she couldn't walk up there, as she'd intended – the view was bound to be magnificent.

She read about the Neptune Fountain and the half-buried Roman Ruins, complete with fragmented Corinthian columns, friezes and archways but she couldn't see them from here. She was raging that she couldn't have a close-up look.

And she'd wanted to visit the little zoo, set up by Franz I. It was infuriating that, having come so far, she should be reading all this from a book and not be able to have a decent look around – like driving out to Fairyhouse at home and then watching the races on a telly in the visitors' tent.

Maybe the rain would stop later or ease off a bit?

As she passed through the sumptuous rooms where Maria Theresa and her daughters had lived, Michelle noticed him again – the man who'd been sitting beside her on the train. He was examining the needlework in the empress's breakfast-room. He looked up as she passed and nodded at her. She ignored him and hurried on.

She passed into a large round room, decorated in the Chinese style with small, highly-decorative furniture and intricate wall hangings. This was Maria Theresa's top secret dining-room, where, during private consultations, a table rose from the floor with a completely prepared dinner, in order that no servant would have to be present at the meal and overhear the conversation. Ken could do with this for his weekly staff meetings in the hotel!

The Hall of Mirrors reminded Michelle of Versailles. Mozart had given his first royal recital here, as a young boy. As she walked by the mirrored walls, she caught another glimpse of her U-Bahn friend walking slowly behind.

Was he following her?

Michelle's favourite was the Napoleon room – originally Maria Theresa's bedroom but later the room where the French emperor stayed on his way to the battle of Austerlitz. As the tape in her earphones played on, Michelle learned that it was in this room also that Napoleon's son had spent his last days. Looking at the boy's death-mask and the stuffed pet bird made Michelle sad.

On the train back to the Innere Stadt, Michelle took a wary look around the carriage. No, there was no sign of the man in the anorak. If he was following her, he was keeping a safe distance between them.

* * *

"Number twenty, please," Michelle said, pointing to her key in its pigeon-hole.

"Ms Bolger?" asked a young receptionist with a swarthy complexion.

"Yes, I'm Michelle Bolger."

"There was a telephone call for you, earlier this afternoon." He handed her a written message. "You're to call back as soon as you can."

"Thank you. Are you, by any chance, Josef?"

"That's right."

"Em, I understand you took a message for me yesterday afternoon."

"Oh? Yes, yes, that's correct, I did. A letter, wasn't it? At least I presumed it was for you. The boy just said it was for – "

"The boy?"

"Yes, the one who delivers the post. Franz – he's our regular postman – he explained that a passer-by in the street asked him to – "

"A passer-by?" Michelle repeated. "So, you never *saw* who handed in the letter?"

"I'm afraid not." He looked at her questioningly. "Is anything wrong?"

Michelle hesitated.

"If there's anything wrong, Ms Bolger, perhaps you'd like to see the manager?"

"No," she replied quickly. "No, no. That won't be necessary. Thanks."

The receptionist went to answer the phone and Michelle glanced down at the message.

Mrs Olive Bolger. Please phone this evening.

Michelle, for once, was relieved to hear from her mother.

"And I had to go back to the doctor, Michelle. Those blood-pressure tablets he has me on don't suit me at all. I swear, I think they're giving me flutters. Poor Declan had to drive me to the surgery this morning. And Fiona's not well. Spent the night throwing up in the loo. In fact, the poor creature didn't make it to the bathroom in time – she vomited all over the bedroom carpet, Declan said."

Did her mother have to go into such vivid detail?

"All over the lovely green carpet. It's cruel. Do you remember when they bought that in Clery's sale? It was a real bargain, very good quality. I suppose it's ruined now. That was a right mess to clean up and Declan, God bless us all, never had a strong stomach."

He could lower eight pints a night, no bother, Michelle thought.

"Fiona swears she's coming down with a tummy-bug, but there's tummy-bugs and tummy-bugs, if you catch my drift. Declan let her have a lie-in this morning. He said she was washed out. He's very good, though, isn't he? Do you know what I'd lay a bet on, Michelle? I'd say she might be pregnant again."

Hopefully not. Fiona was only telling her last week that they could barely afford to clothe and feed the three they had.

"So, to cut a long story short, Doctor Moriarity told me I'd have to take things a lot easier. I won't be able for the garden any more, Michelle."

"We can get someone to come in once a week, Mam."

"Pay someone to come in? I thought *you* loved gardening and sure all I need is the grass cut and a bit of weeding done. Maybe Ken would give a hand?"

Michelle sighed. "Ken has a lot on his plate and I've my own garden to look after and the house is in rag order. I intend to spend the next few weeks painting and decorating."

"Ah, you've your little house perfect, Michelle. I wish this one was as good. I'd never be able to paint here – the ceilings are far too high. It must be great to have your health and be able to do your own painting jobs but, at my age, I suppose there's no sense in worrying about things like that. The way I'm feeling now, I mightn't see out next winter. The house will be here after me."

Could you strangle somebody down the line?

"Listen, Mam, I have to go. I've a dinner appointment in a few minutes."

"A dinner appointment? It's well for you, Michelle. How are you getting on there in Venice?"

"Vienna, Mam. I'm in Vienna."

"Sure they're all the one to me. I never got farther than the Isle of Man with your father. Anyhow, are you having a lovely time?"

"Yes, I am. I'll call you the day after tomorrow."

"OK, love. Don't worry about me, Declan will look in on me. You just enjoy yourself."

Michelle hung up. Mothers!

Five

It was ten past eight when Ruth James, all dickied up in a long, pale green chenille dress with matching sleeveless jacket, joined Michelle in the foyer.

"Hello, there. Sorry I'm a bit late. Gordon's a snail when it comes to getting ready."

"Not at all, Ruth. I've just come downstairs. There's no rush."

"You look very nice," Ruth said, admiring Michelle's royal blue cotton top and trousers. "Gordon's waiting in the car. We're parked down the street."

Ruth led the way outside. The rain had dwindled to a drizzle, although the road was still wet.

"Looks like it might clear up," Michelle said, hopefully.

Gordon James leaned across from the driver's seat of the Bentley to open a door for Michelle. "All set for a night out on the town?"

"I'm looking forward to it," replied Michelle as she sat

in. She ran her hand along the plush leather seat. "This is a lovely car."

"It's belongs to Cyril, my brother," Ruth told her. "He lends it to us while we're here. Saves us hiring a car."

"And it's an automatic," Gordon said. "Easier to drive. No gear changes."

He indicated and pulled out from the kerb. "We're off!"

Grinzing lived up to Michelle's expectations. The road ran through the picturesque village with its cobblestone footpaths. Flowers of every colour were planted in beds, pots and window-boxes and the wine taverns showed off their pretty gardens through archways, where music lilted on the air.

Gordon parked outside a tavern with a farmhouse façade, the Passauerhof.

"You two go in for a drink here, Ruth. I'll head down to the Rottmayr and see about a table. Are you hungry, Michelle?"

"No, not yet. I'd love a look around first."

Ruth opened the back passenger door for Michelle. "Cyril said he might join us later, if he can get away. I hope you don't mind, Michelle."

"Of course not, I'd like to meet him."

The two woman waved goodbye to Gordon as he drove back in the direction they'd come.

"He loves the Rottmayr, knows the owner quite well. It's like his local back home, in a way." She took Michelle's arm.

"Ruth, up there on the door, what are they?"

"The sprig of pine and the plaque?"

Michelle nodded.

"They tell us that the new wine is in and it's been pressed on the premises. It's a nice custom."

Ruth led her into the courtyard of the Passauerhof. There were wooden benches and picnic tables under a canopy of vines. A dozen or so customers sat drinking and chatting at two of the tables, tapping their feet to the music which came from inside the tavern.

"Let's go inside," Michelle suggested. "It looks nice and cosy."

It was. Three musicians – a fiddler, an accordionist and a guitarist – stood by the big, stone hearth, playing lively traditional tunes to an appreciative crowd.

"They're all locals," Ruth explained as she sat at a table by the window and beckoned to the man behind the bar.

Michelle listened to the song the men were singing. She couldn't make out any of the words. "That's not German, is it?" she whispered to Ruth.

"No, no," Ruth replied, nodding to the owner that the white wine was what they wanted. "It's some Austrian dialect. The music is sort of melancholy, isn't it? No doubt they're singing about star-crossed lovers in the Vienna Woods. These old folk-songs are highly sentimental, you know, not unlike the Irish *come-all-ye*!"

The waiter set down two glasses of wine.

"It's called Schrammelmusik," Ruth went on, "after a family who invented it back in the nineteenth century – but you'd want to ask Gordon. He knows more about it."

Michelle felt that Ruth was very ill at ease. She kept looking at her watch or at the door. She chattered on for the sake of chatting, but it was all forced and unnatural. Michelle would just have to be polite and make the best of the evening. She took a sip from her glass and made a face. The taste was sharp.

"Take it nice and slowly," advised Ruth. "You won't feel it, but these first wines are very potent. One night, I'd four or five and I thought I was fine – until I stood up! I think as you're getting older, alcohol has more of an effect."

The Rottmayr didn't appeal to Michelle at all. It was bright and gaudy and packed with the Vienna-by-night tour brigade! As she followed Ruth inside, Michelle was dismayed to hear the crowd singing "Roll Out The Barrel".

Gordon was sitting at a small table by the piano. He filled their glasses as they joined him. "Get that into you, Michelle. Sorry about the noise. I should have realised the place would be crawling with foreigners."

Funny thing to say, seeing that they were foreigners as well.

"We can't stay here, Gordon," his wife admonished him. "It's awful."

"I know," he shouted above the raucous singing. "We could move on, but what about Cyril?"

Ruth pulled her chair closer to the table. "We'll have to hang on for a while. What time is it now? Nine-thirty? We'll wait till ten. If he doesn't show up by then, he's not coming."

Gordon swirled the wine around in his glass. "How about ordering dinner?"

"Not here, Gordon. There are other much nicer taverns in the village."

"Well, why didn't you voice your objections to this place earlier, then?" he snapped.

Ruth ignored her husband's bad humour. "Michelle, what am I thinking of? You must be famished by now."

"No, honestly, no, I'm not. I don't mind when we eat."

She'd gone off the whole idea of food. Sitting with this pair was a strain.

"That's settled then." Ruth smiled at her. "We'll move as soon as Cyril arrives. They serve lovely chicken dishes in Zum Martin Sepp. And the wine's very good there. Much better than this stuff."

Gordon scowled at his wife. He knocked back his wine, poured another glass for himself and Michelle and signalled to the waiter to bring another bottle.

Michelle could sense Ruth's aggravation. She was saved from small talk by the arrival of a photographer.

"You'd like your picture taken? Yes?"

Gordon waved him away but Michelle decided this was a timely diversion. "I'll have one," she said.

She did her best to smile as the photographer adjusted his lens. "Ten or fifteen minutes," he told her as he went to the next table.

"A rip-off, they always are," Gordon said tartly. "Preying on innocent holiday-makers. After a few scoops, people don't mind putting their hands in their pockets."

"Nobody could accuse *you* of that," Ruth retorted.

What had him so angry, Michelle wondered – he was the one who'd suggested this tourist-trap with its exorbitant prices – she might as well go the whole hog and have her photo taken. She could laugh about it with Ken when she got home.

The Dutch crowd at the long centre table started up a loud feet-tapping, table-thumping ballad. This tavern reminded her of the horrendous, organised barbecues she used to go to in Spain when she was young – coaches up the mountains, rubber food, cheap plonk and some mountainy man with a beard, a beer belly and a herd of cows, attempting a drunken seduction.

Ruth waved over to a tall, dark-haired man, dressed in blue jeans and a black T-shirt. "Here's Cyril."

Very nice, Michelle thought. He battled his way over, between the crowded tables. He shook Gordon by the hand, kissed his sister on the cheek and smiled warmly at Michelle. "Cyril O'Connor."

"Michelle Bolger." She shook his outstretched hand.

He sat down on the spare chair beside Michelle and looked around. "Dreadful. Gordon, what were you thinking of?"

Before Gordon could reply, a buxom blonde came to their table, dressed in the traditional costume of a multicoloured, full skirt and a white, low-cut, puffed-sleeve blouse. She was painted like a doll, her hair was in pigtails and Michelle thought she looked absolutely ridiculous. A fifty-something Heidi.

"This is the owner, Brigitta," Gordon introduced her to Michelle. "She's a good friend of ours now, isn't that right, petal?" He squeezed the blonde's waist in a most familiar way.

Sweet Jesus, Michelle thought. Was this the reason Gordon liked this place so much? The pained expression on Ruth James's face spoke volumes.

"You're Irish, too?" the blonde asked Michelle.

"A former student of mine," Gordon said, winking at Michelle. "We want to show her around, so we won't be staying long tonight, Brigitta. I'll drop by again next week."

She smiled her goodbye and went to sing with the musicians who were breaking into a hearty version of "Goodnight Vienna".

The photographer came back with Michelle's photo – a miniature in a brown plastic key-ring.

The Zum Martin Sepp was a definite improvement – plain tables, candles lighting, fresh flowers. No fuss, no ostentation There was a simple folk-song being sung as they made their way to a table in a quiet corner. No tour busloads here, just a few locals and business people who waved over at Cyril.

Ruth and Michelle ordered *Backhendl* – chicken sautéed in egg and breadcrumbs – the dish she was sorry she hadn't chosen in Oswald und Kalb. Cyril and Gordon opted for *Fleischlaberl* – some kind of rissoles, Gordon told Michelle.

Cyril turned to her. "Do you know, Michelle, I'm convinced that we've met somewhere."

"Really?" She looked doubtful. "I've never been to Vienna before."

"No, not here. In Ireland, I mean. Let me see now . . . the Cork jazz festival last year?"

"No, I wasn't there. Maybe you met someone who looks like me. That happens all the time."

"No, no. Hold on, it's coming back to me. It must be about five years ago – more. The wine trade fair in the RDS, that's it! You were with someone from the business – "

"That's right. Ken . . . Ken Leavy," she said excitedly. "My boyfriend. I'm sorry, I should have recognised you but we met so many people that night and – "

"How could you remember me from that far back? Ken, yes. How is he?"

"Fine. He's part-owner of a hotel now. He's doing very well but he's run off his feet. Still, he loves it."

"We hoteliers grumble about how hard we work," he said with a grin, "but we all secretly love it. There's a great buzz."

"That's what Ken says."

"I believe you're a musician. Gordon tells me you're here for piano master-classes."

"Yes, they start on Saturday."

"What pieces have you chosen?"

"Oh, I won't be playing myself," she explained. "I'll just be observing."

"Observing?"

"Yes, you can learn a lot from watching another teacher at work, especially a maestro!"

"I'd say you're a good teacher," he said. "Gordon has the height of praise for you."

"I do my best but there's always more to learn, isn't there? It's important to keep up. Karl Harrach's supposed to be the best there is and I'm looking forward to see him in action.".

"What ages do you teach?" he asked.

"All ages. I've some students who are just starting out and others who are up to diploma level."

"What do you do if you get someone who's just not going to make it?"

Michelle hesitated. "If I believe a pupil has no talent, I have to be honest about it – tell her she's wasting her time It sounds harsh but the parents need to be told. They're the ones paying."

"Is it all girls you teach?"

"No, I have a few boys."

"I suppose you've some who are genuinely talented."

"Oh, I have! There's one young guy, Andrew Watkins, who's brilliant, has a real gift. Actually, it's a pity he couldn't have been here with me. I'm going to enrol him for master-classes in London next year."

"He's lucky to have you."

"You're very kind to say that." Michelle smiled as he filled her glass again. She was beginning to feel quite high.

"What are your plans for tomorrow, Michelle?"

"I might have a lie-in in the morning and I think I'll visit the Belvedere Palace in the afternoon."

"Would you like some company?"

"That would be nice," she said.

Was he coming on to her?

She wondered if he was married. Was she crazy, agreeing to go out with him after they'd just met? Mind you, it would be great not to have to keep scouring around for half-recognised guides or suspicious-looking men in anoraks.

She could do with an escort.

She glanced over at her hosts. They were whispering and Ruth looked annoyed. This was becoming tedious. It was very rude of them, Michelle felt, to be airing their dirty linen in public. Yesterday, when she'd met them in the café, they seemed to be very attached, very united. But tonight, they were like gladiators in the ring – barbing and taunting each other.

"You mustn't mind Ruth and Gordon, they're just having one of their tiffs. Another few glasses and they'll be all over each other. I took a taxi here," he continued, as if reading her thoughts. "I'll be the one driving home."

Their meals arrived and Ruth and Gordon smiled across the table. They seemed to have patched up their differences. At least their arguments didn't last long.

"How long have you been in Vienna?" Michelle asked Cyril, for something to say.

"How long am I here?" Cyril said. "Eh . . . about ten years, I suppose. I was going to go back to Ireland a while ago, take up a partnership in a hotel in Dublin, but the deal fell through, I'm afraid. Someone put in a bigger offer."

"Oh, I'm sorry."

"Ah." He shrugged. "These things happen."

"You seem to be hitting it off well." Ruth smirked. "Is my brother giving you the chat-up line, Michelle?"

"There'd be no point," Cyril assured her. "Michelle's well and truly spoken for."

"Oh? Are you married, then?" Gordon asked Michelle.

"Gordon!" his wife scolded.

"It's all right, Ruth. No, Gordon, I'm not married."

"You have a partner," Gordon said. "Isn't that the current term for it?"

"I do have a boyfriend, yes. His name's Ken Leavy. We've been together for seven years."

"Ah, and no little itch yet?" Gordon smiled but it wasn't a sincere smile. "Must be serious, this friendship."

"You could say that." Michelle tasted her chicken. It was delicious.

"Is he a musician, Michelle?" Ruth asked.

"No, no, although I met him through music in a way.

63

I was introduced to Ken by a friend who's in the concert orchestra. Lynn O'Malley."

"I didn't teach her, did I?" Gordon scratched his head. "I can't remember that name."

"No, Lynn's a violinist. A very good one."

"This Ken must feel out on a limb, Michelle, with all your musical friends. Musicians tend to stick together in a little élite."

"The same could be said for the hotel business. Wouldn't you agree, Cyril? Ken has his own social set. I was just telling Cyril, Ken's in the same line of work as him – he's a partner in the Fullerton Hotel. Do you know it? It's a small hotel, about forty bedrooms. Ken had it completely renovated when he took it over."

"The Fullerton?" Ruth repeated. "Yes, I heard something about it." She stared at her brother. "You mentioned it, Cyril, didn't you?"

"Ken loves it," Michelle went on, "because it's so near the city centre. It means we can sometimes meet for lunch."

"Does he live in?" she asked.

Michelle shook her head. "No, Ken lives with his sixteen-year-old daughter, Beth, in Griffith Avenue."

"That's posh," Gordon said. "And you, Michelle? Where do you live?"

"I have my own house in Collins Avenue – "

"Oh, in Whitehall. They're nice houses. You're quite near the Omni shopping centre."

"That's right," Michelle said. "It's very convenient. You used to live on the main Whitehall Road, didn't you?"

Gordon's eyes burned through her. "We had to move."

"The house was very big for only the two of us," Ruth butted in, almost apologetically. "The new owners converted it into five flats, I believe. Handy for airport staff."

"Indeed," Michelle agreed.

"We're living in a grand little bungalow in county Meath now. Ratoath," Gordon said. "It's Ruth and Cyril's family home." He turned to his wife. "You like living in your old home, don't you, love?"

Michelle thought his tone was resentful.

Ruth fixed her napkin on her lap. "Isn't it dreadful the way house prices have soared nowadays?"

"All this talk of Ireland," Cyril said, ruefully. "You're making me feel homesick."

Michelle smiled at him as he poured more wine. "You'd like to come home, would you, Cyril?"

"Sometimes I think I would but I've a good life here and I manage to visit Dublin quite a bit, especially in the winter. It's funny, when you're away for a long time – in some ways, I feel more of a foreigner at home than I do here in Vienna."

Michelle nodded. "I spent three years in the States. One in New York and then I moved to Connecticut for another two. It took me a good while to settle back afterwards. I used to wonder if I'd done the right thing, going home."

Glenn . . .

Two years living together on his farm. He raised cattle and she taught music in the local school. She almost married him. But the village was small, his parents lived nearby. His sister was married on the next ranch, his uncle was the town vet and his aunt the midwife. It was all very small, very claustrophobic.

Glenn was a good man, hardworking and responsible but Michelle wasn't ready to settle down. A year after she'd come home, he'd written that he was married and expecting his first child.

"Cyril says he's going sightseeing with you tomorrow, Michelle," Ruth interrupted her reverie. "I'm glad. It'll do him good to get away from the hotel for a few hours."

"It's very thoughtful of him to offer," Michelle replied.

Gordon stretched over for the wine bottle. "Fed up touring around on your own, eh, Michelle?"

A dark frown creased his brow.

Six

On Saturday morning after a light breakfast, Michelle set out for the first of the master-classes. It was still raining. She passed the Franciscan Church and, at the corner of the Seilerstätte, she turned right. She walked on, checking her map carefully. She regretted the fact that she'd never learned German – she found the names of the streets difficult to recognise and impossible to pronounce.

She had to consult her map again when she reached the Krugerstrasse so she took shelter in the doorway of a café. Yes, she was heading in the right direction. This street joined up with the Schwarzenbergstrasse and the next left was her turning. Might as well take a look at the menu posted in the window while she was here – snacks, sandwiches and cakes. She could come back for lunch. It looked nice with its marble-topped tables and wicker chairs.

The school was an old building in a quiet street off Walfischgasse. She went in and looked at the notice-board just inside the door. Professor Karl Harrach's class was in the main hall down the corridor. There was a cloakroom to the right and she left her wet raincoat there.

The hall was large with a high ceiling, it would be draughty in winter. There was nothing warm about the beige-coloured walls or the grey plastic chairs arranged in neat rows of ten on each side of the aisle.

Michelle took a seat in the second row and opened her programme. Four this morning: an Austrian boy, a French girl and then two students from North Korea.

There were only about fifteen observers, she was surprised to see, and most of them seemed to be Korean.

"Bonjour," the woman in the next seat said.

Michelle smiled at her. *"Bonjour."*

"Vous avez un élève ici?" The blonde Frenchwoman asked. "Excuse me, do you have a student with you?"

"No, unfortunately I don't. Professor Harrach's marvellous, I believe."

"Yes, the best. I'm with Antoinette, a young student of mine who's about to give her first recital. She's nervous about this class today but she has no need to be."

"It can be a bit nerve-wracking," Michelle said.

"I'm amazed there isn't a bigger audience," the Frenchwoman continued in perfect English.

"Maybe the fee put people off, it's almost as expensive to observe as it is to play."

"That's very true," the woman agreed.

The school had funded Michelle for the classes and would have paid for her accommodation too, but Ken had stepped in. Thankfully he had, as otherwise, there was no way she'd be staying in The Albany!

The Austrian student came out. He nodded to the audience, adjusted the piano stool, sat down and opened up his music.

From the right side of the stage, the maestro appeared and was greeted with a refined round of applause. He was small and dark-haired with a goatee beard. He wore a navy suit and a polka-dotted cravate, faintly Wildean. Early forties, Michelle guessed.

"Very impressive-looking, isn't he?" The Frenchwoman nudged Michelle.

Herr Harrach bowed and went to take his place at the piano. He whispered something to the young pianist, then sat back as the boy began to play Liszt's *"Vier Kleine Kavierstücke"*.

Michelle folded her arms and tried to get comfortable on the hard chair.

The boy was good but this was a difficult piece and he was taking it too fast. Technically he was very competent, but his playing lacked feeling. Professor Harrach stopped him. He turned to the microphone and began to speak . . . in German!

An interpreter in the first row. Good.

She turned to the small audience and started to explain . . . in Korean! It had never entered Michelle's head that there wouldn't be an English interpreter.

The professor carried on explaining, gesticulating and getting quite carried away. Michelle didn't catch one word and judging by the Frenchwoman's expression, she didn't either.

The boy stood up and Karl Harrach took his place. What a transformation! The music flowed in wonderfully executed phrases. That was what it was all about, the phrasing. Michelle scrutinised him. He kept the pedal down for the first few lines and it made such a difference. Then, as the chords changed, he changed pedal. The notes came alive under his fingers. Michelle closed her eyes and was transported. He was dazzling.

The boy took his seat again. This time, he took it more slowly. Better, much better, but he missed the G sharp in an A minor scale passage, possibly due to nerves. Harrach stopped him gently and made him repeat it again and again. Now, he was playing too loudly. Again the maestro stopped him and showed him how. Two lines over and over until he had it perfect.

Harrach addressed the audience. His face lit up animatedly as he spoke. He had a tuneful voice which rose and fell dramatically. He took over at the piano again and played the first two pages. The melody sang out from the right hand – this was the boy's main problem: he was too heavy with the left hand.

The Korean lady kept up the translation for the benefit of her group but Michelle didn't care. She didn't need to understand what was being said. It was the playing that made everything intelligible. The music transcended language.

The French girl played Field's "Nocturne No 4 in A".

He stopped her very little, encouraged her with gentle words. At first, she didn't understand what he wanted – she'd practically no German. But then the realisation would dawn on her and she'd return to the piece and smile as he said, *"Ja, ja, das ist richtig!"* He showed her how to half-pedal and place the first note of the broken chord, how to lead gently on and then build up to an urgency that was haunting.

She got a huge round of applause. Michelle congratulated her teacher.

"I'm so pleased with her," the Frenchwoman said, her eyes shining. "A student like Antoinette . . . she makes all the hard work worthwhile."

By the time they broke for lunch at one o'clock, Michelle was quite tired and very hungry, she'd to hold in her stomach to prevent it from rumbling during the last piece. Sometimes it was easier to perform than to listen and concentrate for such a long period. She got her coat from the cloakroom and left the building.

She hadn't been too impressed with the students at all. Money obviously counted more than talent here. Some of her pupils in Dublin were far superior, especially Andrew.

If he'd only been able to come. Michelle had furiously taken notes during the Bartok piece. She'd now heard a quite different interpretation – less of a slowing-up in the last few bars before the final *diminuendo*. When she went home she'd try it with Andrew. The Grieg sonata was lovely, too, and the tempo wasn't too difficult. She

71

might suggest that piece, especially the *allegro* part, to Barbara Brown. She'd be well able for it and she was looking for something to play in her school concert at Christmas.

Here it was, the small coffeehouse she'd passed this morning. She'd have a light snack here before this afternoon's classes began at one-thirty.

Michelle paid for her lunch, left the café and ambled up the street. She stopped to look at the porcelain in a china shop. Someone tipped her on the shoulder and she swung around.

"Guten Tag!"

It was the guide from the Figarohaus! He looked her up and down slowly, then he smiled slowly.

"Hello," Michelle replied, tightening the belt of her raincoat.

"You have started your classes, yes?"

She nodded. The way he was staring at her made her uneasy. It wasn't exactly a leer but . . . in daylight he seemed older than she'd first thought. He was in his mid-thirties, she reckoned. His little round spectacles gave him a steely-eyed look.

"I'm so glad to meet you again, I've been looking for you. I wanted to talk to you. Could we go for a walk, do you think?"

He'd been *looking* for her?

"I'm sorry, I've no time today. I'm due back in five minutes."

"Tomorrow, maybe?" He raised a bushy eyebrow. "We could meet for lunch, yes?"

No, definitely not. What was he at?

"I've something I'd like to give you back at my apartment," he said. The invitation sounded like a threat. "I live only two streets away. Could you meet me after your class?"

Something he'd like to give her? She'd bet!

"No, no, I have an appointment," Michelle said hurriedly. Why the hell did she have to justify her refusal with an excuse?

"Did you enjoy the Figarohaus the other day?"

Jesus Christ!

"Yes, yes, I did, thank you. Well, goodbye, I have to rush."

"Oh, let me walk – "

"I'm sorry," she shouted back over her shoulder as she rushed on.

Did you enjoy the Figarohaus?

It was *him* . . . it had to be!

Michelle ran on, her heart in her mouth. He was *after* her, she was sure of it. He must have spotted her as she left the café and waited for his chance to accost her in the street.

He was about to ask her to . . . who did he think he was? Go back to his apartment – did he take her for an utter fool? She was out of breath as she ran through the gates of the school.

73

She had to get her mind off this . . . this nuisance. She was here in the hall surrounded by people. *Normal* people. She was all right, wasn't she?

She turned to look at the spectators in the third row. No newcomers since this morning. Grand. Nothing could happen to her here. She nodded at the Frenchwoman beside her and opened her programme for the afternoon.

An Italian girl was on first, playing Schumann's "Romance in F-Sharp Major". Next was a Swiss boy with Chopin's "Nocturne in C-Sharp Minor". Good, she'd have a chance to hear what Harrach would do with this. She might suggest this piece for Elaine for the scholarship.

That's it, Michelle. Forget this pest. You've handled it now and there's an end to it. Concentrate on what you're here for – the music.

Nothing else matters.

Seven

Ruth James brought lunch on a tray to their bedroom. Gordon was edgy after his morning stroll. She'd advised him against going out in the rain but he'd insisted. He got very restless if he was cooped up inside for too long.

"Thank you, Ruth. Vegetable soup, is it? Good, good. What day's today?"

"Wednesday," she answered impatiently. Why couldn't he keep track of the days of the week?

"Would you pass me my glasses? They're over on the dressing-table. Thanks."

"Gordon, I'm worried about Cyril."

"Oh?"

"Yes, do you know he's seeing her again tonight? That's the fifth time in so many days. I don't like it, I thinks he's getting involved."

Gordon shook a liberal amount of salt into his soup. "Ah, it's nothing, Ruth. She'll be going home at the weekend, won't she? He's only being kind to her, knows she's at a loose end in the evenings. I'm sure that's all there is to it."

"Well, I'm not so sure. Cyril talks about her all the time. Remember the last time? He didn't get over that one quickly, did he? She led him a right merry dance and then dropped him when her boyfriend arrived back on the scene. Cyril was besotted by her and then she told him she just wanted to be friends. He took the break-up very hard. I don't want him going through the same thing again."

Gordon didn't answer, his mouth was full. This soup wasn't half bad. Whatever else about Cyril, he knew how to employ a good chef.

"It started with the Belvedere visit last Thursday." Ruth frowned. "A drive on Saturday, then they spent last Sunday together in the Zentralfriedhof. Imagine, wasting an afternoon looking at graves!"

"But sure Michelle would be interested in seeing where all the composers are buried – Brahms, Schubert, Beethoven and the Strausses. Where would you get the like of it, Ruth? So much genius buried in the one place! Many's the day I spent there."

"Buried genius!" she remarked wryly. "Your speciality."

He sprinkled more salt into the soup. "And Cyril wanted to take a photo of the Mozart monument for her. I don't know why you're surprised at that, Ruth. Don't English literature scholars visit Wilde's grave in Paris? And remember the day your cousin went to find Hopkins's grave in Glasnevin? Anyhow, lots of people visit cemeteries on Sundays."

"Yes, to tend to their family graves. Michelle isn't related to the Strausses, is she?"

There was no answer to that.

"And on Monday night he took her to that concert," Ruth went on, getting angrier. "Tonight, he tells me, they're going to watch the outdoor screening of *The Magic Flute*. That's for her benefit, definitely. Cyril has no interest in opera, you know that."

Gordon sighed. "Ruth, I wish you'd stop this. Didn't Cyril say he used to know Michelle's boyfriend, Ken whatever-you-call-him?"

"So?"

"He's not going to fall for her, he's just being courteous. Michelle's not his type. They've nothing in common."

"What's that supposed to mean?" Ruth asked caustically. "Too good for Cyril, is she?"

"She's just filling in time when she's here, told me herself she was glad of his company."

"I don't like her, Cyril, I never did. I was only polite to her because you asked me to be."

"I know that, Ruth. You've made it plain enough."

"She's too cool for my liking. You'd never know what she was thinking."

He buttered another piece of bread. "As you said, she'll be gone home in a few days and then you won't

77

have to like it or not like it. But in my opinion you're making a big fuss about nothing."

"Cyril's my brother, it's only natural that I look out for him."

"Give me strength! He's a grown man, Ruth. What do you think Michelle is – a man-eater?"

"Yes," she said huffily, "she probably is. That night we were in Grinzing she fawned all over him and don't tell me you didn't notice because you commented on it yourself. It was sickening."

"Don't start that again, for the love of Moses. You're jealous, Ruth, jealous of Michelle."

She tugged at the curtain-sash. "Don't be ridiculous. It's *you* who's jealous – jealous of Cyril. Maybe you'd like to be the one showing Michelle Bolger around town? I've seen the way you drool over her."

"Rubbish! You're talking rubbish!" he retorted. "Any man would find her attractive. She's tall and elegant . . . that beautiful blonde hair." He knew his wife was seething. "And furthermore, she has a sense of humour."

"And I don't? Is that it?"

He sighed and bit into his bread-roll.

"Living with you all these years wouldn't make for having a sense of humour, Gordon."

"Ah, drop it, Ruth. You're giving me a headache."

Ruth went into the bathroom and splashed her face with cold water. Gordon was annoying in the extreme. He didn't appreciate anything she did for him: running up and down four flights of stairs with his trays, so that he wouldn't have to put up with the other guests in the dining-room, getting him his morning paper, listening to his damned music and telling him how marvellous he was – massaging his bruised ego every time he needed.

Thirty years of looking after him. No, he didn't appreciate her . . . and he had a very short memory.

* * *

The Swiss boy was the last to play today. Michelle was anxious to hear his approach to the Mozart piano concerto. A hush came over the hall as he began. His fingers glided nimbly over the notes, feather-like in their touch. His playing was smooth and even, exactly how *legato* should be played. He had such control, making the music speak to them individually in its soulful, plaintive way. Michelle was so moved she was close to tears.

Professor Harrach didn't stop the playing at all. He too was moved, it was obvious. He sat in silence when the boy lifted his hands from the piano keys. Then he patted the young protégé on the back and began to clap.

* * *

Michelle had a coffee in the foyer of the hotel before she went up to her room. She took her change from the barman and, not bothering to take her purse out of her handbag again, she shoved the coins into her pocket. She felt paper. She took it out and stared at it. Her blood ran cold. It was the paper napkin she'd used in the café at lunch-time, still smeared with her lipstick.

Hello again!

We were so close today, we almost touched. You're driving me crazy, do you know that? You bent down to fix the strap on your shoe . . . you have such beautiful breasts. I want to feel them. I stared at you today and smiled but you didn't even see me. Why are you ignoring me?

Oh hell, it was starting again.

Why was he picking on her like this?

She left the coffee on the table, stuffed the paper napkin back into her pocket and ran to the stairs. She didn't stop running until she got to the door of her room then, fumbling for the key, she let herself in. She flopped on to the bed and took a deep breath.

What was happening here? He'd stopped bothering her for five days. Five whole days – she'd thought it was over . . .

He had no right to treat her like this. No right. She refused to be victimised – she'd do something drastic, fight it out in the open. She knew who he was now.

She'd call back to the Figarohaus in the morning and confront him. She'd tell Cyril and he'd go with her.

Why? Why? Why? Round and round in her head.

What did he want? Sex?

Could he not see that she had no interest in him whatever? Did he plague other tourists like this? Or did he pick on Austrian women too? If this was his usual modus operandi she could see how frustrated he must be. Frustrated and pathetic.

But why *her*? Why? She lay back on the pillow and closed her eyes. A short nap would be heaven.

The shrill ringing of the phone startled her. Groggily, she picked up the receiver.

"Ms Bolger? Yes, there's a man waiting down here at reception for you."

She shook herself awake. "A man?"

"Yes, a Mr Cyril O'Connor. He says you're expecting him."

"Oh . . . oh, yes. What time is it?"

"It's just after eight o'clock, Ms Bolger."

Eight o'clock! She'd been asleep for over two hours.

"Sorry," she mumbled, "could you tell him I'll be down in a few moments?"

Eight

A huge screen had been erected in Stephensplatz, in front of the main entrance to the cathedral. Crowds of tourists gathered at the outdoor cafés in the square, everyone delighted that the rain had finally stopped. Cyril found them a table with no trouble – he was a friend of the café owner.

"What would you like to drink, Michelle?"

"I'll have a beer, thanks, Cyril. The Gösser's quite nice, I tried it the other night."

"Mmh, a local brew. I think I'll join you. Hans!" he called to the waiter and ordered.

"Are you all right, Michelle? You seem a bit off colour. You're feeling tired? Maybe you should have had an early night – I wouldn't have minded."

"I'm OK, Cyril."

She'd decided not to tell him about what was happening. She was leaving Vienna soon and the whole sordid business would be over.

"It's been a long day," she said, "and I actually fell asleep when I got back to the hotel. I was still asleep when you arrived to collect me. I couldn't believe the time when the phone rang."

He passed her a beer. "Well, you've done a lot of running around and then you had a full day today. The classes are going well?"

"Very well. Not all of the students are as good as I'd expected but this afternoon there was a young Swiss boy – he was only about thirteen. Cyril, you should have heard him – his playing was spellbinding!"

"There's no substitute for real talent."

"No, there isn't. You can teach someone to play proficiently, skillfully even, but it's when there's a natural response, an understanding of the piece . . . that boy today, he was special."

She was so intent, it was captivating.

"He . . . I can't explain it very well," Michelle continued. "It was as if he *became* the music. The notes, the melody, the fingerwork, they all gelled. His mind, his body, his whole spirit was in the music . . . you can't teach that."

"I guess not. Look, Michelle, they're starting the screening. Do you know *The Magic Flute* well? I have to admit I've never heard it through before."

"It's easy listening. A bit like the French comic opera, more of a *singspiel* than opera per se."

He laughed. "What's a *singspiel* when it's at home?"

"It's a . . . a series of songs connected by the dialogue

you know, a musical. Some people find it easier to listen to than heavy opera."

"I bet they still sing their ardent farewell for half an hour before they go!"

"Something like that," she said with a smile.

"Did you enjoy it, Cyril?" Michelle knew it had bored him stiff, but she wanted to see what he'd say.

"Em, kind of." He looked at her out of the corner of his eyes. "To be frank, rites of purification aren't my cup of tea!"

"Get away!" she teased.

"Mind you, there was a lot of truth in it about life. Nothing is what it seems and all that."

"The typical theme of the comic opera." She brushed a crumb from her lap. "Did you like the aria?"

"Which aria?"

"'Queen of the Night'. Strong, dramatic!"

"Yeah, too dramatic. She'd a good voice, I grant you, but it was shrill."

Michelle tutted. "You're impossible to please, Cyril O'Connor! What about Tamino playing the magic flute as he passes through fire and water?"

"Well, you have to admire the poor sod's tenacity! I'm sorry Michelle, but I'd definitely prefer jazz. I'd love to take you to one of the Kellers in Linz."

"The next time I'm in Vienna," she promised. "This evening's a super memory for me, Cyril, one I'll always cherish – sitting here eating and drinking and listening to

Mozart in the Stephensplatz on a warm August evening."
She raised her glass to his.

"I'm glad," he said.

"And it's stopped raining – now that my stay's nearly over!"

"It's been great, these last few days, Michelle. I'll miss you when you go back."

She flushed. Michelle had got to like this man, to value his company. She would have been miserable spending the time on her own. He'd been good to her, kind, attentive. And he'd helped to take her mind off that . . . that . . .

You've lovely breasts.

She could feel the skin on the back of her neck crawl. She pulled her cardigan around her shoulders.

"Are you cold, Michelle?"

"No, no. I just got a bit shivery there for a minute."

"Would you like my jacket?"

"No, no thanks. I'd like to go back to the hotel soon, if that's all right with you. I've another long day tomorrow."

"No problem. I've to be up early myself. I'll get the bill."

As they crossed the square, he took her arm. He had to hurry to keep up with her long strides.

"Hey, hang on. You're a very fast walker."

She slowed down. "Sorry, Ken always says that too."

"Does he?" For a second she saw a flicker of annoyance cross his face. "He must miss you."

"I hope he does," she replied. "They say separations are good for love, help to spice things up – do you believe that?"

"I'm not sure." He guided her across the street. "When I lived in Dublin, I was engaged. She was to join me here but when the time came, she phoned and told me she'd met someone else. Secretly, I think she was two-timing me all along. In my case, separation definitely wasn't good. Maybe I took too much for granted?"

"That's a mistake we all make," Michelle agreed. "When you get comfortable with someone . . . "

"Is that the way you and Ken are? Comfortable?"

"We know each other well. Ken's very balanced. I tend to be the excitable one!"

He squeezed her arm. "Sounds interesting!"

She brushed him away. "No, Ken's good for me, helps to keep my feet on the ground. He's practical."

"Someone you can rely on," Cyril said quietly.

"Are you making fun of me, Cyril O'Connor?"

"Far from it," he assured her.

"I meant to phone him this evening and then I fell asleep. Never mind, I'll get him tomorrow." She turned to look back over her shoulder.

"What's up?"

"Cyril, did you hear footsteps behind us just now?"

"Footsteps? Michelle, there are crowds around. What do you mean, footsteps?" He looked down at her and his eyes shone in the light cast from the streetlamp. "What's the matter?"

She looked at him strangely. "Nothing."

"What's wrong, Michelle? You seem . . . worried."

"It's just that since I - "

"Yes?"

"It's nothing."

"Here we are at your hotel. Are you going to ask me in for a night-cap?"

"No, if you don't mind, Cyril, I'm very tired."

"Of course, straight to bed with you, Miss Bolger. Have a good night's sleep and I'll call you tomorrow evening."

"Ehh, I think I'll stay in, Cyril. I badly need an early night. I'm not used to all this gallivanting."

He looked disappointed.

"I'll be in touch before I go home." She shook his hand. "I'd like to take you and Ruth and Gordon out for a meal. You've all been so kind."

"There's no need for that."

"No, I'd like to. Just a small thank-you."

"OK, I won't argue if you insist."

He walked her to the door. "Goodnight, Michelle."

"Thanks for a lovely evening, Cyril. I really enjoyed myself."

He gave her a kiss on the cheek.

Michelle, her face covered in Oil of Ulay, sat up in bed and picked up the remote control. She'd poured herself a small brandy. She idly flicked through the stations but they were all in German. No, wait, there was some American network station, not NBC, but something like it. She sipped her drink and then the phone rang. She glanced at her watch. Four minutes past midnight.

Good. It would be Ken. She hadn't wanted to phone him this late but she was glad he'd decided to ring her.

"Hello, Ken?"

Silence.

"Ken? Is that you?"

Heavy breathing.

"Hello. Who's this?"

Music came on: Mozart's *"Eine kleine Nachtmusik"*, the first few bars of the *Rondo*.

Michelle recoiled. She held the phone away from her ear but she could still hear the cellos, the violins. Then the music stopped.

"Hello. Hello. Who *is* this?

"Get naked, lover. I'll be up in a minute."

The voice was low. Low and guttural and ugly.

"Please, please leave me alone."

The music got louder but it didn't drown out the manic laughter.

She banged down the receiver as if it had stung her.

Oh, sweet Jesus!

It rang again. Shriller, louder.

No, no, she wouldn't pick it up again.

Ring ring. Ring ring.

She bit the corner of the sheet.

Ring ring. Ring ring.

Please stop. Stop it, stop it, stop it.

Ring ring. Ring ring.

She couldn't bear it. She stuck her head under the pillow but she could still hear the wretched thing, even with her fingers in her ears.

Ring ring. Ring ring. Ring ring.

She jumped out of bed, knocking her book from the bedside table. "Shut up!" she screamed. "Shut up!"

Suddenly it stopped.

Michelle took the phone off the hook and crawled back into bed. She gulped back the brandy. She was shaking all over and now her stomach felt sick. Calm down, she told herself. You're here in your bedroom and you're safe. She glanced over at the door. Had she locked it?

She pushed back the duvet, got out of bed again and crept across to the door. Yes, yes, it was locked.

She'd have another drink, watch TV and forget about it. He couldn't get to her now. Door locked, phone off the hook – she was safe, safe.

Her hands trembling, she poured herself another brandy. She'd put up with a hangover in the morning. Tonight she had to blot this out, get some sleep.

This wasn't fair. Why was it happening to her. Why? She hadn't asked for this . . .

He was some sort of pervert getting his kicks or else . . . or else he was deliberately out to frighten her? Why would anyone want to frighten her?

He was building up to something . . . what? The note,

the dinner paid for, the message scrawled on the napkin at lunch-time. Now this. He'd actually rung the hotel and *spoken* to her. He was getting more daring.

What would he do next?

His voice . . . think, Michelle. Think, think. The accent was different. He didn't really sound like that guide at all. The tone was deep but it sounded muffled, half-choked. This was useless. He'd probably held a handkerchief over his mouth.

She was being stalked. There, she hadn't wanted to say the word before . . . even to herself. *Stalked*. Hunted like an animal.

She'd wanted to explain to Cyril – wanted to ask his opinion. Why hadn't she? How well did she know him? She didn't really know him at all, did she? He'd appeared on the scene, taken a shine to her and then asked her out.

No, it hadn't been like that, exactly. He just seemed to like her company. He didn't have any designs on her or, if he did, he certainly hadn't made a move. He was the soul of discretion and she'd made it quite clear about her feelings for Ken. She'd have sensed something in his behaviour if there had been anything wrong.

But why hadn't she confided in him?

Twelve-twenty. To hell, she *had* to speak to Ken. She dialled The Fullerton and let it ring for a few moments.

"Hello, is Mr Leavy there, please?"

"No, I'm sorry. He's just gone off duty. Is that you, Michelle? This is Paul."

"Hi, Paul. I thought he was working late tonight and I was sure I'd get him. Sorry to have disturbed you."

"No problem. He was supposed to be working late, but you know about the trouble at home."

"Yes."

What trouble at home?

"Beth rang at about eleven and he dashed off. I'll leave a message here that you rang."

"No, it's OK, Paul. I'll phone him tomorrow. Goodnight."

She felt alone. Totally alone.

Nine

Michelle was in the shower when she heard the phone ring. She turned off the taps, grabbed a towel and ran into the bedroom. Should she pick it up?

She stood there stupidly. Transfixed.

It stopped.

Blast, that might have been Ken. She picked up the receiver and dialled his home number.

"Mich! That's weird! I was just trying to reach you. The receptionist put the call through to your room but when I got no answer I presumed you'd gone down to breakfast. Did I wake you?"

"No, no, I was in the shower," she said hurriedly. "I phoned you at work last night but I missed you by minutes."

"It's great to hear your voice," he said. "You've no idea."

"Ken, I wanted to talk to you as well. I've something to – "

"Oh, Mich . . . Toni's back in Dublin. I wasn't going to tell you about it till you came home but the thing is, I mightn't be able to meet you at the airport on Saturday."

"Toni?" she echoed, a brick in her stomach. "Back? What do you mean . . . back?"

"A couple of days ago her mother got some kind of a turn. Gwen, her sister, didn't think it was too serious but Toni phoned and asked me to go and see the old lady."

That's what had him so upset. She'd known there was more to it than Beth's behaviour.

"Then, yesterday Mrs McRory was rushed into Vincent's Hospital. A stroke. Toni got the plane from Gatwick late last night. I met her at the airport."

He'd *dashed off* . . . to the airport to meet his wife!

"Is the old lady bad?"

"I don't think she'll make it. She's in intensive care. Beth went in to the hospital with Toni this morning. I've to work for a few hours and then I'll pop over there."

Michelle bit her lip. "Toni must be very upset."

"She is. I've never seen her so cut up. She was close to her mother – close for Toni, that is. I think she feels a bit guilty as well. She didn't visit as much as she might have. Toni told me last night that she'd intended to take her mother on a holiday this summer. Bit late now, isn't it? Toni's like that, full of good intentions."

"I suppose we all are," Michelle said. "This is hard on her, Ken."

"Mmh, we had a long chat last night, thought it might help to clear the air a bit . . . "

Michelle's heart stopped for a minute. "Is she staying with you?"

"No way, although she wanted to. No, that would have been a disaster. I gave her a room in the hotel – she refused to stay with Gwen. Said it would bring back too many memories if she stayed in her family home. Jesus, she doesn't give a hoot how Gwen feels having to sleep there on her own. I mean, I feel sorry for Toni, but I'm not that bloody forgiving or generous. I'm sorry, Mich, she always brings out the worst in me."

"It's all right," Michelle whispered.

"Still, as you said, this is a difficult time for her and I feel I should try to help her through it."

"Of course," Michelle said.

"Poor Mrs McRory, it's awful to see her like this. She was always very kind to me and she adored Beth."

"How's Beth taking it?"

"She got a terrible shock. She'd visited her granny only last week and they'd gone out for tea together. The old lady was fine then. But she's eighty-four – at that age it's from day to day."

"Yes," Michelle said slowly.

"Mich, I wish you were here with me."

"I'll be back the day after tomorrow, Ken. If . . . if anything happens before – you'll let me know, won't you?"

"Yeah, in one way I'm hoping she'll go quickly. I wouldn't want her to suffer. There's nothing worse than watching someone die slowly. They're very good in the hospital, but Toni's fussing around, bossing the doctors and the nurses and making a nuisance of herself. Sometimes she's an embarrassment."

"She must be up to ninety," Michelle said diplomatically.

"Mmh, she's always up to ninety. Since she's come back she's managed to disrupt everything. This morning she was here at the house shortly after seven, started to clean out the kitchen presses. I was furious, I really was. She didn't say anything but I could see she was critical of my housekeeping. It's none of her bloody business how I live my life – and she wasn't exactly Housemaker of the Year when she lived with me. If you saw her . . . up on a chair cleaning out presses and making comments . . . and her mother dying in the hospital."

"People do funny things at a time like this, Ken."

"Beth's thrilled to see her, as you can imagine. It's strange, Mich, Beth never blamed Toni for anything."

"She's her mother, Ken."

"Yes, that's why I never criticised Toni in front of Beth. I did the very opposite, tried to explain how Toni felt – not that I understood it myself, but it was important that Beth should know it had nothing to do with her. Kids often blame themselves for their parents breaking up."

"You did the right thing, Ken. There's nothing worse than one parent having a go at the other one."

"I don't mind helping out but Toni's hard work – expects to be waited on hand and foot, thinks I should drop everything to be at her beck and call. Anyway, that's my problem. How are things with you? What were you going to tell me?"

Michelle hesitated.

"I forget, it mustn't have been important."

No, it wasn't important at all, she saw that now. It was trivial, not a life-and-death situation.

"I'd better go, Mich. Will you be there tonight?"

"Yes, I'm staying in. Phone me after dinner, if you get the chance. You'll be going to the hospital this afternoon?"

"Mmh, Toni and I have our differences but she needs me right now and I want to keep up some sort of a united front for Beth's sake."

"I'll be thinking of you, Ken. Why not take a couple of days off work? That would ease the pressure on you a bit."

"I might have to," he said thoughtfully. "It depends on how things go. Right, I'll talk to you later, Mich."

"Bye, Ken. Mind yourself."

* * *

On Friday afternoon Michelle sat at the back of the hall, listening to the *Allegro* from Schumann's "Concerto op. 54". The French girl had done her homework well, her *staccato* had greatly improved, it was less harsh. She'd the chromatic runs and the broken chords perfected and she was building up to the *crescendo* very nicely. It was a spirited performance.

The ten-year-old from Korea was next: Chopin's "Etude op. 25". Another *Allegro*. She listened for a few minutes. The piece was slightly frenetic and it was having a funny effect on her. She felt edgy and decided to slip out for a coffee.

She avoided the coffee house where the guide had followed her, there was another one just around the corner. Michelle glanced through the café window. There were small tables with yellow tablecloths and bunches of flowers in blue vases. It looked cheerful and inviting and not too packed.

She went in, had a quick look around and sat at a table by the door. That way she could keep her eye on customers coming and going.

"Yes, madam?" the waitress said as she wiped down the table.

"Just a coffee, please."

"With cream?"

"Yes, thanks."

Ken's phone call this morning had worried her. Mrs McRory had a second stroke in the night and was in a coma. Toni was going to pieces and Ken was spending every minute with her at the hospital. What would happen? There was nothing like tragedy for bringing people together. Would Ken begin to have regrets?

Toni was vivacious, intelligent and witty.

She was also hard, Michelle reminded herself. She'd

97

jumped at the chance of that PR job in London and had sailed off with no compunction whatever, assumed that Ken would up and follow her. No thought about his career or about Beth's schooling.

They were walking in the Furry Glen on their third date, seven years before, when Ken had told her the whole story . . .

"I'd lost her, Mich. Nothing mattered to her by then – not me or Beth or her home or her job in the publishers. One letter from the company in England, an interview in the Gresham and then *wham!* 'I must think about my prospects, Ken.' I just couldn't take it in, Mich. She was a different person from the girl I married. It must have been going wrong before that and I hadn't noticed – I was too busy working. It never dawned on me that she wasn't happy."

"Ken, don't be so hard on yourself. You were a good husband and you're a terrific father, believe me."

"It's difficult, Mich. I love Beth so much, sometimes I think I spoil her, probably to make up for the fact that her mother –"

"I can't understand how she left her daughter, her only child," Michelle said, "I'll never understand that."

"Nor I. At first she suggested taking Beth to live with her in the apartment in Kensington. Can you imagine it? When would she have had time for the child? She was never serious about the idea, though – hadn't even bothered to check out the local schools. I suspect that after a few months Beth would have been shipped off to boarding-school. I simply wouldn't stand for that."

"Maybe she regrets what she did, Ken. She must miss her little girl."

"I doubt it, Mich. Toni's quite hard in many ways although it took me a long time to see it. Parties, publicity events, the races, first nights – they're much more exciting than reading bedtime stories, making packed lunches and joining the school run."

"It depends on your point of view," Michelle said.

"Exactly." He pushed some brambles out of their way. "She sends for Beth to visit her when it suits her. Now that the new boyfriend, George, is on the scene, the visits are becoming rarer and rarer."

Michelle squeezed his hand as they stopped to gaze at the lake. A young couple strolled by with a pram. The man made googling noises at the baby while the woman put on sunglasses.

Ken stared at them for a moment, then looked away. "I've no regrets, not any more. I'm lucky I have Beth. She's such a loving little thing. And there's you, Mich. I'd never have met you if – "

She pulled him to her and kissed him.

Oh, hell. Her coffee had gone cold.

Toni, the beautiful Toni, was back in Dublin. Her mother was dying and she needed Ken. Toni was upset and vulnerable now, not the sophisticated socialite from

London. She was losing her mother and Ken was there, comforting her. Putting his arms around her? They were still legally married and grief has a way of altering your thinking, changing your perspective, of making you take stock of life.

What if . . . what if she wanted to come back to him? Make a fresh start?

And Beth? She idolised her mother. She'd be thrilled if her parents got back together . . . naturally.

* * *

"Thanks, Michelle," Ruth said politely, "I really enjoyed the meal." The four of them were sitting at a corner table in the Stadtbeisl restaurant. "It was very kind of you to take us out this evening and the food was – "

"Excellent, excellent," Gordon interrupted. "The squid was absolutely scrumptious. How was your goulash, Michelle?"

"Delicious," she replied. "And the *Topfenknödel* for dessert was mouth-watering. I don't usually go for desserts."

"Rather you than me – I hate cream-cheese." Gordon made a face. "It doesn't agree with me at all, does it Ruth? Cheese of any kind gives me nightmares."

"I wouldn't know, Gordon," his wife said dismissively. "We haven't come here for a long time, Cyril. This was a good choice. It's very agreeable, I must say. Nice and relaxing."

"Mmh, the dark wood-panelling is kind of old-fashioned and cosy, I like that," Michelle said. "Here, Cyril, pour out the rest of the wine. Will we order another bottle?"

"Is that a good idea, Michelle?" Ruth raised an eyebrow. "You're travelling back tomorrow – you'll want to be fresh for the plane."

"I think we can let Michelle make up her own mind." Gordon frowned at his wife. "Come on, Michelle, it's your last night. What do you say to another? My treat."

"No, no, Ruth's right." Michelle smiled over at her. "My flight's not until the afternoon but I want to have one last look around the shops in the morning, pick up a few presents."

"So, Michelle," Cyril said, "what's your impression of Vienna, then?"

"I've had a great time."

That was the truth as far as it went. But it had also been a very upsetting time. Not much fun being tormented and worried. All in all she'd be jolly glad to get out of this city.

"I'm sorry I didn't get to see more," she added politely.

"You'll have to come back when the opera season starts," Cyril said. "I could get you tickets . . . and bring Ken, naturally. Maybe his daughter – what did you say her name is?"

"Beth."

"Yes, perhaps Beth would like to come too? And the next time you'll have to stay at my place. No, no, I mean it. Why waste good money paying for accommodation when you don't have to?"

Ruth looked anything but pleased.

Michelle gestured to the waiter for the bill. "We'll see."

Gordon played with the salt cellar. "Was your visit worthwhile, Michelle? The classes were beneficial?"

"Yes, they were indeed, Gordon. It's always good for a teacher to watch others teach – it opens the mind, as they say. I learned more about pedalling, properly done it can make a huge difference and it's something I hadn't given enough thought to before."

"It's great to hear you say that you're still learning, Michelle," Cyril said approvingly. "Too many teachers think they know it all."

"Not the ones I know, Cyril. Most of us are always looking for ways of improving our techniques. Another thing, I'm determined to see about that young student of mine, Andrew. He has a rare talent and this trip has convinced me more than ever that he should study music in college."

"And does he want to?" Gordon asked.

"He does but his father's the stumbling-block – he's a doctor and doesn't see any future for his son as a musician. Wants him to go on for medicine."

"Oh, that's typical!" Gordon groaned. "Nothing changes, does it? Parents and their bloody interfering!"

His voice rose and his face went red. "When I think of – "

"Ssh, Gordon," his wife warned, "keep it down, for God's sake." She smiled apologetically at Michelle. "Sorry, he gets so het up."

Gordon muttered into his glass.

"Now, now, let's lighten up a bit here." Cyril flashed a grin at Michelle.

"Why don't you two go back to the hotel, Ruth, and I'll walk Michelle back to hers, all right?"

His brother-in-law glared at him.

* * *

Michelle put her underwear and shoes into the bottom of the suitcase, then she packed the CD of the Vienna Boy's Choir singing the Bruckner motets that Cyril had unexpectedly given her as a parting gift.

She went to the drawer of the dressing-table and took out her hairdryer. She hadn't needed it as it turned out, the hotel had provided one plus an iron.

The note and the folded napkin lay in the drawer. She picked them up and scanned them again. She hadn't heard a word from her mystery man in two days. He'd obviously given up his game, whatever it had been.

Maybe he'd found someone else to pester?

God, that was a thought. Was he out there pursuing some other woman? Maybe she *should* drop these into the police station tomorrow morning and make out a report?

If he got away with this . . . he might go further next time. No, no, it had been a prank, that was all. It was over as far as she was concerned. This time tomorrow night she'd be in Dublin.

Back to Ken, to her own home, her family, her friends, her life – normality. Ken would need her when she got back. She tore the two notes into tiny pieces, went into the bathroom and flushed them down the loo.

Ten

Michelle hauled her luggage down in the lift to reception. The suitcase felt much heavier than when she'd arrived, because of the books she'd bought. Geoff came out from behind the desk.

"Here, Ms Bolger, let me do that." He carried the case over to the desk. "You're checking out this morning?"

"Yes, my plane for London is at three-thirty. Geoff, do you think I could leave my stuff here for a couple of hours? I want to do some last-minute shopping."

"No problem, I'll get your bill ready." He opened a file on the computer. "Gee, your time here sure flew by!"

"Yes, it did. Ten days but it doesn't seem that long and I didn't get to see half the things I wanted to."

"That means you'll have to come back." He looked up from the computer screen. "Won't be a sec now. You've a few phone calls here that have added up to quite a hefty sum."

Michelle nodded. "And I used the minibar more than I'd meant to."

"What the hell?" He grinned. "You were on vacation."

"Geoff, could you order a taxi for me for two o'clock."

"Sure thing, going to?"

"The airport."

He looked horrified. "You don't want to take a taxi to the airport, Ms Bolger, it'll cost a fortune! All you need do is get the underground to the Hilton Hotel. Then there's a direct airport shuttle every twenty minutes. The fare's about 60 schillings. A taxi would be five times that."

"Well, as you said, Geoff, I'm on holiday. No point in stinting at this stage."

He scratched his head as he handed her the bill. "You're the boss!"

Michelle wrote a eurocheque for the amount. "Thanks, Geoff. I'm off into town for an hour or two and I'll see you when I get back. Are you sure the suitcase isn't in your way there?"

"Naw, I'll shove it behind the desk. I might not be here when you get back, Ms Bolger, so I'll say goodbye." He shook her hand warmly. "Have a nice trip home."

"Thanks for everything, Geoff. You've been most helpful."

Another grin. "Just part of the service, ma'am!"

All the same, Michelle would leave him a generous tip.

She bought a silk scarf for her friend, Lynn, a book on baroque art for Beth and a lace tablecloth for her mother. She couldn't find anything suitable for Ken so he'd just have to make do with duty-free whiskey, and she'd get him some chocolates. Ken had a very sweet tooth. Anyhow, at the moment he had more on his mind than presents from Vienna.

Twelve-thirty. She'd a little over an hour left. Almost unintentionally, she found herself walking in the direction of Domgasse – she was going to face the bastard and inform him, in no uncertain terms, what she thought of him. She'd march right up to him, tell him that she knew about his sick games and that she was going to report him to the police.

Nervously, but determined to brave it out, she opened the door of number 5 and climbed the stairs. There was a fair-haired girl writing in some kind of a ledger at the desk.

"Excuse me," Michelle said politely, "do you speak English?"

"A little," the girl replied, without looking up from her work.

"Em, eh, I'm looking for . . . someone who works here. He's got, em, dark hair and glasses."

"Franz?"

"Yes," Michelle said. "I think so."

The girl looked at her suspiciously. "You think so?"

"Yes," Michelle mumbled, "it's Franz I'm looking for."

She shrugged. "He's gone."

"For lunch?"

"No, he's not here."

Michelle hesitated. "Do you know where I could find him?"

"Sorry, he's gone. Holidays. He left three days ago."

"*Three* days ago?"

"He's gone back home maybe, or to Salzburg to visit friends? With Franz, you never know."

"Oh, I see."

The girl put down her pen. "Would you like to leave a message for him. He'll be back next week."

"No, thanks. It's all right. Sorry for disturbing you."

The girl nodded and went back to her work.

Michelle walked back down the stairs. She hadn't been able to challenge him, just as well. It was an impulsive idea and maybe she'd have made a fool of herself. What would she have said to him?

And supposing he wasn't responsible for any of this? She'd no *real* proof that this Franz was her secret pursuer except for the pushy way he'd behaved in the street. Damn! If only she could have checked his handwriting in the ledger. But she couldn't go back now and ask to see the book. The girl would think her crazy.

Right, she'd just have to forget all this, put it behind her. She'd never see the guide again and if he was trailing someone else now, there was nothing she could do about it, was there? A sliver of guilt pricked her conscience.

She knew the *real* reason why she didn't report him. She'd known it all along. She was ashamed. Something in her had triggered off this behaviour. She must have done or said something to encourage him. She didn't know what, but it was a disturbing thought.

Michelle strolled back to Stephensplatz. The sun was shining high in the sky and the horse-and-trap tour guides were doing great business. They'd probably have their second heatwave of the summer in Vienna and she'd be back in the Dublin drizzle in about nine hours' time.

Josef was at the reception desk when she got back to the hotel after a hasty lunch.

"Ah, Ms Bolger. Your taxi has just arrived."

"Thanks, Josef. Could you see that Geoff gets this, please?" She handed him an envelope.

"Here, would you like me to try to squeeze those parcels into your suitcase? We can fit in the other small one as well, I think."

"The other one?" She stared as he pulled out her suitcase. There was a small package on the top. "What's that?"

"It belongs to you, doesn't it? When I came on duty it was there, on top of the case."

"No . . . I didn't leave it there."

The parcel was wrapped in white paper and tied with brown string. Michelle, all butter-fingers, tore off the string. It was a CD of Mozart, performed by the *Capella*

Istropolitana chamber orchestra, conducted by the famous Austrian, Wolfgang Sobotka.

No card or message.

Michelle's hands started to shake. The CD had the *"Serenata Notturna"* and the "Lodron Night Music". It also had *"Eine kleine Nachtmusik"* – including the *Rondo* she'd been subjected to over the phone.

She felt the colour drain from her face.

"Ms Bolger? Your taxi," Josef gently reminded her.

"This isn't mine," she said and left the disc down on the desk. "There's been some mistake."

Eleven

Toni Leavy lay down on the bed in the darkened hotel room. Her head was pounding but she was afraid to take a pain-killer on top of the sleeping pill. Ken had been an absolute pet during the past week. She'd never have got through it without him.

Toni couldn't take it in. Her mother was dead.

She'd never see her again, never speak to her on the phone, never visit her, kiss her or hug her. She squeezed her eyes shut. No more tears, she'd cried herself out.

She hadn't been prepared for this at all. It was so sudden. She'd never given any thought to her mother dying. The old lady had been strong, full of life and very independent. Her own woman, that's how Gwen described her and that's what she was. She was outspoken and honest. Honest to the point of cruelty sometimes . . . when Toni had told her she was leaving for England . . .

"You're what?" Her mother was appalled. "You're going to London? For a *job*? Have you lost your senses, Toni? You've a perfectly good job here – "

"Mum, I need this challenge. It's a great opportunity and – "

"Opportunity?" her mother said mockingly. "Toni, you've had all the opportunities I never had, good schooling, university, a well-paid position . . . what do you mean by *opportunities*? And what about Ken?"

"Ken could get a job in London, no problem. There are plenty of openings in the tourist industry there and – "

"You're totally unreasonable, Toni. I can't believe I'm hearing this. And Beth? Have you thought about *her* at all?"

"Mum, for Pete's sake, don't drag Beth into this. One school is the same as another and I've heard the private ones in London are very well run; efficient, good discipline. There's a much wider choice, for one thing."

Her mother looked at Toni in utter bewilderment. "What did Ken say when you told him?"

Toni flushed. "He . . . he didn't take it too well, but he'll come around, Mum."

"Will he? We'll see, Toni. We'll see. London is no place to rear a child – she'll miss her little friends, not to mention Ken's family. And as for Gwen and myself – " Her mother's eyes filled up. "Don't do it, Toni. Please."

"Mum, London's only an hour away. You can visit as often as you like, once we've invested in an apartment."

"You won't be buying a house?" her mother said,

shocked. "You can't bring up Beth in an apartment, Toni. What about a garden?"

"A garden's not the be-all and end-all. There are parks all over the place and playgrounds."

"Parks and playgrounds! Huh! I think it's terrible what you're doing. The poor little mite living in a smog-filled concrete jungle."

"Mum, don't exaggerate – it'll all work out in time. You'll get used to the idea, just as Ken will."

But Ken hadn't. He'd dug his heels in – she had to choose between him and the new job. She made her decision and she stuck to it, hoping he'd come around eventually . . .

Her mother had been devastated when Toni left but that was to be expected. She didn't understand Toni's ambition or her need to get away. She'd taken Ken's side and, of course, she was devoted to Beth.

Toni regretted now that she hadn't been closer to her mother over the years. But then, she hadn't time to be running back and forward with her heavy work schedule, and she did have her mother over on that holiday. When was it? Some years ago, she realised guiltily, but there was also the fact that her mother wasn't keen on flying.

Gwen.

Yeah, her sister had been good, she had to admit. The dutiful daughter. She'd lived in the family home and kept an eye on things. But sure that hadn't been difficult – their mother had never been sick and wasn't it much cheaper and handier for her sister to live at home? It wasn't as if their mother was ill or doting or incontinent or anything like that.

Toni sat up and lit a cigarette. Another thought struck her. What would happen to the house? It would have to be sold.

She supposed she'd have to agree to Gwen staying on there, at least for the time being. In all fairness, Toni was entitled to half the proceeds from the sale of the house. In any case, why would Gwen, a single woman in her forties, want to live in a big house on her own? Far better to get rid of it and Gwen could get herself a nice little flat in the city. It'd be more convenient for her for work, wouldn't it?

George? Toni was very annoyed with him. He'd phoned her every day since she left their apartment in Kensington, pretending concern about her mother but, when the chips were down, where was he? He couldn't "take time off work to come over for the funeral", had to "finalise the advertising contract with Harrods". OK, it was important, she knew how important but nevertheless . . . her mother was dead, for Christ's sake. Dead.

This bloody sleeping pill wasn't working at all. Toni stubbed out the cigarette and switched off the bedside lamp. The more she thought about it, the angrier she became. George should be *here* with her now. He should drop everything, leave the contract for someone else to sort out. His place was with her at this awful time.

She'd a good mind to phone him this minute, tell him

where to get off. No, she wouldn't bother. To hell with George.

Ken was different.

In spite of everything, their rows and their long separation, he was standing by her. Even Gwen remarked on how helpful he'd been. He'd phoned Massey's to organise the death notices and the funeral cars and the coffin. He'd called on the priest to make the church arrangements. He'd taken over to save them the hassle. Ken was a great organiser.

You could depend on a man like Ken, he was true to his word. When she thought back now she realised what they'd shared together. He'd been supportive of her all the time they were married, when she had Beth, when she'd taken the job in the publishers'.

Ken never made her feel inferior, the way George sometimes did – slagging her about her Irish accent. And she wouldn't mind, but she didn't *have* an Irish accent. George could be a right pain. He wasn't averse to putting her down in company either. Ken would never do that.

Leaving Ken had been the worst mistake of her life.

Beth . . . she was almost a woman and Toni had missed out on her growing up. It was too late to do anything about that now but, in the future, she resolved to play a much bigger part in her daughter's life. Beth could come and live in London if she wanted to . . . no, Ken would never agree to that and Beth would want to finish her schooling in Dublin.

She switched on the light again and lit another cigarette.

What if *she* moved back here? She could set up her own PR business. She'd enough experience. She didn't need George any more. Yes, that was an idea. And who knew *what* might happen?

Michelle Bolger?

What about her? No, no contest. If Ken was genuinely serious about Michelle, he'd have asked for a divorce years ago. They didn't even live together. What did that say about their relationship?

She could see Michelle's side of things. Why would a single woman want to share her home and her life with a teenager who wasn't her own flesh and blood? Of course if she truly loved Ken, she'd be willing to take on his commitments, wouldn't she? So, did this woman love Ken at all? That was the question.

And Ken?

He talked about Michelle a lot but that was probably out of habit. What actually kept them together? Passion? Companionship? She could provide those far better than Michelle Bolger. Yeah, Toni smiled as she remembered sex with Ken.

She got out of bed, switched on the main light, went to the dressing-table mirror and smiled at her reflection. Even now, at this terrible moment of grief, she looked well. No lines, no blemishes – despite her smoking. Her hair was still very dark, only a few little grey strands at the temples and Loving Care saw to them. And she'd kept her trim figure.

She'd be around for another week – plenty of time to seduce her husband all over again. And, legally, he *was* still her husband. One night of passion, that's all she needed. He hadn't forgotten what they were like together. That kiss last night – it was more than a friendly peck.

Toni knew finally what she wanted. She wanted her husband back and she was going to fight for him. Michelle Bolger was no competition. Toni had all the advantages and her main one was that she was Beth's mother. A child was the ultimate bond between a man and a woman.

She'd phone Ken now to see how he was, thank him for all he'd done for her today. She dialled the house. No answer. Maybe he'd gone into work for a few hours? Never mind, she'd see him tomorrow.

* * *

Ken Leavy sat nursing a soda water in the bar of the arrivals building of Dublin airport. He'd a thumping great headache. What a day! He'd finally managed to get Toni to lie down. The doctor had prescribed heavy sleeping pills to help her get a decent night's sleep.

He was glad Beth had insisted on staying with her aunt Gwen in Gran's house. Gwen was worn out running to the hospital, looking after Toni and coping with the rest of their relatives who'd descended on the house in droves. Gwen was finding the house very lonely – not that this would have occurred to Toni. Even now, at her mother's death, she was being selfish. Gwen was kind, good-natured, like her mother. He wondered, and not for the first time, who Toni took after.

The old lady had never regained consciousness. No struggle, no moan, not even a sigh. They say you leave this world as you live in it, perhaps this was true. Only the monitoring machine had registered her death. She simply stopped breathing.

An easy end, the doctor said. She hadn't suffered.

Ken had held his sobbing wife and his grief-stricken daughter. To an outsider it looked like a typical family scene – people brought closer together by grief. But there was a strain, a tension, between Toni and himself that was worse than before.

He'd taken Toni, Beth and Gwen out to dinner last night and he saw a look in his daughter's eyes that he hadn't seen for years. A look of expectation. What was Beth thinking as she sat at the table with her mother and father? She'd smiled and chatted, was her old bubbly self for a few hours, asked her mother all sorts of questions – about her job, about the London apartment, about her plans for Christmas. She touched on every subject except George. Her mother's boyfriend wasn't mentioned. And when Ken had spoken about Michelle, Beth had clammed up.

Toni had kissed him goodnight last night in a way she hadn't since they were together. He'd pulled away and there were tears in her eyes. God, it was so bloody complicated.

The next few days would be taken up with the funeral and then she'd be going back to London. She'd suggested that Beth travel back with her for a holiday. Ken couldn't stop his daughter going but he didn't like the idea.

He glanced up at the arrival times on the television monitor. Michelle's flight from Heathrow was due in five minutes.

Michelle walked down the steps from the plane, carrying her brief-case and the duty-free booze. Surprisingly, it wasn't raining. Hopefully she wouldn't have long to wait for her luggage and, at this hour, she'd have no trouble getting a taxi. Traffic wouldn't pose a problem and she'd be home in less than an hour. She wondered how Ken was. Probably still at the hospital.

She watched the bags come out on the conveyer belt. Hers was practically the last one out. She picked it up, walked under the *Nothing to Declare* sign and through the glass doors to the waiting area of the arrivals building.

The man in front of her pushed a trolley laden with four suitcases. His plump wife marched along beside him, babbling away and laughing. Then a young girl pushed through the crowd screaming at the top of her voice, "Ma! Da!"

The couple were hugged and kissed and slapped on

the back. Michelle sighed. It would be nice to have someone to –

"Michelle!"

He was there! Ken was standing to the side, a big beam on his handsome face. He rushed over and threw his arms around her.

She hugged him with all her might. "Ken."

He bent his head and kissed her tenderly on the lips.

"Oh, Mich. You're home!"

Twelve

Michelle dropped her brief-case on the floor. She opened the tops of the windows – the sitting-room was very stuffy. Then she stood examining the room, as if seeing it for the first time. It was always like this after a holiday, things caught your eye that you hadn't spotted before. What she noticed now was the grubbiness. The cream-coloured walls badly needed a coat of paint, as did the doors and the skirting. The three-piece suite looked very drab; she'd gone right off peach, but if she changed that, she'd have to change the curtains as well.

"Have you checked your post?" Ken called in from the hall, as he carried in her suitcase.

"The post? Why? What's there?"

He came into the sitting-room with a bundle of letters.

"I've just got in the door, Ken. Give me a minute!"

"OK." He put the letters on the arm of the couch. "Take it easy."

"Sorry, I didn't mean to be tetchy. I'm tired."

"Tired and emotional! I don't care what humour you're in, Mich, I'm just so relieved to have you back!" He hugged her. "Relax, put your feet up and I'll pour you a drink."

She lay on the couch and flicked through the letters. "Nothing much here – the usual bills. Oh, here's a card from Portugal from Lynn. She went to the Algarve with her sister – a holiday after the break-up with Fred."

"Fred the flautist?" Ken laughed.

"Not funny. I forgot to send Lynn a card from Vienna."

"She'll understand – yours was a working trip more than a holiday. Will I close the window, Mich? Are you in a draught there?"

"In a minute," she said, stretching her legs out. "I'd like to air the room a little longer. Ken, thanks for getting in the groceries for me."

"Well, it's Saturday evening and I knew you wouldn't want to spend Sunday in a supermarket."

"No," she said. "I'll never understand why anyone goes to a supermarket on a Sunday. I mean, they've late-night shopping now practically every evening of the week. Wouldn't you think they'd have something more exciting do with their time on a Sunday? Like visiting their beloved mothers. Hmm, maybe trolley-pushing's not such a bad idea, after all."

When would she have the guts to get around to the subject of Toni? She'd been dying to ask him but if he didn't mention his ex-wife, maybe he'd a good reason?

"Your mother's not the worst, Mich. She was delighted to see me the other day, never stopped thanking me for bringing her to Omni. At least she's appreciative."

Michelle stretched again. "She'll have you wrapped around her little finger if you don't watch out . . . but thanks, Ken. What would I do without you?"

"You'd manage fine, as you always do. It's good to have you back, Mich."

"It's good to be back," she said and she meant it. "Where's that drink you offered me?"

"What'll be? A gin?" He stood up. "Are you hungry? Will I fix us something to eat?"

"Not for me, I ate on the plane. I could do with a drink, though."

"I'm ravenous. I bought some pies in Marks and Sparks – I'll stick one in the oven. The chicken and broccoli's quite tasty. Right, a drink coming up."

"Actually, forget the gin. I bought some nice red wine. Look, there in the bag on the chair."

He went to the kitchen to get the corkscrew. Michelle kicked off her shoes, fluffed up a cushion and placed it under her head. The ceiling was brown and blotchy in parts. She'd definitely have to get the paintbrushes out next week. How long would it take her to redecorate this room and the dining-room? The folding doors meant she'd have to paint them both or one room would show up the other. About four or five days, she reckoned. It wasn't as if she'd have to wallpaper. If she used a roller, it would speed things up.

MARY McCARTHY

Ken came back from the kitchen with two glasses, the corkscrew and a packet of pistachio nuts she'd bought for him in the Duty Free.

"What time do you have to go home?" Michelle asked.

"I don't. I'm all yours! Beth's staying with Gwen tonight and Toni should be out for the count by now in room three on the first floor – sounds like a line from a song, doesn't it?" He opened the wine and left it on the coffee table. "We'll let it breathe for a while."

"So, you can stay?" She was delighted.

"Indeed I can. You look well, Mich. The break did you good." In reality, Ken thought she looked tense. "Will I shell a few nuts for you?"

"No, thanks. Mmh, I've had an interesting few days."

She wouldn't tell him *how* interesting. If she didn't talk about the stalking episode, she'd be able to forget it. Anyway, lying here on her couch, chatting with Ken, watching him shell nuts . . . the whole thing seemed so bizarre now – it was as if it had never happened.

"Tell me about the classes?"

"Nine to six every day with an hour for lunch. It was pretty heavy going but I've plenty of new ideas, which was the object of the exercise." She moved her legs to give him room to sit down. "I'd have loved more time for sightseeing, though. Maybe we could to go back together sometime, Ken?"

"It's a wonderful city but you do need time to have a good look around. When I was there, I was caught up in

124

business meetings, so there are places I never got to see either. Did you like Schönbrunn?"

Michelle took his hand and curled her fingers around his. "Fabulous, except I didn't manage a proper visit to the gardens – the bloody rain spoiled the day. The evening I spent in Grinzing was good fun, though, with Gordon James and his wife."

"They seem to have been friendly." He'd piled about twenty nuts into a bowl on the coffee table.

"They were OK, I suppose. Ruth's brother, Cyril, joined us. He was good company."

He munched. "Yeah?"

"He showed me around. It was handy to have the car although you don't really need one in Vienna, but I definitely got to see more places than I would have trucking around on my own."

"It's more fun with somebody else, too. So, come on, out with it. Tell me all about this Cyril."

No, she wouldn't be side-tracked any longer.

"Your news first, Ken. How's Toni?"

"She's . . . what can I say? Toni is Toni. I'd rather not discuss her. I've had a bellyful for the past few days. If I talk about her, I'll only get into a bad humour and I don't want to spoil your first night home." He smiled. "Tonight I want everything to be perfect. Let's not talk about our families at all. Let's pretend they don't exist – for a few hours!"

"All right, so. I'll bore the pants off you talking about Vienna instead!"

"You never bore me." He took the wine bottle and poured each of them a glass. "Mmh," he said as he had a sip, "this is a bit of all right." He read the label: *"Blauer Burgunder*. It's strong, not as light as the usual Austrian red, is it?"

"I like it," Michelle said. "Cyril ordered it one night and I thought it was rich without being too fruity."

"So long as this Cyril wasn't too fruity!" Ken leaned over and pecked her on the cheek. "So, what was he like, my competition?"

"No competition. Not half as nice as you."

"Nice? Jesus, she thinks I'm *nice!* What a blow to the ego, Michelle Bolger!"

"You've absolutely nothing to worry about. Cyril was very polite and kind but I didn't remotely fancy him."

"Glad to hear it." He took her bare feet onto his lap and gently massaged them.

She closed her eyes. "Ooh, that feels good."

"So do you," he whispered as he moved his hand up her leg and under her skirt, stroking her thighs.

"He's Ruth James's brother. Oh, I already told you that. Actually he said he knew you, remembered you from some wine fair we went to years ago. He's manager of a hotel, you'd have a lot in common with him."

He continued to caress her, making little circling motions with the tips of his fingers. "Cyril what?"

"O'Connor."

He pulled his hand away abruptly. "Cyril O'Connor!"

"Yes. Do you know him?"

"Do I what! Mich, you really met up with that chancer? It's incredible."

She sat up and took a sip from her wine glass. "What is?"

"Cyril O'Connor's the guy I nearly went into business with. Remember? I told you about it at the time."

Michelle stared at him. "You told me some con man was trying to go into partnership with you but you never told me his name," she said, aghast. "It couldn't be the same man."

"Tall, dark hair, blue eyes?"

"Yes," she said slowly. "Nice accent."

"And he's in the hotel business? Oh, it's the same all right. This really takes the biscuit. Cyril O'Connor – such a scam merchant. And he threatened to sue me for pulling out of the deal!"

Oh hell! It was *Ken* Cyril was talking about when he told her that he'd almost gone into a partnership in Ireland. He'd sounded peeved . . . all the time he'd spent with her . . . he must have resented her. And he'd spoken about Ken without as much as a flicker of animosity.

"I can't believe it – he was so kind. Thoughtful."

"Thoughtful! I'd say he was. That's the way these guys operate, Mich. Did you tell him you were my girlfriend?"

She nodded.

"He was obviously trying to upset *me*." Ken poured more wine. "He knew full well you'd tell me all about it."

She blushed. She'd thought that Cyril had *liked* her,

fancied her even. He'd showed her a really good time. Why would he have gone to so much trouble if he hadn't liked her?

"I'll never forget that bollocks, he spun me such a web of lies," Ken continued, not knowing he'd irked her. "Said he had money stashed away in a foreign bank account – cash he'd accumulated from savings bonds and investments. What's this Terry nicknamed him? 'The great pretender'. I gave him quite a different epithet!"

"I thought he was charming." Michelle's anger rose. "I fell for his act completely."

"So did I, Mich. He was so bloody plausible – had falsified bank records, the lot. Luckily, Terry had him thoroughly checked out. Phoney address, no capital or assets whatever – he was flat broke. The last business he was involved with went to the wall."

"Well, he's not broke now, Ken. He drives a Bentley."

"He might be *driving* a Bentley, Mich, but he sure as hell doesn't own one," Ken insisted.

"No, you must be wrong. The hotel is right in the centre of Vienna, an old established hotel, and business is booming. I saw it with my own eyes. Cyril told me he had a financial interest – that he'd invested in the hotel. He's loaded, Ken."

"Not unless he won the Lotto, he's not. Did you meet the owner?"

"No, I didn't," Michelle admitted. "He was away."

"There you go. Cyril was spoofing. He's the manager and, as such, he'd be on a fairly good salary but there's no way he'd have the money to *invest* in a Viennese hotel, take my word for it." He saw her crestfallen expression. "Don't feel bad about it, Mich. He's quite convincing, I'll grant you that. I would have fallen for his spiel myself if it hadn't been for Terry."

"There I was, thinking that he actually *liked* me . . . I feel like such an idiot."

"Why should you? You took him on face value, there's nothing wrong with that. It's not as if he conned you out of money . . . Mich, you didn't lend him money, did you?"

"No, no, there was no question of that – he was spending money like water."

"There's no harm done, so."

No harm done?

But there *was*. *He* was the bastard who had almost ruined her holiday . . . he was taking his anger out on her and disguising it in a pretence of friendship and she'd trusted him, thought of him as her escort, her protector. Bloody ironic, wasn't it?

It all began to make sense in a perverse kind of way. She had her motive now: revenge. Cyril O'Connor had gone out of his way to get into her good books, to be courteous and helpful to her and all the time he detested her boyfriend.

He'd known all along who she was, from the time Ruth had innocently mentioned her name and talked about bumping into her in the café. He'd made it his business to join them that night in Grinzing and *she'd* made it plain sailing for him from then on. What a moron she'd been. He couldn't get to Ken, so she was the next best thing.

A sitting duck.

"I'll just check the oven, Mich. Have a little piece of the pie, why don't you?"

"No," she said absent-mindedly, "no thanks, Ken."

But what had *he* got out of it? What satisfaction could there be in frightening her? Funny way to get his kicks. He'd had plenty of opportunity to come on to her, but he hadn't. He'd behaved like a gentleman, hadn't laid a finger on her. A chaste kiss on the cheek in the doorway of her hotel – that was it.

And the notes? She took another long sip of wine. They were disgusting. To think that he must have been ogling her and fantasising about her all the time he was with her. What a creep!

And the CDs? He'd given her the one of the Vienna Boys' Choir *as a present*. Nothing but a front to conceal his real intentions. The Mozart one he'd deposited on her suitcase in the hotel. He'd sneaked in like a thief in the night and left it there . . . just to freak her out . . . the same piece he'd played over the phone for her. He knew she loved Mozart.

He'd sat through *The Magic Flute* even though he hadn't enjoyed one minute of it. He was hoping she'd confide her fear to him and he'd have been caring and solicitous but secretly been having a good laugh at her expense.

What a twisted mind.

"Not done yet, another ten minutes or so," Ken said as he sat down beside her again. "Cyril O'Connor. Well, that's a good one."

"Ken, did you say you parted on bad terms?"

"Bloody sure we did. After he threatened to sue me, I threatened to report him to the gardaí. Of course I didn't, I just wanted to scare him. There are lots of his type around, Mich. Some of the scams that go on are something else!"

"*Thanks a million big fella* kind of stuff?" She tried to make light of it.

"Cyril O'Connor wasn't in *that* league, I can assure you. I heard he went abroad and I thought no more about him. I was just glad to have him out of my hair."

"How long after that did you settle the partnership deal with Jonathan?"

"A few weeks later. Remember I went to London? We bought The Fullerton at the beginning of October."

"Yes, yes, I do. That was the year I started working in the music school."

"And I was up to my tonsils organising the renovation and hiring the staff. Mich, I don't know how we survived that time – we hardly saw one another. If we got through that – we'd get through anything. Here." He topped up her glass. "Well, Cyril O'Connor. Talk about a blast from the past!"

Michelle sighed. "I didn't realise I was such a bad judge of character."

"You're not, Mich. You were on holiday and you met someone who was kind to you. He was introduced to you by people you knew. Why should you have been suspicious?"

"Because I . . . ah, it makes no odds."

"Cyril's just a chancer, not an out-and-out crook. He hasn't the intelligence or the right connections to be truly dangerous. But his personality is a bit off, if you ask me."

"A bit off? What do you mean, Ken?"

"There was something else . . . there was an English girl he brought out for a drink with Terry Scott and me one evening."

"What about her?"

"He introduced her as his fiancée but that was all rot, seemingly. Terry met her months afterwards and she'd married someone else. She told Terry she'd only gone out with Cyril a few times but he'd got very possessive, you know, read more into it than there was."

"Go on."

"Terry was the accountant for the girl's father – he was a solicitor. Corcoran, I think their name was. The law firm is in Merrion Square. Mmh, I think Corcoran was the name."

"It doesn't matter. Ken, tell me what happened with Cyril."

"Apparently, Cyril plagued this girl a lot after she broke up with him, threatened to sue her for breach of promise, or so she told Terry. Another scam of course, but the girl got quite frightened."

"Frightened?" Michelle repeated, numbly.

"I think he pestered her – phone calls at work, hanging around her flat, that kind of thing. She was silly to have got involved with him in the first place. In the end, her father had to step in and warn Cyril off."

"Silly," Michelle mumbled.

"Let's not waste any more time talking about Cyril O'Connor. Though," he said, squeezing her knee, "maybe it's just as well you left Vienna before he took a shine to *you*, Mich!"

That settled it. There was no way now she'd tell Ken what happened. She'd feel like a worse fool. Cyril O'Connor was in Vienna and she was in Dublin.

End of that particular story.

Ken kissed her, his lips gently parting hers. Michelle arched her back and held him closer. She wanted him now. She needed the physical closeness, the touching, the intimacy. She slowly probed his mouth with her tongue.

"Mich." His voice was husky. "Let's go to bed."

"What's wrong with right here?" she said as she lifted his hand to her breasts.

He grinned. "Absolutely nothing."

"Ken . . . "

"Mmh." He kissed her neck. "Oh, Mich . . . "

He was nibbling her ear now. "Ken . . . "

"Mmh? Oh, Mich, you feel so good."

"Ken . . . I – "

"Me too."

"Ken . . . Ken, I smell burning."

"Oh, shit." He sat up with a start. "The pie."

* * *

The sun shone through a tiny slit in the pink curtains when she opened her eyes. The digits on her alarm clock read seven-sixteen. She yawned and stretched her right leg down the bed and tickled Ken's foot with her own. Ken sighed softly and turned to her, still fast asleep. His brown hair lay tousled on the pillow and his eyelashes fluttered gently for a moment. He looked innocent in his sleep, young. His breathing was calm, soft. There's a certain vulnerability about someone sleeping.

Michelle filled up with love for him. Love and warmth and tenderness. She ran a finger down the side of his cheek.

He stirred. His hand crept up to her breast. "Good morning," he whispered as he touched her nipple.

She moved her lips to his, tracing her tongue around the contours of his mouth. "Do you want breakfast, love?"

"Not yet." He put his arms around her and drew her closer. "Not yet."

* * *

"Michelle!" Olive Bolger stood on the doorstep of her semi-detached in Shanowen Road and threw her arms around her daughter. "Come in, come in."

Her mother shuffled down the hall to the kitchen in her old red slippers. "I've just finished lunch, but I've some ham in the fridge. Will I get you a salad?"

Michelle plugged in the kettle. "No, Mam, you sit down and I'll make us both a cup of tea. I had lunch with Ken in town." She pointed to the parcel she'd left on the pine chair. "That's for you."

"For me?" Her mother picked up the package and eagerly tore it open. "Oh, Michelle, it's lovely." She spread the tablecloth out to admire it. "Lace, it's so delicate. It looks handmade."

"It is, I thought you'd like it."

"I do, I do. It'll be gorgeous on the dining-room table when Declan and Fiona come over for tea next week."

"Great." Michelle got the tea-bags from the cupboard. "So, you've been keeping well, Mam?"

"What's the point in complaining?" Her mother folded the tablecloth and put it in a drawer in the dresser. "I'm not too bad, all things considered."

"Good." Michelle poured the boiling water into the teapot. "You heard about Ken's mother-in-law?"

"Dreadful, the poor woman, it was sudden, wasn't it? When's the funeral?"

"The removal's tomorrow at five and the burial's on Tuesday morning." Michelle brought the tea to the table and her mother opened a tin of biscuits.

"You'll have to go, Michelle, won't you?"

"No." Michelle took a Mikado from the tin. "No, I

don't think it would be wise. Toni wouldn't want me there."

"You know best." Her mother stirred three spoonfuls of sugar into her tea. "I'd have thought Ken would have needed your moral support."

"No, he agrees with me. I'll keep out of the way for the next few days. It's only fair to himself and Beth. My presence there might be an embarrassment to Toni and her family."

"It's not easy for you, Michelle." Olive Bolger looked at her daughter in a pitying way which was irritating. "You know I've never agreed with divorce but . . . I think it would be far better if Ken sorted out something definite for himself. After all, you're with him seven years – that's as long as he was with his wife. I'm very fond of Ken, he's a decent man."

"Yes he is, Mam, but neither Ken nor I want to get married, so a divorce isn't necessary. Ken would hate to do anything that would upset Beth."

"What about you, though? Doesn't his situation bother you?"

"Quite frankly, no. I told you years ago that I'd no wish to be married. I like my life the way it is."

Her mother wasn't convinced. "I'd rather see you properly settled, Michelle."

"I *am* settled." She forced a smile. "Is that a new plant on the windowsill?"

"Do you like it? I won it and the pot-holder in a raffle

in the Church draw. Fiona thinks it's lovely. I might give it to her."

"How is Fiona? Is she better?"

"She is. It was just some kind of gastro-enteritis after all. She's not pregnant."

"That's a relief."

Her mother stared hard at her. "Not a nice attitude, Michelle. Children are a blessing."

"Some are," Michelle agreed with a grin. "I just meant that Fiona might not be overjoyed to find herself back to the nappy stage. Ben is nearly five now, isn't he? She told me she wanted to look for a job when he started school. Anyway, three children are quite enough for anyone."

"Easy for you to say that. You don't want children."

"That's not a crime." Michelle poured her mother another cup of tea. "I'm very fond of children, as it happens. I like most of my students. But having a baby of my own isn't a huge priority. You've nothing to complain about, Mam, you have three grandchildren."

"I was thinking of *you*, Michelle, not myself."

"Come on, get your coat. It's a nice afternoon. We'll go for a walk."

"I was going to watch the film on Channel 4," her mother replied.

"OK, if that's what you'd prefer."

"No, no, if you want to go for a walk, that's what we'll do."

"Mam," Michelle said impatiently, "I don't care, we'll do whatever you choose."

"Ah no, I know you'd prefer to go for a stroll. While we're out, you can tell me all about Venice."

"Vienna."

"What, love? I'll get my jacket. It's hanging under the stairs."

How was it, that no matter what she did or said, her mother was always able to make out she was doing Michelle a favour?

Thirteen

Toni Leavy had a lump in her throat as they lowered her mother's coffin into the cold earth. A small group huddled around the graveside: Gwen, Toni, Beth, Ken, a handful of neighbours and close friends and a few of the staff from Arnotts, where Gwen worked. Mrs McRory had outlived most of her contemporaries, the downside of growing old.

Ashes to ashes, dust to dust.

Gwen tried to join in the prayers for the repose of her mother's soul but the words became a blurred chanting – a mocking reminder of her schooldays, when they were subjected to continual lectures and repetition of "Hail Mary"s, "Our Father"s, "Glory Be"s, the "Angelus" and the "Litany of the Saints" . . . freezing classrooms, blue knees, black-garbed nuns glaring at them and occasionally brandishing the *strap*. Gwen closed her eyes.

Toni mouthed the responses. Although it wasn't a

cold day, the wind whipped around her ankles and she shivered. She gripped Ken's arm more tightly and smiled through her tears at her daughter. Beth stood stoically, refusing to cry.

"May she rest in peace." The priest said solemnly, sprinkling the grave with holy water. "Amen."

"Amen," they choroused.

The priest shook hands with Gwen and Beth and then he moved among the crowd.

"Ken," Gwen whispered, "I've invited some people from work back to Hedigan's. I'm just going to ask Mr Dunne to tell the neighbours."

Ken had organised drinks and sandwiches in the pub nearest to Glasnevin Cemetery.

"Right, I'll bring Beth back to the car, she's very upset. We'll see you there. Toni can go with you."

Gwen accepted condolences from her colleagues from work while her sister chatted to some neighbours from the street. Ken took his daughter by the arm.

"You OK, Beth?"

"I hate this, Dad. I hate to think of Gran lying alone down there . . . look!" Her voice was choked up. "They're filling in the clay now." She turned away.

"Come on, sweetheart." Ken led his daughter through the rows of graves back to the gate where he'd parked his Audi.

She sat in. "It's so final, isn't it?"

Ken switched on the engine. "Yes, love, it is. I know how much you're going to miss your gran."

"I will, Dad. I mean she was always there for me with the cup of tea and the chocolate biscuits, ready to listen to all my stories and problems."

Ken patted his daughter's knee.

"And Gran was a good laugh," she added. "She used to tell me all about Mum and Gwen when they were growing up. Sometimes she talked about her old home in Mayo, about Granda and herself sneaking out to the fields for walks in the summer and all about their honeymoon in West Cork during the war. Gran was a great talker. Gwen's going to be very lonely without her."

"Mmh," her father agreed, "you'll have to keep up the weekend visits, Beth, and we can ask Gwen out now and again. Your aunt likes musicals. I think the Rathmines and Rathgar Musical Society are putting on *HMS Pinafore*. We could get tickets for it. Michelle might come with us."

"Gilbert and Sullivan?" Beth looked sceptically at her father. "Michelle?"

He pulled out and drove in the direction of Phibsborough. "What do you mean?"

"Hardly what you call opera, is it?"

"Michelle likes all sorts of music. Anyhow, we can think about it." He didn't like Beth's tone when she talked about Michelle but he wasn't going to scold her now, not after the burial.

As they got to the traffic lights at Hart's Corner, Beth tugged at his sleeve.

"Dad, Dad, honk the horn quickly," she shouted excitedly. "Look, there's Mark! He's back!"

Beth's boyfriend, dressed in denims and a white T-shirt, was hurrying along in the direction of the cemetery. Ken hooted the horn and his daughter waved furiously. The boy looked over, saw them and waved back.

"I can't stop here, Beth, the lights have changed." Ken hooted again, pointed down the street and raised his cupped hand in an imitation of drinking.

Mark gave him the thumbs up.

Ken drove on, indicated right and pulled in from the busy Phibsborough Road to the pub's carpark.

"Great." Beth grinned. "Mark must have got my message from his boss in New York. Wasn't it good of him, Dad, to come back early for Gran's funeral?"

"Yes," Ken said slowly, "very considerate."

"He's the best." She jumped out of the car, slammed the door shut and ran to meet him.

Although he had misgivings about Mark Patterson, Ken was glad for his daughter. Mark's presence here would make the day a lot easier for her.

* * *

Michelle lugged the five-litre cans of undercoat and silk vinyl emulsion up the three steps to her front door and into her hallway. She'd forgotten to buy white spirit. With any luck there'd be some in the garden shed. She shut the front door and the phone rang.

"Hello, Ms Bolger? Hi, this is Andrew."

"Andrew! How are you?"

"Fine, thanks. Did you have a good time in Vienna?"

"Terrific."

Apart from being scared half to death.

"I was raging you weren't with me, Andrew. You'd have knocked the socks off everyone there! How have you been doing?"

"Not too bad. I've worked hard on the Debussy."

"Good for you."

"I'm just checking in with you to confirm the lesson on Thursday."

"Right, eleven o'clock, isn't that what we said?"

"Yeah. I made a start on the Chopin – "

"How do you find it?"

"It's OK, but it needs polishing. I'm having trouble with the second page."

"We'll sort it out when you come over, Andrew. See you on Thursday morning."

"Bye, Ms Bolger."

Wouldn't it be marvellous if all her pupils were as earnest as Andrew? Michelle didn't usually teach during the summer holidays but Andrew was an exception. He was sitting Grade VII in December and after that, it would be the diploma. Then, she'd have a word with his father about his career. Andrew really did want to study music.

Michelle plugged in the kettle and glanced at the front page of the morning paper: a huge drugs haul on the northside of Dublin, mostly cannabis and Ecstacy; a rape case in Carlow; floods in the south and south-east.

Depressing.

She made herself a cup of tea and glanced up at the clock on the kitchen wall. One-thirty.

They'd be out of the cemetery by now and back in the pub. How was it going? What was Toni doing and saying? How was Ken coping? Michelle hoped Ken's wife wasn't making things too awkward for him.

Ken's wife.

Yes, her mother had hit a nerve on Sunday. Ken's marriage didn't sit comfortably with her. It was all right when Toni was at a safe remove in London but . . . her being *here*, seeing Ken every day, talking to him, looking to him for advice and consolation, calling him on the phone and going to his house . . . a new turn of events and Michelle didn't like it one little bit.

* * *

Beth and Mark sat in a corner of Hedigan's, away from the rest of the funeral crowd who'd assembled in the glass-enclosed garden bar. Beth sipped a soda water and lime.

She gazed at Mark. "I'm so glad you came home early. I've missed you, I really have. The summer's been an awful drag and now Gran . . . it's lousy."

"Yeah, it's tough." He put his arm around her shoulder. "Your gran was a nice lady."

"What do you think of Mum? You were away the last time she was over. Isn't she gorgeous? I hope I look like that when I'm her age."

He smiled. He'd only met Mrs Leavy for a few moments and he hadn't liked her. She'd gushed all over him, bombarded him with questions without waiting for a reply. He hated blatant insincerity.

"She's asked me to go back to London with her for a few days, Mark," Beth went on. "I suppose it's not very fair to you, seeing as how you've just came back from the States to be with me."

"No worries. It's right you should spend some time with your mother."

"That's what I thought. Do you know, Mark? I think there's still something between them."

"Between who?" He took a long gulp of his Guinness. "God, I really missed this as well."

"As well as what?" she asked coyly.

"You, you monkey!"

"About time you said so."

He took another long drink and sighed with satisfaction. "You can get a decent pint of stout only in this country, that's for sure."

"As I was saying before I was rudely interrupted – I think there's something going on between Mum and Dad. They've been spending a lot of time together and so far there've been no rows."

"Rows? There'd hardly be rows at a time like this, Beth. Your dad's doing his best to help out. He must feel sorry for her, losing her mother. I wouldn't read too much into it, if I were you."

"You're wrong," she insisted. "I'm convinced there's more to it than that. Even looking at them standing side by side at the grave today . . . they looked right together."

Mark nodded and finished his pint. He wouldn't argue with her but he thought this was definitely a case of wishful thinking.

"How's Michelle?" he asked.

"I don't know, I haven't seen her." Beth frowned. "She was away on a holiday. Vienna, I think. She brought me back a book on art."

"Vienna – probably went there for the music."

"I don't know and I care less." Beth shrugged. "I don't want to talk about Michelle, all right?"

"Fine, fine." He stood up and held out his hand to her. "We'd better go and join your folks, Beth."

"But I want to hear all about America."

"Later. Come on, I want to have a chat with your aunt. Oh, by the way, I bought you a present."

"What did you get me?"

He tapped the side of his nose with his index finger. "Nosy, nosy. You're going to have to wait."

"You're mean." She pouted. "Tell me what it is."

"No, you'll just have to have patience, my pet. Patience."

"You're a desperate tease, Mark Patterson, you really are. Do we have to go and talk to that shower? I hate this

– everyone chatting and laughing and Gran only buried an hour ago. Jesus, I don't believe it. Look at Mr Pearse, Gran's next-door neighbour. I think he's actually humming a song!"

"Beth, you'd be a dead loss at a wake! Sorry, sorry, wrong choice of words! Sure the Irish always have a hooley when someone dies, it's healthier than moping around with a long face. Your gran would be delighted if she thought there were people singing at her funeral. That's the way she would have wanted it."

"Well," Beth said crossly, "I think it's the pits."

"Maybe you could come too, Ken?" Toni suggested. "Just for a few days. We could bring Beth to see the sights together. I might be able to get tickets for that new play in Drury Lane. Beth would enjoy it."

"It's impossible, Toni. I've taken far too much time off work as it is."

She ran her hand up his thigh. "I know, darling. You've been absolutely wonderful and I appreciate it. Nobody could have been kinder." She smiled coyly at him. "In some ways during the past few days it was . . . it was like old times."

Ken balked at the thought. Rows, scenes, tears, depression . . . unkept promises and broken vows. *Old times!*

"I want to get a drink for Gwen," he said, edging away.

"Get one for me too, darling, would you? A brandy and ginger, please." She kissed him on the cheek. "And don't be too long, there's a lot more I want to discuss with you."

Ken escaped to the bar and ordered the drinks. While he was waiting, he went over to chat to Gwen and a friend of hers. "Sorry to interrupt, ladies. Gwen, Beth says she'll sleep in your house for the next few nights if you like, before she goes to London with Toni."

Gwen McRory, dressed in a simple black dress, took her brother-in-law by the arm. "Ken, it's awfully good of her but there's no necessity. She was great company last night but I'm certainly not going to play on her good nature. Look at her over there with Mark. She's thrilled to have him back. Let her enjoy herself for the next few days, Ken. She deserves it."

"All right," he agreed, "but I know she'd like to stay with you, if you need her, Gwen."

"No, I'll have to start as I mean to go on. Of course the house will be lonely for a while . . . this morning I started to move the furniture around, just to make it look different. I shifted Mum's chair out of the corner." Her eyes brimmed. "If I left it where it was I'd still see her sitting in it."

Ken handed her a sherry. "Maybe you should think about redecorating? Give the place a whole new look."

"No point," Gwen said thoughtfully. "Toni wants to sell."

"What?" Ken's voice rose. "She's talked to you about selling the house? Already?"

"Mmh. I was a bit annoyed, to tell you the truth."

Ken bit his lip. "I'll sort it, Gwen, don't worry."

He moved away from the bar and headed back to his wife. She was talking to a cousin, sniffing into her handkerchief. He could feel the anger rising in his throat. He took a deep breath to calm himself down. He wouldn't make a scene here but he'd get his point across.

Quietly.

* * *

Michelle's neck had gone stiff from looking up at the ceiling. She'd a roller stuck on to the end of a sweeping-brush handle which saved her going up and down the ladder, but it was awkward and laborious.

The phone rang in the hall.

It startled her and she jerked her arm, causing a huge blob of white paint to plop on the carpet – a spot she hadn't covered with the old sheet – naturally.

She carefully laid the roller back on its tray, rubbed her hands in the damp J-cloth and went to answer the phone.

"This is the Telecom Éireann Answering Service with a message for Michelle Bolger. Please check your mailbox."

Michelle replaced the receiver and dialled in the four digits of her password.

An ear-splitting sound reverberated down the line. No voice, no message . . . just music played at a deafening volume – and not just any music. What Michelle recognised at once were the frighteningly familiar notes of the *Rondo*.

Fourteen

"To erase this message, press seven; to save it, press nine."

Angrily, Michelle pressed seven.

"You have no more messages in your mailbox. To review your personal options, press four."

Personal options. If only she could opt to erase this . . . predator. How dare he pursue her like this?

She didn't have to put up with it – she dialled the emergency number. It rang three times before she hung up – she couldn't go through with it. How could she explain her plight over the phone to a faceless voice? She'd have to do this in person.

She'd call right this minute to the garda station and make a full report – tell them everything about Vienna, about the notes, the harassment, her suspicions about Cyril O'Connor. That's what she'd do. They'd take it from here. They'd ask her questions, get information, then they'd deal with it.

Questions.

Why do you think you're being harassed, Ms Bolger? What makes you think it's this Cyril O'Connor? Did you do anything to encourage him? You say went out with him a few times? For dinner? Do you think that was prudent, Ms Bolger, going out with a complete stranger in a foreign city?

No, not *prudent* at all. But it's easy to be wise after the event. Why should she torment herself now with guilt? She'd trusted him, that was all. No sin in trusting, was there?.

What proof have you got, Ms Bolger? We need some concrete evidence. You destroyed the notes, did you say? *Why* did you do that?

Stupid, stupid, stupid, Michelle.

You thought the harassment had stopped until this phone call to your home? Did you give him your number, Ms Bolger? No? But you told him where you lived? That was unfortunate.

Why did you erase the message on your answering machine, Ms Bolger? Yes, we understand it was frightening for you and that you panicked . . . would you say you were suffering from stress? Is it possible that you . . . that you're overreacting, maybe even imagining some of this . . . ?

And she'd sit there squirming with embarrassment, in the interview room, with a detective and a sympathetic policewoman listening to her sordid little story, giving her a cup of tea and trying to calm her down.

Has this kind of thing ever happened to you before, Ms Bolger?

In other words, was she a silly neurotic female, who lived alone and suffered from delusions?

No, she wouldn't go to the police. She'd deal with this herself.

But how?

What was Cyril O'Connor up to? Why was he picking on her? For revenge on Ken? In the cold light of day, it all seemed so outlandish. It wasn't Ken he was getting at, it was *her*. He wanted to hurt her.

Why?

Had she done something unwittingly to cause this? She must have done or said something to upset him, to annoy him . . . what? Why was he bullying her like this? What did he hope to achieve by it? If he had something against her, why didn't he speak out? Making these phone calls wasn't normal – not the act of a rational human being.

No, not normal at all. It was some kind of an obsession. She stared at the phone. It had taken on a life of its own that was threatening, menacing . . . disturbing.

It's good to talk.

The British Telecom jingle ran round her head: *It's good to talk, it's good to talk.*

She got really angry. This bastard hadn't the nerve to talk. He got his fix by leaving musical messages . . .

She came back to the sitting-room and sat at the piano. Playing would soothe her, give her some sense of normality. Anytime she was upset or edgy or down in the dumps, playing the piano restored her to a state of calm.

She took up her music book and it slipped from her hands onto the chair, opening at Mozart's "Fantasia in D Minor".

The Fantasia . . . from that nightmare of long ago. It was years since she'd played this. Years. As her fingers moved shakily over the keys, Michelle's breathing quickened. She tried to think her way into the piece but it was useless – she couldn't block out what was happening. Her fingers kept moving, flying over the notes, programmed by some deep, inner compulsion.

You're all right, Michelle. You're safe. He can't get you here.

No, no, she was fooling herself. He was out there . . . coming after her to scare her, to turn her life upside down. Wait a minute, calm down . . . messages on an answering service couldn't harm her. He couldn't harm her *unless she let him*.

That was it in a nutshell. Michelle *wouldn't* let him. He couldn't control her . . . couldn't dictate how she felt or what she thought. He was making a big mistake if he thought he had power over her. She couldn't stop him from making the calls but she could stop him from upsetting her. She'd listen to his wretched attempts to unnerve her, then she'd laugh and erase them. She'd *press seven* and the world would return to normal.

If she got any more malicious phone calls, bizarre more than malicious . . . if she got any more, she'd contact Telecom Éireann. She could change her number. Yes, that's what she'd do.

Nothing simpler.

She was safe in her own home, playing and teaching her music, going about her business, living her life. At least she *had* a life.

This sick, twisted individual . . . what had he got?

Michelle smiled as she gained control of the piece. She performed the chromatic run to perfection. There, he hadn't even affected her playing for long.

How could he have any *real* impact on her life at all? He was in Vienna.

Fifteen

Beth dipped her spoon into a huge banana split. She loved the desserts here in Captain America's.

"Thanks for the clothes, Mum. The black mini's deadly and the top you bought me goes great with it. I know you preferred the red one, but I adore black."

She let the ice cream melt slowly on her tongue and swallowed, then she frowned. "Dad will think it's too skimpy."

Toni, straining to hear above the loud music, stirred her coffee. "He needn't see it, it's for London."

"He's always on my case," Beth said, angrily attacking the second half of the banana. "Lately I can't do a fecking thing right. Remember that silver tank top you sent over last month? I wore it to a disco and he nearly freaked. You could barely see the top of my boobs but he said it was far too low-cut and revealing and that I was turning into a Jezebel, whoever the hell she was."

"Your dad's conservative. He never liked me to wear anything he considered risqué, either."

"You know, half the time I go out with the gang, I have to call over to Carmel's house to change. Her mother's terrific, doesn't mind what we wear and we swop clothes as well. Carmel lent me her denim mini last week and I was never off the dance-floor! But Dad expects me to dress in polo-necked jumpers and long skirts. Even when I have my jeans on, he's moaning that they're too tight. Jesus, he hasn't a clue."

"He still sees you as a little girl. Never mind your father, I'll take you to a night-club in London, an exclusive one in the West End. We could go with the Frawleys, they've a son of about your age. We must buy you a nice jacket to go with the skirt. They've some fabulous things in Richard Alan's at the moment."

"A jacket? Cool." Definitely not in Richard Alan's, though. She'd be laughed out of it. "I don't want anything too expensive, Mum. I saw a waisted yellow corduroy jacket in Miss Selfridge. Could we go and have a look at it later?"

"As soon as we're finished lunch." Toni took another sip of coffee. "How are you for underwear?"

"Gone grey from washing."

Toni lit a Rothmans. "Your gran always insisted that Gwen and I had good underwear, in case we were involved in an accident!"

Beth grinned. "I'd love a black Wonderbra or the red matching cami and knicker sets they have in Penneys. They come in navy, too. The thing is, I hate asking Dad for money for clothes. He's not mean or anything, but clothes don't seem to matter to him."

Her mother blew out a large puff of smoke. "Beth, I have an idea. Why don't I open a bank account for you and I could deposit money every month in it?"

"A bank account? Brill!" Beth laughed. "My own bank account." Then she bit her lip. "I don't know, though, Dad mightn't like it. He's always on at me about getting a part-time job. Can I have a fag? Thanks. He doesn't believe anyone should get things too easily, says it makes people irresponsible."

"Well, we needn't tell him." Toni handed her daughter the silver lighter. "It'll be our secret. I want to do this for you. It's just pocket-money. You're my daughter, after all."

"The money would certainly come in handy," Beth admitted. She pushed her dessert dish away from her. "I can't swallow another mouthful – that Hawaiian burger has me stuffed. I shouldn't have had the onion rings with it."

Toni called the waiter for the bill. "Was your dad working last night?"

"I don't think so." Beth knotted the sleeves of her blue sweater around her shoulders. "He went over to Michelle's as far as I know. I was in bed by the time he got home."

"I see."

"He goes over to her house two or three nights a week and she spends most weekends in Griffith Avenue."

"Does that bother you, Beth?"

"It used to." Beth shrugged. "I can't understand what Dad sees in her. She's OK I suppose, but she's kind of . . . stodgy, boring, which probably suits him. The state of her clothes – down to the ankle. And her hair's dead boring too – that long, curly style went out with the flood. She could look quite attractive if she put a bit of effort into it."

"Perhaps she's more important things on her mind." Toni didn't want to seem too pleased by what her daughter was saying, but pleased she was. "Speaking of hair, Beth, your own could do with a trim. Is that henna you've put in?"

"No, it's hair mascara, it's great as long as it doesn't rain! It's weeks since I put in a rinse – that's another thing Dad moans about. He says I'm ruining my hair as well as the bathroom. Two little splashes on the woodwork last month and he lost it."

"I remember doing that when I was about your age, black dots all around the sink. We had wood in the bathroom, too. I managed to hide the stains, though."

"How?"

"I stuck blobs of toothpaste over the marks. The paintwork was white so it was weeks before your gran discovered it."

Beth smiled at her mother. "Any more tips?"

"Plenty, but back to your hair. Why don't we get a professional job done? Auburn highlights would suit you really well, bring out the colour more." Toni glanced at the bill the waiter had brought.

"Highlights? Brilliant. Can I get them done today?"

"If we can get an appointment. Go over to the desk and ask them for a telephone directory. I hope Sebastian still works in the Grafton Street salon. He's a marvellous colourist." She took her mobile phone from her handbag as Beth went off.

Toni rang home.

"Gwen? Hi, I won't be over to you till about six, I'm taking Beth for a haircut. Don't bother with lunch, we've eaten and I've plans for dinner this evening, all right? No, no, leave it till we get there. I think she has most of her packing done. Did Ken phone? Oh, did he not? He said he'd ring to confirm the arrangements for tomorrow morning. Never mind, listen, if he does get in touch, tell him to phone me on the mobile. What do you mean he's working? It's no big deal. All right, all right, see you later. Bye."

Gwen was hopeless.

"Here's the book, Mum."

"Oh, darling, look up the number will you? I haven't got my lenses in."

Beth dialled the number of the salon and got an appointment for four-fifteen.

"Thanks, Mum. I might get it cropped."

"Nothing too drastic, darling, it takes time to grow back." Toni finished her coffee. "Beth . . . what do you make of Michelle?"

"Not much. She's Dad's girlfriend but I don't have to like her. Imagine going out with someone who plays the organ at Mass! He's got so bloody *old*."

"Watch it," Toni said with a grin. "Your father's only two years older than I am. To think I'll be forty soon!"

"You don't look it, Mum. Compared to Dad, you're from a different time zone – the way you dress, the way you think . . . there's no comparison."

"Thanks for the vote of confidence but we mustn't forget how kind your dad is, Beth. He's very good to you."

"I know he is, I just wish he wasn't such a worrier." Beth groaned. "It drives me bonkers the way he goes on: 'What time will you be home?' 'Who are you going out with tonight?' 'How long did Mark stay?' What difference does it make how long Mark stays, for Christ's sake? If we were going to do it, we could just as easily do it at eight o'clock in the evening. Dad seems to think that after midnight Mark grows horns!"

"All parents are like that, Beth."

"You're not. At least you can see my point of view. It's great to have you here – you're more like a friend than a mother – oh, I didn't mean – "

"It's all right, Beth. I know what you meant and I'm glad. It's important we get on together, that you feel you can talk to me."

"I envy Carmel because she has a sister. They tell each other everything. When I got my periods, it was Carmel's sister, Anne, I told first. I couldn't bring myself to talk to Dad about it."

Toni rummaged in her handbag for a biro. She felt a twinge of guilt. Growing up with no woman in the house must have been hard for her daughter.

"What about Michelle? Would you ever confide in her?"

"No way! She says I can go to her anytime but I . . . I wouldn't. I used to talk to Gran, she was great." Beth looked sad. "And Gwen's good too but she's very . . . old-fashioned. You know, I could never discuss . . . personal things with her."

"Neither could I." Toni took out her hand-mirror and checked her make-up. "Gwen was old even when we were young. I had all the boyfriends and I think she was jealous, to tell you the truth. Gwen and I weren't close, Beth. Having a sister doesn't necessarily mean you get on."

"I suppose not."

Toni zipped her handbag. "So, you're not overfond of Michelle, then?"

"No, to be fair, it's not her fault." Beth stubbed out the half-smoked cigarette in the ash-tray. "I don't have anything in common with her, that's all. Dad thinks he loves her . . . but I'd say he was just lonely when he met her."

Toni ran the tip of her tongue around her lips.

"Mum, you and Dad . . . you still like each other, don't you?"

"Of course we do. I've made some mistakes, Beth, I'll freely admit it. I was too rash, too impulsive." She took her daughter's hand. "I've always wanted to ask you this but it never seemed to be the right time – "

"Ask me what?"

"How you felt about me. You're not angry with me, are you, for leaving? I couldn't bear it if you were."

Beth squeezed her mother's hand. "Of course I'm not. You didn't leave me . . . you just moved away. You had to go but you didn't want to uproot me, I can understand it. You thought it would be better for me to stay with Dad."

"It wasn't that," Toni said. "I was sure your father would follow me to England. I counted on the three of us being together but . . . it didn't work out that way. This sounds selfish, Beth, but if I'd stayed in Ireland, I'd have been miserable and where would that have left you?"

"You were right to go away if you were unhappy. I hate martyrs, there's nothing worse. People often blame their kids for tying them down. I admire you, Mum – you had the guts to do your own thing."

"You should travel too, when you've finished school. You could come and live with me for a year in London – that's if I stay there."

"If you stay? Are you thinking of leaving London?"

" . . . I'll have to see. But you should go there for a while and then head off to Europe or America. It's not good to go to college too early. See a bit of life first."

"Mmh," Beth said dreamily. "I'd love to go to New York. Oh, do you know what Mark brought me back from the States? A pendant watch. Knocked him back mega bucks, I'd say."

"He's very generous."

"Isn't he?"

Toni hesitated. "I hope you don't think I'm sticking my oar in, but you're not getting too serious about Mark, are you? You're only sixteen. Plenty of time to play the field."

"There's nothing heavy between me and Mark, Mum, and despite everything Dad believes, we're not sleeping together."

Toni nodded.

"You're not going to give me a lecture too, are you?" Beth moaned.

"No, I'm not. I know you're a sensible young woman. If you do intend at any time to – "

"I know, Mum, I know. I'll head straight to the Well Woman and get myself fixed up."

"Good. Are we right?" Toni stood up, went to the cashier's desk by the door and took out her Visa card. She was glad to be out of there. Burger-joints were not her scene and the loud music was getting to her, but she wouldn't let on to Beth.

Sixteen

Gail Loughlin, the head receptionist who doubled as Ken's private secretary, knocked gently on the door and walked into her boss's office. He was scrutinising the computer screen.

"Gail, be with you in a moment, I'm just checking last night's audit. Where are the FXB invoices?"

"I've left them on the desk there, Mr Leavy. There are two bills outstanding. Could you sign the cheques?"

"Right, right," he said absent-mindedly.

"Norman Daly's in the outer office, Mr Leavy."

Ken turned from the screen. "Send him in, Gail, and don't put any calls through for an hour or two, I don't want to be disturbed. I've a pile of paperwork."

Gail nodded, walked to the door and showed in the sous-chef. She quietly closed the door behind her.

"Sit down, Norman," Ken said, pointing to an easy chair opposite his page-littered desk.

The chef, visibly nervous, took the seat and folded his hands in his lap.

"Now, you know why I sent for you, Norman?"

" . . . Em, it's about . . . yesterday?"

"Yes, it is."

"Mr Leavy, things have been getting . . . eh, I'm finding it difficult . . . to settle in – "

"To settle in? How long are you with us now, Norman?".

The chef cleared his throat. "Em . . . six months."

Ken stared hard at him. "Six months. I'd have thought that was time enough to have found your feet."

" . . . Yes."

"Is it your workload?"

Norman Daly shook his head. "No, I've no complaints about the work as such, it's . . . " He clenched his hands and looked down at the floor, hoping he might find some excuse written there for him.

Ken picked up the time-sheets for the previous week. "An hour late last Wednesday, fifteen minutes on Thursday and yesterday you didn't show till eleven o'clock. You were supposed to be on breakfasts, Norman." Ken's voice rose. "You heard what happened?"

"I . . . em – "

"You know full well that we only have one breakfast chef on duty, which is quite sufficient – *if* that chef bothers to turn in for work!"

Norman Daly knew enough to keep his mouth shut and let the boss get on with the tirade.

"At one stage we'd a party of four important guests sitting in the dining-room twiddling their thumbs, admiring the decor, while the night-porter tries to figure out how to work the grill. The night-porter, Norman! *He* was not hired to cook breakfasts – *you* were! I was told it took him ten minutes to find the right switch!"

Norman Daly had heard all this from the kitchen porter. It was the talk of the hotel this morning.

"As he's frantically tearing open cartons of orange juice and serving up undercooked rashers and sausages and – how did Mr Rahilly describe his poached egg?" Ken checked his notes. "Ah yes, here we are: 'a slithery lump of rubber.' Not exactly good for our reputation, is it, Norman? Is it?"

"No, sir."

"Meanwhile, Hilda the waitress is busily burning the toast!" By now Ken's voice had reached falsetto level and his face had turned beetroot. "It is *not* the waitress's job!"

"Mr Leavy, I'm terribly sorry – "

"As well you should be, Norman. As well you should be. This is The Fullerton not Fawlty Towers!"

"Yes, Mr Leavy."

"It could have proved disastrous, Norman. These Americans bring us a lot of business. It was lucky for me that they were regulars, that they actually *like* this hotel, God bless them. I sincerely hope they don't think this bungling is part of our native charm."

"I'll apologise to them – "

"Too late, I've done that for you. They've gone off on their coach tour of Ireland. But I've had to make amends – a free weekend for the four of them before they go back to the States, do you hear me? I don't like giving away free weekends – it goes against my principles! Empty bedrooms freak me out, Norman, but *free* weekends . . . " Ken drew his index finger across his throat. "Suicide, Norman. Economic suicide."

"Mr Leavy, I promise you, it won't happen again." Norman took a handkerchief out of his pocket. He blew his nose soundlessly and coughed.

"Partying, Norman?" Ken poured him a glass of water. "Suffering for it today, are you?"

"It was Deborah's twenty-first." He laughed nervously, noting his boss's confused expression. "Deborah Bennett, you know, the restaurant supervisor," he explained. "We got in free to The Pod and – "

"What do I care about The Pod, Norman? It doesn't matter *what* the occasion was," Ken snapped. "This hotel is not a social club, it's my *business*. It's your livelihood, too, you'd do well to remember that. It's wonderful that you all get on so well, Norman – staff morale is very important but – and this is a big but – you'll have to cope with hangovers on *your* time, not mine. Understood?"

The chef nodded apologetically.

Ken swivelled around in his chair to face the window. He was finding it difficult to keep this up. The poor bugger!

Ken remembered doing exactly the same thing when he worked as a duty manager in that hotel in Wexford. Duty manager! Straight out of college with his B Comm and a load of bright ideas. Shitty hours, really crappy pay. A gang of them on the piss one Saturday night had arrived hours late for work on the Sunday and were hauled over the coals. At the time, Ken had thought the general manager a complete bollocks!

"Are you on lunches today, Norman?"

"Yes, Mr Leavy."

"I'll be in at twelve-thirty as usual."

Part of his *quality control* operation. Norman would serve up the best bloody salmon that Leavy had ever tasted. And he'd go to town on the sauce!

"Norman, get back to work now." Ken arched an eyebrow. "As far as I'm concerned, this matter's over and done with. Just see that it never happens again."

"Yes, Mr Leavy. Thanks, Mr Leavy."

Gail looked up from the desk as the chef walked by.

"You look chirpy enough! How did it go?"

Norman shrugged. "The usual. Gave me a rollicking and I swore to be a good boy for the future. Leavy's a bit of a gobshite but he's not a bad bastard – not the worst I've worked for."

"No, he certainly isn't," the receptionist agreed.

Orla, the conference manager, snatched a menu from the desk, shot a smile at them and hurried off.

"She's flying around as usual. What's going on in the function room today?" Norman asked.

"A sales conference for some motor company, followed by a dinner. The boys getting together to bond!"

"Not very PC, Gail. If I said that about women, you'd call me a sexist swine!"

"That's 'cause you are! What time are you finished today, Norm?"

"Four o'clock."

"A few of us are going to celebrate Paul's promotion – "

"Promotion? Paul's been promoted?"

"Mmh, did you not hear? Oh, you were out yesterday. Yes, he's now officially the deputy general manager."

"That's great. He must be thrilled."

"Yes," Gail said, "he is. Especially since he's been doing the bloody work for ages – I'm glad he's finally got the title."

"Big salary increase as well?"

"I suppose so."

"Nice one. I'll go to the pub for an hour but . . . " Norman reflected. "I'd better take it easy today – just two pints."

The phone rang and the secretary turned to answer it.

"Gail? Hi, it's Suzanne. Is his nibs there? I want a word."

"Told me to hold his calls, doesn't want to be disturbed. He's checking the accounts. Will I buzz him for you later?"

"No," the head housekeeper replied, "I'll call by his office. I'm going from crisis to crisis here."

"I know the feeling. I saw Claire Mooney slinking off an hour early. Is she sick?"

"No, I sent her home. I came down from the second floor and was greeted by the charming sight of a pool of vomit on the stairs just outside number eight. I don't know how the night cleaners could have missed it."

"It's that football crowd, Suzanne. They left this morning, thank Christ."

"Well, when I asked Claire to clean it up, she started to give me lip, so I did it myself but, I can tell you, I'm not one bit happy about it. I have to speak to Mr Leavy."

"Drop by on your way home, Suzanne. He's working till six tonight. Talk to you later." Gail put down the phone.

"That was our salubrious housekeeper, I gather?" Norman asked.

"Yeah, she's bulling. One of the accommodation assistants is giving her grief and – "

"That's not the only thing giving her grief!" He leaned over the desk and whispered. "Suzanne found Colin in bed with one of the lounge girls – a uni student."

"Colin! You're kidding!" Gail gasped. "I was sure that was the real thing – that Colin was totally into Suzanne."

"He's into Suzanne, all right. But that doesn't stop him from being into every other woman as well! The bed-hopping in this place!" Norman tutted in mock horror. "And yer woman's a right little goer by all accounts!"

"That's desperate. Colin should have his balls . . . oh, hello, Mrs Hughes. Off shopping, are you?" Gail smiled broadly as the woman in number two handed in her key. "Have a nice day!" Gail turned back to the chef. "Tell me more, Norman!"

"Can't. Have to get back to my hell-hole."

"So, are you coming with us this evening?"

"I don't know." Norman scratched his head. "I'm dying. I really am."

Gail smiled. "A hair of the dog?"

"OK, just for the one. Then I'll head home."

"That's what you always say, Norman!"

Ken glanced at his watch. Four-thirty. He picked up the phone and dialled Michelle's number again.

Hello, this is Michelle speaking. I'm sorry I'm unavailable to take your call at the moment but if you leave your name and number I'll get back to you as soon as possible. Begin speaking after the tone. Thanks.

He hung up without leaving another message – this was the third time he'd tried to speak to her this afternoon. She'd said she'd be at home, hadn't she?

Ken had a word with the bar manager about stocks, then he called into the restaurant, to check the till. He'd just come back to his office when the phone rang.

"Hi, Ken. Got your messages."

"Mich? At last! I rang at two and then again at three. I thought you told me you were painting today."

Michelle smiled. Ken didn't like the unexpected.

"I was here all afternoon,' she said.

"Why didn't you answer the phone, then?"

Michelle hesitated. "I was up the ladder. I'm almost finished the ceiling in the front room. I couldn't come to the phone," she lied, "I'm in a difficult corner."

She hadn't answered the phone in the last forty-eight hours because she was afraid to. Although she'd heard nothing from *him* since Tuesday . . . *not* hearing was just as worrying. Every time the phone rang she jumped, expecting it to be him. When it wasn't, it meant that she had to wait for the next call.

"It's like having a love affair with your answering machine these days," he said bemusedly. "I'm in a difficult corner myself."

"What?"

"Nothing. Are you free for the cinema tonight?"

"Yes, I'd like to see *The Full Monty*. It's meant to be a good film, a comedy."

"I don't like comedies," he muttered.

"Well, it's not just comedy. Fiona told me it was very true to life and we shouldn't miss it."

"OK, we'll go to Omniplex, it's handier for you than coming into town. What time is it on at?"

"Hang on till I check the newspaper."

He drummed his fingers on the mahogany desk as he waited for her to come back to the phone.

"Ken? Hi. There's a screening at seven-twenty-five and another at nine-thirty."

"OK, we'll go to the earlier one. I should be finished here by six-thirty at the latest and I'll pick you up at about seven."

"Right. Is Beth all set for her London trip?"

"She's on high doh. Toni took her into town today to get new clothes. She'll buy up town. I hate the way she does that – buys Beth's affection. Anyhow, Beth will be busy packing tonight so I'm better off staying out of the way. We'll go for something to eat after the film."

"Great. Why don't I book us a table in Il Corvo?"

"Do we have to book?"

"Definitely, it's got very popular. You'd never get a table after nine without booking."

"Even mid-week?"

"Yes, we should book, Ken. It's no problem, I'll phone straight away."

"OK, reserve a table for nine-thirty."

"Are you all right, Ken? You sound a bit frazzled."

"Hassles here. Never mind, I'll see you at seven, Mich."

* * *

Michelle rubbed body lotion all over her legs and arms.

Her skin felt smooth and silky. She went into her bedroom and plugged in the hairdryer. Bending forward, she finger-dried her hair, making it fuller and curlier. She tossed her jeans and paint-splashed shirt into the bottom of the wardrobe and took out her good navy trousers and her pale mauve top. She pulled the top over her head and looked in the full-length mirror on her wall.

It didn't look right on her. The last time she'd worn it, she had a tan. Now her face was pale. She took it off and slipped out of the jeans. The red T-shirt and the black skirt would be better.

The front doorbell rang – it always did when she was half-naked or in the shower. She pulled on her white silk dressing-gown. She wasn't expecting anyone, maybe it was Declan? He sometimes called on his way home from the office. She wasn't in the humour to see her brother, but she'd give him a quick cup of coffee and explain she was going out in an hour.

The bell rang again.

She raced downstairs and opened the door.

"Ken! You're early. I'm only out of the bath."

"Hello, Mich."

He stepped in to the hall and kissed her on the cheek. Then he handed her a large box of Cadbury's Milk Tray.

She smiled. "What's this in aid of?"

He followed her into the kitchen. "An apology," he said sheepishly.

"Why? What have you done?"

"It's what I'm going to do, Mich." He sat down at the kitchen table. "I have to cancel this evening. I'm awfully sorry, but there's nothing else I can do."

"What's up? Work?" She sat down opposite him. "Will I make some coffee?"

"No, not for me. It's not work, Mich. It's Toni."

"Toni?"

"I'm furious with her. She decided that she was taking Gwen, Beth and myself out for a meal tonight as a farewell do for their going away tomorrow. She never thought to consult me about my plans, naturally. She booked a table for four in Al's for nine o'clock and I – "

"It's all right, Ken. We can go to the film some other time."

"Mich, I'm really sorry about this. They called to see me at work an hour ago, laden down with parcels. Wait till you see Beth's hair – it's multi-coloured. They were both giggling and laughing and acting like idiots."

"At least Beth's in better form, Ken. Toni must have cheered her up."

"Mmh . . . I swear I think Toni brought her for a few drinks – the woman has no cop-on at all."

"Maybe I should get us that coffee?"

"No, no, I haven't time. Sorry, Mich. This is dreadful, ruining your night like this – "

"It doesn't matter – "

"It does. I tried to get out of it, but then Beth kicked up a fuss, started to whinge. Told me I didn't care about her, that I was always spoiling her fun. Toni played on that and reminded me it was her last night in Dublin. She even suggested that I invite you to join – "

"Oh, no, Ken. I don't want to – "

"I know, I didn't land you in it, don't worry, but I agreed to the dinner in the end. I should have stuck to my guns but when the two of them started at me . . . "

"It's OK, Ken."

"What about tomorrow evening?"

"No, I can't. I've two piano lessons and I told Mam I'd drop over to her for an hour."

He nodded. "I'll see you at the weekend, so?"

"Sure."

Ken stood up, pulled her to her feet and kissed her lightly on the lips. "I'll make it up to you, Mich, I swear."

She saw him to the door, waited until he got into the car and waved. Michelle came back to the kitchen and stared at the huge box of Milk Tray on the dresser.

She didn't even like chocolates.

Seventeen

Mark rang Michelle's doorbell at nine-thirty the following morning. She opened the door, wearing jeans and a T-shirt, a scarf tied around her hair.

"Hello, Michelle."

"Mark! This is a pleasant surprise."

"Hope this isn't a bad time. I'm on my way back from the airport and thought I'd drop in. Then, I looked at my watch and I said to myself, she'll still be in bed – "

"Not a bit of it, I'm up since the crack of dawn – painting, as you can see by the state of me. Come in."

"I don't want to disturb you if you're busy." He shifted from one foot to the other.

"No, Mark, your timing's perfect, I've just brewed up, taking a tea-break from this bloody job. I've aches and pains in places I never knew existed!"

He stepped in to the hall.

"Go on down to the kitchen and pour yourself a cuppa. I'll join you in a minute."

"Right you be," Mark said.

The overpowering fumes of paint pervaded the house. He opened the kitchen window.

"Your clothes are getting a good blow on the line," he shouted in at her. "My mother loves this kind of weather – great for drying, she says. She spends her life filling the washing-machine. I think it's a fetish with her. If you stand near my mother for more than a second, she's liable to whip the clothes off your back. The poor father's shirts are threadbare from the amount of times they've been washed and tumble-dried."

He laughed.

"What were you saying about your father?" Michelle, asked as she came in to the kitchen. "I didn't catch it."

"Don't mind me, I'm just blabbing on. Do you know your back gate's open, Michelle? I'll go out and shut it, you don't want stray dogs tramping through the garden. While I'm at it, I'll bring the clothes in from the line."

"Thanks, Mark. The wind must have blown the gate open. I thought I heard banging in the night. I've been meaning to replace the bolt, it's faulty."

"I could have a look at it for you."

"Would you? Are you hungry? Will I make us breakfast."

"You know me, Michelle. I'm always ravenous."

She opened the fridge. "What about poached eggs on toast?"

He made a face. "Could you scramble them?"

"Certainly," she said with a smile, "if you agree to wash the pot afterwards."

"Done!"

"I'll grill a few rashers and sausages while I'm at it."

"Terrific. I could eat a horse!"

Mark went out to the back garden and Michelle opened the rashers. She put four on the grill-pan along with six sausages – she knew Mark's appetite of old. Then she cracked four eggs into a saucepan and added a dollop of butter and some salt and pepper.

While she whisked the eggs, Michelle went to the window and watched Mark grapple with the plastic clothes-pegs.

He piled the laundry in his arms and pushed the kitchen door with his foot.

"The bolt's OK, Michelle, not broken. You must have left the gate open."

"Did I?"

"Your clothes are bone dry."

"Thanks, Mark, just dump them there on a chair. I'll sort out the ones for ironing later. So, you went to the airport to see Beth off?"

"I drove them, actually. Ken, I mean, Mr Leavy – he hates me to call him Ken – anyhow, he was too busy this morning so I borrowed my father's car and dropped them up. It was no big deal. I think Mrs Leavy was a bit miffed, though."

Mrs Leavy. Michelle bristled slightly.

"It's good Beth's getting away for a holiday," she said, hiding her irritation. "Ken tells me she's very cut up about her gran's death."

"Yeah."

"I think she was delighted you came back for the funeral, Mark. She missed you. Will you set the table? I don't want to burn the eggs."

Michelle poured tea into two mugs. "If you take your eyes off scrambled eggs for a minute, they stick. The cutlery's in that press beside the door."

He moved some books off the table and laid two places. "Beth's been in funny mood all week."

"It's to be expected."

"No, not about her gran, it's something else. She's peculiar when Toni's around – sort of silly and superficial . . . schoolgirlish."

Michelle turned to him, still stirring the eggs. "She *is* a schoolgirl, Mark."

"You know what I mean. She acts differently, puts on airs and graces, changes her accent – it's annoying. Yesterday she got her hair dyed purple, definitely Toni's influence."

"Purple!"

"She calls it auburn but it's purple and streaky. And the two of them are in cahoots, ganging up on Mr Leavy. I swear, I was embarrassed in the hotel lobby this morning by their carry-on."

Michelle turned off the gas.

"That man has the patience of a saint," Mark went on. "She keeps nagging and telling him what to do."

"He should be firmer with her – "

"No, not Beth. Toni. I shouldn't say this but . . . no, I'd better shut up."

Michelle brought plates of buttered toast to the table.

"Toni's . . . shallow," he went on. "That's my opinion, for what it's worth. You know someone who's pretending to listen to you but they're fixing their hair or looking in the mirror or staring beyond you at something more interesting."

"I hate that," Michelle agreed. "The last time I met her, she was very chatty, gushing. That was a good while ago."

"She blows hot and cold, all over you one time, and the next practically ignoring you."

Michelle smiled. "Maybe she's insecure."

"And pigs might fly! It must be awkward for you," Mark said, taking the plate from Michelle, "having her around. Thanks a mill', Michelle, you've enough to feed an army here!"

"Enjoy."

Michelle joined him at the table.

"Toni doesn't approve of me." He cut into a sausage. "I know from the way she went on this morning. She's polite up to a point but . . . she dismisses me. You know what I mean?"

"Eat your eggs before they go cold, Mark. Yes, I do know what you mean. I wouldn't say she's enamoured of me, either."

"No, you wouldn't be flavour of the month."

"I was dismissed too." Michelle buttered a slice of toast. "You see those chocolates, there on the dresser?"

Mark nodded, his mouth full.

"A peace offering from Ken. He broke off our date

last night because Toni booked had a meal for them without even consulting him."

"Tell me about it! I wanted to see Beth last night but Toni put the kibosh on that, too." Mark sighed. "I feel as though I'm being pushed out of the way."

Michelle poured them each another cup of tea. "Well, I for one am glad she's gone back to London."

"You know she's thinking of moving back?"

Michelle dropped her knife on the plate. "What?"

"That's what I gathered from the conversation this morning. She was talking about setting up her own business here in Dublin, said she was going to make inquiries and try and build up some contacts."

Michelle swallowed. "What did Ken say to that?"

"Precious little. She did all the talking, he answered in grunts. I'd say he wasn't elated, to put it mildly." Mark poured more milk into his tea.

Toni back in Dublin . . . for good. She'd never leave Ken alone. She'd be calling for Beth, phoning all the time, turning up at weekends . . .

"We won't worry about it till it happens." Mark stood up and put his dirty dishes in the sink. "May I have a look at your painting job, Michelle?"

"It's not finished yet, the ceiling's still blotchy. I missed a few bits. It could do with another coat."

She scraped the leftovers from her plate into the bin and followed Mark into the back room.

"See, over there, the left-hand side near the window. It's such an awkward angle and I – "

"Say no more," Mark said and pulled his T-shirt over his head, revealing a broad, tanned chest. "I'll have it done in no time."

He was up the ladder before she could protest.

"I've nothing planned for the rest of the morning, in any case. I've Toni to thank for that. I'd saved enough to take Beth down the country on a holiday – thought we'd be in Lahinch by now."

"Ah, Mark. Does Beth know that?"

He dipped the paintbrush in the can. "No, I didn't say anything – not when I saw the way things were." He shrugged. "It doesn't matter. I might take a job with my uncle for the next three weeks, before I go back to college. He's a landscape gardener and he's plenty of work on at the moment. No point hanging around, I like to keep busy."

"Me too. I'm looking forward to the new term."

"If we get through here by lunchtime, would you like to go to a film? I want to see *The Full Monty*. The da said it was hilarious. Why are you smiling?"

"At the coincidence," Michelle replied. "Ken was supposed to take me to see it last night."

"Right, it's time we suited ourselves, so."

"I have to be home by seven o'clock. Andrew's coming for his lesson."

"We'll be back long before that if we go to the afternoon screening. You bring those chocolates, Michelle. We'll guzzle them like partners in crime." He noticed her wistful expression. "Only kidding!"

"You're more than welcome to the chocolates, they'd choke me! Thanks for helping out today, Mark."

"No sweat, I like painting, actually. You can see things happening before your eyes. When the job's done, it's done – not like studying. Sometimes I feel I'm getting nowhere."

"A creative block, that's what I used to call it."

"A creative bleeding wall! It's really a matter of getting into a regular study routine, that's what I keep telling myself, anyhow."

"Don't think about it now. Enjoy your last few weeks of freedom."

"I will. Come October, I'll have the head buried in the books, that's for sure. Second Year's serious business, according to my tutor. The history course is so damned wide."

"And the politics?"

"I get a real buzz out of it. I grew up on politics, what with Dad being a councillor."

"Of course. What would you like to do when you're finished? Would you go into politics yourself?"

"Haven't made up my mind yet. I don't think so. Research maybe, or journalism, I'm not sure."

"You've two more years to make up your mind."

Michelle opened a tin of gloss. She could make a start on the door. "You might even decide on a post-graduate course, Mark."

He stretched forward on the ladder to reach the corner. "Be an eternal student, I like the sound of that."

They were finished the room by one o'clock.

"You've done a great job, Mark. Very professional."

"Not bad, though I say so myself. I'll just have a quick wash in the bathroom. Shit! I've a huge stain on these jeans. I'll have to scrub them."

"Use lots of water, it'll come off easily enough."

Michelle went back to the kitchen to sort out the pile of laundry. She folded the sheets neatly and put her blouses and skirts in the ironing-basket. Then she placed her underwear on top of the folded towels. Something seemed to be missing.

She counted the panties again. Seven pairs. Where were the red ones? She was sure she'd put them in the wash yesterday.

She went upstairs, neatly stacked the sheets on the bottom shelf of the hot press, draped two towels over the chrome rails in the bathroom and the third over the bath.

In her bedroom, she opened the underwear drawer in the double bed. No, the red panties weren't there. Maybe Mark had dropped them in the garden?

When she went downstairs, she opened the back door and had a look out – nothing on the ground or on the grass near the clothes-line. It had been such a wild night, the wind must have blown them away.

She grinned at the thought of her Dunnes knickers landing in a neighbour's garden. So long as they hadn't been swept into the street, she didn't mind.

Eighteen

"I'm very pleased with the Scarlatti, Andrew, but you'd need to keep going over the last two lines of the Debussy, make the ending more closed."

"I know." The boy nodded gravely. "I can't seem to get it right, maybe I should have chosen the Gershwin."

"Well, it's not too late if you want to change," Michelle said. "Perhaps the tempo would suit you better."

"I'll give it another shot, put in more hours."

Andrew didn't like to be defeated. He was the most determined student Michelle had ever taught.

"Will I play the Chopin now?"

"Yes, and don't run away with it, OK?"

The "Nocturne in E flat". His fingering was excellent, light and nimble. The phone rang but, as usual, she ignored it. She'd check the call-answering service later to see if it was . . . to see who had phoned.

"Keep going, you're doing beautifully," she told Andrew as she walked up and down behind him, around the sitting-room, tapping the rhythm against her thigh. He played a wrong note in the last bar and cursed under his breath.

"Easy, Andrew, easy. Try it again."

He turned to her. "You're making me nervous, walking up and down like that."

She laughed. "Tough."

"Ms Bolger, I prefer you to sit beside me," he pleaded.

"The examiner won't sit beside you," she pointed out. "They usually hover, as you well know. Now, once more, Andrew."

He tried it but again he missed the note. He hunched his shoulders stiffly and sighed.

"Take it nice and slowly a few more times and I'll make us some tea. Two sugars, isn't it?"

"Yes, thanks."

"I'll leave the door open so I can hear you from the kitchen. Take it from the top of the second page, all right?"

She plugged in the kettle and put two mugs on a tray. She could hear him faltering at the end of the piece.

"Again, Andrew," she called in to him.

"Slave-driver," he shouted back at her but he laughed.

She went out to the hall and stared hard at the phone. Who had rung? Her mother? Ken?

Him?

Did she really want to hear the message? Be subjected to more of this prurient nonsense? Damn you! I'll listen to you later, when and *if* I feel like it and then I'll erase you, blot you out, annihilate you – you bastard.

The kettle had boiled and she made the tea. Andrew banged the piano in his frustration.

"Tut, tut," she said, smiling, as she came back with the tray. "You're not going all temperamental on me, are you?"

He groaned. "The more I go over it, the worse I get. Honestly, I played it perfectly at home."

"That's often the way," she said sympathetically. "Here, have your tea." She put an ash-tray on the coffee table. "And a cigarette."

He looked surprised. "You're always nagging me to quit smoking."

"This mightn't be the best time," she said. "Go on, light up. I don't mind. We'll leave the Chopin for this evening and get down to scales."

"Scales?" He grinned. "Goodie!"

"Just for that, young sir, you're going to begin with the contrary motion chromatic, two octaves starting on F."

"Starting on F? Thrilling!"

Michelle raised the back of her hand, pretending she was about to deliver a slap.

He laughed and ducked. "Ms Bolger, I'm seriously beginning to think you've a very cruel streak!"

"That's me, Andrew, tough as old boots."

He took a long drag on his cigarette. "Whew, that's better. I get into a tizzy when things go wrong."

"So do I," she said. "Relax for a few moments. Have you thought about what you're going to do after your Leaving Cert?"

He shook his head.

"What do you want to do, Andrew?"

"The diploma."

"Are you certain?"

"Yes. In the long-term I'd like to try the Licentiate, but maybe next year I could take the Diploma of Associate Teacher. It's easier, kind of like a stepping-stone. I might be able to do the Pre Med at the same time. What do you think?"

"That's a good idea. Have you spoken to your father about it?"

He stirred his tea. "No point. Every time I broach the subject, another row flares up. He wants me to pack in the music and concentrate on my other subjects."

"And your mother? How does she feel?"

"She just wants me to be happy." He smiled sadly. "My sister's in second-year medicine now. Wouldn't you think Dad would be content with that? But he's not. If he had the slightest clue that I was considering the performer diploma, he'd go mental. Not that he wants me to be a teacher, either. Sorry, no insult intended."

"None taken."

Andrew pulled thoughtfully on the cigarette. "I admire teachers, Ms Bolger, but I wouldn't be cut out for it. I think I'd slaughter the pupils."

"Oh, you admire me, do you?" She raised an eyebrow. "A few minutes ago you told me I was a slave-driver!"

"I was joking. Where would I be without you? You've always given me great support and encouragement."

"That's my job, Andrew."

"No, it's much more than a job for you, anyone can see that. I don't know how you have the patience – "

"It's not hard when I have a student like you. I love to see how well you're doing – how much you've come on in the past few years."

"That's what I mean, you give so much," he said, stubbing out the cigarette, "and what do you get in return?"

"I've often told you, Andrew, teaching's all about empowerment. You've learned the basics from me but now you've made your own of that knowledge. You've developed your own strengths, your own interpretation."

"With your help – "

"I've only equipped you with the mechanics."

"No, no, you've done far more than that for me, Ms Bolger. You've given me a belief in myself."

Michelle smiled ruefully. "You're on your way, Andrew. Pretty soon there won't be much left for me to teach you."

"That's not true – "

"It is," she insisted. "It's time you spread your wings a little. If you seriously intend to go on with your music,

I'm going to recommend you to someone in the academy."

His jaw dropped. "I presumed I'd be doing the diploma course with you."

"Time for you to move on, Andrew. There's a wonderful teacher I know, a graduate of the Hochschule für Musik in Vienna."

"I just can't imagine learning with anyone but you!"

"We'll talk about it again. For the moment let's concentrate on the job in hand – scales. OK, on we go."

Andrew played the F chromatic contrary motion without a hitch.

"Now G."

Again, no mistakes.

"Good, Andrew, very good. You've obviously practised them well. Now double octaves, hands separately, in the key of G, then C and F sharp."

Andrew, his mouth set resolutely, began. The doorbell rang and Michelle went to answer it.

"Come in, Aoife. You're a bit early. Did your mother drop you over in the car?"

"Yes, Ms Bolger." The little girl followed her teacher into the back room.

"Sit over there, on the armchair, pet. Andrew's just finishing." Michelle picked up the tray. "Coke, Aoife?"

"Oh, yes, Ms Bolger, that would be lovely."

She went to open the door for Michelle, who hid a smile as she hurried out. The eight-year-old was almost prim in her manner.

Andrew turned to the little girl. "Are you doing an exam?"

She nodded enthusiastically. "Grade II. I'm hoping to do Grade III next May. Ms Bolger said I'd be well able for it."

"Great."

"I'm practising like mad," she went on, "because I want to enter for the Feis Ceoil as well. My dad's very excited about it. He plays the cello in the Symphony Orchestra," she added proudly. "And my brother's learning the violin. He's brilliant."

Andrew nodded. A musical family – this kid was lucky.

Michelle came back with a large glass of Coca Cola and handed it to Aoife. "Would you like to hear Andrew play one of his pieces, Aoife?"

"I'd love to." She turned eagerly to the boy at the piano. "Would you mind?"

"I don't want to be taking up your lesson time," he said.

Aoife folded her arms. "Oh no, you wouldn't be. It would be very good for me to hear you play. Please."

"In that case, I'd be delighted." The boy was genuinely touched by this little girl's enthusiasm. He winked at Michelle. "Who could refuse such a charming invitation?"

He opened the Scarlatti and began to play.

The child sat in awe as she watched and listened. Some day, she'd be able to play like that . . . if she worked very hard at it.

Eight-thirty. Michelle was tired, too tired to call over to her mother's. Could she put it off till the morning? She picked up the phone and heard the jingling tone which reminded her to check her answering service. She waited for the signal and keyed in her personal number.

You have two new messages in your mailbox.

Half in dread, Michelle pressed one.

Hello, Ms Bolger. My name is Patricia Hanley. Father Noonan gave me your number. I'm getting married in the parish church on September the twenty-second and I was wondering if you'd be free to play the organ. I've a singer organised so perhaps you'd need to meet up with her? I'm not sure of the procedure.

A little giggle ensued. The bride sounded very young.

Could you give me a call as soon as possible? I'd be very grateful. My number is 8563029. Thanks.

Michelle pressed nine to save and waited for the second message.

Michelle? Hi. This is Mark. You won't believe what happened after I left you home from the cinema. I had a bloody flat tyre on my way into town. Must have been a slow puncture. Anyhow, when I went to the boot – which wasn't locked, by the way, the da would kill me if he knew I left his precious car unlocked – when I went to get the spare, I discovered a parcel that was addressed to you. I don't remember you putting anything in the boot? I'll drop it over some time tomorrow. See you.

A parcel addressed to her? What was he talking about? She hadn't put anything in the boot.

Could it be . . . ?

No, he was in Vienna.

Mark had left Beth and her mother to the airport this morning. Maybe Beth had left it there and forgotten to tell Mark? But why? A present?

The last time Michelle had spoken to Beth on the phone, the girl had been very abrupt. Was this her way of making up?

It didn't seem like Beth but wonders never cease.

Michelle felt like taking a walk. She'd visit her mother after all.

* * *

Her sister-in-law opened the door. "Oh, Michelle, thank the Lord! I rang you earlier but I didn't leave a message. I hate those bloody answering machines."

Michelle shut the front door. "What is it, Fiona? You look worried. Is Mam OK?"

"The house has been done," Fiona whispered. She pointed upstairs. "I finally got your mother into bed. I gave her a large brandy. She's in shock."

"A burglary?" Michelle said, alarmed. "When? Was Mam here when it happened?"

Fiona shook her head. "Come down to the kitchen with me and we'll have a drink. Sorry to spring it on you like this but – "

"No, no, go on. Tell me." Michelle accepted a glass of brandy. "First, is Mam all right?"

"The doctor came and gave her a light sleeping pill. Luckily, she wasn't here when it happened. She was over in our place for tea and at about eight o'clock she insisted I drive her home because you were calling, she said."

Michelle nodded. Thankfully she hadn't put off her visit. She'd never have forgiven herself.

"The minute she opened the door," Fiona continued, "I could see what had happened. The scullery window was wide open and the sugar bowl and a bottle of vinegar were knocked over. They obviously forced the lock – we'll need to have it repaired or replaced. Declan came over and did a temporary job on it – "

"She can't be left here on her own tonight," Michelle said.

"Declan wanted her to sleep in our house but she wouldn't hear of it. She's terribly stubborn. She didn't even want me to phone you."

"Fiona, was there any damage done?"

"No, apart from the window. There's a few things missing but your mother got confused and – "

"Did you call the police?"

"Of course." Her sister-in-law topped up Michelle's drink. "They checked around for fingerprints and asked a lot of questions. She'll be able to claim on the insurance. We'll have to look again to see what's missing."

Michelle nodded. "She had some nice jewellery upstairs."

"That's the weird thing, none of it was taken, not even your father's wedding ring and gold watch which were worth a few bob. And the telly. I can't understand it – they didn't touch the telly or the stereo."

"So, what *did* they take?"

"I'm still not sure. Your mother had a few pounds in the wardrobe, not much, about forty quid, she thinks. That's gone. The drawers were pulled out and everything was thrown around. They went into your room as well."

Her room. She hadn't lived here for years but the family still referred to it as "Michelle's room".

"They wouldn't have got anything in there," Michelle mused aloud. "I haven't left anything valuable in this house. Come to think of it," she added with a smile, "I haven't really got anything worth stealing, even in Collins Avenue – apart from the piano."

"Your mother said something about your Feis medals and cups. She had them in the china cabinet in the sitting-room."

"My medals? They wouldn't get much for those. What about her Waterford crystal?"

"I don't know, there may be one or two pieces missing. Your mother was so agitated with the police being here – I didn't want to hassle her."

"No, you were right, Fiona. Look, I'll stay here tonight and tomorrow we'll sort something out."

Fiona stood up and put on her jacket. "I better be getting home. The kids will be driving Declan up the walls. I'll give you a ring in the morning. Your mother's more than welcome to stay with us for a few days, Michelle."

"You're very good."

Her mother would never agree to that, though. Much as she loved her grandchildren, she wouldn't want to spend days with them. No, Michelle would try to persuade her to come to Collins Avenue. But that was only a short-term measure.

"She'll have to get a security alarm," Michelle said, as she walked her sister-in-law to the door. "I've been telling her that for years."

Fiona raised her eyes to heaven. "So have we. Mind you, I hate the damned things – they're always going off and nobody pays a blind bit of attention."

Michelle waved her sister-in-law off, then she locked the front door and bolted it. She went upstairs to her mother's bedroom. Her mother was sleeping, her breathing soft and regular. Michelle crept over to the bed. Her mother looked old suddenly. Shrunken and old. Old people living on their own were vulnerable.

Michelle quietly shut the bedroom door and went into the spare room. The drawers and the wardrobe were open. A red cloth doll with yellow hair was thrown on the floor. She picked it up. Imagine her mother keeping it all these years!

Memories came crashing back . . .

This was the room where Michelle had spent the first twenty years of her life, studying for her school exams at a desk that used to be in that corner by the bed. She remembered the transistor she'd buried under the pillow and listened to for half the night; the walls, now bare, which had once housed posters of Mozart, Beethoven, Lizst – posters she'd saved up her pocket-money for week after week and pictures she'd torn from her collection of *The Great Composers*. Her mother had thrown them all out when she'd had the room re-decorated a few years earlier.

But she'd kept that doll.

Michelle could feel her eyes smart. There was something sad about seeing it again like this, a bit of straw stuffing protruding from a rip in one of the legs.

Where had her mother kept it? Hidden in the wardrobe?

Why?

Sentimentality?

There'd been so much unsaid in this household, they'd never been good at showing their feelings. Even when her father died, Michelle hadn't told anyone how she was feeling. Neither had Declan, to her knowledge. After the funeral, they hardly spoke about him again. That's the way her mother seemed to want it.

All through their childhood, she and her brother had laughed, fought, argued, teased each other like all siblings do, but they'd never, never *talked*. And her mother . . . her mother had retired into herself, erected a wall of silence.

Were all families like that?

The eiderdown on the bed was tossed to one side. Michelle pulled back the bedclothes. The carving-knife from the kitchen drawer was lying on the sheet. Its jagged edge gleamed up at her.

Jesus Christ.

Nineteen

Michelle's stomach turned a somersault as she stared in horror at the knife. Imagine if she'd got into bed without checking and lain on it? She shuddered.

What kind of blackguards were they? Why would anyone do this to an old lady living alone? Were they not satisfied with breaking and entering and petty pilfering? Did they want to frighten the life out of her as well?

She took the knife and went quietly downstairs to the kitchen to slip it back inside the cutlery drawer before her mother found out.

Eleven-thirty.

She went to the phone to report this latest turn of events. Which police station had the gardaí come from?

Fiona had left a contact number on the telephone pad: Dave Lacey, Santry Station. Lacey – a good name for a cop! Michelle dialled the number and the desk sergeant put her on hold for a few moments.

"Hello. Dave Lacey here."

"My name is Michelle Bolger. You were here earlier tonight with my mother. The robbery at – "

"Shanowen Road, yes, I remember Ms Bolger. It was your sister-in-law I met."

"That's right. I came over later and I'm spending the night here."

"How's your mother?"

"She's sleeping. I'm phoning to tell you about something else, actually."

"Yes?" The voice was unhurried and reassuring. The voice of a man who had everything under control.

"The burglars hid a carving-knife in one of the beds. I was . . . upset when I discovered it. Luckily, *I* was the one who found it and not my mother."

"A carving-knife? Theirs?"

"No, the knife belongs to my mother. They took it from the kitchen."

"I'm making a note of it, now."

Michelle drew in a long breath. "Is it some kind of a warning?"

"I doubt it, Ms Bolger. They probably took it for protection, to use as a threat if they were disturbed."

"My God! If my mother *had* come in on top of them . . . "

"Luckily she didn't. What did you do with the knife?"

"I put it back in the kitchen of course . . . oh, sorry. I shouldn't have touched it, should I? Fingerprints."

"It's all right, Ms Bolger. We gave the place a good dusting over tonight and got a few prints. I suggest you pour yourself a stiff drink and get some sleep."

She thanked Dave Lacey and hung up.

He'd been kind, done his best to reassure her.

But she was far from being reassured. Finding a sharp carving-knife in her bed was not conducive to a good night's sleep. She felt a little better after the conversation with the policeman . . . but only a little.

* * *

Michelle woke to the smell of coffee wafting up from the kitchen. She'd left the bedroom door open all night to listen out for her mother. She struggled into a sitting-position and glanced bleary-eyed at her watch. Nine-fifteen.

Her head felt fuzzy. She hadn't intended to sleep this late but she hadn't dropped off last night till after three – too many frightening thoughts. And when she had nodded off, she'd landed slap back in the middle of that awful nightmare. The candles, the Mozart, the hands around her throat . . . she'd woken at four in a lather of sweat.

Michelle hoped it wasn't back for good, that blasted dream. Her mother had always told her she'd grow out of it. Thirty-two years of age and here it was back again.

It felt very odd to be getting dressed in this bedroom. For a second she had the fancy that it was time to put on her school uniform and go downstairs to face the morning porridge, lumps and all.

Her father would peck her on the cheek and head off for work, whistling. He was always whistling or singing around the house, light-hearted and cheery, that was her father – not the typical heart-attack candidate at all.

Michelle's childhood . . . music, laughter, friends, the tennis club, holidays in Bundoran with her grand-parents, school. Happy times. A nice, uncomplicated life.

It had all changed overnight.

Sixteen years ago, on a sunny spring evening on his way home from work, her father dropped dead in O'Connell Street, outside Clery's. On his own, he died on his own – none of his family there to hold his hand, tell him how much they loved him, kiss his cheek or say a prayer over him.

On that horrible day – sixteen years ago – a light went out in the Bolger household. And shortly after that, Michelle's nightmare began. Her mother was convinced it had been brought on by the shock of her father's death.

"Oh, you're up, Michelle? I hope I didn't wake you." Olive Bolger smiled and handed her daughter a cup of coffee. "Would you like some breakfast?" she asked cheerfully.

What was happening here?

"No, no breakfast for me, thanks." Michelle stared curiously at her mother. "How are you feeling?"

"Tip-top, thank God."

Had her mother *forgotten* last night?

"Mam, I'm sorry about the burglary. It's awful for you."

"Could have been a lot worse. Thankfully, I wasn't here when they broke in and they didn't do any damage."

This was *not* her mother speaking.

"All things considered, I was lucky." She sat at the table and buttered a scone for herself.

"Lucky?"

"You hear such awful stories, don't you? People's houses vandalised, ornaments broken, clothes ripped up . . . sometimes, they do disgusting things, Michelle . . . even defecate on the carpets." Her mother shook her head slowly. "No, I was lucky. I was visited by the good thief."

The *good* thief?

Bullshit.

Michelle sat and sipped her coffee in silence. She'd let her mother talk this out of her system. Judging by what she was saying and her unnatural high spirits, she must be in denial.

"Last night I got a terrible fright when I first discovered it," her mother admitted. "But after a good night's sleep – those pills Dr Driscoll gave me would knock out an elephant – I felt better this morning. I came down to the kitchen at about seven o'clock and opened the curtains. The sun streamed in, Michelle, and you know what? A little robin landed on the branch just outside the window. Do you know how long is it since a robin came into this garden? Years. Donkeys' years. They've been hunted away by the magpies. All the little birds have, the sparrows and finches as well. When I saw that robin on the window-sill, 'Olive,' I said to myself, 'this is a good omen.'"

How could her mother sit there and witter on about robins, finches and sparrows? What about the bloody robbers who'd broken in and rifled through this house?

Michelle got madder and madder the more she thought about it. They'd gone through her mother's private belongings and coldly chosen which items they were going to rob, pinch, take as their own . . . without any qualm of conscience.

"Will you help me to make a list of what's missing, Michelle? In case you spot something I miss."

"Of course, but there's no rush."

"No sense in putting it off," Olive said with a resoluteness Michelle hadn't ever noticed before. "The quicker I make the claim, the quicker the insurance company will cough up."

She tried to analyse her mother's behaviour – up much earlier than usual this morning and ready for action – out of character. It certainly wasn't the reaction Michelle had expected.

"First things first, Mam. We'll have to see about getting the window fixed."

"No need, Declan's sending over someone this morning. He phoned earlier. There's some fellow calling after ten."

Declan was certainly on the ball.

"Another coffee, Michelle? I wish you'd have something to eat. Even some toast? No? Oh, blast. There's the phone again, probably Fiona ringing to see if I'm still alive and kicking. I hope you're not all going to fuss over me from now on. I'm perfectly all right."

Olive Bolger went to answer the phone. Michelle simply couldn't believe how her mother was taking all this. It actually seemed as if she was *enjoying* herself.

"It's for you, love. Ken. He was phoning your house all night, worried about you. I explained."

Ken.

With all the comings and goings, she'd totally forgotten about him. She went out to the hall to take the call.

"Hello, Ken. Sorry to have worried you. Did Mam tell you what happened here yesterday? Mmh, desperate." She lowered her voice. "No, she doesn't seem to be. In fact, I think she's revelling in it. I haven't seen her this lively in years. It's very peculiar."

"Maybe she's in shock?"

"I think she is. Listen, I'm going to ask her to spend the weekend in Collins Avenue, so I don't know how I'll be fixed for Saturday night."

"Do whatever you think best, Mich."

"You don't mind? Good. I'll phone you later today. Oh, did you get that hassle in work sorted out?"

"Not yet. I think I might have to fire one of the accommodation assistants – maids, to you. She refused to follow an instruction from the housekeeper. I don't want to fire the girl but it was downright insubordination. Maybe if I have a talk with her?"

"Firing should be the last resort, Ken."

"Yes. It's a delicate kind of an issue and I have to be careful – don't want to draw an unfair dismissal case on myself. At the same time, I have to placate the housekeeper." Ken sighed. "I'll work it out. Would you like me to drop over to you this morning?"

"No, no, you've enough going on at the moment, Ken. Where would you get the time?"

"I'll make time, Mich."

"There's nothing you can do here. No, really, Ken. Everything's under control."

"By the way, did Mark give you your present?"

"What present?"

"A little gift from Toni," he said sarcastically.

"What? Are you serious? Mark said he found a parcel for me in the boot of his car."

"Toni obviously forgot to tell Mark to give it to you." He sighed down the line. "A large bottle of *Dune*."

"Perfume from Toni for me? Why, for God's sake?"

"Atonement, she said." Ken sounded doubtful. "To make up for spoiling your night."

Michelle paused to digest this. "There was no need for it, Ken. I don't like – "

"I told her not to, but you can't talk to Toni. Any advice there always falls on deaf ears."

"I suppose it was . . . thoughtful of her, but there was absolutely no need."

"Toni? Thoughtful? No, Mich, she's up to something."

Michelle *knew* that but hadn't wanted to say it.

"I better go, Ken. I'm going to make an inventory of what's missing and then I'll take Mam out to lunch. I should be back home after four, so you can catch me then. If not, I'll phone you tonight. OK? Fine. Talk to you later."

A present from Toni . . . from *Mrs* Ken Leavy.

What was she up to? Plotting and planning. She could leave Michelle out of her little intrigues.

How dare she?

But part of Michelle was relieved.

At least the parcel hadn't come from *him*. Since Mark's phone message, it had played on her mind that maybe, just maybe, Cyril O'Connor had left Vienna and followed her back to Dublin.

Was it possible?

Lately Michelle's thoughts were in turmoil – about Beth and her frosty behaviour, about Toni and her scheming, about Cyril O'Connor, a sicko, who seemed determined to make her life a misery.

And now, to cap it all, this burglary.

Olive Bolger dried the dishes and lined them up on the dresser. She wasn't going to let these scoundrels grind her down. She'd thought about nothing else since she'd got up this morning.

This burglary was a God-send, in a way. It made her focus on what she'd become: a dependent, nervous woman who'd relied too much on others, especially her children. From now on, things would be different. She'd have to take back control of her own life.

OK, they'd broken in and stolen from her. These things happened every day of the week. She was just another casualty of the drug-related crime rise in the city. It wasn't a nice thing to have happened but it wasn't the end of the world.

When she'd lost her husband, it hadn't been easy but she'd wallowed in the part of the lonely, bereaved widow, she realised guiltily. She'd refused to mix socially, not bothered to get out and find a job, made do with the widow's pension.

Made do. That described her life to a T.

She'd given up on ambition, enjoyment, fun – that must have had a traumatic effect on Michelle and Declan.

Her daughter had borne the brunt of it. It wasn't right. Things were going to change and change dramatically. She refused to let herself be seduced into the victim role.

They finished making the list of the stolen goods by twelve o'clock.

"Right, that's grand, Michelle. Thanks for your help, another pair of eyes is useful in situations like these. I think we've got everything noted. I'm furious about the Waterford decanter and even more so about your medals and stuff."

"Like you said, Mam, it could have been a lot worse. What about the insurance claim forms? I'll drop into the Hibernian for them."

"You'll do no such a thing. I'll phone and ask them to post out the forms."

"Well, I'll help you fill them in when they arrive."

Olive sighed. "Listen to yourself, Michelle."

"What do you mean?" Michelle replied defensively.

"You don't think I'm capable of looking after myself at all, do you?" A sad expression crossed Olive Bolger's face. "It's my own fault, of course. I've relied on you for far too long and before that, on your dad. He did everything, I never had to think."

"But, Mam, he just wanted to save you the bother. He worshipped the ground you walked on – "

"That's true, Michelle but . . . you know he never even let me pay a bill? He looked after all the household accounts, and as a result, after his death, I was hardly able to write a cheque." Her mother paused. "Maybe . . . maybe the best way to help people isn't by doing everything for them."

Michelle nodded.

Empowerment.

She'd been going on about it to Andrew last night. She loved to see her pupils thrive and grow and become self-reliant . . . but when it came to her mother, was it a different story?

Had she actually *contributed* to her mother's dependency, albeit unintentionally? Secretly delighted in her "good daughter" image? Michelle the reliable, the responsible, the dutiful? Had she, in fact, *enjoyed* her self-made martyrdom?

"I was going to ask you to stay with me for a few days, Mam." Michelle took her mother's hand. "Not a good idea?"

"No, thanks, love. I'll be fine here on my own. I mean it – you're not to worry. That man did a good job on the window. It's very secure now. In any case, lightning never strikes twice in the one place, isn't that what they say?"

"Yes."

"And I can't let those thugs get to me, love, can't let them win. This is my home and I have to feel safe in it. I won't *let* them turn me into a nervous wreck. I will see about getting an alarm, though. They're a deterrent. Now, you run along, Michelle, you've done quite enough for one day."

"What about lunch? I was going to take you to the Regency."

"Some other time. I've a nice piece of beef for tonight's dinner. You go home and get ready for your weekend with Ken. Beth's away, isn't she? Make the most of his free time, then. It can't be easy for him to combine parenting with romance."

"Tell me about it!"

Her mother kissed her on the cheek. "It's never too late to change, I've discovered."

"Is that a hint, Mam?"

"If the cap fits!"

"Well, Mother dear, you'll have to give me time to come to grips with your newly-found – what's that the term is? Self-esteem!"

"Isn't it desperate?" Olive groaned. "All these bloody American terms creeping into our speech – it's scary! We never had self-esteem in my day, I can tell you. Just a large dose of cod-liver oil – for whatever ailed ya!"

Michelle hugged her mother. "Is it all right if I phone you tonight?"

Olive tittered. "I'm not breaking off all communication with you. It's time you had breathing-space, that's all."

Breathing-space.

Yes, that *would* be nice.

Twenty

"What's up, Mich? You're very quiet." Ken turned down the stereo. "Are you OK?"

She stretched out on the sofa in his sitting-room. "Yes, just exhausted after my first week back in college. I'll get used to the routine in a week or two."

He mussed her hair. "You look tired, actually."

"I haven't been sleeping well."

That bloody nightmare . . . and now it had got worse. It started as usual at the piano in the darkened room, but then the scene shifted and changed and became a bedroom. Her mother was sleeping peacefully in her bed when a masked man appeared. He had a carving-knife in his hand. Michelle wanted to scream out and warn her mother but of course she couldn't. She wasn't in the room, she was just a silent witness to this horrifying vision. The burglar crept around the bed and stared down at the sleeping woman. He raised the knife slowly . . .

"Mich, are you OK?"

"Oh . . . oh, sorry, Ken. I was miles away. Sorry."

"I was just saying, the dinner will be ready in about ten or fifteen minutes."

"Great, thanks."

"I'll go and check the oven."

Michelle lay back on the cushion again. She had a pain across her shoulders. Tension probably. Tonight as she left the music school, she was convinced that someone was following her. Even after she got on the bus, she couldn't shake the notion.

Ken came back and uncorked a bottle of red wine.

"Where's Beth this evening? Has she gone out?"

"No, she's in her room. Studying."

Michelle puffed up another cushion and put it behind her back. "That's good."

"If you can believe it," he said sceptically.

"Give her the benefit of the doubt," Michelle advised. "At least she's settled back in school. Three weeks ago, you were afraid she wasn't going to come home from London, remember?"

"She's not the same since that trip." He ran his hand through his hair. "She's jumpy, edgy, ready to explode. And . . . there's something I can't put my finger on."

"Have a talk with her, Ken."

"Have a talk with her?" He laughed bitterly. "I barely ever see her these days. She comes in from school at four while I'm still at work. By the time I get home, she's ensconced in her bedroom pretending to do her homework – in reality, she's wired into her *music* – or else she's lying comatose on the couch here, vegetating in front of the TV. She has a better relationship with the Klingons than she does with me!"

"What?"

"*Star Trek*," Ken said angrily. "I can't get a *word* out of her, let alone have a talk."

Michelle closed her eyes for a second. "I could try, if you want me to."

"I don't know if that's a good idea."

"Maybe not." She shivered.

"Are you cold? It's got a bit chilly, hasn't it?" Ken went over and switched on the gas fire. "There, that's better. I like a glow in the room."

Michelle lay there, her eyes still closed. "Have you heard from Toni?" she asked, not really wanting to hear the answer.

"Every bloody day." He groaned. "She's coming back next week to look for a suitable office."

Michelle sat up. "She's really going to do it then, move here?"

"Looks like it." He shrugged. "I think she's making a big mistake. Dublin isn't London. She'll be bored in another few months and then she'll high-tail it off somewhere else. You haven't heard the latest, though – she's thinking of renting an apartment in town, in the city. She rang this morning to tell me. Then Gwen rang, she's not too pleased. I think she prefers her sister to be at a safe distance."

Michelle suddenly felt queasy.

"Where is this apartment?

"In one of the new blocks on the quays, if you don't mind, near the new Financial Services Centre. Very chic, very up-market and very bloody expensive. Two bedrooms. Says she'll have Beth to stay at weekends. I wonder how long that will last."

He went out to the hall and shouted upstairs at his daughter.

"Beth, come down. Dinner's ready."

Michelle, still not over the shock, followed him out to the kitchen. "And the boyfriend, George? What does he have to say about all this?"

"According to Beth, Toni dumped him last month." Ken took a large casserole from the oven and placed it on a serving-mat in the centre of the table. "Chicken *à la* Ken! Hope you like it."

Michelle, in a daze, set the table as Beth came in and took her place. "Oh, Dad, not your gooey chicken!"

"It's delicious," Ken insisted. "Chicken breasts, onions, peppers and a can of Campbell's mushroom soup. Nothing simpler, nothing tastier."

"Nothing more disgusting you mean," Beth muttered as she buttered a large chunk of baguette for herself.

"Help yourself." He placed a large bowl of fried rice in front of her.

"Dad! You know I *hate* rice. You know I can't stand the smell of that bloody chicken dish and – "

"Sit down, Beth," he warned. "Apologise to Michelle."

"No way." She threw her napkin on the table. "Why should I apologise? I haven't done anything – "

"It's all right, Ken."

"No, Mich, it's not all right at all." He turned angrily to his daughter. "Sit down, madam, and behave yourself." He lowered his voice in a serious way. "This is inexcusable, Beth. I won't tolerate any more of your tantrums. I – "

"Ah, shut it, shut it, shut it," she screamed. "You make me puke, the pair of you!"

Beth dashed from the kitchen and Ken made to follow her but Michelle jumped up and stood in his way.

"Ken."

Ken took her by the sleeve. "Out of the way, Mich." His face was a purple rage. "I'm going to kill her!"

Michelle led him back to the table. "Have a glass of wine and calm down."

"She can't be let get away with it," he snorted. "She's turning into a right little bitch. Last week I was called into the school by her form tutor. The poor woman is demented with all the complaints she's getting from the other teachers."

Michelle was surprised. "You never said anything."

"It's not your problem."

"But – "

"No, you don't come running to me every time something goes wrong in your life, do you? You've your mother to worry about, but you don't dump on me."

"Ken, I hope you can talk to me about . . . things. If we can't tell each other . . . "

Who was she kidding? Could *she* discuss her problems with Ken? Sure, she'd talk about college, her students, her mother, her brother, the neighbours . . .

Her *stalker*?

"I thinks Beth's very unhappy, Ken."

"What are you saying?" he asked sharply. "That it's *my* fault?"

Michelle took his hand. "Of course not. She's going through some kind of a crisis, I think. Maybe it's about her . . . mother."

"Toni? Do you think so? I doubt it. She's on the phone to Toni every single day, had a ball in London – can't wait for her mother to move back here. No, everything's OK between Beth and her mother, Mich."

"I don't think she's over her granny's death yet. She's exactly the age I was when my father died. It's . . . hard. And Beth's granny was very close to her – in a way she was more like a mother."

"That's true," Ken said. "I'm sorry I lost my cool, Mich. Beth has this effect on me – I know, I know, I'm the adult here. But she pushes me too far."

"You need a break from one another."

"Yes, I think we do. The one parent, one child thing can become a bit fragile. It's hard for her as well – nobody else to diffuse our rows."

"And Mark? How is she with him?"

"He hasn't been around in days," Ken admitted, helping himself to some rice.

"Really?"

Ken stopped eating and stared at her. "Do you think . . . "

"A squabble? It's possible."

Ken nodded slowly, realisation dawning. "Mmh, I think you could be right. It's unusual for him not to have phoned. There's something up, definitely."

"Let her sort it out herself, Ken."

"Naturally."

Michelle went into the bathroom to wash her hands. She heard muffled sobbing coming from Beth's bedroom. Should she try to help?

Sixteen years old.

Beth was a miserable sixteen-year-old who was madly in love or out of love or love-sick or love-weary or disillusioned, depressed, despairing . . .

A miserable sixteen-year-old who despised, loathed, detested her boyfriend for some perceived wrong. How could he? How could he do this, say this, *think* this? He was a selfish, unfeeling, callous cad. He didn't understand her at all.

He was a *man*.

Michelle smiled ruefully into the bathroom mirror. Beth needed a woman to talk to, someone who'd been miserable, in love and pre-menstrual, all at the same time.

She'd knock on the bedroom door this minute.

Ken stacked the plates and glasses in the dish-washer. What had become of his daughter? Where was the Beth he *knew*?

He sat down at the table, lit his after-dinner cigarette and mentally planned the following morning. At ten o'clock there was the weekly Heads of Department meeting. The projections for Christmas were the most important thing on tomorrow's agenda. They'd had a terrific summer season, a boom time, it was vital that they kept it going.

The new deal they were negotiating with The Olympia Theatre looked promising. Two nights accommodation in The Fullerton and tickets for the show.

Ken would have to remind the department heads of the importance of this weekly meeting. He'd overheard the housekeeper saying to one of the bar staff that it was "nothing but hours of drivel!" And Paul, he wanted to see him privately and discuss his plans for building a new extension. They were badly in need of a proper conference centre.

"Go away, Dad. Leave me alone."

"Beth, your dad's downstairs. It's Michelle. Can we talk?"

Silence.

"Beth? I'd like to help."

anded Michelle something damp and soft. She
make it out clearly in the semi-darkness of the

they came into the kitchen she saw all too
hat the intruder had left behind him.
ir of *red lace knickers*.

"Go away. Please."

Michelle tapped lightly on the door again.

No response.

"All right, Beth. This mightn't be a good time for you."
Michelle turned to walk down the stairs.

The bedroom door opened. Slowly.

Ken heard the crackle of branches in the back garden.
That blasted mongrel from next door! He'd managed to
dig up the rhubarb the last time he'd got in. Ken would
have to repair the fencing again. He pulled open the
kitchen door, grabbed the sweeping-brush from beside
the fridge, yelled at the top of his voice and ran out.

"Aagh!" he screamed as he bounded down the back
steps. "Get out of there! Go piss in your own place!"

Beth sat at her dressing-table and puffed on a cigarette.

"You're right, it's Mark," she admitted.

"You've had a row?" Michelle sat down on the bed.

"Not exactly." Beth didn't turn around, she answered
to the mirror which was slightly disconcerting for
Michelle. "We're cooling it for a while. My idea."

"I see."

Beth tapped the ash from her cigarette into an empty
cold-cream jar.

"I mean, Mark's lovely and . . . " Her voice shook.

"Yes, he is, Beth. I – "

"Michelle." She half-smiled. "I know what you're
going to say – you're very fond of him."

"I am," Michelle agreed.

"He likes you, too." She stubbed out the cigarette.

"Does he?"

"Yeah." Beth stared into the middle distance. "He thinks you've had a hard time of it with . . . my mother and . . . me. He thinks you're being pushed aside . . . "

Michelle said nothing.

"He thinks he is, too." Beth frowned. "I didn't mean to push Mark away but things have gone funny for me . . . I'm not sure how I feel any more. When I was in London, something happened. I . . . I – "

Michelle looked at her. "You met someone else?"

Beth blushed. "I didn't mean anything to happen but . . . well, it happened. There's nothing I can do about it now."

"And you like this boy?" Michelle prompted.

Beth shook her head. "No, nothing like that. Not the way I like Mark but I let him . . . " She shrugged. "It doesn't matter. I don't want to talk about it."

A crash came from downstairs.

Michelle jumped up from the bed. "What was that?"

Beth laughed. "Just Dad doing his nightly freak-out. Wait. You'll hear the shouts now in a minute and a wallop if he makes contact!"

"Makes contact?"

"With the arse of next-door's dog!"

Scurried movements at the back of the garden.

"I'm coming, you smelly flea-ba[...] once and for all!"

He didn't care if the Sweetmans [...] was sick of this pest coming in eve[...] up his garden. It wasn't right. Do[...] locked up.

A rustle of leaves and a laugh.

Not a bark, not a growl, not a yelp.

A *laugh*!

There was a man in the garden.

He was crouching down, in between[...] bushes.

Ken felt a rush of adrenaline. "Right, yo[...] brandished the sweeping-brush high over[...] ran like the clappers down the long gard[...] give you something to laugh at, you slimy sc[...]

The man laughed again and raised two fin[...]

Then he disappeared.

Ken wheezed and puffed down to the fe[...] was a wide gaping hole where four or fi[...] wooden slats had been ripped off.

"Ken, Ken. Are you all right?" Michelle switch[...] outside light and ran into the garden.

"A prowler, Mich!"

He walked up the path and put his arm arou[...] couldn't catch him. He was away into the othe[...] like a scalded cat. He dropped this."

Twenty-One

Four am.

Michelle turned over on her right side and stretched her leg down the bed, desperately trying to find some sort of comfortable position. Ken's shallow breathing beside her did nothing to calm her – in fact it irritated the hell out of her.

How could he sleep?

The night's events churned round and round in her head . . .

Two detectives from Whitehall Garda Station had arrived at the house within minutes of Ken's phone call. They scoured the area for the garden visitor but he'd scarpered by then.

Ken had only been able to give a vague description, medium to tall, average build, some kind of a dark woollen cap on his head. Dark clothes, possibly jeans or a track suit. The sole clue left by the trespasser was the pair of ladies' red panties.

"Not much good as evidence," the older detective said

solemnly. "He must have stolen them from someone else's garden. Very few women would come in to the station to report these missing!"

Ken had laughed but the younger detective noticed Michelle's frightened expression.

"Nothing to worry about, miss."

She could feel her blood pressure rise. "No?"

"This type of offender isn't usually dangerous," he explained.

Michelle recalled the flasher. He'd been going into the grounds of one of the local girls' schools and exposing himself. A neighbour had described him as a harmless old guy, looking for attention, who was stoned out of his head when he was picked up.

That wasn't the way Michelle saw it. What about the schoolchildren and the fright they must have got?

"We treat this kind of behaviour very seriously," the older man said. "The man was trespassing on your property, apart from anything else."

"Exactly!" Ken butted in.

"Detective Rowley meant that these individuals aren't usually violent," the detective continued. "Not dangerous, in that sense."

What were they at? Trying to pacify her? To calm her down? To assure her that she was *safe*?

If so, they were far from convincing.

"Sad, when you think about it, isn't it?" The younger man said, adopting a graver tone. "Robbing women's underwear from clothes-lines."

"Closet knicker-sniffers", they called them down at the station but there was no point in sharing this with these good folk. He could see that the woman was upset.

If she only knew what real trouble was – the nightly horrors he came across in this job: battered bodies with their skulls bashed in; women who'd been beaten, bruised, burned with cigarettes, attacked with broken bottles; children who'd been thrashed, raped, buggered; drunks who'd been stabbed in alleyways; druggies who'd choked on their own vomit . . .

"Is he some kind of . . . pervert?" Michelle blurted.

The older detective stopped writing in his note-book and looked at her straight in the face.

"I wouldn't hazard an opinion on that, miss. He might be some local kid out to make mischief. From my experience, these individuals rarely go on to commit eh . . . serious crimes."

He meant rape, Michelle realised.

"What are you going to do about it?" Ken got a bit stroppy. "I have a sixteen-year-old daughter asleep upstairs. How do I know this bastard wasn't after *her*?"

The older detective turned to his partner. "Rowley, bag the . . . underwear for forensics." He ushered Ken and Michelle back into the kitchen.

"I'll make a full report, Mr Leavy, but really, we don't have much to go on at the moment."

Not much to go on.

She should have spoken out, told them everything,

admitted that the red panties belonged to *her*, that they'd been stolen from her garden, that the bastard had been hounding her, following her, menacing her for the last six weeks.

Notes.

Phone messages.

Now this.

Taken one by one, these incidents didn't amount to much but together . . . tonight had offered her an ideal opportunity to get it all off her chest.

She *should* have told them.

Michelle turned onto her left side. Ken was now in a heavy sleep. The sleep of the innocent. She'd tell him tomorrow. Come clean. But she couldn't imagine saying the words . . .

Oh, by the way, Ken, did I mention that I was being stalked? No, didn't I? It must have slipped my mind. How long? About six weeks. Why didn't I tell you before? Well, I must confess . . .

Confess.

What had *she* got to confess? She'd done nothing wrong. So, why hadn't she told him before? Weeks ago? Why hadn't she confided in him?

She hadn't wanted to bother him.

That was understandable. After all, he had Toni to contend with and Beth and the hotel. The last thing he needed at the moment was her troubles. And he'd want to know why she hadn't trusted him, wouldn't he? He'd be furious with her.

Hurt.

No, it was too late now to say anything to Ken.

Her eyelids grew heavy and she fell into a light sleep.

* * *

Ken's side of the bed was empty when Michelle awoke after ten the next morning. The lemony scent of his shampoo still clung to the pillow. She heard Beth down in the kitchen, singing.

Michelle had a quick shower in the *en suite*, but it didn't get rid of her groggy headache. She went to the wardrobe where she kept half her clothes. She'd go for jog this morning. She needed fresh air. Where was her track suit? Must be in Collins Avenue. Ken's house. Her house. She'd been living two lives for the past few years and it was beginning to get to her.

"Morning." Beth looked up from her cereal. "Coffee? I've just percolated."

"Thanks, Beth. Have you any aspirin?"

The girl pointed to the press above the sink. "Should be some Panadol there, I think."

Michelle swallowed two with a drink of water. "I didn't get much sleep last night." She joined Beth at the kitchen table.

"Is Dad at work this morning?" Beth poured more Crunchy Nut Cornflakes into her bowl. "That's a bummer, isn't it? Having to work on Saturday."

Michelle took a long sip of coffee. Her head throbbed. "Beth, we never got to finish our conversation last night. With all the commotion and – "

"What a gas!" Beth laughed. "Talk about excitement. Deadly. Gives me loads to tell Carmel and the gang tonight."

"Didn't it frighten you?" Michelle had to admire the resilience of the young. "Having someone lurking in your garden?"

"Naw! Actually . . . do you know what I think?"

"What?"

Beth pushed away the cereal bowl and lit a cigarette. "Do you mind if I smoke here? When Dad's out, I always do."

"Go ahead. Your dad knows that you smoke, Beth."

"Well anyway, do you know what I thought last night?" She blew out the match and looked conspiratorially at Michelle. "I thought it might be Mark."

"Mark!"

Beth exhaled loudly. "Yeah, remember I told you I'd been avoiding him? Well, maybe not avoiding him, but you know what I mean. Anyhow when I looked out my bedroom window last night I was convinced it was Mark who was running away. The guy had a kind of navy or black track suit on. Mark bought one in Lifestyle recently."

Michelle stared at her. "Why would Mark do something like this?"

Beth shrugged and pulled on the cigarette again. "For a gag, a mess. To get my attention. Who knows?"

"Do you think so? Surely not," Michelle exclaimed. "It doesn't seem the sort of thing Mark would do, Beth."

"Go away. Please."

Michelle tapped lightly on the door again.

No response.

"All right, Beth. This mightn't be a good time for you." Michelle turned to walk down the stairs.

The bedroom door opened. Slowly.

Ken heard the crackle of branches in the back garden. That blasted mongrel from next door! He'd managed to dig up the rhubarb the last time he'd got in. Ken would have to repair the fencing again. He pulled open the kitchen door, grabbed the sweeping-brush from beside the fridge, yelled at the top of his voice and ran out.

"Aagh!" he screamed as he bounded down the back steps. "Get out of there! Go piss in your own place!"

Beth sat at her dressing-table and puffed on a cigarette.

"You're right, it's Mark," she admitted.

"You've had a row?" Michelle sat down on the bed.

"Not exactly." Beth didn't turn around, she answered to the mirror which was slightly disconcerting for Michelle. "We're cooling it for a while. My idea."

"I see."

Beth tapped the ash from her cigarette into an empty cold-cream jar.

"I mean, Mark's lovely and . . . " Her voice shook.

"Yes, he is, Beth. I – "

"Michelle." She half-smiled. "I know what you're going to say – you're very fond of him."

223

"I am," Michelle agreed.

"He likes you, too." She stubbed out the cigarette.

"Does he?"

"Yeah." Beth stared into the middle distance. "He thinks you've had a hard time of it with . . . my mother and . . . me. He thinks you're being pushed aside . . . "

Michelle said nothing.

"He thinks he is, too." Beth frowned. "I didn't mean to push Mark away but things have gone funny for me . . . I'm not sure how I feel any more. When I was in London, something happened. I . . . I – "

Michelle looked at her. "You met someone else?"

Beth blushed. "I didn't mean anything to happen but . . . well, it happened. There's nothing I can do about it now."

"And you like this boy?" Michelle prompted.

Beth shook her head. "No, nothing like that. Not the way I like Mark but I let him . . . " She shrugged. "It doesn't matter. I don't want to talk about it."

A crash came from downstairs.

Michelle jumped up from the bed. "What was that?"

Beth laughed. "Just Dad doing his nightly freak-out. Wait. You'll hear the shouts now in a minute and a wallop if he makes contact!"

"Makes contact?"

"With the arse of next-door's dog!"

Scurried movements at the back of the garden.

"I'm coming, you smelly flea-bag! I'm going to fix you once and for all!"

He didn't care if the Sweetmans heard him or not. He was sick of this pest coming in every night and digging up his garden. It wasn't right. Dogs should be kept locked up.

A rustle of leaves and a laugh.

Not a bark, not a growl, not a yelp.

A *laugh*!

There was a man in the garden.

He was crouching down, in between the gooseberry bushes.

Ken felt a rush of adrenaline. "Right, you bastard!" He brandished the sweeping-brush high over his head and ran like the clappers down the long garden path. "I'll give you something to laugh at, you slimy scum-bucket!"

The man laughed again and raised two fingers.

Then he disappeared.

Ken wheezed and puffed down to the fence. There was a wide gaping hole where four or five of the wooden slats had been ripped off.

"Ken, Ken. Are you all right?" Michelle switched on the outside light and ran into the garden.

"A prowler, Mich!"

He walked up the path and put his arm around her. "I couldn't catch him. He was away into the other gardens like a scalded cat. He dropped this."

Ken handed Michelle something damp and soft. She couldn't make it out clearly in the semi-darkness of the garden.

When they came into the kitchen she saw all too clearly what the intruder had left behind him.

A pair of *red lace knickers*.

Hurt.

No, it was too late now to say anything to Ken.

Her eyelids grew heavy and she fell into a light sleep.

* * *

Ken's side of the bed was empty when Michelle awoke after ten the next morning. The lemony scent of his shampoo still clung to the pillow. She heard Beth down in the kitchen, singing.

Michelle had a quick shower in the *en suite*, but it didn't get rid of her groggy headache. She went to the wardrobe where she kept half her clothes. She'd go for jog this morning. She needed fresh air. Where was her track suit? Must be in Collins Avenue. Ken's house. Her house. She'd been living two lives for the past few years and it was beginning to get to her.

"Morning." Beth looked up from her cereal. "Coffee? I've just percolated."

"Thanks, Beth. Have you any aspirin?"

The girl pointed to the press above the sink. "Should be some Panadol there, I think."

Michelle swallowed two with a drink of water. "I didn't get much sleep last night." She joined Beth at the kitchen table.

"Is Dad at work this morning?" Beth poured more Crunchy Nut Cornflakes into her bowl. "That's a bummer, isn't it? Having to work on Saturday."

Michelle took a long sip of coffee. Her head throbbed. "Beth, we never got to finish our conversation last night. With all the commotion and – "

"What a gas!" Beth laughed. "Talk about excitement. Deadly. Gives me loads to tell Carmel and the gang tonight."

"Didn't it frighten you?" Michelle had to admire the resilience of the young. "Having someone lurking in your garden?"

"Naw! Actually . . . do you know what I think?"

"What?"

Beth pushed away the cereal bowl and lit a cigarette. "Do you mind if I smoke here? When Dad's out, I always do."

"Go ahead. Your dad knows that you smoke, Beth."

"Well anyway, do you know what I thought last night?" She blew out the match and looked conspiratorially at Michelle. "I thought it might be Mark."

"Mark!"

Beth exhaled loudly. "Yeah, remember I told you I'd been avoiding him? Well, maybe not avoiding him, but you know what I mean. Anyhow when I looked out my bedroom window last night I was convinced it was Mark who was running away. The guy had a kind of navy or black track suit on. Mark bought one in Lifestyle recently."

Michelle stared at her. "Why would Mark do something like this?"

Beth shrugged and pulled on the cigarette again. "For a gag, a mess. To get my attention. Who knows?"

"Do you think so? Surely not," Michelle exclaimed. "It doesn't seem the sort of thing Mark would do, Beth."

"Oh, and you'd know, would you?" Her tone became prickly, hostile.

Michelle held her tongue.

"I'd say he did it for a joke," Beth said casually, "but he wasn't expecting Dad to attack like that, so he ran away . . . Jesus, if he heard the squad car he probably had a heart attack."

Beth laughed and poured herself another coffee.

"Phone him now." Michelle stood up. "Come on, Beth. Phone him."

The girl shook her head. "No way. He's looking for attention like a spoilt little boy. He can piss off!"

Looking for attention.

"I'll ring him, then," Michelle offered.

Beth's expression of amusement changed to one of rage. "Keep out of it, can't you?"

"Sorry?"

"It's got nothing to do with you." Beth mashed the cigarette-butt into the half-eaten cereal. "Not that *that* ever stopped you before!"

"Beth, I – "

"No, no, I'm not listening to you. Mind your own business. You're always meddling in my life. I'm sick to bloody hell of it."

Michelle sat there, open-mouthed.

"I'm really cheesed off having to put up with you, if you must know," Beth ranted on. "You're here every weekend poking your nose in. This is *my* home. Not yours. Why don't you go back to Collins Avenue where you belong?"

"Beth – "

"Ah, fuck off! Dad never stops talking about you –
Michelle this, Michelle that, Michelle said this, Michelle
thinks that . . . that's OK, you're his girlfriend but . . .
when Mark starts it . . . that's something else – "

"Beth, please stop – "

"No, I shagging-well won't stop! Why should I? I've
had enough of you, Michelle Bolger. Mark's always on
about you, how nice you are, how good you are, how
talented, how sincere . . . how bloody wonderful. I'm fed
up with it."

She stood up, her hands on her hips, roaring at the
top of her voice. "Then he goes off and helps you to
paint your house. 'Michelle has such good taste', he says.
'Michelle's so artistic.' And the latest? He thinks you're
'passionate'! What do you think of that, Miss High-and-
Mighty Bolger? My boyfriend thinks you're *passionate*.
Sick, isn't it? He has a *thing* about you. Likes to help you.
Huh! Maybe he'd like to *help* you to a lot more, Michelle.
Yeah, maybe he'd like to . . . "

Beth burst into tears and fled from the kitchen.
Michelle sat there, shaking.

Mark . . . the prowler? A dark track suit. Medium height.
Average build. He'd dropped something. A calling card.

Her red knickers.

No, no, no. What possible motive could he have?
There was no sense to this. She was at it again, jumping
to conclusions, giving in to all sorts of wild and crazy
imaginings.

I'll bring in your clothes from the line, Michelle.

A wave of nausea rolled over her.

Twenty-Two

Beth lay on her bed, eating a Mars bar and listening to her Jean Michel Jarre cassette. The front door banged. She turned down the volume on her Walkman and went to the window which overlooked the busy tree-lined Griffith Avenue.

She watched Michelle close the gate behind her and head off in the direction of the bus-stop.

Beth was sorry she'd lost her temper – when her father found out about it, he'd go ballistic – but she wasn't sorry to see Michelle leave. She'd the house to herself now, the way she liked it. She'd have a bath and laze about for the morning and this afternoon she might drop into town for a look around the shops and a coffee in the Bad Ass Café. Maybe Carmel would meet her?

She stared at the phone on her bedside table. Should she ring Mark? Apologise? Ask him to come over? No, if he wanted to see her, he knew where to find her. Beth fixed a second pillow under her head and closed her eyes. It was nice lying here, relaxing.

The phone rang. Beth unplugged her earphones and stretched over to answer it.

"Hello, Beth?"

"Mum!"

"How are you, darling?"

"Don't ask!"

"I *am* asking."

"Nothing changes here." Beth groaned. "I'm in the wars again!"

"Your father?"

"No."

"Mark?"

"He's not my number one fan at the moment, but no, it's not Mark. I've really blown it this time, Mum."

"It can't be that bad. Is it school? Miss Rent-a-moan again?"

Beth half laughed, then she sighed. "It's not funny, Mum. It's eh . . . Michelle."

"Oh, dear." Toni tutted. "Did you two have a row? Poor darling!"

"She stayed here last night and tried her nicey-nicey act with me. I can't stand it when she does that. Does she think she's my surrogate mother or something? It gets on my wick. Tried to cheer me up because Dad obviously told her I was in bad form – "

"And are you, sweetheart?"

" . . . no, I don't think so."

"Good."

"Anyhow, this morning at breakfast she started on at me again and I told her . . . I can't believe I did this, Mum, I told her to fuck off!"

A loud laugh down the line.

"I'm glad you think this is funny, Mum, but Dad will gut me when he finds out."

"How would he find out? Michelle's hardly going to tell him, is she? Don't waste your time worrying about it, it's not important, Beth. What's done is done."

"And cannot be undone."

"You *do* sound a bit down. You'll have to meet me for lunch."

"Meet you for . . . where *are* you, Mum?"

"I'm in Dublin. I landed this morning."

Her mother made it sound as if she'd swooped in.

"Aubrey Malone, you remember him, darling? I introduced you to him at that dinner party in the Frawley's – "

"Black moustache, glasses and bad breath?"

"The very one. To cut a long story short, he's gone off to Brussels for six months and he's offered me his apartment to rent. I'm in it as we speak and I'm quite impressed. Come on in here and I'll show it to you."

"Does Dad know you're back?"

"No, it's a surprise. I thought I'd get myself settled and then spring it on him."

"Cool! Where *is* this apartment?"

"Custom House Harbour. Wait till you see it, Beth.

Right in the heart of Dublin's financial centre. Very posh!"

"On the quays?"

"Yes, just five minutes from the city centre." Her mother's voice rose in excitement. "Hurry in."

"I'm not sure how to find it. Is it near The Point?"

"Not as far down. It's just beside Connolly Station. Tell you what, I'll meet you on the steps of the Custom House at – let me see now, one-thirty – OK?"

"Right." Beth giggled. "This is hilarious, Mum."

"Isn't it? Now, remember, Beth. Not a word to your father."

* * *

The Harbourmaster Bar was atmospheric in that wood-and-glass, simple-but-classy sort of way. Upstairs, they served soup and sandwiches while downstairs the well-heeled clients tucked in to more substantial meals. Beth followed her mother upstairs.

"What's the soup today?" Toni inquired of the young, friendly barman.

"Leek and potato, madam."

"Lovely." Her mother turned to her. "Beth? Soup?"

"No, thanks."

Toni read the menu from a blackboard. "I'll have the soup, a Cajun chicken sandwich, and a glass of white wine, please."

"One Cajun chicken coming up. White, brown or rye?"

"Brown, I think."

"I'll have that, too." Beth said and went to sit at a window table.

Toni brought the food on a tray.

Beth examined the view. "Fisherman's Wharf – straight out of a Steinbeck novel or something. Wright's Sea Food Bistro. What's that beside it? A laundry? Looks *very* up-market for a laundry."

"Does it?"

Toni sat opposite her daughter and passed over a plate, a knife and a paper napkin.

"You didn't like the apartment, then?"

"Wouldn't be my scene. It's so . . . perfect." She cut her sandwich in two. "It's too . . . sterile for you, Mum. Cold."

Toni was amused by her daughter's description.

"More like a show-house than a real home," Beth went on. "How could you possibly relax in it?"

"But the location's fabulous, Beth, and it's so self-contained. I like it – it's different, not like being in the city at all. Another world."

"Overlooking that fake lake with the gushing fountain? All those art-deco office-blocks around it? Sick! Look out the window, for God's sake, Mum. La Touche House, IFSC House, AIB International, Anderson House. Jesus, it'd be weird going to bed every night in the middle of all these fecking banks."

"Ssh, Beth."

Toni glanced surreptitiously at the smartly-suited

business-woman sitting at the next table with her immaculately-dressed colleague.

"Another world is right." Beth sipped her wine and made a face. "The whole complex is so . . . false. It's phoney, Mum, like stepping into an alien existence. And then when you come out you're in bloody Amiens Street!"

"I'm disappointed, Beth. I thought you'd love it."

"Well," Beth said, plucking out a leaf of lettuce from her door-stop sandwich, "if it suits you, so be it. You're the one who's going to be living there."

"I haven't made up my mind yet. There are plenty of other places." Toni looked downcast. "I'd prefer somewhere you liked as well."

"I thought you were supposed to get a place on the other side of the quays, nearer to O'Connell Bridge."

"I was." Toni hesitated. "The deal fell through. My loan was . . . delayed."

"Oh."

Was her mother having money problems?

"George refused to sell the London apartment and of course that meant that I – never mind, I'm not going to bore you with the details. Let's just say that for the moment I'll be renting."

"George is acting up, then? It's to be expected, I suppose. You weren't very nice to him, Mum. Dumping him like that."

"How can you say that, you monkey! You always *hated* George!"

"Now that you've ditched him, I feel kind of sorry for him. It's a typical Irish thing – "

"What is?"

"Championing the underdog!"

Toni beamed at her daughter. "You've cheered me up, do you know that?"

"How did I manage that? I've been moaning all morning."

"But a lot of what you said is right. Maybe that apartment wasn't right for me after all. I'd have been living practically on top of the river."

"Mmh," Beth agreed. "Great if you were a smuggler or a drug baron. Moor your yacht and then off up the Liffey in the dead of night. A clean getaway and nobody the wiser!"

"You always had a great imagination, Beth. You know, when I was your age, the docks were dangerous – not a place where respectable people would be seen but . . . my goodness, if your grandfather came back now, he wouldn't know the city."

"This place doesn't feel like the docks to me, Mum, it doesn't even feel like Dublin. More like some strange satellite land in a different orbit!"

"I thought you'd like it here," Toni said impatiently. "It's so central."

"For what?"

"For me when I set up my business and for you at weekends – a stone's throw from all the shops and you could have met your friends on Saturday nights. Temple

241

Bar is only across the Liffey . . . hey, that's not a bad idea. There are nice apartments in Temple Bar, aren't there?"

"Mum, I don't want to *live* in Temple Bar, much as I like it," Beth protested. "My friends would think that was seriously sad."

Toni arched an eyebrow. "What's got into you, love? There's no pleasing you today."

Beth pouted.

"Well? Out with it!"

"Mum, I don't want to talk about it, OK?"

"All right, darling."

Beth flicked her hair behind her ears.

Toni had a good look around. "What do you think of the colour scheme in here? Is that deep purple on the walls? No, it's more of a plum colour. I like it, it catches the light, doesn't it? Complements the wood."

Beth couldn't have given a monkey's about the colour scheme.

She *had* wanted to talk.

"Mum?"

"Yes, darling?" Toni took out a diary and started to write. "I'll borrow Gwen's car tomorrow and take a trip out to Howth. There are some new apartments on the coast road, I believe. Will you come with me?"

"Howth? Mmh, that'd be much nicer. Near the sea."

Toni turned a page. "Oh, I mustn't forget this." She underlined something. "I've an appointment on Monday with an old friend of mine. Well, she's more of an acquaintance than a friend – an interior decorator. I'm going to get her to do my curtains, maybe a few wall-hangings as well."

"Really?" Beth said indifferently.

She'd wanted her mother to give her advice, but Beth was beginning to realise that Toni wasn't the best listener in the world.

"She designs for the Dublin 4 set," Toni went on. "You choose the material and then she makes up the curtains to your specification. Would you like to come shopping with me this afternoon, Beth?"

She didn't wait for Beth to answer.

"We could call into Arnotts to see Gwen. She'd probably get me a discount on the material. May as well use her, she's my sister, after all."

Beth helped herself to one of her mother's cigarettes.

"What's the point in buying material if you haven't even decided on *where* you're going to live, Mum?"

"I'd like to have a look and see what's available. Get some ideas, colours, fabrics, you know."

Beth yawned. "I think I'll give it a skip."

"You'll have to pick out some bedclothes and curtains for the bedroom you'll be in, anyway."

A bedroom in an apartment which existed only in her mother's head?

"I'm not in the mood for shopping, Mum."

""Course you are, darling," Toni said absent-mindedly. "And afterwards we could meet your father. What time is he finishing work today?"

"Haven't a clue. He's seeing Michelle later. They usually go out on a Saturday night."

Toni took her mobile phone from her handbag. "I'll ring him."

"He doesn't like to be disturbed at work, Mum."

"Beth, don't be so silly. Take that frown off your face. You remind me of Gwen when you scowl like that. All right, I won't phone your father now. I've a better idea." She smiled to herself.

Beth had seen that look before. Her mother was plotting again.

"Would you like another glass of wine, darling?"

"No, thanks."

"Well, let's go then. Arnotts, here we come."

"Great!"

"What's up with you, Beth? Couldn't you *pretend* to be a bit excited about my being home?"

"Sorry, I *am* glad. It's great to have you back. To be truthful, I can't take it in. I keep thinking you're going to disap – "

"Oh, Beth, don't lay a guilt-trip on me. I'm home and I'm here to stay. You'll see."

Beth kissed her on the cheek. "In that case, Mum, I'm very happy."

"That's better." Her mother smiled. "And the shopping? You don't mind? I really *would* like your advice about fabrics and cushions and things. When I get the apartment I want you to think of it as your home as well . . . your second home."

"OK. It might be fun doing up a new bedroom. My weekend pad."

"Exactly." Toni got excited. "That's exactly the way I want you to look on it, Beth. Your weekend pad. I'll get a key cut for you and you can come and go as you please."

"Are you serious?"

Toni was gratified by her daughter's belated surge of interest. "Oh yes, I'm deadly serious. We'll be like flatmates."

"Flatmates!"

"You can come every Friday night and stay till Sunday." Toni paused. "You'd be more than welcome to stay with me all the time, but your father wouldn't approve."

"Well, I'm probably better off staying in Griffith Avenue, Mum. Nearer to school and I've more room for study and – "

"Room? More room? Do you imagine I'm going to get a pokey little place?"

Beth was conscious of her *faux pas*. "No, not at all. But the house in Griffith Avenue is big, you have to admit."

"We'll have some good times from now on, Beth. I can feel it in my water, as your gran used to say. And you won't be sorry to get out of the house every weekend, will you? It can't be easy for you having Michelle there all the time."

"No, it's not." Beth finished the glass of wine and

wiped her lips. "I'm being selfish, I know. Dad has his own life to lead. It's just . . . there's no privacy when Michelle's around. She probably finds it hard as well – "

"How *she* finds it is of no interest to me, Beth, but I do think you need your weekends to yourself. Your dad's been great but it's time he let go a little. When you stay with me I won't be coming the heavy with you."

"That'll be a relief!"

"No, there won't be a curfew or anything like that. I trust you, you're a big girl now and you have to learn to look out for yourself. I'm glad we sorted out the contraception thing. How are you finding the pill? Any side-effects?"

"No, Mum. I wanted to talk to you about . . . that night in London."

"The Frawley boy?"

" . . . yes. And the morning-after pill."

"Don't dwell on it too much, love. These things happen and at least you're not pregnant. It was a silly mistake. Put it down to experience and move on."

Beth blushed. "I feel so guilty about it."

"Guilty? Why?"

"It wasn't right, what happened. I did it . . . out of curiosity, I guess. But I don't feel right about it, Mum. And there's Mark. I can't look him in the face any more."

"Forget it, Beth. There's nothing more time-consuming and wasteful than guilt."

"But – "

"You think you made a mistake, OK? Fine, learn from it."

"I wish it hadn't happened. I'd give anything to be able to turn the clock back."

"Wouldn't we all?" Toni said with a groan. "You're an adult now, Beth, and I intend to treat you as one. But," she went on sagely as she zipped up her enormous handbag, "freedom brings with it a certain amount of responsibility."

Beth nodded.

"You'll have to be accountable for your own decisions, your own actions."

Responsibility. Was Beth expected to look to her mother as a role model?

Twenty-Three

"I'm glad you've installed the alarm system, Mrs Bolger."
Dave Lacey said approvingly.

The detective spooned more sugar into his tea. His
large bulk filled her kitchen, dwarfing the chair he sat on,
making the table seem miniature. He was a big man, big
in every sense of the word.

Generous.

"It'll help you sleep soundly in your bed at night."

"It's not *me* who's losing sleep, Detective Lacey, it's
my daughter Michelle. She's been awfully upset since the
night of the burglary. It's not like her to be nervous. She
used to be the one who calmed me down but . . . "

"Funny, isn't it?" He smiled warmly at her. "Parents
spend their lives worrying about their offspring and then,
before they know it, it's middle age and role reversal –
the kids try to take over the parenting role."

"Have you any children, Detective Lacey?"

"No, Mrs Bolger, I'm not married."

"Nowadays," she mused aloud, "that's no guarantee."

"Lovely fruitcake," Dave Lacey said pleasantly. "Just like my mother used to make, God rest her. Poor Dad misses her fruitcake." He paused. "Of course he misses her as well."

Olive Bolger was charmed by this big handsome man who was so polite and well-spoken. "It was very kind of you to call to see me, Inspector."

"Well, I wanted to let you know that we got those two young hooligans. Put your mind at rest."

"Fast work, wasn't it?" Olive was full of admiration. "They can say what they like but I, for one, think the gardaí do an absolutely marvellous job. First class."

"Thanks for the vote of confidence," Dave Lacey replied. "Of course we can't do our jobs properly without the help of the general public, who, for the most part I'm glad to say, are extremely co-operative."

"Proper order. We all have a role to play in the fight against crime."

"Indeed," he agreed.

"A woman down the road had garden furniture stolen during the summer. She didn't bother to report it, she told me, didn't think it was worth her while. I was scandalised. How can people expect the guards to act if they don't inform them about what's going on in the area? I thought her attitude was dreadful and I didn't pull any punches with her, believe you me. That's how these young blackguards get away with it – people not reporting them."

"It's a problem all right, but I think things are improving. You'd be amazed at the number of people who *do* get involved. The Neighbourhood Watch scheme is a case in point."

"That was a great idea, whoever set it up. I must find out who's in charge in this area, maybe volunteer my services. Sure I could help with the distribution of the literature at least. Lick a few stamps."

"Bernie Fitzgerald. He's the man to get in touch with. He'd be delighted to have a new recruit."

"Do you know, Inspector, *Crimeline* is one of my favourite programmes on the telly?"

"You don't say."

"Yes, I find it totally absorbing, wouldn't dream of answering the phone or making a cup of tea when it's on. All those photo-fits and re-enactments of the crime scene, then the videos of the actual robberies, fascinating, aren't they? Like watching *Hill Street Blues* – only for real."

Dave Lacey cleared his throat. "I'm not sure if it's intended as entertainment, Mrs Bolger."

Olive had the good grace to look contrite. "So, you've got the two brave buckos?"

"Hardly *brave*, Mrs Bolger."

"Just an expression, Detective Lacey, I didn't mean it literally. Prison's the only answer, I'm sorry to say. Of course the way the courts operate, they could be out in a day or two, roaming the streets and getting into all sorts of mischief again. Disgraceful."

"The police have no control over the legal system, Mrs Bolger. We've charged them, at least."

"Thank God," Olive said gravely.

"We've been after them for the past two years but, if you want to make it stick, you have to catch them *in flagrante delicto* – which, I'm happy to say, we did!"

"Go on!"

Dave Lacey lowered his voice in a conspiratorial way. "Setting fire to a warehouse near the markets, they were."

"Despicable!"

Olive poured the nice detective another cup of tea and this time cut him a bigger slice of cake. "And you're sure they're the ones who robbed me?"

"We found most of your stuff back at their squat – the Waterford glass decanter and the silver photo-frame. No sign of your daughter's medals, though."

"It's very odd about that photograph. I didn't even miss it, you know. But when I think about it, it was on the dressing-table in Michelle's old room. Funny I didn't miss it."

"And you say there *was* a photo in it?"

"Yes, a beautiful picture of Michelle playing the piano at one of her school concerts. It was a lovely photo." Olive Bolger's face lit up. "She couldn't have been more than fourteen years old at the time it was taken. She was wearing a simple blue dress that evening and there was a vase of magnificent red roses on top of the piano – leave it to the nuns for that extra little touch, I always say. She looked so . . . serene, sitting at the piano. That's the only word to describe her: serene."

An indulgent nod from the detective.

"I'll never see it again. Pity. Imagine those two young louts stealing Michelle's photo? What would they want with it?"

"It was the frame they were interested in," he explained. "Silver. Worth a few bob."

"I don't even have a negative." Olive sighed. "Photographs. They tell a story, don't they? Capture a moment in time. I was never great with a camera, I left all that to my husband."

She went into the sitting-room and came back with a small cameo-like wooden ornament with a tiny snapshot inside. She handed it to the detective.

"That's my Joe. He went especially and sat for that in a photographer's studio in Berkeley Road. I've always cherished it."

Dave Lacey studied it politely. The man in the photo was in his late forties, he guessed. Blonde wavy hair and big, dark eyes.

"Very handsome," the detective said.

"Isn't he? Michelle takes after him in looks. My son Declan resembles my side of the family. Joe was a real gentleman." She sighed. "A gentle man, yes."

"He looks it – gentle, I mean."

"He was. Never raised his voice in anger, not once in all the years we were together. He was placid, you see, easy-going. Not like me," she added.

"Ah now, Mrs Bolger – "

"No, no, I'm a terrible fuss-pot – at least I was. Always saw the bad side to every situation, always worried about things that would never happen. I must have driven my children mad."

"I'm sure you're exag – "

"But I've changed, do you know that? Changed since the robbery. I've switched myself off." She folded her arms, proud of herself. "That's what I've done, switched myself off."

The detective stroked his chin. "Have you now?"

"Indeed I have. 'Olive,' I said to myself, 'this has got to stop. All this worrying and fussing and fretting over things you can do nothing about.' That's exactly what I said to myself – in this very kitchen the morning after the robbery, and since then, Detective Lacey, my life has changed."

"Is that a fact?"

"It is, changed beyond belief. You see, it's all about how you *look* at things, isn't it? It's taken me sixty-three years on the planet to figure that out." She smiled shyly at him. "I must be a bit slow."

"Mrs Bolger, some people *never* figure it out."

"Perhaps you're right. The two . . . the two lads who robbed me, what age were they about?"

"One was eighteen, the brother was only sixteen."

"Two brothers?" She gasped. "Isn't it woeful? Their poor mother."

"Their mother?" he scoffed. "Therein lies the tale."

Olive was all ears.

"In jail for the last six months."

"Mountjoy?"

"The Joy, yes. Robbery and aggravated assault." He sighed loudly. "She's a heroin addict."

Olive shook her head sadly. "Have they no father?"

"The husband – that's what he calls himself at any rate – he's supposed to look after the two lads but sure he spends most of his waking hours in the boozer."

Olive had a change of heart. "It's in *care* those two boys should be, not in prison at all."

"They've been in and out of care all their lives, Mrs Bolger. And this won't be the first time the older one will appear before a judge. Not by a long shot."

"A vicious circle, isn't it? When they have kids of their own, it'll be the same story, history repeating itself."

"They live in a dog-eat-dog world, Mrs Bolger. They have a different sense of values from us."

"Us and them. The haves and the have-nots. It would make you think."

The detective stood up to go. "Of course they denied the robbery flat out, swore blind they found the stuff dumped in the laneway down the street. Compulsive liars. They'd sell their granny to the glue factory for a fix."

"Desperate," she said, shaking her head. "The drugs. Terrible business."

"Some of the stories I come across are gruesome, all right. It's the young kids I feel sorry for."

Olive opened the hall door for him. "They've no chance in life at all, do they?"

He shook her hand and walked down the path. When he got to the gate, he turned back.

"Some of them don't. No," he agreed.

Twenty-Four

Michelle had a headache – from tension, she guessed. After a warm bath she felt a bit better. She came down to the kitchen to make soup for her lunch, took a tin of Campbell's Cream of Tomato from the press but then changed her mind. She wasn't hungry. This morning's row with Beth had upset her more than she'd realised at the time.

Would she tell Ken? Maybe Beth had told him herself? She could imagine the spin the girl would put on it.

Michelle didn't know where she'd gone wrong. She'd tried very hard to get on with Ken's daughter, but Beth was becoming impossible. Hopping hormones or not, there was no justification for her insinuations. She'd practically accused Michelle of trying to seduce Mark.

OK, she was jealous, that much was obvious. Jealous of the time her father spent with her and now, it appeared, she was jealous of her friendship with Mark. Things had never been easy between Beth and herself but there was no doubt about it – the situation had deteriorated rapidly since Toni had taken up with her daughter again.

Luckily Toni was in London . . . but for how much longer?

Michelle decided to take *one* bull by the horns. She took the phone into the sitting-room.

"Mark?"

"Michelle? Hi. How's it going?"

"Could be better."

"Same here. I've just spent three hours pouring over the Constitution and I'm going bananas."

"Fancy an hour or two away from the books? I'd like to have a chat."

"Fair enough, will I call over?"

"No, not here. I'll meet you in town for a coffee."

"I want to leave some books back to the Ilac Library but I'll see you after that, OK?"

"I've a wedding at three in Corpus Christi. I could be in town by five-thirty. Is that too late for you?"

"No, but forget the coffee, at that stage I'll be in the mood for a pint. There's nowhere decent around O'Connell Street . . . what about Sinnotts?"

" . . . it gets very packed, Mark. I'd prefer somewhere quieter."

"Nearys?"

"Nearys is perfect. The snug? See you at half-five."

"Fine. Michelle . . . have you seen Beth?"

"Mmh, last night and again this morning."

"She's giving me the cold shoulder at the moment. I

don't know what I'm supposed to have done but she's angry with me."

"Mark, Beth's the reason I'm ringing you. There's something she said this morning . . . something I need to discuss with you."

"Sounds ominous." He laughed nervously. "I'm not in *your* bad books as well, am I?"

"See you later."

She hung up, leaving Mark very puzzled by her tone.

* * *

Mark kissed her on the cheek and took a seat beside her at the bar.

"You look very nice," he said. "New top? Green suits you."

"Thanks."

"I thought you wanted to sit in the snug, Michelle?"

"There are two couples in there, I didn't want to intrude . . . and I wanted to be able to talk to you without being overheard."

"Curiouser and curiouser! Sorry I'm a bit late."

"Traffic?"

"No, it wasn't too bad."

"Parking? You should have tried Drury Street, that's where Ken usually parks."

"I got a place on the Green, across the road from the Shelbourne. That wasn't what delayed me. You'll hardly credit this but I'd another flat tyre."

"*Another* one? That's the second in a week, isn't it?"

"They say they come in threes. I swear the da thinks I'm driving over tacks or broken glass on purpose!"

"Where did it happen?"

"After the library, I drove over to Griffith Avenue to see Beth. I know, I know, I shouldn't have gone running after her but I wanted to clear the air. I parked in front of the house on the footpath, where I always park, and when I came out the back tyre on the left was down. Last time, when I left your house, it was the one on the right. I'm beginning to think that car's jinxed."

Jinxed or . . . *interfered* with? Michelle didn't like the sound of this.

"What'll you have, Mark? Smithwicks?" She signalled to the barman and he came over to take her order.

"This place is jammed, isn't it? At this hour on a Saturday – I didn't realise people came out so early for a drink."

"The shoppers, I suppose, in for a quick one before they go home," Michelle said. "Town is buzzing!"

"Yeah," Mark agreed. "All those weekend trippers over from the UK. Dublin's hot at the moment."

"So, you spoke to Beth? How did it go?" Michelle wished she didn't care. The girl's morning's tantrum was still playing on her mind.

"There was nobody in. First I thought she just wasn't answering but when I went around to the back garden – "

Michelle stared at him. "How did you get into the back?"

"Through the garage door, it's an up-and-over job. Ken – you don't mind me calling him that, do you? He never locks it. I often go in that way. Sometimes Beth leaves the back-door key under the geranium pot and – "

"You *often* go in through the back garden?" Michelle was flabbergasted.

"Oh, Christ, don't tell Mr Leavy, will you? I've only done it once or twice. I creep in the back way at night, through the kitchen and upstairs into Beth's bedroom. It's a kind of game and she thinks it's exciting. Then I sneak out early the next morning – "

"I can't believe what you're telling me, Mark – "

"Oh, please, Michelle. Don't look at me like that. We don't *do* anything." His face went bright red. "She's only a kid. I wouldn't do anything to harm Beth or take advantage or anything – "

"No, no, no. You don't understand. Did you come in that way last night?"

"Last night? Eh . . . no, I was at home, studying. And I told you, Beth's not speaking to me at the moment. I don't think she'd have welcomed one of my surprise visits."

"Come off it, Mark. Tell me the truth. It was you, wasn't it?"

"What was me?"

"The midnight prowler. It was you, Beth said it might be."

"Michelle. I was nowhere near Griffith Avenue last night, I swear . . . *what* prowler?"

259

"You really don't know?" She scrutinised his expression and saw only confusion, faint alarm.

He shook his head. "I haven't a notion what you're talking about. Someone broke in to Beth's garden last night, is that what you're telling me? And you thought it might be *me*?"

"No need to adopt a huffy tone, Mark. Not when you've just informed me that nocturnal visits to Beth are a regular occurrence."

She was getting very bitchy, he thought. "Another drink?" he asked coldly.

"No."

She stared at the rows of bottles on the mirrored glass shelves.

"Sure you don't want one?"

"No, I said. Thank you."

Mark lit a cigarette. If she wanted to sulk like a petulant child, so be it. He looked down the bar and spotted a guy from his history class. He might go and join him.

Michelle swirled the nearly-melted cubes around her glass.

"Trying to break the ice?" he joked.

No response.

"Michelle?"

"What?"

"This is getting us nowhere. What's the use in us falling out? We used to be allies." He looked at her sheepishly. "Remember?"

"You're right, I'm sorry." She patted his arm. "I'll have another G and T. But let *me* get them."

"No, you got them last time. Fair is fair."

She smiled at him. "You're very stubborn."

"So are you." He nudged her playfully. "Truce?"

"Truce."

"Good," he said with a grin, "I hate fights."

"Me too. They're a waste of energy. I'm sorry I had a go at you. I'm in a bad mood, Mark."

"I can see that. What is it?"

"Something terribly weird happened last night and I was afraid that you . . . "

"That I what?"

"That you were responsible." She lowered her voice. "This . . . prowler, he was . . . after something – "

"They usually are."

"I know . . . but this was different, Mark. He left . . . he dropped something. I think he did it deliberately like a . . . I'm not sure, some kind of a warning or . . . "

Mark leaned closer to hear better. "Dropped what?"

"Underwear."

"Underwear? What do you mean? His vest, his underpants, what?"

" . . . Women's underwear. A pair of . . . knickers, to be precise."

"Knickers!"

"Ssh, ssh." Michelle cringed.

"Sorry." Mark put his hand over his mouth to stop himself from laughing out loud.

"You think this is *funny*?" she demanded.

"Michelle, if I didn't laugh at this, I'd be furious. Would you think about it, please? This guy was skulking in Beth's garden last night and he dropped a pair of knickers and you thought it was me! Charming, I'm sure. I can't *believe* you thought it was me. Christ on a bike, what do take me for?"

"It wasn't like that," she explained hurriedly. "It never occurred to me that it could be you until Beth said . . . she thought it was you messing. She – "

"*Beth* thought it was me?"

He gulped at his drink, then he sat back on his stool and folded his arms, an incredulous expression on his face.

"She actually said that, did she? This is getting better by the minute."

"Mark, listen – "

"No, Michelle, you listen. My girlfriend thinks I'm some kind of a *perv* who goes around dropping ladies' knickers all over the gardens of the northside of Dublin. What does she think I *do* with the underwear? Wear it in secret? Ha! Tonight, under his Levis, Mark is wearing a frilly black pair and a matching halter-neck bra. To complete the outfit a black boa and over-the-knee leather boots!"

"Ssh, Mark," Michelle whispered, "calm down."

"Calm down? Calm down? *How* can I bloody well calm down after what you've just said? I thought you knew me better than that. As for Beth – "

"Beth didn't know anything about the underwear. She stayed upstairs during the whole thing. It was this morning at breakfast that – "

"She said this creep might be me, so why didn't you – "

"After the police came – "

"The *police*? Holy shit, it was a right old circus, wasn't it? I'm sorry I missed it. I'd have charged admission. Ken phoned the police?"

"Yes, Mark, he had to. It was a break-in."

"Well, I presume Ken didn't think it was me . . . or did he?"

"Don't be silly – "

"Don't be silly, she says. Jaysus! Look, if Beth thought it was me larking about, why didn't you tell her about the knickers?" he challenged. "That would have cleared up the matter there and then. Beth knows I'm not *into* women's underwear." He chuckled. "At least not in that way. Why didn't you set her straight, Michelle? What were you thinking?"

Michelle sighed. "Oh, I don't know what I thought. In a way, I was hoping it *was* you . . . "

"Pardon!"

"You see, those knickers . . . they were . . . "

"Christ, wait a minute . . . they weren't *yours*, weren't they? Oh hell . . . they *were*."

She nodded dumbly.

"But how? . . . Why?"

Michelle shrugged her shoulders despondently. "They

went missing a while ago. Remember one morning you brought my clothes in from the line?"

"The day Beth went to London with her mother? Yeah, of course I remember. There'd been an awful storm the night before. Your gate had blown open."

"That's right, I assumed the panties had blown away. Then, last night . . . I really got a shock, Mark. Seeing them again . . . and in Ken's garden. For a split second I suspected *him* of playing a joke on me. Luckily I didn't say anything."

She fiddled with the beer-mat in front of her.

"Mark, you must think this is all highly amusing but . . . it's had an awful effect on me. The whole thing makes me feel . . . ill. Defiled or something . . ."

"Yes, it's not a pleasant experience – "

"I'm trying not to take it too seriously, but the idea that someone actually came into my garden and robbed my personal belongings . . . why would anyone do that? I don't want to think about it and yet I can't stop thinking about it – "

"I know."

"What *kind* of a person would do something like that?"

"Someone who wasn't the full shilling, if you ask me. You're sure they belong to you?" He coughed. "I mean . . . knickers are knickers. One pair is the same . . ."

"They were mine all right. I checked last night before the police bagged them as evidence. The little bow – ah, what am I doing? Look they were *mine*, Mark, take my word for it."

Mark scratched his head. "This is unreal, isn't it?"

"You can say that again."

"What did Ken say when you told the police?"

"I didn't."

"You didn't? Why the hell not?"

"I didn't want them to know," she admitted. "Or him. Especially not him. I couldn't tell him. You see . . . "

"Yes?"

"It would have meant that I'd have had to tell him . . . "

"Tell him what, Michelle?"

"Nothing." She stood up. "Excuse me, Mark, I'm going to the loo. Be back in a moment."

*   *   *

Michelle stared at her reflection in the mirror and dabbed cold water on her face.

She was sweating.

She'd been on the verge of telling Mark everything – just stopped herself in time. It would have been nice to have got it all off her chest.

But how would *he* have reacted?

Thought her crazy? In need of help?

She *was* in need of help but somehow she couldn't reach out and ask for it. What was happening to her? She used to be so competent and pragmatic, had an answer for everything. That's what she used to believe – that there was a reason for everything and an answer to every problem.

Now, she wasn't sure.

If there *was* a reason for this . . . this outrage, this abuse, Michelle wasn't sure she wanted to know it.

He was sick, disturbed . . . insane?

He'd chosen this course of action and carried it through. He was plotting all the time – the notes, the phone messages, the CDs. All planned and organised – not a random thing. He was on some sort of a crazy campaign . . . out to destroy her.

She was the innocent victim in all this . . . *victim*.

No, no, no, she *wasn't* a victim. She refused to accept that she was. She was her own person. She would not, could not, be threatened or harmed or damaged by this . . . depraved, demented clod. She wouldn't allow it.

There *was* an answer to her problem . . .

One of these days Cyril O'Connor would give up, become bored by his stupid games and her lack of reaction. He couldn't carry on like this forever.

She smiled at her reflection.

Inaction.

That was her answer.

She wouldn't report him to the police as he probably expected her to do. Maybe that's what he *wanted* her to do? Deep down, was Cyril O'Connor looking for help? Crying out to be noticed? Hadn't he done this very thing before? Wasn't that what Ken had told her?

He was still at it.

That girl years ago, whoever she was, she'd got her father on to it. Her father was some important solicitor who'd succeeded in frightening Cyril off . . . but now he was at it again. Michelle would have to play the game differently – not tell *any*one. She'd ignore him – wipe out his messages, destroy any subsequent notes or letters. It would unnerve him. Eventually he'd lose interest – when he saw he was getting no reaction, he'd give up.

And last night's prowler?

How could she have thought it could be Mark? He'd never do anything to upset her – never mind this kind of seedy stuff. Was Cyril the prowler? Did that mean he wasn't in Vienna at all? He was back?

In *Ireland*?

Was it *Cyril* who'd got into her back garden, broken the bolt on her gate and actually got in? Had he gone to her clothes-line, removed her underwear and then brought it to Ken's house?

Cyril O'Connor . . . back in Dublin. Had he followed her all the way from Vienna?

Was he following her now?

Tracking her around the city? Was he trailing her to work each day? Had he been waiting for her outside the music school last night? Got on the 11 bus after her and followed her to Ken's house? Had he been sitting behind her on the bus *all the way from town*?

Suddenly it hit her . . .

The robbery in her mother's house. Her medals were missing. Had *that* been him, too?

No, no, no.

Cyril O'Connor couldn't be responsible for everything

that went wrong in her life. She was becoming paranoid. She couldn't go blaming him for every little mishap. Her imagination had gone to the fair and was roller-coasting.

But . . . just supposing . . .

Was he watching every move she made? Following her everywhere? Trying to create havoc? Interfering with the people she loved? Getting at her by bothering them? Her mother? Ken?

Mark's car . . . two flat tyres in one week?

Was he . . .

Was he watching her *now*?

Twenty-Five

It was almost seven o'clock as Ruth James was making her way out of the Mace supermarket when she bumped into the last person on earth she wanted to see – Emer Thomas, the pharmacist's assistant and the village snoop.

"Hello, Mrs James. Haven't seen you in an age. Keeping well, I hope?"

"Yes, thank you, Emer."

"The evening's are drawing in, aren't they? There's a chill in that wind that'd go right through you. A lot of 'flu knocking about. You'd want to wrap up warm."

"Yes, I didn't realise it was so cold when I came out. I don't usually shop on a Saturday but Gordon went off early in the car this morning. It doesn't matter though, I only had a few things to buy. I ran out of milk and bread."

"One extra mouth makes a big difference, doesn't it?"

Ruth looked blankly at her. "Sorry?"

"I hear your Cyril's home. On holidays, is he?"

"Eh . . . that's right."

Ruth shifted the shopping bag to her left hand. "I must fly, Emer, I'm expecting visitors." A blatant lie but how else could she get away from the third degree?

"And Mr James himself? How is he?"

"He's in fine fettle," Ruth said pointedly. "Never been better."

The younger woman took her by the arm, which was much too familiar for Ruth's liking. "We miss him something terrible at the committee meetings. You can tell him that from me – he's sorely missed. He used to keep things moving, too. There was no messing when Mr James chaired the meetings, no time-wasting on silly issues. He cut through the red tape and got on with the business in hand."

Ruth wasn't sure how to respond so she merely nodded.

"We're trying to organise an event for the Sunday after Hallowe'en," Emer went on. "Margaret Turner and her cronies want a funfair, stalls and pony rides and the usual boring old stuff. I wanted something different – something that would have a wider appeal. A concert in the parish hall."

"A concert? Yes, that's a possibility."

"And, Mrs James, we'd be relying on you to sing."

"Oh no, Emer," Ruth said hurriedly. "My singing days are over."

"That's not what I heard, didn't you sing at young Delia Martin's wedding in July?"

"I do the odd wedding," Ruth admitted. "But a concert . . . I don't think so."

"Nelly O'Halloran still raves about your performances in Jurys' Cabaret. Said you had a marvellous repertoire."

"That was many moons ago," Ruth pointed out.

"Well, would you think about it, Mrs James? It'd be a treat for us all and Mr James could accompany you, just like in the old days."

"I'm not sure Gordon and I would pack them in for you, Emer. I think you'd need something more . . . modern. My version of 'I Dreamt that I dwelt in Marble Halls' is no match for Enya's!"

"You have your own style, Mrs James."

"Such as it is."

"The older folk prefer simple singing, not all these strange-sounding echoey gimmicks. But you've put your finger on it. What we'd need is a few different acts, a variety show – something for everyone. For the teenagers we could find out who's in vogue now. Sure aren't there plenty of groups around we could ask to play?"

"Are there?"

"Oh, yes. The secondary schools are crawling with young lads in groups, thinking they'll be the future U2. A lot of these bands would give anything to perform at a venue like ours – free promotion, plenty of publicity."

"I never thought of that," Ruth said.

"They'd be delighted to give their services free, that's what I thought anyway. But would that shower listen to me? Not a bit of it!"

"Em, what could Gordon do to help out, Emer? He wouldn't have much connection with younger bands – "

"No, no, I didn't mean that. I know Gordon's not interested in pop music. I wasn't thinking of him in his musical capacity at all – apart from his accompanying your song. It was more to do with his . . . his inventiveness."

"His inventiveness?" Ruth echoed.

"Yes," Emer enthused. "Gordon was always the one with the bright ideas."

"Gordon?"

"Oh yes. He was so enthusiastic about everything, like a breath of fresh air in the fog of bureaucracy."

A breath of fresh air?

"He'd never have left us if it wasn't for that Gertie Fox. Just because she was married to the rector, she thought she knew everything. Uppity she was. But that's all history now since the rector moved to Kilkenny."

Ruth said nothing. She didn't want to be reminded of Gertie Fox and all that unpleasantness.

"I don't suppose he'd consider coming back to us? Maybe you could persuade him to join our ranks again?"

"I don't think so, Emer. He's very busy lately."

"Oh?"

Her sceptical expression angered Ruth.

"Is he teaching again?"

"No, no," Ruth said quickly, "but his music is taking up all of his time at the moment. You know he's converted the barn into a music room?"

"The barn? That must have been expensive."

"You can't put a price on happiness, Emer, can you? I'm very glad Gordon's found an interest. It's given him a new lease of life."

"I'd say that," Emer said, a smile creasing her mouth. "He's looking very sprightly these days. A music room. Fierce posh." She laughed. "He must intend to give recitals – to cover his costs."

"I'm not *au fait* with all of Gordon's plans, Emer," Ruth retorted. "But money was never his first priority."

Easy for Ruth James to say that. No mortgage and no children. She'd inherited their cottage from her dying father. As soon as the old man popped his clogs she was back like a shot to live here. Back to her roots! She hadn't bothered to look after her father when he was alive and then, the minute the poor sod shuffled off his mortal coil – back she comes with the mad musician in tow. Nixers for weddings and funerals. Nice work if you could get it!

"Gordon's composing at the moment," Ruth said haughtily.

"Composing, is he?

"Yes. A piano concerto."

"A piano concerto? Fancy! He hasn't given up the advertising jingles, has he? That last one he did for Burchall's Tea was very catchy, I thought."

Ruth flinched.

"And I heard he's a good artist too. Must be wonderful to live with such talent," Emer remarked dryly. "My Danny hasn't a note in his head and as for sketching – he couldn't draw water from a well. He's more your feet-on-the-ground, practical kind of a man, which is a good thing for me as I can't even change a light bulb."

Feet on the ground? Not the last time Ruth saw him. Danny Thomas was a drunken sot, an oaf, a ne'er do well, a waster. No wonder Emer Thomas had money problems, when her husband squandered everything he earned in Ryan's pub and Molloy's bookies, and they'd insisted on having seven children. Seven children!

"Well, Emer, I must be off."

"Mrs James, I was wondering if . . . of course I don't know how much he charges but I'd be willing to pay the going rate . . . "

"I'm sorry?"

"Lessons. Piano lessons for Ivy."

"Ivy?"

"She's the ten-year-old, our youngest. I'm only asking because her teacher, Ms Fallon, said she thought that Amy was very musical, has a good ear, apparently. So, I thought that music lessons would be just the ticket. What do you think?"

"I'm sure it's a good idea, yes, if the child's showing an interest."

"Oh, she is, she is."

"But my husband doesn't teach any more. He . . . retired from teaching a long time ago."

"I know, but I thought he might . . . he might make an

exception in my case – seeing as how we're neighbours and all."

And all? Ruth had never understood that expression.

"I'm sorry, Emer. The answer has to be no."

"That's a pity."

"There are plenty of other teachers. In fact there's one living in Ashbourne. I heard she was very good. A Mrs Costello. That'd be quite handy, wouldn't it?"

"Mrs Costello?"

"Yes, she teaches piano and violin."

"I'll speak to Danny about it," she said abruptly. "Give my regards to Gordon, won't you? And Cyril, of course."

Ruth was about to move off but Emer Thomas drew her back again. "Listen, why don't we all get together one of these evenings? Meet in Ryan's for a drink? Danny would be thrilled. Himself and Cyril used to be quite good pals, remember?"

Ruth didn't.

What she *did* remember was that Danny Thomas, a snotty-nosed, scabby-kneed brat, was forever robbing the priest's orchard and putting the blame on Cyril. Her brother was always blamed in the wrong.

* * *

Cyril O'Connor hung up the kitchen phone.

"Any luck?" his sister asked, as she served his dinner. "Beef casserole, OK?"

"Thanks, Ruth, you're very good." He smiled. "No, no

275

luck. I was on to Roddy McGrath. He has nothing at the moment. That new Merrion Hotel might have something in the New Year. Where's Gordon? Isn't he joining us?"

"Down in the music room. Doesn't want to be disturbed. I'll keep some dinner for him, he can reheat it later. It's a terrible pity you gave up the job in Vienna, Cyril." Ruth poured her brother a glass of water. "You were earning good money and you had the car."

"True," he agreed. "I was lonely, though."

"I know that. When we visited you this summer, I noticed a big change in you. I said it to Gordon."

"Mmh, it was coming on me for a while but I think it was meeting up with Michelle Bolger that brought things to a head for me."

"Michelle Bolger?" Ruth frowned. "What has *she* got to do with anything?"

"I'd been thinking of coming home – she helped me to make up my mind. Pass me the salt, will you?"

"You discussed it with Michelle Bolger?" Ruth's voice rose.

"No, no, I didn't."

Ruth glared. "What then?"

"It was just being with her and talking about Dublin and the scene here in Ireland, it made me realise how homesick I was."

"Cyril, have you . . . have you contacted Michelle Bolger since you got back?"

"Why?" he asked suspiciously.

Ruth averted her gaze. "I was wondering, that's all."

"I haven't been speaking to her, no," he said cautiously.

"I'd keep well away, if I were you."

"It's quite clear you don't like her, Ruth. Why not?"

Ruth shrugged. "Whether I like her or not is of no consequence, Cyril. I simply think you should leave well enough alone."

"Don't worry, Ruth. I won't do anything . . . stupid."

"You said that before, Cyril," his sister reminded him. "Remember your infatuation with – "

"Ruth, for God's sake, are you ever going to let me forget that? It was years ago – "

"That woman had an awful effect on you, Cyril. You became obsessed. You wouldn't listen to reason."

Cyril got angry. "This is totally different, Ruth."

"Is it?"

"Yes. Michelle Bolger was good company, that's all there was to it, I swear. Some day I might look her up again, but – "

"I'd prefer if you didn't, Cyril. I have my own reasons."

Cyril cut into a succulent piece of meat. It had been a mistake coming back to live with his sister in the family home. She was kind and caring but she was far too possessive. Interfering. The quicker he found a job and new lodgings the better. He couldn't let her dictate to him as she'd done in the past.

"You got good references from Hans?"

He nodded.

"You worked very hard for him and I just hope he appreciated it."

"He did, Ruth. The references are brilliant. I come highly recommended."

"I'm glad to hear it."

"Hans and the rest of the staff were easy to get along with. It was a great place to work, friendly – "

"So, why did you leave so suddenly?"

"I had to," he said simply. "Once I make up my mind to do something, I – "

"You could have stuck it out, Cyril."

"I couldn't, Ruth. Life's too short for sticking things out. I enjoyed the few years I spent there but it was time to come home."

"Impulsive," she admonished him. "You're too impulsive."

"Impulsive? I'm almost forty, Ruth. You're the one who's always nagging me about settling down – well, that's precisely what I intend to do. I don't want to be wandering around Europe for the rest of my natural."

"Of course not. Cyril . . . did you manage to save any money?"

"A bit." He smiled. "Not a fortune, Ruth, but I've enough to tide me over for a month or two. I lived well and Vienna was expensive."

"I realise that. I don't want to see you short of – "

"Will you quit doing the big sister bit? Don't worry about me, Ruth. I still know quite a few people around town. Maybe I should give Ken Leavy a bell? See if he has anything in the pipeline."

"Ken Leavy?"

"Mmh."

"Leavy?"

"The Fullerton Hotel."

"Not the man you had the run-in with a couple of years ago, Cyril? Are you *mad*?"

"Ah, he'll have forgotten all about that by now," Cyril said nonchalently. "I'm damn good at what I do, Ruth. So, if Ken Leavy wants an efficient and experienced assistant manager he need look no further – "

"Cyril, have you lost your senses altogether?"

"What do you mean?" her brother asked innocently.

"Didn't he threaten you with *fraud*? You can't go knocking on his door again. Cyril, are you listening to me? And . . . and isn't he – "

"Isn't he what?"

"Michelle Bolger's boyfriend?"

"He is, you're perfectly right."

"Cyril O'Connor, what are you up to?"

"Nothing."

He grinned cheekily and daubed a potato with a big lump of butter.

"Cyril, what are you thinking of? You're not *thinking* at all, that's the trouble – "

"Just pulling your leg. You should see your face!"

"I don't find this amusing at all, On the contrary."

"Ah, relax, will you? I've no intention of asking that

twit for a job. I have my pride. I wouldn't be caught dead working for him."

"You'll have to keep looking. What about Sid? Is he still in Buswells?"

"I don't want to contact Sid. Haven't been speaking to him in years. No, something will turn up, Ruth. It always does."

Her brother's lackadaisical attitude was most annoying. He was a harum-scarum – no sense of responsibility at all. Cyril had always been a Walter Mitty type. She was worn out worrying about him.

Twenty-Six

Cynthia Fadian, the pretty red-haired night receptionist, gave Michelle her friendliest smile.

"Hello there, looking for Mr Leavy? I saw him go into the bar with the accountant about half an hour ago. Will I page him for you?"

"It's OK, Cyn." Michelle smiled back, crookedly. "I'll foll-follow him in." She glanced at her watch and swayed slightly. "Eight-thirty. With Terry Scott, you said. He's not still working, izee?"

"Does he ever stop?"

The girl turned away to answer the phone. Why was she grinning?

No sign of Ken or Terry in the bar. Michelle tried to walk normally as she made her way into the lounge. The select lounge, to be more precise. It was a spacious room, with soft lighting, old-fashioned green leather armchairs and couches, round highly-polished mahogany tables and wall-to-wall leather-bound books.

The effect was supposed to be *olde worlde* but Michelle privately thought it was a bit *de trop* – too fussy to be truly elegant.

She spotted Ken sitting at the circular bar with Terry. He gestured over when he saw her.

She tottered towards them, banging into the edge of a table as she passed.

"Zorree! Zo Zorry!" She nodded formally at the three girls who were sitting there having drinks, but had to hold on to the back of one of their chairs to stop herself from falling forward. "Hello there, you two." Michelle kissed Ken on the cheek. "Sporting a moustache, now, Terry? It suits you. You're looking ver-very well."

Terry pulled out a stool for her. "You too," he replied politely.

But she wasn't looking well at all. Terry couldn't get over how Michelle had changed since the last time he'd seen her. She was clearly under the weather. Her hair was tossed, her make-up messy and her eyes had a strained expression he'd never seen before.

"May I join you?" Michelle tried to sit up on the high bar stool between them but she faltered.

Ken reached out to steady her. "Are you all right, Mich?" he whispered, quite sternly she thought.

"I'm . . . fi . . . I'm fi . . . I'm grand."

Her lopsided grin irked him.

"Michelle," he hissed. "You're drunk."

"I know!"

She giggled at Terry.

"Excuse me a sec," Ken said to his friend. He led Michelle over to an armchair in a corner, at the back of the bar and out of sight. "Sit there, I'll get you a coffee."

She tugged at his arm. "No, Ken. I want a G and T." She stretched up and landed a sloppy kiss on his mouth. "Mmh, I mizzed ya."

"One large strong coffee coming up. Where the *hell* were you?"

"Out with my . . . boytoy. My *toy*boy!" She hiccupped. "Why? Are you zealous? Ha! I mean jealous!"

"Jesus, Michelle, you're in a right state. Where *were* you?"

"I met Mark in Nearlys. Nearys," she corrected herself.

"You've had way too much to drink. How did you get here? I hope Mark wasn't driving."

"Driving?" She looked at him quizzically.

"Did Mark have his father's car?" he asked sharply.

She shrugged.

"Michelle." He gripped her arm. "Was Mark driving tonight?"

" . . . Mmh, I think so."

"Christ, that's very bloody clever of him, isn't it?"

"He left the pub at six – or maybe it was seven." She chortled. "He only had doo pints." She raised two fingers to illustrate her point, then she yawned and stretched.

"And where were *you* since then? That's over two hours ago."

Why the hell was he so cross?

"What's the matter with you? Did your goldfish die or

something? I stayed on, read the *Evening Heller – Helard* . . . paper. The evening paper. Then I relaxed for a while and had a few more drinks. It's Saturday night – I'm entitled."

"A *few*?"

"Two, maybe three. A drop in the . . . " Her eyes began to close. She tried to open them but she found it hard to focus.

"Michelle," he said quietly, "you never drink like this so early in the day."

"Zorry. That's all I seem to be say-saying tonight. Zor . . . sorry. I'm sorry, all right?

"Take it easy. Mich. Now, tell me – "

"Ken." She grasped his hand. "Don't leave me."

"Of course I won't leave – "

"No, no, swear it, swear it. Say you'll never leave me."

"I'll never leave you, Mich."

"Ken, I'm af . . . afraid."

"Afraid? Of what?"

"Of him."

"Last night's prowler?"

"Yes." She nodded slowly and her eye-lids drooped again. "And the burglars and . . . "

Her voice trailed off sleepily.

Ken stroked her face gently. "Listen to me, Michelle. Your mother phoned earlier. They *got* the burglars."

A momentary spark of awareness. "Did they?"

"Yes. The detective called to see your mother and – "

"Ah, Ken, you're so good. You called to see my – "

"No, not me. The detective, Mich," he explained irritably.

"The detective," she repeated. "The detective."

"Try to concentrate, will you?"

She nodded but her eyes rolled in her head.

"Right, Mich, are you listening? The police got the two burglars."

"Two? There were two?"

"Yes. Two kids, drug-addicts. Your mother's very relieved, so you don't have to worry about her any more, OK?" He shook her gently. "Open your eyes, Mich. Did you hear what I said."

"Yes." She squinted again and then she leaned towards him. "But what about him? They haven't got *him* yet."

"Who? Haven't got who?"

"Him, him, him. The mystery man."

"What are you talking about, Mich? What do you mean?"

"*Him!* I'm talking about him!"

"Who, for God's sake?"

She started to hum a tune which he vaguely recognised. "Mozart," she said with a sigh. "Mozart."

Ken had had enough of this. "What are you saying, Mich?"

She sniggered. "Yes, Wolfgang Ama-Amadeus . . . phones me all the time, you know, gives me private performances down the line . . ."

"Michelle," he said firmly. "Pull yourself together."

"Pull myself together?" She tittered into her hand. "I'm not a pair of curt . . . curtains, Ken."

Ken stood up angrily. "This is hopeless."

Her bottom lip quivered and dropped.

"No, no way. Don't start the water-works, for God's sake." He sat down again and put his arm around her. "I'll get you that coffee." He made a sign to the waiter. "Have you eaten?"

"Not hungry."

"You have to eat, Michelle. I'll order you a beef salad."

"Order me? Will you?" She tried to glare. "No, you won't. Stop ordering me," she said crankily. "You're getting too bos-bossy." A loud hiccup. *"Don't be cruel to a heart that's true."*

She sang the last bit.

Too loudly for his liking.

Then she hiccupped again.

"Michelle, you're tired. Would you like to lie down?"

"Lie down?" She thought about it. "Ooh, yes please."

She started to undo the zipper at the back of her new green top. "This is stuck, Kenny. Come on, help me, will you? Help me out of it."

"You don't need help, Michelle, you're well and truly out of it!"

She was comical in a way, but infuriating too.

"You're no fun." She puckered up her lips. "Kiss me."

"Michelle, stop it. The bar staff are staring at you."

"Kiss me, kiss me, kiss me."

"Here's Alan with your coffee. Sit up straight. Come on, there's a good girl."

Ken took the coffee from the waiter and Michelle pushed the cup away, spilling its contents over the saucer and the table.

"Oops! I've made a mess, haven't I? Don't give out to me, Ken. I couldn't bear it." Tears formed at the corner of her eyes. "Be nice to me, please."

His heart melted.

"It's all right, Mich. Why don't we go upstairs for a while? To number six. You remember that room, don't you?"

"Mmh," she agreed. "Our special r-room. Let's make love. For hours and hours and hours. For da-y-y-ays. Yes, Kenny. Let's stay awake all n-night and make mad bash-passionate love. And all day tomorrow as well." She hugged him tightly to her. "Will we?"

"Yes," he agreed, kissing her lightly on the lips. "Whatever you say, Mich."

He nodded over at Terry as he linked her out of the lounge, across the hall and into the lift. She snuggled into him like a little child.

Ken felt protective of her. Tomorrow, when she was sober, he'd have a long conversation with her. Try to get to the bottom of this.

He got her safely to the first floor and let her into the room. She was still unsteady on her feet so he had to keep a good grip around her waist. The bed was already turned down.

"Ooh, lovely."

She sank down on top of the duvet and closed her eyes.

"Undress me, will you, Ken? I feel . . . woozy."

He barely had her shoes off when she fell fast asleep.

"Not like Michelle, is it?" Terry passed a pint to Ken. "I never considered her a drinker."

"She's not, usually. A glass of wine or two with dinner, maybe one or two gins after. She never drinks during the day, not like that and she hadn't eaten."

"We're all entitled to a slip-up, Ken."

"I know . . . but she's been in very bad form lately. There's something on her mind but I couldn't get any sense out of her tonight."

"Toni?"

He lit a cigarette. "No, I don't think so."

Terry wasn't convinced.

"I left the house early this morning. Michelle was still asleep and I didn't get a proper chance to talk about last night."

"The prowler? Yes, that probably shook her, all right. Women get nervous about these things. It's understandable, Ken. And Michelle lives on her own."

"That's her choice, Terry. Not mine." Ken flicked the ash into a teeming ash-tray. "Alan, when you have a minute, could you get me a clean ash-tray and check the other tables?"

"Yes, Mr Leavy."

"That burglary in her mother's house knocked her for

six but the strange thing is, her mother has risen to the occasion heroically. In fact, her mother has never been stronger."

"I don't think that's what bothering her at all, Ken. You've every right to tell me to butt out and mind my own business but . . . I think Michelle has a lot to contend with and – "

"And what?" Ken sensed he wasn't going to like what he was about to hear. "A lot to contend with? For instance?"

"Beth."

Terry looked at him, waiting for the expected outburst. But Ken just sat there. Sat there and rubbed his chin, thoughtfully.

"Ken, wouldn't it be better for all of you, if you gave some serious thought to getting a divorce?"

"Yes, it would."

Terry was surprised.

"It would tidy things up considerably. It'd even be better for Toni if she could only see that . . . but I never wanted to do anything drastic because of Beth . . . "

"She's sixteen, Ken. She'll be up and gone before you know it. I wouldn't risk losing Michelle, if I were you."

Ken looked shocked. "Losing her?"

"Things don't look all that healthy between you two from where I'm sitting," Terry said quietly.

"What do you suggest?"

"What I'm always suggesting. Ask her to marry you."

"But Michelle doesn't *want* to marry me?"

"There's only one way of finding out." Terry gulped back the rest of his pint. "I'll tell you, it wouldn't be me!" Terry was in full stride now. "There's no way I'd let anyone stop me from marrying the woman I loved. Michelle's a terrific person, Ken. You two are . . . I was never much of a romantic but, all joking apart, you two were meant for one another. Since Michelle came into your life, you're a new person."

"Very true. She's good for me."

"It works two ways. Don't risk losing that, mate."

"I'm not convinced this is the best time to talk about marriage."

"When *is* there a good time?"

"Michelle's . . . preoccupied. That's putting it mildly."

"So? Give her something else to be preoccupied about. There's nothing like a wedding to grab a woman's attention. Will I ever forget June? And her mother! Such a goddamn awful fuss – invitations, flowers, bridesmaids, booking the organist and the singer and the altar boys, the cars . . . it was a major miracle I turned up at all, the way they went on at me for the month before the big day."

"Thanks, that's very heartening. My memories of my own wedding aren't much better. Maybe once up the aisle is enough for anyone."

"Michelle's different, and you're a lot older this time around. I think you should go for it, Ken. I really do. You could have one of those foreign weddings, on a beach in the Caribbean or somewhere."

"You're forgetting one thing, Terry. I'm still married."

"You call it a marriage, Ken?"

"But a divorce . . . how long would that take?"

"Don't know," Terry admitted. "You've been living apart for ten years, that should go in your favour. Get yourself a good lawyer. I'll find out who's the best."

Ken stubbed out his cigarette. "I'll have to discuss this with Michelle. See what she wants."

"You might get a pleasant surprise, Ken. I think you will. Sleep on it, anyhow."

"Speaking of sleep, I'd better go check on her. I'll leave her here for tonight, no sense in disturbing her."

"Why don't you stay, too?"

"No, I have to go home. Beth will – "

"Ken! There you go again!"

"What?"

"Beth. Couldn't you put Michelle first for once?"

"Beth's my responsibility, Terry."

"You have some responsibility to Michelle, too."

"Michelle's an adult."

"Beth isn't a *child* any more."

"That's exactly what she is."

Terry pulled on his cigarette. He wasn't going to wear himself out trying to argue.

"Come off it, Terry. I'm not going to leave a sixteen-year-old alone all night in a house where there's already been an intruder."

"I suppose not."

Terry offered Ken a Major which he refused. He'd make one last effort.

"You know, it's not just you who's getting older, Ken. Beth won't let you fuss over her for much longer."

"I don't fuss," Ken protested.

"You could have fooled me."

Michelle was out for the count. He turned down the controls on the radiators and opened the window slightly. He got the duvet from the other single bed and draped it over her.

On the drive home, the conversation with Terry went round and round in his head. He didn't fuss, did he? Beth was only a kid. She needed guidance, protection. And she needed supervision. Terry hadn't a clue what went on these days – drink, drugs, casual sex. June and Terry hadn't got kids so how the hell would *he* know what went on?

Maybe parents couldn't be prepared for every eventuality but it was their duty to be vigilant, at least.

And Michelle wasn't bothered by Toni. She didn't like the idea of Ken's wife settling back in Dublin and that was understandable but she didn't have any *real* worries about it.

Did she?

Michelle was happy the way things were. They saw each other a few times a week, went on holidays, rarely fought. They lived their own lives but they had each other as well. The best of both worlds.

Wasn't it?

Ken turned right into Dorset Street. Gangs of youths were spilling into the streets from the cluster of pubs. Many of them were singing, laughing, horse-playing. Others were floundering around, footless. One wrong word and a row would erupt.

He drove on, past Whitworth Road, Botanic Avenue and St Pat's Training College. The Skylon carpark was full, he noted. He glanced at the car clock.

Ten-thirty.

He hoped Beth would be at home. He *did* need to talk to her.

The minute he opened the hall-door, he heard the gushing sound of his *en suite* shower and that annoyed him. He'd told Beth time and time again to use the bathroom down the landing. Her own bloody private bathroom wasn't good enough for her – she had to use the shower in his room.

He hated that, there'd be a godawful mess, a pong of that cheap perfume or deodorant or whatever the hell she wore and a clump of tangled wet hairs blocking the plug-hole. If she'd dyed her hair in there tonight, he'd swing for her.

"Beth!"

He took the stairs two at a time and dashed into his bedroom. Some skimpy black underwear was strewn across his bed. He lifted it up in disgust. Ken could feel his blood pressure rising. What was a sixteen-year-old doing wearing *this* sort of stuff?

"Beth?"

He knocked on the door.

Now he heard singing.

"Beth!"

The singing got louder.

He thumped the door.

"Beth!"

The singing stopped and the water was turned off.

Good. About time.

"Hurry up and finish your shower," he shouted. "You're not supposed to be in there, you know that damned well. I'll be downstairs in the sitting-room. Get dressed and come down immediately."

He threw the underwear back on the bed and stormed to the door.

"Hi, Ken!"

He whipped around, surprised by the deep voice.

She stood there, all wet and long-legged and sexy, dressed only in a hand-towel which she'd draped around her waist, leaving her breasts exposed. The dark nipples pointed upwards under her long wet tresses.

Christ, she was beautiful.

"Surprise, surprise!"

A seductive smile as she walked slowly towards him – cat-like, sleek and sensuous.

"Toni! What the hell are *you* doing here?"

Twenty-Seven

Toni grasped Ken's hands and pulled him close. She stretched up on her toes and was about to kiss him on the lips but he drew away.

"I wanted to surprise you, Ken!"

"You've done that, all right."

Ignoring her calculated display of warmth and affection, Ken went to the wardrobe. He took out the silk bathrobe, the one Toni had sent him last Christmas, which he'd never worn – he hoped she'd notice that.

"Put this on and follow me downstairs."

He threw it to her and left the bedroom before she'd a chance to say another word.

She was up to her old tricks – a sudden dramatic entrance, guaranteed to take him unawares and make it easier for her to manipulate the situation. She'd wanted to *surprise* him, her favourite ploy in the past but this time, it wouldn't wash with him.

Toni drew in her breath and tied the belt on the navy silk robe very tightly. Great, it emphasised her tiny waist. She pulled the top of it open a little wider – just a hint of cleavage.

The full frontal a minute ago had already whetted his appetite. She'd recognised that glazed-over look in his eyes, she'd seen it often enough when they were together. Ken still wanted her.

He had the hots for her.

She'd play this coolly at first, sit opposite him on the couch and casually let the robe fall open . . . accidentally.

Thankfully, she'd kept her body fit and toned. Ken was a passionate man – he'd never be able to resist her . . . but she'd take it slowly. She checked the radio alarm clock.

Ten-forty.

Why was he home so *early*? What had happened to his sizzling date with Michelle? Home by ten on a Saturday night – it didn't smack of wild passion, did it?

She preened in the mirror as she dabbed some *eau de cologne* behind her ears and down between her breasts. No make-up, Ken liked the fresh-faced, wholesome look – but how would *he* know she was wearing Clarins Gel Auto-Bronzant? She was blessed with blemish-free skin, not like Gwen who was prone to broken veins. All the same, a little extra colour never did a brunette any harm. Would she sneak some blusher? She had another look at herself. No need. The gel had given her a translucent, healthy glow.

Better not to overdo it.

Toni glanced around the bedroom. Michelle's influence was all too obvious – ornaments on the shelves, a Technics hi-fi system in its own mahogany unit and classical CDs stacked in a floor-to-ceiling matching mahogany rack.

Making out with Mahler, Liszt for lust!

She opened the wardrobe. One side was taken up with Michelle's clothes – or what passed for clothes. She lifted out a grey skirt. God, how middle-aged! And this navy one? Long and pleated, in what Michelle must imagine to be the *classical* style. Two blazers – talk about drab! Anyhow it didn't matter even if Michelle was a Naomi Campbell lookalike.

She was only his girlfriend not his *wife*.

Toni *Leavy* was the mother of his daughter, a bond that could never be broken by Michelle Bolger or any other woman. Having a child with someone counted. You couldn't dismiss or deny a relationship which had produced a child.

It was too important, a lifelong pledge.

Beth was right – Ken couldn't possibly love Michelle Bolger the way he'd loved her. He'd made her his wife. They'd made public vows to one another. He'd been lost when she walked – when she left for London. He'd needed a woman in his life. He'd been lonely. All men were like that.

They weren't able to survive on their own.

So, Michelle came along – a port in a storm. A

friendly, warm, safe port. A haven of calm and tranquillity for poor forlorn Ken whose wicked wife had . . . what was the point going over old ground?

Ken must be quite fond of Michelle, really. She'd been good to him, even good to Beth in her way . . . but Michelle had been, and still was, a stop-gap. Ken needed more than that – *deserved* more than that.

What had Beth told her? Michelle stayed an odd mid-week night here and every weekend? Playing house with Ken, that's all it was – playing. Make-believe. Ken didn't belong to Michelle. She hadn't been his first choice. She was second fiddle . . . peculiar role for a pianist!

Michelle had tried to put her stamp on this house but it hadn't worked. Toni's glance fell on the lamp in the corner. A wedding present from her friend, Alison Geoghan. This bedroom was where Ken and she had started their married life. This was where she'd slept with Ken for six glorious passion-filled years. This double bed was where they'd conceived their beautiful daughter.

Michelle couldn't compete.

It wasn't too late for herself and Ken and she'd make him see that. She was back with her husband in her home – her rightful place.

"Where's Beth?" Ken poured her a glass of Merlot.

"Gone to a party and she's staying over in Carmel's." Toni switched on the TV.

Ken took the remote control and turned down the sound. "We have to talk."

"Yes, Ken, we do need to talk."

"Tonight isn't a good idea, I haven't much time. I'm going back to the hotel."

"Going back? Tonight? It's Saturday, for God's sake. Why are you going back? You're not working again – "

"No, I'm not. I left Michelle there. The only reason I came home early was to check on Beth. Since she's not here, I'll – "

"Ken, don't rush away. We can use this time for a chat. There's something I *have* to discuss with you."

Toni uncrossed her legs provocatively, giving him a glimpse of naked thigh.

"Look, Toni, I'm still not sure why you're here but – "

"Are you not, darling? I was going to tell you all about it." She licked her lips slowly. "Later."

"I'd prefer to hear *now*, if you don't mind. What exactly are your plans?"

He was very gruff. She hadn't expected him to be so abrupt. Another drop of wine might thaw him out a bit.

"It's so nice sitting here with you in our sitting-room." She topped up his glass and smiled beatifically. "Isn't it?"

Our sitting-room. It would be hilarious if it wasn't so outrageous.

"Carry on, Toni. You have my undivided attention."

"The apartment I was looking at, on the quays, remember I told you? Well, it fell through and then I was offered another one but Beth doesn't like it and . . . "

He looked at his watch. "Yes?"

Jesus, this was maddening. Was he timing her? She'd hardly call this his *undivided attention.*

"I thought I could stay here . . . for a while, I mean . . . just for a week or so until I find somewhere else. I don't want to stay with Gwen, we'd fight like a couple of bitches in heat."

Lyrical as always, he thought.

"You've lots of space here, Ken, and I wasn't sure if you'd a room available in the hotel – "

"I have, as a matter of fact – "

"But I thought it might be nice for Beth to have me here and – "

"Did you? You thought it would be nice for Beth?" he replied bitterly. "You've obviously done a lot of thinking, haven't you? Pity you left it so late – "

"It's all right, Ken," she said stiffly. "I had no idea you'd take it like this."

A tear in the corner of her right eye. If he counted to three another one would appear in the left. He didn't know how she managed it, but she had this down to a fine art.

She sniffed. "I'll pack in the morning and – "

Ken lit a cigarette. "It's OK, Toni. You can stay . . . for a few days."

"Really, darling? You're sure?"

He nodded and clicked the top of his silver lighter shut.

"Oh, that's marvellous. It makes sense. I hoped you'd agree. Ken, I was wondering . . . "

He stared hard at her.

She bent forward to put her wine glass on the coffee table. The robe fell open, as she knew it would, revealing her perfect pert breasts. She smiled up at him from under her long dark lashes – blatantly coming on to him.

When she sat back into the couch, she crossed her legs again. Her thighs were slim and long and sensual. There was no denying it – she was one of the most beautiful women he'd ever seen in his life.

* * *

Michelle woke with a start. The room was in darkness. She lifted her throbbing head off the pillow and turned to look at the alarm clock. It wasn't there on the bedside table where it always was. Groggily she put up her arm and felt around for the overhead light switch.

Nothing.

What was going on here?

She sat up and the duvet slipped off the bed. To her amazement, she was fully dressed, lying on top of the sheets.

Blurry images crowded her brain . . . drinks on a table, chatting to people she didn't know, walking through Stephen's Green.

A ray of light escaped through a slit in the curtains and landed on a painting of a lily pond.

Room six. She was in room six in The Fullerton.

"Ken," she called out.

No answer.

"Ken," she called more loudly.

Silence.

She hauled herself out of the bed and groped for the switch on the wall to the left of the bed. She shivered in the night air. Some idiot had opened the window. Michelle staggered over to close it and went to the bathroom for a drink of water. As she gulped at the cold liquid, which snatched her breath, she caught a glimpse of herself in the mirror.

She looked like something the cat had dragged in.

* * *

"I'm so glad you're going to let me stay." Toni hummed happily. She'd her feet up on the couch and had draped herself against the cushions in what she considered to be an abandoned way. If she'd been modelling for a *Penthouse* centrefold shoot, she couldn't have taken more pains to get the pose right.

"I think Beth will be glad to have you here. You two have a lot of catching up to do."

"Yes, darling. Beth needs a woman in her life. Don't get me wrong, Ken, you've done a wonderful job with her. No father could have done better but – "

"No need to explain or apologise," Ken said resignedly. "You're right. Beth needs you at this stage.

Michelle does her best but she doesn't like to interfere and Beth can be quite – "

"Yes, she's sorry for having a go at Michelle. She didn't mean to be so rude but she was – "

"Had a go at Michelle? When?"

Toni, conscious that she'd made a gaffe, took another sip of wine. "This morning, Ken. It was nothing at all. Beth's going through a difficult patch at the moment and – "

"Michelle never said a word about it – "

"Didn't she? Well, there you are, then. She didn't even think it worth mentioning."

Michelle had been extremely agitated this evening and it was because of Beth. Terry was right. What had his daughter said? She had a very sharp tongue sometimes. She'd have to learn to control these outbursts.

Michelle hadn't said anything to him because she didn't want a row, didn't want to create any unpleasantness. It *was* difficult for her. And Michelle had gone to meet Mark this evening for a drink. Why?

Could she talk more freely to Mark than she could to him? He didn't understand . . . did he *want* to understand?

He let his mind wander as Toni talked on . . . and on and on.

Wouldn't it be nice to have a few weeks away from this house? To escape? Let Toni take over with Beth for a while? A few weeks of peace . . . no more tantrums or sulks or cheeky answers, no shouting matches, no more slammed doors, milk left out to go sour, clothes strewn around the hall, copies and schoolbooks all over the kitchen table . . .

"We could start doing things together again . . . " Toni was oblivious to the fact that he was miles away.

No more make-up smeared on the mirrors, bottles of nail polish left lying around, dirty cups and glasses behinds the sofa or under her bed for months growing strange fungi and other vegetation sprouting on stale crusts of bread.

A few days to think only of himself. And Michelle.

* * *

Almost midnight. How long had she been asleep? Three hours? Four? Where was Ken? Why had he left her here in this room on her own? And Mark, where had he got to?

Mark.

She vaguely remembered a row, some kind of a disagreement with Mark. She'd accused him of . . . what had she been thinking of? She was losing it, definitely. The poor guy. Imagine thinking him capable of . . . but she hadn't actually *accused* him, had she? It was Beth's fault for putting the idea in her head in the first place.

Beth. What was she going to do about Beth?

Another image floated by. A green tie and a salt-and-pepper moustache . . . Mark didn't have . . . oh, no!

Terry Scott.

Oh holy divine, it was all beginning to come back in

spiteful flashes – the room spinning, Terry's embarrassed smile, the three women at the table she'd practically sent flying, the coffee she'd spilled . . . and she'd tried to strip and have her wicked way with Ken on top of a table in the *select* lounge.

He'd kill her!

* * *

Toni got off the sofa, slithered to the floor and settled herself at his feet. Ken hadn't been listening to a word she'd said for the past ten minutes.

"After my mother's funeral, I began to see things in a new light. Losing someone you love, Ken, it makes you realise what you've missed, the mistakes you've made."

"Sorry?"

"My mother, Ken. Since she died, I've had a long hard look at myself – "

"Your mother loved you, Toni."

Despite all your shortcomings, he wanted to say but didn't.

"I know she did, Ken, I loved her too. She was a great woman, kind and good-natured, always thought of others before herself."

"Indeed," he agreed.

"I wasn't just talking about Mum. I meant . . . you and me, Ken. I think we should try again. Mum would have wanted it, she said so the night before she died. It might take a little while, but with both of us making an effort – "

"Toni, hang on a minute . . . "

She ran her hand up the back of his leg and he pulled away as if he'd been scorched.

She laughed. "Jumpy, aren't you?"

"What the – "

"Relax, Ken, it's OK?" This time she laid her head against his thigh. "Given time, we'll adjust."

"Adjust?" He stared down at her. "Adjust to what?"

She smiled sexily up at him, brought her knees together and then slowly parted them giving him a full view. "To each other, darling." She stroked her thigh, running her fingers lightly up and down in a tantalising way.

He stood up and walked away in disgust.

"Ken." She got up from the floor, went quickly to him and put her arms around his neck. She couldn't stop now. This was a crucial moment.

He still had his back to her but she hugged him tight.

"Ken, don't fight this."

He removed her arms gently but firmly and turned to face her. "Toni, you have it all wrong."

Her eyes hardened. "What do you mean?"

"You've misinterpreted everything I've been saying."

She took a step back. "Misinterpreted . . . "

"Yes, we won't be getting back together, Toni. It's too late for – "

"No, Ken, no, it's not." She threw herself at him, clung to him. "Don't say that . . . "

Again, he extricated himself from her grip.

"Toni, listen to me. Whatever we had is over. A long time ago – "

"It's not," she cried in dismay. "It's not. It was my fault, all my fault, I admit that. I shouldn't have left – "

"But you *did*," he said, raising his voice. "You made your decision, Toni."

"It was a wrong decision, Ken. I made a mistake, a big mistake, the biggest mistake of my life and – "

"Maybe not," Ken whispered.

"Maybe not? Why are you saying that?"

"It wasn't a mistake, Toni."

"It was, it was," she insisted. "I was young, immature. I didn't know what I was doing. I wanted freedom – "

"I know," he said. "I understand it now, even if I didn't at the time. I was so angry with you – "

"You were right, right to be furious, Ken." She grabbed him again. "I love – "

"Toni!" He pushed her away from him and she dropped back on the couch, startled.

"I'm sorry," he said quickly. "I didn't mean to hurt – "

"I know, I know," she replied eagerly. "I didn't mean to hurt you either, Ken. I want – "

"Toni, *please* listen to me. You left ten years ago because you needed your free – "

"Oh, don't say it again, Ken. Please don't say it again. I bitterly regret what I did and – "

"No regrets, remember?" He knelt on the floor in front of her. "That's what you always used to say. No regrets.

You were right. And I think you were right about us, too."

"No." She burst into tears. "No, Ken, I wasn't right at all."

Ken put his arm around her and gently stroked her hair. "Toni, let's not pretend. Things can never be as they once were between us. It's best if we can come to some amicable arrangement . . . "

She wiped her eyes in the sleeve of the bathrobe and sniffed again. Ken went to the sideboard, opened a drawer and got her a packet of tissues.

"What do you want, Ken?" She gulped.

"A divorce," he said quietly.

He patted her knee in a fatherly way.

She'd been so bloody stupid. The big seduction scene! How could she get out of this without making a bigger fool of herself?

"Yes," he continued, "I think a divorce would be for the best . . . for both of us."

She blew her nose and tried to smile. "You've made up your mind?"

He nodded.

"And Beth? Have you spoken to her about it, Ken?"

"No. I'll make it my business to see her in the morning."

Toni took his arm. "What about telling her together? It might be easier if she heard it from the two of us . . . she's not going to like it, Ken."

Toni didn't like it either.

"No, Beth won't like it. We'll have to be open with her, though. The truth this time, the full truth."

"Yes," Toni agreed.

The full truth? What was that?

"You know," she said, squeezing the tissue into a ball, "ten minutes ago I was overjoyed because you said I could stay here. I thought you meant that we – "

"I know what you thought, Toni." He took the wine glasses from the table. "I'll move into The Fullerton for the time being. We'll take it from there."

"Ken? May I ask you something?"

"Shoot."

"What about . . . Michelle?"

"I love her, Toni," he said simply. "I love her."

Toni swallowed hard.

"I'm hoping she'll agree to marry me."

It was after four am when he drove back to the hotel through the almost-deserted streets. A light drizzle misted the windscreen. He parked in his space, dashed into reception and nodded to the hall porter as he hurried up the stairs to the first floor.

Would she be asleep? Damn, she would be. Should he wake her to tell her what had happened with Toni? His heart beat faster and faster as he opened the door to number six.

He was free.

Free!

Well, almost free. Free to love Michelle and marry her, if she'd have him. He'd make a clean legal break from Toni now, and Michelle might feel differently? He hoped so.

He switched on the main light. The window was closed and the bed made.

She was gone.

Twenty-Eight

After the eleven o'clock Mass the next morning, Michelle gathered up her music sheets and locked the organ. Despite a dreadful hangover, she'd played quite well, she thought. She liked the O'Riada Mass and the choir hadn't sung too many wrong notes, which made a nice change.

She came down from the organ gallery as Father Noonan was chatting to one of the parishioners in the porch.

"Lovely, Michelle," he said, shaking her hand. "You outdid yourself today."

"Thanks, Father. Hello, Mrs Wilson."

"Ms Bolger, what a treat that was! Your little troupe sang beautifully this morning. They're a credit to you."

"Yes," the priest agreed, " Michelle has them well-rehearsed, devotes a lot of her time to the choir."

"They're very eager,' Michelle said, "and good attenders for the most part."

"I was telling my Niall he should come down to you for an audition." Teresa Wilson tied a scarf around her neck.

"What age is he now?" Michelle asked.

"Nine and a half. He has a good strong voice, like a lark on the top notes, Ms Bolger. I'd love him to join the choir before his voice breaks and it'd be good for him, he's a bit shy."

"Nice to think there's a few shy ones left," Father Noonan piped in. "The way some of the young ones carry on at the local dance-hall!" He groaned.

"Teenagers, Father!" Teresa Wilson adopted her world-of-experience manner. "I've three of them at home and how I've escaped the Valium I'll never know."

"You've good children, Mrs Wilson." He lit a cigar. "Not like those Perry girls – they'd have the heart scalded in you. Last night at the disco, I had to take them aside and speak to them about self-respect. 'Just dancing, Father', they told me, as brazen as you like."

"Shocking!" Teresa whispered to Michelle.

"I'd love you to see what they call dancing. Mouth-to-mouth resuscitation more like!" The priest was in full flight now. "Glued to the lads they were, didn't even come up for air!" He scratched his head. "I'm telling you, in the old days the parish priest used to prise them apart with a big stick!"

"You're right there, Father," Teresa Wilson said. "I don't even understand the lingo mine use anymore. 'She's a ride, Ma!' That's what Derek said to me last week. Imagine describing a girl like that!"

"I've heard a lot worse," the priest said sadly. "The

language is gone to the dogs altogether. They've no respect any more. I pity the parents."

"Don't waste your pity, Father," Teresa said caustically. "I *blame* the parents. They let the children away with murder at home. How can we expect children to behave properly when they've never been taught manners or how to behave decently? What do you think, Ms Bolger? It must be desperate in the schools. It's the teachers *I* pity."

"I have to say the pupils I have are great," Michelle said, drawing puzzled looks from both of them. "I like to think I get on well with them."

"I'm glad," Teresa said dubiously. "If you could hear the way my lot go on about their teachers! Derek's maths teacher is brilliant, works very hard to push the class along and what did Derek say when I pointed that out to him? 'She has no life!' I was fit to be tied."

"I'm lucky because I work with them on a one to one basis," Michelle continued. "It must be totally different teaching a class of thirty."

"Mmh," Father Noonan reflected, "and your pupils *choose* to study music. You don't have to spend your time persuading them to practise. "

"They enjoy it," Michelle agreed. "I try to make it enjoyable for them – "

"Ah, I've no truck with that theory at all," Teresa grumbled. "That's all they want nowadays – to enjoy themselves. They haven't a clue about the real world. Can't wait for anything, must have everything they want immediately or sooner, no patience. They'll learn. They don't know the meaning of hard work – "

"I can't agree with you there, Mrs Wilson," Michelle interjected. "I think they've a tougher life than we had. Some of them have a much *better* clue about the real world than we'll ever have – unfortunately. There's far more pressure on schoolchildren nowadays."

"Pressure?" Teresa scoffed. "Yeah, pressure to get Nike runners!"

"Peer pressure," Father Noonan agreed. "They've more temptation, more free time, more money – "

"Now you've said it! They're spoilt rotten, so they are." Teresa took a pound from her purse to buy the *Sunday Independent* from the newspaper seller who'd installed his stand in front of the church. "Parents give in to them too easily."

Michelle thought about Beth.

"They think they were put on this earth to enjoy themselves," she went on bitterly. "Half of them are high as kites on that bloody old Ecstacy. Even the ones you'd least expect – I pray to God none of mine get involved, but if they do, I'll . . . "

Michelle saw her frustration.

"And the drink's a worse problem," the priest joined in. "The publicans should be shot for serving them. It's a perfect disgrace selling alcohol to underage children. Of course they're only interested in their profits. Down the laneway the other morning, what did I discover? Empty bottles and cans of every description: beer, cider, naggin bottles of vodka, if you don't mind!"

Michelle didn't want to talk about alcohol. Not this morning.

"And," he added, lowering his voice, "as for the used condoms strewn around . . . "

"Say no more, Father Noonan." Even Teresa had had enough.

"Send Niall down to see me, Mrs Wilson," said Michelle. "We'd be delighted to have a strong soprano, especially another male. As usual there's a shortage of boys, they don't think singing in the church is cool!"

"Niall's not at that smart-Alec stage yet, mercifully. When do you have the weekly practice, Ms Bolger?"

"Wednesday nights at eight sharp," Michelle told her, as she bid them both good morning.

She was glad to get away.

Her mother was waiting on the doorstep when she got home.

"Hello, love." She kissed Michelle on the cheek. "Have the O'Rourkes got visitors staying with them?"

"Don't know. Why?"

"It's just there was a green car parked outside your gate. I've seen it a few times before. He pulled away when I came along."

"You're early." Michelle opened the hall door. "I haven't peeled the potatoes yet."

"No cooking for you today, Michelle. I'm treating you

to lunch." Her mother followed her into the kitchen. "You're very pale, are you all right?"

"Fine, Mam." She plugged in the kettle. "Dying for a cup of tea. You look nice, is that a new coat?"

Her mother twirled around. "Do you like it? I got it in Marks. I'm not sure about the mauve . . . "

"It suits you. Look, it won't take me long to roast the chicken. I don't feel like going out to a restaurant. I – "

"Nonsense, it'll be good for you. I booked a table in Rooks. We can walk there in five minutes. A good juicy steak, that's what you need. Put a bit of colour back into your cheeks."

The thought of it made her want to vomit. Michelle, her back to her mother, sneaked some Alka Seltzer from the press and into a glass. She poured in the water and the mixture fizzed noisily. Shut up, she told the glass.

"There, I knew it!" Olive came up behind her. "Upset tummy, have you?"

"Just a few too many last night," Michelle admitted. "Self-inflicted sickness doesn't count."

"Sit down, Michelle. I'll make the tea. Maybe lunch out isn't a good idea. Would you like to lie down?"

"No, Mam, I'll be fine in a minute." She sat at the table and put her head in her hands.

"Right," her mother said firmly. "I'm going to phone and cancel Rooks. Go upstairs and have a lie-down. I insist, Michelle."

"I can't go to bed. I – "

"Why not?" her mother demanded, hands on hips.

"There's lunch for a start. It wouldn't be fair to . . . "

"Me? Don't be silly, Michelle. I'll cook the chicken. Haven't I been doing the Sunday roast for longer than I care to remember?"

"And the veg – "

"I'm more than capable of peeling a few spuds, Michelle. Get up those stairs before I lose my patience!" Her mother's face softened. "Do as you're told. Go on."

Michelle stood up. She felt queasy. "I have to phone Ken."

"I'll do it." Her mother went to the phone in the hall.

"No . . . wait a minute, Mam. I want to check my answering service."

"Can't I do that for you – "

"No, no, it won't take a second." Michelle grabbed the receiver. She got the normal dialling tone.

No messages.

"Here, it's OK." She handed the receiver to her mother and made her way upstairs.

Now, what was all that about? Michelle was acting most peculiarly. Olive shrugged and dialled Ken's number.

"Hello." A female voice.

"May I speak to Ken, please?" Olive said guardedly.

"I'm sorry, he's not here at the moment. May I take a message? Oh, could you hold on a moment? I have to turn down the oven."

Turn down the oven? Who was this? A new housekeeper?

"Hello."

"Is that Beth?" Olive asked, trying to make her tone friendlier.

"No, did you want to speak to Beth?"

Olive didn't like the voice. It was controlled, husky, kind of superior. "Em, no. It's all right. I'll phone later." She was dying with curiosity. "With whom am I speaking?" she added in a posh voice.

"I'm Ken's wife."

"Oh, I see. Thank you."

Olive hung up.

I'm Ken's wife.

The bloomin' cheek of her answering the phone like that as if it was *her* house. Lady Muck!

Wait a minute, Olive Bolger. It is her house. She still has a legal stake in it. But what was she doing back in Griffith Avenue staying with her *separated* husband? Having a little holiday with her daughter?

This wasn't right at all. She'd give Ken a good telling-off when she saw him. What did he think he was playing at? His wife back in his home? Did he think he could have his cake and eat it?

No wonder poor Michelle wasn't feeling well.

Olive had the potatoes peeled and scrubbed when the telephone rang. Right, Mister Ken Leavy, you're going to get an earful now. This isn't Michelle you're dealing with. No more excuses, no more shilly-shallying.

Action time.

She wiped her hands on a tea-towel and answered the phone.

"Hello," she said in her best telephone voice.

"I'm looking for Michelle Bolger."

A man's voice. Not Ken's.

"I'm very sorry, Michelle isn't available just now. May I take a message?"

"Em . . . no, it doesn't matter. I'll phone again."

Nice accent.

"Are you looking for an organist?"

"Pardon? Oh, no. No. Nothing like that. It's . . . personal."

"Perhaps you'd like to leave your name and I could get her to call you back?"

"That's all right, thank you. I'll phone her in a day or two."

"Right you are. Thank you, Mister . . . ?"

The man laughed. A little tickly laugh. Most appealing.

"O'Connor. My name's Cyril O'Connor."

"I'm Michelle's mother, Mr O'Connor. Will she know who . . . "

"Oh, yes, Mrs Bolger, she'll know who I am. Michelle and I met recently – in Vienna, in fact."

"Really?" Olive was getting more and more interested. "In Vienna? How nice."

"It was."

The way he spoke made Olive's heart quiver. He had such a seductive voice. "And Michelle will know what it's in connection with, will she?"

"Indeed. There'll be no need to explain. Michelle and I are old friends."

"Fine, Mr O'Connor. I'll tell her you rang."

"Much obliged. Sorry for troubling you."

Cheerful and well-mannered too!

"No trouble at all, Mr O'Connor."

"Thank you, you're most gracious. Will you tell her I'll be in touch again *very* soon."

"Certainly. Goodbye."

He sounded nice, this Cyril O'Connor. Rich. Yes, sure of himself in that way rich people are. Olive sang as she basted the chicken and turned the roast potatoes. Michelle was a sly old thing, hadn't as much as mentioned his name before. Who was he? Lovely accent, cultured. Finished his words beautifully, like a foreigner. Was she having a secret fling with him?

No, Michelle wouldn't do a thing like that.

More's the pity. It might shake Ken up a bit. Olive knew precisely what she'd do in her daughter's situation. She'd invite this Cyril for lunch some day, or better still for dinner. If he looked half as good as he sounded, Ken would be seething with jealousy.

That was the trouble with Michelle. She was too open, too forthcoming and too damn trusting. Didn't believe in playing games, she said. But with men, you *had* to play these little games sometimes. Her daughter was very intelligent and talented, but sometimes, Olive surmised, she was a bit naive.

Blast it, the phone again.

Twenty-Nine

"Did you have a nice sleep, love?" Olive took the Erin Gravy Rich from the cupboard.

"Yes, thanks. I feel a bit more human."

"Good. Set the table there, will you? I'm not sure where you keep your cutlery. It's taken me ages to get this dinner ready. I think you're slower in someone else's kitchen."

"Here are the knives and forks, Mam. You set the table and I'll carve."

"Good, I'm useless at carving, I usually end up throwing out half the chicken. Declan bought me an electric carving-knife for my birthday but I'm terrified of using it – don't say that to him, though."

"When I was talking to Declan the other day, he told me you'd joined some sort of a committee."

"Mmh, the Santry Community Association."

"Very impressive!"

"It's time I took more of an interest in the area."

"The Community Association? Are they the ones trying to save Santry Woods?"

"Yes, Fingal Council want the site for development, worth twenty million if it's rezoned, they say."

"Twenty million!"

"But without rezoning the land's worth only about two and a half million – although that's not the point."

Since when had her mother become environmentally conscious?

"We'll have no natural amenities left at all the way those developers ride roughshod over everybody."

Michelle put the condiments on the table. "I saw something about it on the RTÉ news. The protesters from the Glen of the Downs are going to give their support, I believe."

"Mmh." Olive stirred the gravy. "The eco-warriors. It's great publicity. Once you get the story out there in the public arena, you'd be amazed at how things can change. I'm helping to write the notices," she continued, "petition the local politicians, that sort of thing."

She made it sound as if she'd been doing it all her life.

"Well, Mam, so long as you don't intend to take up residence in a tree!"

Olive laughed. "You'd never know. Oh, by the way,

there was a phone call for you earlier. I didn't want to wake you."

"Ken?"

"No. A Cyril O'Connor."

No, no, no.

The carving-knife slipped and gashed Michelle's left hand, just above the thumb. The blood spurted out and she grabbed a tea-towel. She pressed it to her hand to stem the flow of blood.

"Michelle!" her mother cried in alarm.

She rushed her daughter over to the sink. "Let me look at it. It's not too bad. Keep it there under the water for a few minutes. Have you any bandages?"

"Bathroom cabinet," Michelle gasped. The cut was small but it stung.

Olive dashed upstairs.

Cyril O'Connor rang. *Cyril O'Connor rang.*

"Down in a minute!" her mother shouted from the landing.

He'd phoned and given his name.

His name.

Oh, Christ.

The floor came up to meet her and the room swayed.

Her mother hurried back with the bandages and a bottle of Savlon. "Michelle, sit down, come on love, sit down here. You've gone as pale as a sheet. Give me your hand. There, it's not too bad. Look, it's not deep at

323

all." Olive dabbed gently with a piece of cotton wool soaked in the disinfectant. "That'll clean it out properly." She expertly fitted the bandage.

Michelle nodded.

"We don't want you getting tetanus. Maybe we should go the hospital for a shot, just to be on the safe side?"

"No," Michelle said feebly, "it'll be all right. It's throbbing a bit but I'll be OK."

"Sure? I'll get you a drink of water."

"Thanks." Michelle, her hands shaking, took the glass from her mother.

"Take it easy, Michelle. Drink the water slowly. You've had a shock. I hate to see you like this."

"Like what?"

"Jittery, fidgety."

"I'm all right."

"No, you're not. I'm worried about you. Even Declan said he'd noticed something about you recently . . . what's the matter, love?"

"Nothing. Nothing's the matter."

Michelle sat and sipped the water as her mother fussed around with the dinner pots. She turned on the radio but Michelle went over and turned it off.

"Mam, what did . . . Cyril O'Connor say?"

Olive put a plate of chicken in front of her. "Try a little bit, Michelle. I don't think you're looking after yourself. You look drawn."

"I'm not hungry."

"Come on, love. Just eat a little bit. I gave you the breast – you don't like the leg, do you?"

Michelle sat at the table, staring into space.

"Some gravy? You always liked my gravy."

Food was her mother's solution to every problem.

"Tell me again, Mam. What did he say? Word for word."

"He didn't say much at all, Michelle. He was barely on for a minute." She spooned some gravy from the roasting-tin onto her daughter's plate. "He asked if you were here and I said that you – what's that I said? You weren't available, I think, something like that – "

"What did he say *after* that?"

Olive put roast potatoes on Michelle's plate. "Would you eat another one? They're quite small."

"No, no, two's plenty. Never mind that, what did he say?"

Olive dished up the vegetables. "Here, I'm giving you extra green beans, they're full of vitamins. I can't remember, Michelle. He mentioned something about Vienna, I think. Eat up before it gets cold, there's a good girl."

"Mam! This is *important*. I need to know what he said."

"Oh, for Pete's sake, Michelle, will you quit? You've me moithered with all these questions. I don't know what the hell – there, you've *me* at it now and I hate bad language – I don't know what he said. He gave his name and said he'd be in touch soon."

"He had the cheek to give his name!"

"Why wouldn't he?"

Because it brought the whole thing to a new level.

Now he *wanted* her to know who he was.

"Then Lynn rang, she said something about the lunch-time concert in the Hugh Lane Gallery. You're to give her a call about it if you want to go."

"OK, I'll phone her later. Cyril O'Connor, did he – "

"Listen, Michelle, I'd a much more worrying phone conversation. One I think you *should* take seriously."

"Oh?" Michelle moved her chicken around the plate.

"I rang Ken's house and – "

Michelle's thumb throbbed like an extra pulse. "Is he coming over this afternoon?"

"Ken was at the hotel, I was told."

"I didn't think he was working today. Were you talking to Beth?"

"No, Michelle, I wasn't. That's the point." Olive's eyes narrowed. "Do you *know* who answered Ken's phone? Toni, that's who."

Michelle tried not to register on her face the surprise she felt.

Her mother cut a piece of chicken and speared a green bean. "You never told me she was back."

Michelle stared out of the kitchen window. The

rosemary bush could do with a trim, she'd get around to it soon before the frosty weather arrived.

"Why is that woman staying in Ken's house, Michelle?"

Michelle pushed her dinner plate away.

"Well?" her mother persisted.

She couldn't handle *this* now.

"I don't know how you put up with it, Michelle, it wouldn't be me!"

Shut up, shut up, Mam.

"You'll have to be a bit more assertive." Olive clacked her fork on the plate. "She's very sly, Michelle. She'll worm her way back, I'm warning you."

"How do you know she's staying in Ken's house? She probably just dropped in for a visit. Toni always stays in The Fullerton when she's in Dublin."

"This time, she isn't." Olive opened the kitchen door. "I'll throw out the leftovers for the birds. You hardly touched your chicken, Michelle. No, Toni Leavy's back living in Griffith Avenue, all right."

She looked as if she was ready to come out of the red corner, gloves on, fists clenched.

"She was making the dinner, Michelle. You don't make the dinner if you've just *dropped in for a visit.*"

"*You* did!"

"Very funny. Here, I'll get dessert. You'll have to eat something, no wonder you're weak. You've an apple pie in the fridge. I could heat it and make custard."

Michelle gagged and rushed to the sink. Then her stomach heaved and she dry-retched, gasping for breath.

"Right, right, back to bed with you this instant." Olive put her arm around Michelle and led her out to the hall. "I'm going to phone the doctor."

"No, Mam, no."

"But – "

"No, the doctor can't do anything. I just need sleep," Michelle said wearily. "Sleep."

She opened her eyes slowly. Her body was sticky, damp. Her throat was raw and her tongue seemed to be swollen. Her legs felt like lead in the bed, it was painful to move them.

She closed her eyes again. Red-hot lights pricked her eye-balls, like needles piercing jelly.

She felt a cool hand on her forehead.

"Michelle, are you awake?"

"Sort of," she answered sleepily. "What time is it?"

"Twenty past five. I brought you up a drink of water and some ice cream."

Michelle struggled into a sitting position. "Thanks. No, don't open the curtains."

Olive leaned over the bed. "Are you feeling any better?"

"A bit. When I went to the bathroom, I actually vomited. I can't remember the last time I got sick like that. Not since I was a kid."

"I'd like you to see the doctor, Michelle."

"It's a hangover, Mam. A bad one but just a hangover."

"It's not like you to drink too much."

"No, and I won't be doing it again in a hurry."

Her mother paused. "I wish you'd tell me what's wrong."

"There's nothing wrong." She couldn't look her mother in the face.

Olive handed her the dish of ice cream. "Ken phoned. He's on his way over."

"Did you tell him I . . . I wasn't well?"

"Naturally."

"I'm glad he's coming. I want to apologise to him."

"Apologise for what?"

"Making a show of him last night."

"You will not. Don't dream of it. It's Ken who should be apologising to you. Bringing his wife back to his house and – "

"It's not like that at all."

"Isn't it?"

"No," Michelle insisted. "Ken isn't interested in Toni any more – not romantically."

"I wish I had your confidence. I don't like the idea of her being under the same roof as him. Ken's one of the best, Michelle, but at the end of the day . . . a man's a man and a woman's a woman."

"Very perceptive of you."

"Oh, this is just your bravado act, Michelle. Admit it, you don't like her being there any more than I do."

"No, I don't, but I'm going to wait until I've a full explanation from Ken before I go accusing him of . . . anything."

"I'll never understand you, never. Do you love Ken? You can tell me to mind my own business but you're my daughter and I hate to see you being . . . used, Michelle."

"Used? How can you say that?"

"Easily. Ken has you, he has his daughter and now he has his wife ensconced in his house. His wife, Michelle. *Ménage à trois*, is that what they call it?"

"Mam!"

"Don't 'Mam' me, Michelle. I never took Ken to be the Clintonic type but – "

"The *Clintonic* type?" Michelle laughed. "Did you make up that word just now?"

"Yes," Olive said, with no trace of a smile. "It might be appropriate."

"Look, you're jumping to all sorts of conclusions without knowing the facts and – "

"Right, so. Give me the facts."

Michelle sighed. "What's the point?"

"I'm beginning to think that this arrangement suits you, Michelle."

"What arrangement?"

Michelle was badly dehydrated. She swallowed a

mouthful of ice cream. Its cold softness soothed her throat.

"Because Ken's still married . . . it saves you from making a decision. The more I think about it, the more I think I might be right. Wasn't that what happened between you and Glenn?"

"That wasn't the same thing at all. I didn't want to settle in the States."

"But sure he was cracked about you, Michelle. Told me himself he was willing to come over to live in Ireland."

"No, Glenn would never have left his home, he – "

"Rubbish! Everything was fine when you were living together but the minute he mentioned marriage, you upped and left America without a backward glance. Michelle, are you afraid of getting married? Is that it? Afraid of commitment?"

"Of course not," Michelle retorted. "I'm with Ken for seven years. What's that if it isn't a commitment?"

"An easy option," her mother said quietly. "Ken has his career, his home, his daughter, a family life and you on the side."

"On the side? Don't be ridiculous. I have my home, my career, my friends and I have Ken."

"Have you, Michelle?"

"Yes, yes, I have."

How dare her mother speak to her like this?

"Well, that's what you say, Michelle, but I'm not sure what you have."

Michelle was boiling mad.

"What have you got?" she asked cruelly. "You had Dad but he's gone. You had Declan and me but you're living on your own now. What difference does it make? At the end of the day a lot of us end up living on our own. Fact of life. And I'm happy the way – "

"Are you?"

"Yes," Michelle said defiantly.

Her mother took the dish of ice cream and put it on the bedside table. "All right, love. I'm sorry. I don't want to upset you. I care about you, you know that."

Michelle looked at the worry lines etched on her mother's face. "I'm sorry too. Sorry for what I said."

Her mother kissed her forehead.

"We're a right pair, aren't we?" said Michelle.

"What you said, Michelle. You were wrong, you know. Things change and life moves on but some things last. I'll always have you and Declan."

"And I'll always have Ken."

Would she? Olive hoped so.

"Michelle, I want you to know that I'm here for you. I don't want to be interfering or bossy or needy but I do want you to know that I'm always ready to help, to listen."

Michelle squeezed her mother's hand.

"I know that. Please tell me again, Mam. I need to know exactly what Cyril O'Connor said."

"Oh no, not that again." Olive frowned. She couldn't make out the look in her daughter's eyes. Fear? Loathing? "He said he'd be in touch and I asked him for his name and he gave it to me. There, that's it. Now forget about him, Michelle, whoever he is."

"And he actually gave you his name! Said he was Cyril O'Connor!"

"No, told me he was Julio Inglesias."

"Ah, Mam. I'm . . . I really *am* angry with him."

"Why? What has he done?"

"Things. Some weird things . . . I don't want to speak to him and I hate the idea of his having my number. He . . . he gives me the creeps."

Olive put her arm around her daughter. "It was just a phone call. No harm done. If you don't want to see him or speak to him . . . "

Just a phone call.

"Mam, don't ever give him any information about me. You don't realise – "

"I didn't, Michelle, I didn't. I'd never tell a complete stranger anything over the phone. Mind you, I didn't think he was a stranger. He seemed to know you well – "

"He doesn't know me at all. And I don't *want* to know him, do you hear me?" she shouted. "I don't want to know him."

"When he said he met you in Vienna, I presumed – "

"I am *not* a friend of Cyril O'Connor's and he certainly

333

isn't a friend of mine. If he ever rings here again, just hang up. He's a weirdo."

Olive was taken aback by Michelle's vehemence. If her daughter didn't calm down, she'd make herself really ill.

Thirty

Ken looked at her, waiting for some response. Michelle lay back on the pillow and closed her eyes.

"So, what do you think, Mich?"

"You've moved into The Fullerton?"

"Yes. It makes sense. Toni will stay with Beth for a few weeks. She's welcome to the house and all that goes with it. I'm looking forward to the break."

"I see."

"The truth is, she came back to Dublin with no definite plans. Toni always gives the impression that she's on top of everything but it's the opposite. She's quite scatty. Unpredictable. Her apartment deal fell through – trouble getting a mortgage or something. Then Beth put her off the other one she was offered."

"Why couldn't she stay in her mother's house?"

"She doesn't get on with Gwen." He shrugged. "It might be nice for Beth to have her mother around," he added. "I'm tired dealing with all the problems on my own. Maybe I've created some of them by being too easy on her, I admit that. Beth's getting beyond me, Mich. When she was small, it was easier, I knew where I was but . . . her friends, they seem to have taken over. Nothing I say means anything to her any more."

"Ken, that's not because you brought her up on your own, that can happen anyway – "

"Yes, but Beth's right about one thing – I do take everything seriously and that is because I'm on my own. Two parents can share the responsibility . . . I'm afraid for her, Mich. I don't want to see her hurt or – "

"She knows that, Ken."

"Does she? Beth's sixteen, thinks she's a woman, sees me as some kind of a tyrant who's deliberately trying to spoil her fun. It's not that I don't want her to enjoy life but . . . "

"She knows you care about her."

"That's not the impression I get." He paused. "Sometimes I think she blames me for the split up – "

"I'm sure you're wrong about that."

"I'm not apportioning blame here, but – I resent Toni. I was the one who stayed and got on with it. Toni left and saw Beth when it suited her but she's the big cheese. As far as Beth's concerned, Toni can do no wrong. It aggravates me, Mich."

"It would annoy me too."

"Do you know something? I'm *glad* Toni's back. Let her deal with Beth for a while. Maybe she can sort out the problems. She can't do any worse than I have."

"Don't be so hard on yourself, Ken. Beth will be fine, you'll see. You've always been there for her. You've done your best."

"Maybe my best wasn't good enough," he said despondently.

"There's not a parent alive who doesn't feel that at some stage."

"This sounds daft, but I'd love a second chance. I can't have that though, can I? I feel I've made so many mistakes with Beth, that I was only learning and if I could just . . . what's the use?"

"You're feeling edgy, Ken. I don't know if letting Toni stay in the house was wise. It might make things more awkward."

"No, it won't. I'll be much freer, have more time for you. I've been neglecting you."

"I've been busy." She hated the way he did that, assumed she needed looking after. "You don't have to worry about me."

"I know that, I just think we should spend more time with each other."

"Difficult. Neither of us works regular hours."

"That's what I want to discuss with you, Mich. I've been giving it a lot of thought. I think we should move in together."

. . .

Beth came downstairs, dressed in a very short black mini,

a red boob tube, long black boots and an ankle-length red coat, which she left swinging open to accentuate the shortness of her skirt.

"You look gorgeous, Beth. Would you like a drink before you go?"

"Better not, Mum. I'm meeting Carmel and Sophie at eight."

"You look absolutely stunning. The other two won't be a patch on you. You've lovely long legs. You get them from my side of the family." Toni giggled and took another sip of gin. "Ooh, not enough tonic. Be a pet and hand the bottle to me, would you, Beth? Thanks. So, you're not too upset about your dad moving out?"

"Not if it means you're here, Mum. It's deadly having you back."

Toni raised her glass. "I'll drink to that."

"If only . . . if only you – "

"What, darling?"

"I wish you and Dad – I wish you'd rethink this divorce thing."

"Don't worry. I haven't given up yet, Beth. Not by a long shot."

"Are you serious, Mum?"

"I certainly am. I don't like defeat, Beth. Never did. I'm not giving up your father without a bloody good fight, I promise you."

Beth hugged her.

"Now, go off and have a good time. Tell Carmel I was asking for her."

"Will do, if Mark phones . . . "

"I'll put him off in a nice way," Toni assured her. "Where are you going, anyway?"

"For a drink, then The Back Gate."

"Is that a club? Where is it?"

"Cathal Brugha Street. Don't worry. I'll get a taxi home. I should be back at about three."

"I'm not worried. I'll be fast asleep, so don't wake me."

"This is so cool."

"What is?"

"Not getting a lecture about the time I'm to be in at. Gee, Mum, you've no idea how great it is to have you back!"

Toni blew on her fingernails. "This pink is a new shade, what do you think of it?"

"Not bad. I prefer mine, though." She showed off her black nails. "Mark hates me wearing this. Says it look cheap."

"Have you finished with him, Beth?" Toni asked hopefully.

" . . . Not exactly. I just told him we were seeing too much of one another. He agreed . . . kind of."

"You've gone off him, haven't you?"

"I'm not sure how I feel anymore. He's nice, generous. He's very good-looking and I fancy him . . ."

"Yes, he is handsome," Toni agreed. "In a dark smouldering way! But isn't he a bit too serious for you, Beth? Mark struck me as being the studious type."

"He is," Beth said, "but that's OK, Mum. He's ambitious, I guess. The real problem is . . . "

Toni picked up the newspaper to check the TV programmes. "What? What's the *real* problem?"

She smiled at her daughter. What she'd give to be sixteen again! The clothes, the make-up, the romance.

"He's always broke. The money he made in the States, that's going to pay for books and stuff. His parents aren't that well off, so he can't look to them for support."

"I thought Mark was living at home?"

"He is. I mean they feed him, obviously, but he can't go scrounging money for socialising. You know he saved enough to bring me away for a few days – "

"Where did you go?" Toni asked, her eyes glued to the televsion.

"We didn't. I went to London with you, so he gave the money to his mother for board and lodging. Gross!"

"Mmh."

"Mum, if he phones tell him . . . tell him I'll get back to him, OK?"

"What, love?"

"*Mum!* Have you been listening to me at all?"

"Of course I have."

Beth kissed her mother on the cheek. "It's brilliant having you back." When she got to the door, she turned back and blew her mother a kiss. "Tell Mark I'll definitely phone him tomorrow night."

Toni would do no such thing.

* * *

Michelle looked at him. "Move in together, Ken?"

"I'm forty-one, Mich. I don't want to spend the next twenty years working, squeezing you in at weekends, living on my own, not having time for . . . us. If we lived together, at least we'd – "

"But what about Beth? You always said you didn't want to disrupt her life."

"I was wrong, Mich." He leaned over and kissed her forehead. "Beth would have adjusted."

Michelle closed her eyes. She should have expected this, but even though she knew things couldn't go on forever the way they were, it was still a shock hearing the words. *Move in together*.

"We love each other, Mich."

"But living together, Ken – it's a huge step."

"Yes, it is, but it's the right step for us . . . isn't it?" He looked at her earnestly. "Don't you want us to be together?"

She took his hand. "I thought we *were* together."

"You know what I mean. Maybe this isn't the best time to discuss it, you're not well. I'll go downstairs and make you a cup of tea, or would you like a drink?"

"No, thanks, I couldn't look at a drink. Ken . . . if we decide to . . . live together, how would it work? I mean would we live in your house or mine or – "

He came back to the bedside and smiled down at her. "We don't have to go into all that now, Mich. I only brought up the idea today so you could think about it, OK? We don't have to rush."

"But we do have to consider Beth – "

"Of course. I'll say nothing to her yet. At the moment she has enough to cope with, hearing about the divorce."

"How did she take it?"

"Hard to say. I don't think she believes it's going to happen." He looked hard at Michelle. "It is, though, this time I'm determined. I feel as if a huge weight has been lifted off my shoulders. Other things are falling into place too. I've talked to Jonathan about my ideas for extending the hotel and he's all for it. I'm going over to London soon for a meeting with him."

"You're never happier than when you're organising, Ken Leavy!"

"True and this is the ideal time for us to sort out our lives, Mich. We have to move forward."

"Yes, I know, but you're right, not today. I've already had a gruelling session with Mam."

"One thing at a time, eh?" He ran a hand through her hair, pushing it back from her forehead.

"I'd better get up."

"No hurry. I'll bring up the tea."

* * *

Ten-thirty. Nothing on the bloody box. Toni poured herself another gin. She'd drunk half the bottle. She was bored, bored.

Bored.

Miley from *Glenroe* was having a better sex life than she was. She wondered would Gwen come into Leeson Street for an hour or two. Toni wanted a bit of excitement. A few drinks, a few laughs. It was obvious Ken wasn't going to fall into her lap as easily as she'd thought. How long would it take? Three weeks? Longer?

She couldn't wait around for a month without . . . without some excitement. Dublin wasn't shaping up the way she'd expected. If only she could get her PR business off the ground. Maybe setting up on her own was a bit unrealistic? That new contact, Sam Mulligan, maybe he'd be some help? Said he'd an interesting proposition for her. She'd have to wait and see. Ah hell! She picked up the phone and dialled her sister's phone number.

"Hello."

Deep voice. Male. Definitely male.

"May I speak to Gwen, please?"

"Who's speaking?"

What a cheek!

"This is her sister speaking," Toni said frostily.

"Hold on a moment, please."

Who the hell was *he*? Did Gwen have a *boyfriend*?!

"Hello, Toni. Heard you were back. Beth called me this afternoon. She's delighted."

"Mmh, she is. Listen Gwen, do you feel like going out tonight?"

"Tonight? It's a bit late, Toni."

"Not for a nightclub, it's not. Come on, Gwen. We'll have a laugh."

"And it's Sunday. Work in the morning."

"So what? Don't be such a misery-guts! Come on, it'll be fun!"

"I've . . . I've somebody here, Toni."

"Ah ha! I wanted to ask you who answered the phone."

"That was Robert, my . . . friend."

"Your *friend?* Come off it, Gwen. He's your new fella, isn't he? Where did you meet him? At work?"

"No . . . actually. I met him at Mum's funeral."

"What!"

"I'll tell you all about it when I see you, Toni," Gwen whispered into the phone. "I'd better go."

"Phone me tomorrow, Gwen. I want all the intimate details!"

Toni replaced the receiver. Gwen doing a line! Robert. Robert who? Wonder what he did? Probably a department manager from Arnotts? Sounded like a bit of a prat.

Toni flicked off the TV. At least Gwen *had* a date!

* * *

"What was that?" Michelle pulled away from Ken.

"What?" He kissed her neck.

"A noise. I heard a noise downstairs."

"It was next door, Mich, the O'Rourkes. Someone banged a door."

"I think it was down in the sitting-room, Ken." Michelle got out of bed and pulled on her dressing-gown.

"Come back, Mich. It's nothing."

"I'm going down anyway, I have to lock up."

"I'll do it."

"No, it's all right."

"I'll do it, Mich," he offered. "I can see you're nervous – "

"I'm not," she insisted. "No, stay where you are." She tucked the sheet around him. "I have you where I want you!"

She tiptoed downstairs, her bare feet sinking into the carpet. She passed the hall mirror and stopped to look at herself. She looked much better, the colour was back in her cheeks. She smiled at her reflection. Then she spotted him . . . in the mirror . . . behind her.

She whipped around. "What are you doing? I – "

He grabbed her and crushed her body to him. He kissed her hard on the mouth, taking her breath away.

"You can't get away from me, Michelle!"

She tried to fight him off. "Let me go."

He backed her up against the wall.

"Let me go," she squealed.

"No chance. You're driving me crazy."

"Yes, you're crazy. Completely craz – "

"I have to have you." He crushed his lips to hers again. "No, don't bother to put up a fight, Michelle. You want this as much as I do."

"Stop – "

He laughed. "I love it when you struggle – can't wait, can you?" He pulled her down on the carpet. "This is going to be one night you'll never forget. I'm going to . . ."

He entered her quickly.

"I'm going to devour you. Ooh, you feel so good!"

"So do you, Ken!' She bit his shoulder. "So do you! This is highly debauched, making love on my hall floor."

"Yes, it is, but isn't it fantastic?" He rolled onto his back, still inside her, taking her with him. He grasped her shoulders.

She thrust her hips forward, pushing him deeper inside.

"I love you, Michelle."

The gnawing sensation began slowly and wound its way down, down, circling deeper, deeper within her. Her insides turned fluid and she felt herself being lifted, higher and higher, up, up, up.

Ken adored her. He loved this woman with every atom of his being. He wanted to be with her always, to love her, care for her, protect her.

She laughed into his chest. "God, we're both soaking."

"'Slick with sweat,' isn't that what they say in the books? Their bodies were *slick with sweat*."

"Who cares what they say in books?" She kissed him. "The doors, Ken. I came down here to lock up!"

"We both came, Michelle. And it was heavenly." He nuzzled her neck. "I'll see to the locks. You go back upstairs. Let's have a shower together."

"No, a bubble bath."

"Mmh, a bath!"

"Race you!"

She was up and off before he could catch her.

Thirty-One

Beth,

There's a quiche and some coleslaw in the fridge. I've gone to meet Alison Geoghan and her husband for a few drinks. Her brother Sam is having a party for his advertising friends, so I'll go on to that. Need to make more contacts if I'm ever to get my business off the ground. Hope your German exam went well.

I'll see you some time tomorrow – not at breakfast, though!

Love,

Toni.

Beth crumpled up the note and dumped it in the bin under the kitchen sink. She hadn't seen her mother in three days. Yesterday didn't count – Toni had been twisted after her liquid lunch with other *contacts*.

Beth wasn't in the mood for quiche – if she ate one more she'd turn into an egg, and she was sick of sausages and chips, too. Last Saturday, Toni had decided that Beth needed a good nourishing meal, so she'd presented her with a Chinese takeaway.

And what really got on Beth's wick was this latest effort of having to call her mother "Toni". Did it make her feel younger or something? Hadn't taken her long to grow tired of the nurturing role, had it? Two fun-filled weeks.

Beth went to the fridge. A salad would be a welcome change from all the stodge. What happened to the tomatoes? And Beth could have sworn there'd been a green pepper on the bottom shelf yesterday. She pulled out the vegetable tray but all she found were a few soggy leaves of lettuce and a bunch of scallions which had seen better days.

Toni had obviously been too busy to go shopping. Beth would have to make do with coleslaw and cold ham. She took the meat from the plastic bag and smelled it. Gone off!

Shit, shit, shit, shit. *Shit!*

Beth was exhausted after eight classes, a basketball match at lunch-time and a particularly difficult French test. At least when her father was here, he'd made some effort at preparing dinner. She was sorry now she'd bitched about his cooking.

Hope your German exam went well.

I don't do German, Mother dear. I study French.

Carmel's mother had a hot dinner waiting for her kids every day. Mrs Richardson was a super cook – rustled up roasts, casseroles, lasagnes, stir-fries – whatever took Carmel's fancy.

Lucky Carmel.

There was some Brie in the egg compartment of the fridge and Beth found some crackers in a press which, thankfully, hadn't passed their sell-by date. Where were all the plates?

No. Please no!

There they were – stacked high in the water-logged sink with cups, saucers, mugs and bowls. The foul-smelling water had gone a pinkish red and there were disgusting-looking green objects floating on the top. Scummy!

Did her mother never wash up after herself?

Beth threw down the pen in dismay. Her copy page was covered in red marks and mad Mac, the psychotic who taught (tried to teach) French, would refuse to look at the next exercise till Beth had done all these corrections. Fecking hell!

Beaucoup d'erreurs.

She knew it was full of bleedin' errors. What she didn't know was how to correct them.

Time for a blow.

She opened the side pocket of her schoolbag and got her pencil case. She took out a Tampax applicator where she kept her precious supply hidden. Clever, wasn't she? No teacher would dare to search there.

Josie had passed two joints to her under the jacks door today. Beth had nearly died when "Freyne the Pain" came into the loos on her rounds. Pity Sara and Orla had been nicked, but the stupid little bitches nearly set fire to the wooden frame as they puffed out the window. Good job it was only Silk Cut Purple! Three days' suspension for their trouble.

Mad wagons.

Beth inhaled deeply, held it in her lungs and counted to ten, then blew out slowly. Another few puffs and she'd be feeling no pain!

Michelle stepped back out of the porch and looked up. There was a light on in Beth's bedroom. She must be listening to her music – couldn't hear above the noise. Michelle tried the doorbell again. Still no answer. Ken had told her that Toni wouldn't be there and this would be a good time to pick up her CDs. He'd forgotten them when he'd packed her clothes and other stuff.

She rang again.

Had Beth looked out the window and decided not to open up when she's seen who it was? Michelle wouldn't put anything past her.

One more try.

"Someone's knockin' at the door, somebody's ringin' the bell." Beth giggled as she mimed Paul McCartney's words into the mirror.

A long peal made her chuckle even more.

"Open the door, let them in!"

She collapsed on her bed, laughing loudly. The yellow walls of her bedroom looked bright and beautiful, much more yellow than she'd noticed before.

"All things bright and beautiful," she sang at the top of her voice, as she admired her duvet. She loved her blue duvet, sky-blue.

"Sky of blue and sea of green, in our yeh-hell-o submarine."

Another puff. Another cackle.

Three sharp raps on the front door knocker. Ooh, whoever was there was getting very very ma-ad!

"Knock three times on the ceiling if you wa-ant me! Twice on the pipe, if the answer is no-oh-oh!"

You couldn't beat the old songs. Her mates slagged her off for being into this music – what did *they* know?

Let's have a little peek out the window and see who's there. Might be Mark. Would he fancy a quickie?

Or, with any luck, a slowie?

Ah, he never went beyond a good feel. Wonder how he'd *feel* if he knew what his little Beth had been up to? She giggled as she pulled back the curtains. It was dark outside, too dark to make out who was standing at the door.

Mark should look on the bright side – he wouldn't have the trouble of breaking her in.

"Always look on the bright si-ide of life. De-dum, de-dum, de-dum, de-dum."

Maybe he'd be glad?

Maybe not.

One more drag and this baby would be floating.

"I am sailing, I am sailing home ageh-hen 'cross the sea."

Another long, loud ring.

Ah, fuck it! She'd have to go down and answer the shagging thing.

Michelle was about to give up and go away when the door opened. Beth, her hair dishevelled and her eye make-up smeared, stood there grinning.

"Hi!" She sniggered. "Dad's not here."

"I know," Michelle said. "I just called to collect my CDs, Beth. Is it OK if I come in?"

Beth stood to one side and bowed. *"Entrez!"*

"Thanks."

Was Beth drunk?

"Your dad said he'd packed them in a box. Do you know where he left them, by any chance?"

"Nope. Sorry."

Beth didn't look sorry.

"Maybe I could have a look in the sitting-room?"

"Sure, why not?"

Beth skipped ahead of her and opened the sitting-room door. Michelle spotted a large cardboard box under the sideboard.

"Great, here they are! Ah, I see you're doing your homework. Sorry for disturbing you, Beth."

"You're not." The girl pouted. "French. Can't do it."

"Maybe I can help?" Michelle moved over to the coffee table where Beth had laid out her books. She picked up the copy. "Do you mind if I have a look?"

Beth shrugged. "Be my guest."

Michelle poured over the page. "It's years since I studied French but I used to like it."

Probably brilliant at it, Beth surmised spitefully. Clever Clogs Bolger. The lick-arse of the class.

"Look, Beth. It's the past tense you've the problem with."

"I know."

Mistress of the bleedin' obvious!

Michelle ignored her tone. "If you're using a verb that's – what do you call it? Conjugated, yes – conjugated with *être* you have to add an *e*, because you're writing in the feminine form. You see there, *je suis sortie*. Do you know what I mean?"

Beth looked at it. "And *s* for the plural. Yeah, but it's the *avoir* I don't understand."

"Hold on, let me think. Do you have a grammar book there?"

Beth handed her the textbook. "The grammar section's at the back."

Michelle studied it for a few minutes. Ken's daughter had been smoking, she could smell it from her breath. A

353

pungent aroma hung in the air; Michelle had noticed it the minute she'd walked in the door. Would she say something?

No, none of her business.

"Right, Beth, now I remember. If the sentence has a direct object and if – "

"Oh yeah, if the object goes before the verb then the past participle agrees."

"Exactly. You do know how to do it. Look, here's one in the second paragraph with *faire* and another one further down with *écrire*. Do you want to correct them and I'll check them for you? Another pair of eyes comes in handy."

"I couldn't be arsed."

Fine with Michelle.

"On the other hand, I don't want a detention this Friday – we're all going to The Mean Fiddler. I hate the place but the others like it for some odd reason." Beth looked at her doubtfully. "Would you mind going through it? It's only two pages."

"No, I'd be glad of a few minute's rest before I go on to choir practice. Wednesday is my busy afternoon in the college. I'm exhausted."

"How about a cup of tea?"

Michelle was taken aback by the girl's offer. It wasn't like Beth. "Tell you what, you go ahead with the corrections and I'll make us both a coffee . . . if that's all right."

Beth nodded. "Great, you know where everything is."

Was that a smart remark?

Beth saw Michelle wrinkle up her nose. "What's the matter?"

"Nothing," Michelle said quickly. "I got a funny smell."

Beth blushed. "I've been burning some incense sticks upstairs."

"Oh, is that what it is?" Michelle nodded innocently as she went out.

"Mmh."

Jaysus! Michelle bloody well knew. Would she tell her father? Ah, shite, anyway.

"Thanks for helping me with the French, Michelle. Mad Mac will be floored when she takes up my copy. It'll ruin her day, she'll have less to moan about. That woman wrecks my head. So, thanks again."

"No problem. Are you meeting your dad tomorrow?"

"I think so." Beth opened the hall door. "He told me to call in to the hotel after school. We're going bowling."

"Good."

"Michelle . . . do you . . . do you want to come with us?"

"I have to work, but thanks for the offer."

"What a pain! Most of your evenings are taken up with work, aren't they? I don't know how you stick it."

"That's the way it goes, Beth. My pupils are in school during the day. Music lessons are for afters!"

Beth nodded. "Anyhow, thanks again for your help."

"Any time. See you."

"Michelle, when you're talking . . . when you're talking to Dad, you won't say anything – "

"About the incense?"

Beth stuck her hands in her jeans' pockets. "I'm not really into it, I mean it's not a problem . . . I can take it or leave it."

Michelle hesitated. "I'd leave it so, if I were you."

* * *

It was after nine-thirty by the time the choir practice had ended. Michelle spoke briefly to some of the parents who'd driven down to collect their children. She was anxious to get home and put her feet up; it had been an extremely long day.

She said good night to Paddy, the sacristan, left the church grounds and crossed the road at the traffic lights at Collins Avenue. She entered the laneway which connected with her road and looked over her shoulder. Not a sinner around.

The October evening was blustery so she kept in near to the wall for shelter. The bushes and trees from the neighbouring gardens whooshed and sighed eerily in the wind. The street lamp on the corner threw ghostly shadows and shapes all around.

Footsteps behind her.

Michelle swallowed.

One set of footsteps.

Her heartbeat quickened but she tried not to break into a run.

The footsteps grew louder. She could hear *breathing* now. Louder and louder, nearer and nearer.

Footsteps.

Breathing.

Footsteps.

Breathing.

Louder, louder, louder.

Nearer, nearer, nearer.

Michelle's knees wobbled. Her stomach floated up under her ribs and back down again. Her chest tightened.

She half-turned her head but didn't slow down.

The man was five or six yards behind her. He wore a dark hat and an overcoat with the collar turned up. She couldn't make out his features in the dusky light.

The lane got longer and longer.

The footsteps grew nearer and nearer.

She couldn't help it – she panicked and started to run.

The man ran, too.

Her heart in her mouth, Michelle tightened her grip

on her music-bag and dashed on, towards the exit. Just a few more yards and she'd be there. Five, four, three . . . almost . . . two . . .

She tripped over a stone and went crashing to the ground, face first.

"Ms Bolger, are you all right?"

The voice came from very far away.

"Ms Bolger? Ms Bolger? Can you hear me?"

Pain pounded.

"She's coming to. Got a big cut on her forehead. Get her a glass of water, someone."

"Come on, out of the way. No, don't move her. She might have broken something."

Pain pulsed.

"Thanks. Look, here's a glass of water, Ms Bolger. Can you sit up? Here, have a little sip of this."

Dots danced in front of her eyes.

Pain.

"That's right, good girl. Sit up there, that's it. You're OK, aren't you? Have another sip."

Her throat was sore. Scratchy.

"Come on, Ms Bolger. You'll be fine now. You just had a little turn. Lucky for you that Mr Nealon was walking behind you, wasn't it? Try another little sip, go on now."

Water.

"Ah, you'll be as right as rain now, so you will. You tripped, that was all. Could happen to a bishop. Mr

Nealon, God bless you, you got a bit of a fright too, you poor man."

A face swam into view.

"There, there, Ms Bolger. It's Charlie Wilson from across the street. You know me now, don't you?"

Michelle squinted.

"That's right. And here's Mr Nealon. Wasn't it lucky he was right behind you? Said he thought you had some sort of a funny turn, a dizzy spell or something."

Michelle tried to focus.

"Here, have another sip of this water. You could do with a brandy, I'd say."

Michelle gulped at the drink. The pain in her brain hammered and pounded but her eyesight began to return to normal.

"I'm sorry," she mumbled.

"Don't be apologising. Mr Nealon and I are going to help you up now and then we'll walk you to your door. All right?"

Michelle stiffened as the two men linked her into a standing position. "Thanks," she mumbled. "Sorry to cause you all this bother."

"No bother at all, Ms Bolger." Charlie Wilson would have lots to tell Teresa and the kids around the dinner table this evening. "Isn't that what neighbours are for?"

Was she *on* something? Drugs, maybe? Musicians were a funny class of people. Arty-farty. No, probably not. She was a very down-to-earth woman, judging by what his Teresa said. Michelle Bolger kept herself to herself, no nonsense, no trouble, no complaints. But she was there if you needed her. Hadn't Teresa borrowed a ladder from her only the other day?

Ian Nealon opened Michelle's gate. "Can you make it up the step? You're a bit shaky after the fall but you'll be fine when we get you inside."

Thirty-Two

Ian Nealon handed Michelle a mug of hot sweet tea. It was the strangest thing to see him in her kitchen – like a dream where you know it's your house, but it's not like your house at all. Distorted, not quite right.

Michelle hadn't spoken more than two or three words in her life to this man. He was a neighbour, someone she said "hello" or "good evening" to on her way back from work, someone she nodded to as he weeded his front garden or got into his car.

"You should get that cut seen to, miss," he mumbled.

He closed the top of the carton and put the milk back in the fridge. Michelle was hoping he wouldn't notice the dirt – she'd been meaning to clean the fridge for ages.

He was as uncomfortable as she was. "Is there anyone you'd like me to phone?"

"No, Mr Nealon, I'm grand now. You go on home.

Please tell Mr Wilson I said thanks. You've both been very kind."

Relief spread over his face. "Not at all." He edged his way to the kitchen door.

"Mr Nealon," she said, standing up shakily.

"Yes?" he asked, praying she wouldn't detain him further.

"Did you . . . did you notice anyone else in the lane?"

He looked perplexed.

"A man?" Michelle prompted. "Behind me?"

He shook his head. "No, I was behind you. There was no one else in the lane."

"I see. Thanks again."

He left the kitchen door ajar, walked up the hallway to the front door, had his hand on the latch to open it, changed his mind and tottered back to the kitchen. For the first time, Michelle noticed that he wasn't too steady on his feet. He hadn't got his walking-cane, she realised. Mr Nealon always carried a walking-cane.

"I didn't see anybody walking but there was a man getting into a car, near the entrance to the lane. I noticed him because I'd seen the car a few times before, parked on our street. A dark green Corsa."

"Dark green?" Michelle said faintly.

"Mmh. He's been here a lot lately. Must be visiting. At first I thought he was a parent, collecting one of your piano pupils. But he parks here at different times, sometimes in the morning. You don't usually teach in the mornings, do you?"

"No."

Ian Nealon saw quite a lot.

A retired postman – a widower, as far as she knew. Lived on his own a few doors down on the other side of the street. Late sixties or thereabouts. He must spend a lot of his time looking out of his window.

"Thanks, Mr Nealon."

"Ian, please call me Ian . . . I'll look in on you tomorrow, miss. You might need shopping or something."

"Oh, there's no need. It's very thoughtful of you to offer but – "

"Right you are." He nodded politely and left.

A dark green car. Her mother had mentioned a green car, hadn't she?

* * *

"Merciful hour, Michelle!"

Olive hauled her daughter in off the doorstep in Shanowen Road. "What happened? You look as if you've gone a few rounds with Mike Tyson."

"I tripped, it's nothing."

"Nothing? A big gash on your forehead and you call it nothing? Shouldn't you have a bandage on it?"

"I think it'll heal quicker in the air. I've put some antiseptic ointment on it."

"What's come over you?" Her mother looked at her suspiciously.

"I don't know what you mean."

"First your hand, now your face. You're like the walking wounded."

"Stigmata!"

"Michelle, don't blaspheme! Look under the eye – a big yellow bruise on your cheek. That'll go purple."

"You're a great comfort!"

"How did it happen this time?" Olive ambled down the hall into her kitchen.

"What do you mean *this time*?" Michelle followed her, wishing she'd stayed at home. "I've cut myself twice and you're going on as if I was indulging in some kind of masochistic ritual."

"All I asked was how it happened."

"Last night in the laneway, I fell over a stone or something."

"Did you go to the hospital?"

"Don't be silly, it's a scratch. No fussing, Mam. Come on, I'm off to Omni for my groceries. You can get yours at the same time. Where's that shopping-thingy on wheels I bought you?"

"I'm all right for groceries, Fiona was here yesterday. She brought me in the car."

"Well, I'll treat you to lunch in Bewley's, then. Get your coat on."

"Fair enough. Oh, I want to call into Books Upstairs

and have a word with Claire. The book she recommended to me last week – I was reading it in bed last night and I nearly had a stroke. Full of sex it is, I don't know how they get away with it."

"Who?"

"Those writers. It's scandalous. Mind you, I'm not sure if Claire actually read it. Maybe it was Maura who told me about it? I think it was. That one's a holy terror!"

"Get away out of that, Mam. You love the juicy bits. I'll bet you skim through the books first to see where the steamy scenes are."

"God forgive you!" Her mother grinned. "No, but this one was all about . . ." She lowered her voice as if there was someone else listening. "Orgasms and . . . other things I couldn't bring myself to talk about."

Olive stopped at the kiosk just inside the door of the shopping-centre. "I want to do the Lotto, Michelle. Will I get one for you?"

"A two pound quick-pick, Mam. I'll go on to Crazy Prices."

"I'll call to the bookshop and then I want to buy tights in Penneys. I'll have a look into Vero Moda as well, I have to get something for Fiona's birthday."

"Right, see you at Bewley's in about half an hour."

"Michelle, could you get me some tea? I forgot it yesterday. Barry's. Thanks, love, the large packet."

"Ninety tea bags?"

"Yes, I hate to run out of tea."

"Anything else?"

"No. Oh, wait. Could you get me some marmalade? The lime. I like it with my slice of toast in the morning."

"Lime it is. See you in half an hour."

"Look, Michelle, they sell concert tickets here. Weren't you supposed to buy them for that Leviathan concert?"

"Max Levinson, Mam! No, Lynn phoned last night. She got them at the Concert Hall."

Olive polished off a mixed grill, two slices of brown bread and apple-pie and cream for dessert. She had a good look around while Michelle finished her coffee.

"This place does a great trade, doesn't it?"

"Yes, it's always packed."

"I used to meet your dad in the one in Westmoreland Street." Olive pulled on her gloves. "Your poor dad. He was very partial to black and white pudding. He'd have enjoyed this, what's it you call it?"

"Brunch." Michelle stood up. "Are we right?"

"Don't look now! Here's Mrs Sullivan from Majenta Crescent. Oh, no, she's coming this way. I hope she doesn't spot us, Michelle. I wouldn't like her to see your face."

"Shall I put a paper bag over my head, Mam?"

"What, love?" Her mother was flustered.

"Nothing."

"She's gone. That was a close shave. Here, Michelle, pass me a few of those bags. What are you grinning about?"

"Nothing."

"You can poke fun at me all you like, Michelle, but I'm telling you that one spreads stories like other people spread butter. So, Lynn got the tickets. I'd have liked to have gone with you, Michelle."

"The next time, Mam. I didn't invite you because Catherine Ryder's going and – "

"Catherine's going to the concert too?" Olive sounded more peeved than ever. "I haven't heard you talking about her in a long time."

"She's taken a year off from school. New baby. She's still with the Chamber Orchestra, though."

"New baby? Her second?"

"Third. Her eldest started school this September."

"Imagine! Where does the time go? She's married to that cellist, isn't she?"

"Keith's a viola player."

"Bet their children will be musical, bound to be. I haven't seen the chamber orchestra for a while."

Michelle knew this was another hint.

"I'll pick up the programme in school. They're going to run a series of concerts in the Irish Museum of Modern Art on Sunday afternoons, Catherine told me."

"In the Royal Hospital? Get away. I'd love to go to a few of those. Will Ken be going with you on Saturday night?"

"No, he's working."

"That's a pity." Olive took Michelle's arm as they walked through the carpark.

"He wouldn't have come anyway, it's a girls' night out." Michelle waited for a break in the traffic before she linked her mother across the road.

"Quick, Michelle! Over there!" Olive pointed excitedly. "The car, the green car, do you see it?"

"Where?"

"Just going past the petrol station. That's the car I've seen near your house. Same driver, I think, but I didn't get a good look at him. This is the third time I've seen that car in a week. Are you sure the O'Rourkes have no one staying with them?"

"How would I know, Mam?" Michelle snapped. "I'm not in the habit of spying on the neighbours."

"Don't bite my head off."

Michelle stepped into the road without looking.

"Watch out, Michelle! There's a car coming on your left."

"OK, OK."

"I'd like to get home in one piece," Olive said icily, "if it's all the same with you."

A stony silence settled between them. Michelle stared straight ahead as she marched on, military fashion. Olive trotted alongside.

"Michelle, please tell me what's going on."

"Nothing. There's nothing going on. Would you leave me alone, Mam?" Michelle stood on the path, eyes blazing. "Stop nagging. You're at me and at me all the time."

"That's because you're – "

"What? I'm what?" Michelle shouted.

"Michelle." Olive lowered her voice – *she* wasn't going to behave like a fishwife on the street. "Since you've come back from Vienna, you've been . . . different. You're a bundle of nerves. If I say anything at all, you jump down my throat. I can't look crooked at you these days and . . . I'm not the only one who's noticed. Fiona says she thinks – "

"I don't give a hoot what Fiona or anyone else says, all right? Just leave it."

"But will you see the doctor, Michelle? I'd be happy if you just agreed to go to the doctor."

"Why should I?" Michelle took the bags of groceries from her mother. "I've work to do. I've to go over Mozart's *'Alleluia'* for a wedding next week. It's a tricky piece and the singer's coming over at three for a trial run. I want to have it right. Maybe you should go on home?"

Olive tried not to look hurt.

"Is it Ken, Michelle? Has he changed his mind about the divorce?"

"No, he hasn't. Ken's already been in touch with the solicitor. Now, does *that* make you happy?"

Olive sighed.

She was anything but happy.

Thirty-Three

"Well, did you enjoy the first half?" Catherine asked Michelle while Lynn made her way to the bar in the main foyer of the Concert Hall. The place was packed to capacity, making it difficult to get a drink.

"He's super, isn't he? I loved the Schubert, especially the *scherzo* section."

"Yes," Catherine agreed, "and the waltz."

"I wasn't mad about the Kirchner pieces. I'd never heard of him before this evening," Michelle confessed

"Me neither." Catherine rolled her programme into a tube. "Levinson apparently performed them for the piano competition in May and didn't Lynn say they were included on his first CD?"

"Yes, I must buy the CD for Mam. I think she was a bit annoyed I didn't bring her along."

"You should have, Michelle. She loves the piano."

"She does. I think she regrets she never had the chance to learn to play. I got her John O'Conor's last CD for her birthday and she plays it at full volume with the windows open – thinks she's impressing the people on the street, neighbours, even passers-by."

"John O'Conor's sitting a few rows in front of us, did you notice?"

"No. I guessed he'd be here, though."

"Your mother's keeping well?"

"She's turning into an eco-warrior. At last, here's Lynn with the drinks."

"Lynn, you look very disgruntled." Catherine moved aside to give her room.

"I am."

"Here, I'll pass this to Michelle. Give me your glass, I'll hold it while you put away your purse."

"Thanks, Catherine. The bar's bedlam. Some ignorant lout kept elbowing me, I deliberately wouldn't let him in."

Catherine took a large sip of her brandy. "Your hair's fabulous, Lynn, no sign of the grey. Did you get a colour in?"

How did Catherine manage to turn a compliment into an insult?

"Did it myself. L'Oréal."

"You did a great job. I might try it, my roots need touching up. I usually get it done in the salon but I haven't a minute to myself now with the baby."

"How is he?" Lynn felt she had to ask.

"Very cute. We're calling him Leo after Keith's father."

"Nice," Lynn murmured vaguely.

"I'm not mad about the name, but I was the one who chose Chloe's and Sorcha's, so I can't complain." Catherine looked over their shoulders, to see who else she could spot. "How are things in the school? Any scandal or gossip?"

Lynn took a piece of Nicotinell from her handbag. "Just the usual bitching. Claire's busy rehearsing with the musical society at the moment so I don't see much of her."

"The R and R? What are they doing? Gilbert and Sullivan?"

"Mmh, *HMS Pinafore*. It'll be on next month. I suppose you heard that Amy Regan's youngest daughter got ninety-four per cent in Grade V? She's going for a scholarship."

"I thought she was past the age," Catherine replied.

"No, she's only thirteen. Still eligible for group B."

"Amy must be delighted. She's very ambitious for her offspring! Come on, Michelle, You must have something more interesting to tell me? I know you're only in there a few days a week but often I think the part-timers know more about what's going on than the full-time staff. More time for chit-chat!"

"If only," Michelle said.

"*Some*thing must have happened since I took my maternity leave. No mad affairs? No sex-changes? Did Bren make a pass at Sylvia yet? Come on, guys, shock me with some electrifying news."

"We've a new microwave in the tea-room," Michelle obliged.

Catherine laughed. "I see you're off the cigarettes, Lynn . . . again!"

"Yes, this time I'm determined. I'm saving thirty quid a week from not smoking. I'll put the money away for a holiday."

"I didn't know you'd given them up," Michelle said. "Fair play to you, Lynn. How long are you off them?"

" . . . two days."

"You have the taxi fare to the airport already!" Catherine laughed again.

She'd a very annoying laugh, Lynn decided. Snide.

Catherine lit a cigarette and made a drama about finding an ash-tray. "Peter Langton told me Bill Elliot's most likely moving to the Limerick college next year. That would mean vacancies in high places, wouldn't it?"

"Who do you think'll go for his job?" Michelle asked them.

"Your guess is as good as mine, Michelle." Lynn chewed harder. She smiled sweetly at Catherine. "Are you thinking of applying, yourself?"

"No, Lynn. Too busy on the home front."

Another dig.

Lynn decided it was her turn. "You won't be able to tour with the orchestra this year, Catherine, will you?"

"I'm not ruling it out yet. I'd love to go on the Milan trip in the spring. Keith's all for me going, he's very supportive. I'm lucky."

Smug bitch, Lynn told herself.

"If we can find a decent nanny, I'll go. The last girl we had was excellent. An Italian, very refined. My mother's offered to mind the kids, but I don't like the idea. One family is enough for anyone to rear."

"I agree," said Michelle.

Catherine waved over at a man at the far side of the bar. "There's Simon Davis. I haven't seen him in an age. I'll be back in a sec, folks!"

She swept her scarf over her shoulder and headed off across the room.

"Who's Simon Davis?" Michelle asked.

"He's a big nob in the Arts Council, used to be on the Board of Governors for the Academy. I'm glad she's gone for a minute. Sorry, Michelle, but Catherine's getting to me tonight. She rubs me up the wrong way."

"I don't think she means to be bitchy."

"No," Lynn agreed, "it comes naturally to her! So, how are things with you? How's Ken?"

"Busy as usual, planning to extend the hotel."

"Really? More bedrooms?"

"A conference centre, no less. It'll take time and a lot of money but you know Ken, he enjoys a challenge."

"Yes, he does. Why do you think he pursued you? The first night I introduced you two, he told me he didn't care how long it took, that he was going to end up with you!"

"He did not!"

"He did . . . and he was right, wasn't he?"

"The arrogance of it!" Michelle pretended to be annoyed.

"And how's everything else?"

"You mean Beth?"

"Yes."

"Difficult, Lynn. And to make matters more complicated – keep this under your hat for the moment – Ken's filing for a divorce."

Lynn beamed. "Michelle, that's wonderful news. I can hear the wedding bells – "

"No, Lynn – "

"Please, oh please let me organise the music! I can get Anne and her group to play. You'd like that, Michelle. We could – "

"Hold on, hold on. I never said *any*thing about a wedding, Lynn."

"Oh, Michelle!" Lynn was all starry-eyed.

"Don't get carried away, Lynn. I'm treading very carefully."

"If I were you, I'd jump in there while the going's good. Ken's a dote. Stop arsing around, Michelle. Sign on the dotted line. Michelle Leavy, yes, it has a certain ring to it."

"I like things the way they are."

"Do you? I don't think the single life's all that great and I've had enough experience to know."

"It's not all that bad either, Lynn!"

"There's the bell for part two and here's Catherine back. We'll continue this conversation later." She gave Michelle a meaningful look. "Later!"

Michelle handed Catherine her programme. "I'm looking forward to this. The Chopin Preludes."

"Me too," Catherine replied. "Oh, I meant to ask you, Michelle, how's that student of yours doing? Andrew Watkins, is it?"

"Yes. I'm going to enter him for the Vandeleur Scholarship."

"You should. Simon was just talking to me about the supposed plans for the *conservatoire*. This building would be ideal, wouldn't it? It's so stately."

"And it's central as well," Lynn joined in. "I've always loved Earlsfort Terrace. Could you imagine it? All the rooms given over to classical and traditional music, opera, dance and then a recital room at the back."

"I heard the Taoiseach gave the idea the thumbs up," Catherine said.

"He did," Michelle agreed. "They're going to appoint a committee."

"A Committee!" Catherine groaned. "In that case we'll be six feet under before anything happens!"

"There's the problem of moving the Veterinary Faculty to Belfield," Michelle pointed out. "How many millions are we talking about?"

"What about Lotto funds? Dublin deserves a suitable place for the performing arts. There's a lot of musical talent in Ireland. We must be one of the few European cities without a conservatory – and we were promised." Catherine was disgusted.

Lynn put her empty glass on a table nearby. "You'll never guess who's been accepted into the Dublin Youth Orchestra?"

"Janet Shortt?"

"Yes, I'm thrilled. She's a great kid, works brilliantly."

"You must be very proud, Lynn," Michelle said. "How long have you been teaching her?"

"Five years, since she started," Lynn replied. "Hey, it's yer man, the ignorant lout from the bar. He's making his way over here."

"Must be following you, Lynn," Catherine said, with a smirk.

Lynn imagined every man she met fancied her. She was still doing the rounds at thirty years of age. Catherine wondered what had happened with the flautist. Lynn never lasted more than six months with anyone – she was too needy.

This guy coming over was handsome in an older-and-definitely-married kind of way. Catherine would have to warn Lynn. But it wasn't Lynn he approached. Michelle felt a tip on the shoulder. She turned around.

"Hello, there. I thought it was you."

Michelle, hesitantly, shook his hand.

"Haven't seen you since Vienna. How have you been keeping?"

"Fine, thanks, fine." Michelle stared into the bespectacled, green eyes of Gordon James.

The bell sounded again.

Gordon took her by the arm. "Perhaps we could meet after the performance for a drink?"

" . . . em, I'm not certain if I – "

"With your friends, of course," he added quickly, nodding at Catherine and Lynn.

"Delighted. We'll see you here after." Lynn dragged Michelle away.

"Who is he?" Lynn asked as soon as they were back in their seats.

Michelle put the programme up to her face. "His name's Gordon James."

"Why are you whispering, Michelle?"

"I didn't know I was."

"You were. In any case, who is he, this Gordon James? Should I know him?"

"An organist. He used to teach me," Michelle explained.

Catherine leaned across. "Did he? Not in St. Augustine's, by any chance?"

"Yes, I'm going back a long time. He doesn't teach any more."

"There was a girl who did piano with me in the College of Music, I can't think of her name. She used to learn the organ from him too. She gave it up suddenly, I think. I can't remember the full story now."

"Ssh, Catherine,' Lynn interrupted, "Max Levinson's back on stage."

The short Prelude No 1 had a restless plunging theme and mirrored Michelle's uneasy mood. Gordon James had been a bit too pushy for her liking.

"This second one's more like Liszt," Catherine said,

out of the side of her mouth. She nudged Michelle. "See who's sitting to your left."

Michelle looked and saw the unmistakable profile of Don Cockburn, a retired RTÉ newscaster.

"You could meet anybody in the Concert Hall," Catherine said.

A man in front turned around and glared. That shut Catherine up.

"I have to fly, girls." Catherine buttoned her jacket. "I promised Keith I'd be home early. Isn't it well for you two single ladies?"

"I'm going to throttle her," Lynn muttered as she groped under the seat for her umbrella.

"You go ahead, Catherine," Michelle said pleasantly. "Tell Keith we were asking for him."

"We must do this again some time soon," Catherine said. "Give me a tinkle, Michelle. See you, Lynn."

Another flourish of the scarf and she was gone.

"I need a drink, Michelle. She has me worn out. Come on, let's meet your dishy friend."

Michelle hesitated. "Lynn, I'd prefer not to."

"Why?"

"I just don't want to talk to him, that's all. You know the way, once you start – "

"Michelle, you're just meeting him for a drink. It'd be rude not to, when you said you would."

Michelle followed her up the steps and through the doorway into the foyer.

"When I got a second look at him, I decided I fancied him." Lynn grinned. "The glasses give him a kind of distinguished look and I love that shock of silvery hair. You're going to tell me he's too old for me and that he's happily married, aren't you?"

"No, I'm just going to tell you he's married."

"Here he is, say no more."

Gordon had a tray of drinks in his hand. "I noticed you were both drinking G and T so I took the liberty of getting them for you and a brandy for your friend. Where is she?"

Michelle was stunned. "You bought . . . that's very kind of you, Gordon, and very observant. This is Lynn, a friend of mine from the music school. Gordon James, Lynn."

"Catherine had to go." Lynn accepted the proffered glass.

"Not to worry. I'm delighted to run into you like this, Michelle. Ruth was talking about you only last week."

"Was she?"

"I've been extremely busy since we met in Vienna – built myself a music room at the back of the house." He handed Michelle her drink and put the tray down on a nearby table.

"A music room?"

"Yes, a builder friend of mine converted an old out-house for me. It's terrific. Three rooms: a tiny bathroom, a kitchenette and the music room with my piano and organ – the ceiling's quite high and the acoustics are first class. It's my own place, a haven." He smiled. "It's important for a musician to have privacy, you'll agree. I'm working on a concerto which I'd love you to hear. Would you come over some evening? You and . . . Ken?"

"Em, that's very nice of you, Gordon. We're both very busy at the moment, I'm afraid. Perhaps later on . . . "

He frowned. "When?"

Michelle got flustered. "I'm not sure, in a f-few weeks' time."

"Ruth's brother isn't well at the moment," he said suddenly.

Michelle's stomach turned over. "Cyril?"

"Mmh, Cyril. Not well at all." Gordon's face had gone an odd shade of purple. "My wife's younger brother," he explained to Lynn. "He's just back from abroad. But he's . . . not well. It's worrying."

"What's the matter with him?" Lynn inquired politely.

"Not sure." Gordon looked away.

"I must go to the ladies'," Lynn excused herself.

"Gordon, I have to talk to you . . . it's about Cyril. I'm . . . worried myself."

"Are you, Michelle? You've heard from him, have you? Ruth was afraid you might have."

"This is hard for me to say, Gordon. Is Cyril . . . has he ever had any kind of a . . . problem with his nerves?"

"Nerves?" Gordon shook his head.

"Or any . . . any trouble with the . . . police?"

"Police?" He looked at her harshly. "What do you mean by that?"

"I'm sorry . . . it's just that I've had some very peculiar – "

"Cyril's a bit of a dreamer, that's all. He suffers from . . . delusions, you might call them."

"I need to talk to him," Michelle said.

"I'd be more than willing to tell him that but I don't know where he is."

"You don't know – "

"He was staying with us but then he left, packed his bag and left suddenly. Cyril's like that. You'd never know what he'd do next."

"Here's the car, Michelle. I was lucky to get parking in Hatch Street."

"Thank God you came back when you did, Lynn. I was sure Gordon James was about to offer me a lift home."

Lynn opened the passenger door of her Fiat Uno. "He seemed nice enough. Friendly."

"I found it hard to get away from him."

Lynn indicated and pulled out. "He's a bit obsessed about the brother-in-law, Cecil, isn't he?"

"Cyril," Michelle corrected her. "Cyril's been . . . "

She was about to say "pestering me', but it might sound as if she was trying to get rid of a persistent young suitor and Lynn would get the wrong idea.

When they reached the traffic light at the end of the road, Lynn turned right into Harcourt Street.

"Do you want to call in to The Fullerton and see your beloved?"

"No, I'm ready for bed, Lynn. I'm playing at the ten o'clock Mass tomorrow as well as the eleven."

"No rest for the wicked." Lynn smiled over at her. "I'll have you home in no time. I enjoyed this evening."

"Me too. We'll do it again soon."

"You'll have far too much to be doing, Michelle."

"Funny you should say that, there's a spate of weddings around my area. I've four to play at in the next month."

"I meant *your* wedding, you idiot!"

"Do you ever give up, woman?" Michelle smiled. "And if I ever *do* take the plunge . . . "

"Ye-es? If you ever take the plunge . . . what?"

"I wouldn't want a fussy wedding – it'd be small, intimate and – "

"And lovely!" Lynn enthused.

"There's one minor detail, Lynn. Ken hasn't asked me to marry him."

"You ask him, then." Lynn braked suddenly at the next red light.

"Not a bad idea," Michelle said slowly. "I'll think about it."

"That's your trouble, Michelle. You think too much!"

Thirty-Four

The O'Rourke's Siamese cat sat preening on Michelle's garden wall. She bent to pat the silky head.

"Hello there, puss. Keeping watch for me, were you?"

The cat purred and arched his sleek body.

Michelle opened the hall door. "Coming in for your usual?" The cat dashed between her legs, down to the kitchen and sprang up on the windowsill without as much as a by-your-leave.

Michelle was amused. She loved this little creature, he was so affectionate but independent at the same time. She put a saucer of milk down for him and went back to the hall to get her post from the doormat.

The usual bills: Gas, VHI, home insurance, TV licence.

How did they all manage to arrive in the one month?

The fifth envelope was some sort of a catalogue – more rubbish to be discarded. The amount of paper that came through the door on a weekly basis was sinful; ads, brochures, give-aways, reminders, notices. Anything and everything.

Michelle was about to throw the catalogue in the bin when something caught her eye: the word *knickers* in big black capitals.

What?

She tore open the envelope. It was a mail order catalogue – for sex aids. Lingerie, rubbers, dildos . . . and other exotica she didn't bother to look at. She examined the front of the envelope again – *M Bolger* and the address typed clearly.

Someone had posted away for this stuff and given her name and address. No, not someone.

Him.

Cyril O'Connor.

Cyril's not well. Gordon's words.

No, Cyril was not bloody well. He was very, very sick. It was time to confront him. The next time he rang, she'd answer the phone. Tell him what she thought of him.

The policeman in Ken's house, what had he said? That these types were rarely dangerous. But it depended on what you called dangerous, didn't it?

Cyril O'Connor was a coward, hadn't the gumption to face her, say what he wanted. He scribbled notes, like some silly infatuated schoolboy; paid for meals and then ran away; handed presents to complete strangers in the street to leave at hotel receptions – he hadn't the balls to speak to her, just played Mozart to an answering machine. He parked his car on the road, watched her house, but when any neighbour came along, he scurried away like a rat from a trap.

What did he *want*?

To scare her? To keep her intrigued? What was it all leading to? Seduction? No normal man who wanted to seduce a woman went about it this way. There was something very warped about his thinking. Michelle had looked for logical explanations, rational answers. There were none. The only thing she knew for certain was that he liked playing games. Maybe the only way to deal with him was to join in?

She poured herself a large gin and tonic and sat down to think. She was going to take control. There was nothing to fear but fear itself. The phone rang.

Good. Great.

Michelle gritted her teeth and picked up the receiver.

This is the Telecom Éireann Answering Service with a message for Michelle Bolger. Please check your mailbox.

Michelle keyed in her number.

You have one new message. To review your message press one.

She was surprised at how calm she'd become.

Hello, Michelle.

Not as calm as she'd thought. Hearing his voice, his normal voice, was unnerving.

I need to see you.

Did he? He needed to see her. Didn't he see her every blasted day when he ogled her from his car?

We must talk.

Oh, yes, Cyril O'Connor. We certainly must, only this time I'll be doing most of the talking, you bastard.

There's something you have to know. I was hoping it wouldn't come to this but . . . I don't want to say anything over the phone . . .

You two-faced moron! Why don't you put it to music?

I'm going to drop by your home tomorrow, Michelle. I'll explain everything then.

The phone clicked.

Right, Cyril O'Connor. Call here tomorrow, by all means. I'll be waiting for you. Showdown time. You're going to explain everything, are you? That'll take some doing.

Thirty-Five

"Mich? I'm running a bit late. I'll be over for you at eight-fifteen."

"Take your time, I've my last lesson in ten minutes. Nicola Jones, Grade VI."

"You make her sound like a vegetable."

"A good analogy . . . seriously, she'll be with me for about forty minutes so there's no rush."

"Good. Everything else OK?"

"Fine."

"By the way, I ran into an old friend of yours in Grafton Street today." Ken paused for effect. "Cyril O'Connor. He's back in Dublin."

"I know."

"You *know?* How do you know?"

"I met Gordon James at the Concert Hall."

"Oh? You never said."

"It slipped my mind."

"He was asking for you – as brazen as you like!" Ken

laughed. "In a way you'd have to admire him. The gall! Said he'd invested in some hotel in Killiney. He was all dressed up, expensive-looking suit. He wanted me to go for a drink with him, as if we were bosom buddies. Then he told me he'd met you in Vienna and what a nice time you both had."

Michelle felt angry.

"He actually suggested that we all go for a meal some night."

"Ken, I – "

"Ah, don't worry, Mich, I put him off. I've a feeling he's going to phone you, though."

"He already has."

"What?" Ken sounded reproachful. "When was this?"

"Mam took the first call and I've just got a message from him now on the answering machine. He's calling here tomorrow."

"To the house?"

"Yes."

"You're full of surprises, Mich. Why didn't you say anything?"

"It . . . it wasn't . . . you've more important things on your mind."

"Michelle Bolger, are you harbouring some dark secret from me?" Ken's attempt at levity didn't fool her. "Is there something going on I should know about?"

"Going on? What's that supposed to mean?"

"Don't get mad." Ken could hear the tension in her voice. "I'm joking."

"Are you?"

Best to drop this subject. "Mich, I wanted to ask a favour."

"A favour?"

"Don't feel you have to say yes."

"I never do anything I don't want to, Ken."

That wasn't quite true but he wasn't going to argue with her. She was very touchy today. "Would you mind if I dropped in to Griffith Avenue on my way over to you and asked Beth to come out to dinner with us?"

"Of course I don't mind." She sounded relieved, as if she was glad to hear such a harmless request.

"I wouldn't ask but I'm a bit worried about her. Anytime I phone she seems kind of . . . lost."

"That's the impression I got when I called in the other night."

"She told me about the French homework. Thanks."

"She told you?"

"Yes, she was very grateful and . . . touched."

Michelle was pleased. "It was nothing."

"She said you were 'sound', and I'm quoting. I didn't point out to her that you were always sound if she'd only bothered to see it."

"I was glad to be able to help."

"I don't think herself and Toni are hitting it off too well. It's a case of 'If you want to know me, come and live with me'. From what I gather, Toni's running around a lot."

"Ken, phone Beth now and invite her to join us. Say it was my idea, if you like."

"No, I'd prefer to drop in, make it look casual. I don't want her to think I'm checking up on her. It drives her crazy when she thinks I'm fussing."

"We're all the same."

"Mich, I appreciate this."

"Will you stop! She's your daughter."

"Maybe it's time we had a fresh start, you, me and Beth?"

"I think so. Since you've moved out of the house, you've broken a pattern. You needed space from one another."

"Exactly. You know, there's a touch of the *déjà vu* about this."

"About what?"

"Remember the last time we booked for Il Corvo?"

"You're not breaking the arrangement this time, Ken!"

"No. I saw Terry today, about the other arrangements. He's sorting out the finances. I'm going to London to meet up with Jonathan. I could do it over the phone but – "

"No, it'd be better for you to meet him in person."

"Yes, that's what I figured. I'm going in the morning on the early flight."

"No problem. Are you going to spend the night with me? It'd be handier for the airport."

"No, I don't want to disturb you so early in the morning. I'll stay in the hotel tonight and book a taxi for six am. I'll be back in Dublin tomorrow night. What will I bring you from London?"

"Just yourself. How's Toni?"

"Not answering my calls. I don't know what she's playing at."

"She's not going to make it easy, Ken."

"She said she wouldn't contest the divorce but she's . . . I'm not sure – "

"Not to worry. It'll work out."

"Until later, Mich. I see Gail making faces at me through the window. Another crisis, no doubt."

* * *

The waitress took their jackets and led them to a table for two by the window, overlooking the Drumcondra Road.

"A bottle of Corvo red." Ken smiled at the girl as he pulled out the chair for Michelle.

"Beth wasn't in when you called by the house?"

"No, unusual for a mid-week night. I'd never let her go out when she's supposed to be studying. Toni wasn't there either. If you saw the state of the place, Mich!"

"You'll have to get the Mini Maids in before you move back."

"If I go back." He looked at her. "I might give Toni the house."

"*Give* it to her?"

"Yes. Terry went into the figures very carefully. She's entitled to half, anyway. This could be the best way of making a clean break and it's Beth's home. If Toni is serious about wanting to live with Beth, this could be the ideal way."

"I see."

Ken handed her a menu. "Mich, I'm glad Beth decided not to come. We need to talk."

Everybody "needed to talk" lately.

The waitress came back with the wine and Ken tasted it. "That's fine, thank you."

The girl poured Michelle's, left the bottle on the table and went to serve the young couple at the next table.

"Have you thought any more about us getting a house together?"

"I'm starving," Michelle said, scrutinising the menu. "I might go for the cannelloni, what are you having?"

Ken lit a cigarette. "Did you hear what I said, Mich?"

She nodded but she didn't look at him.

"Well?" He moved the menu down from her face. "Stop hiding behind that!"

"Yes, I have thought about it and . . . "

"And?"

The waitress came back again and Ken ordered cannelloni for both of them.

Michelle looked at him.

He was wearing his cream-coloured trousers and his navy silk shirt. She loved that shirt. It made him look . . . boyish and clean-cut, like a well-behaved schoolboy. He was smiling up at the waitress. He'd a lovely smile.

She tried to imagine it. Waking up every morning with Ken. Having breakfast together. Kissing him on the

doorstep as he went to work. Making love every night . . .
but that wouldn't last.

Where would they live?

A little cottage by the sea? Springtime walks at dawn
and dusk on a wind-swept beach? Summer sex on the
seashore with the waves licking their feet . . . winter
storms and the tide flooding their kitchen?

A mews in a fashionable suburb on the southside?
Coffee mornings with the social club? Musical *soirées* in
the evenings? Were there stalkers on the southside?

A cabin in the mountains? A love-nest tucked away in
a hilly glade, watching the sunset and –

"Talk to me, Mich. What are you thinking?"

"I'm trying to imagine what it would be like."

"You don't have to imagine, I can tell you. It'll be
fantastic."

"I'm not sure, Ken. It's a huge step."

"I love you, Mich. I want us to be together."

"To make a commitment?"

Ask me the right question, Ken. Come on, out with it.
It's not that hard to say – you asked Toni. *Will you marry
me?* If you've done it before you can do it again! Hmm . . .
maybe having done it before you never want to do it again.

"A commitment, yes, Mich." He leaned over and took
her hand. "What we have is great but it's kind of
piecemeal – we see each other once during the week
and most weekends if neither of us is working. We fit
each other in. If we lived together we'd be together all
the time, no more snatched moments."

Michelle nodded. When would he say the magic word?

"Wouldn't it be better if we could share our lives, Mich? Be a proper couple."

Yes, be a proper couple. Married.

"It's about change, Mich. I'm going to make big changes in my life. I want you to be part of them, no, not part of them . . . I want you to share them with me."

Michelle stroked his fingers. "And Beth?"

"Beth's almost seventeen. Like I said earlier, she can live with her mother in Griffith Avenue and – "

"What if it doesn't work out with Toni? I don't want to see Beth unhappy, Ken."

"Neither do I. If she wants, she can live with us. Let her have the choice. Or, better again, she can divide her time between Toni and us, have the best of both worlds."

"I wonder what she'll think."

"She'll be finished school in another year, then it will be college and before you know it, she'll be gone. Beth has her own life now. She . . . she doesn't rely on me the same way she used to. It's taken me a while to see that. I need you, Mich. I love you."

This was so unlike Ken. Words like these didn't come easily to him.

"Mich, think about it carefully, will you, before you dismiss the idea?"

"I'm not going to dismiss the idea. Here's the food. Let's eat." She spread her napkin on her lap. "And there's my house to think about, Ken. And my piano pupils."

"I knew you'd bring up your house." He stroked his chin thoughtfully.

He watched her. She ate so daintily. She looked radiant tonight in her black dress. He loved that dress, it was sophisticated, understated. Just like her. Michelle had a quality he couldn't resist, a serenity – at least she used to have. He could never make out exactly what she was thinking. She intrigued him.

"I'm not asking you to give up your life, Mich, or your house. I wouldn't."

"But if we live together?"

"You can let your house. Extra income."

"Typical of you, Ken, to think of the money." She smiled.

"It's your independence I'm thinking of and I admit I'm practical – you once told me you liked that. Said you needed someone to organise you."

"I meant it. And my pupils?"

"Logistics, that's all. I'd never let logistics stand in the way."

"I know!"

"What about letting the upper part of your house and keeping downstairs as your work area? The pupils could still come to you there."

"You really have given this a lot of thought."

"Yes, because I know what you're like." He sipped his wine thoughtfully. "Your mother was on to me today, Mich. She's worried about you."

"Ken, Mam exaggerates, you know that."

"I told her you were all right and if there was anything wrong you'd have told me." He looked hard at her. "You would tell me, wouldn't you?"

Michelle avoided his eyes. "I'm not sleeping very well, that's all."

"You're still not sleeping?"

"No, but Mam and I were in Omni today, she went into a natural food shop and got me some sort of a concoction to try. Fiona swears by it. I'll take it tonight."

"Should you be drinking?"

"It's only some herbal remedy, Ken, and we're not exactly knocking the wine back here, are we?"

"I think your mother's right about one thing, Mich. It would do no harm to see a doctor."

"I'll go tomorrow," Michelle agreed.

She didn't want Ken on her back, too. She had to admit that she hadn't been feeling all that well lately – queasy a lot of the time and she had this heavy feeling in the pit of her stomach. For the last few days she'd felt a bit light-headed.

Panic attacks? The quicker she met Cyril O'Connor and cleared up this mess, the better.

"I'll be back in a sec, Ken. I'm dying to go the loo."

Michelle walked past the other tables and up the two steps to the back of the restaurant where the toilets were situated. She didn't notice the coat-stand to her left, or the man with his hand in Ken's jacket pocket.

Thirty-Six

Ken pulled up at her gate. "Would you like me to stay, Mich?

"No, you go back to the hotel as planned. Have a good night's rest – you want to be fresh in the morning."

They kissed briefly.

"Good luck tomorrow in London. I'm sure things will go fine. Tell Jonathan I was asking for him. 'Night, Ken."

"I'll go in with you for a minute."

He knew Michelle didn't like going into the house late at night on her own. "You didn't leave the lights on," he remarked.

"I thought I did."

Ken went ahead of her to open the hall door. He searched his jacket pocket. Nothing.

"Michelle, give me your key. I must have left mine in my other coat."

She opened her handbag and rifled through the three compartments before she found her key. "This damned bag. I can never find anything in it. Oh, Ken, I left my gloves in the car."

"It's open."

Michelle went back and got her gloves. When she came into the house, Ken had switched on the hall and upstairs lights.

"Ken? Where are you?"

"In your bedroom," he shouted down. "Just turning on your electric blanket."

"Thanks." She went into the kitchen, filled the kettle and got the milk from the fridge.

He came up behind her and kissed her neck.

"Will you stay for a cuppa?"

"No, I'd better head off." He turned her to him and kissed her softly on the mouth. "If I stay for a while," he whispered, "I won't be able to go."

"Phone me tomorrow night and let me know how you got on."

"No, I'll come here straight from the airport."

"What time is your flight due in?"

"Some time after nine, I think."

"I'll cook us a meal to celebrate. Do you want to invite Terry and June?" She laughed. "You know, it never struck me before: *Terry and June* – it used to be a comedy show on telly."

"Sometimes I think they *are* a comedy show!" Ken kissed her again. "No, we'll have them over another time. Tomorrow night I want you all to myself."

Michelle took the little brown bottle from the kitchen press. Bioforce. Fresh Herb Extract. Dormeasan. It reminded her of *"Nessun Dorma"*! She read the ingredients. *Humulus lupulus* and *Valeriana officinalis* which translated as hops and valerian. Michelle had never heard of valerian.

These herbs were known for their soothing properties, she read on the bottle, helped to maintain a normal sleep pattern. Sounded good. It was weeks since she'd had a decent night's sleep.

Following the directions, Michelle poured a little water into a glass and added thirty drops of the tincture. Then she read that it should be taken half an hour before retiring.

Time for a long, hot bath.

She went up to her room to get undressed. Ken had the blanket turned to high. She'd barbecue at that temperature. She lowered the dial then turned back the duvet to get her nightdress.

A single red rose lay on the pillow.

She picked it up and sniffed. It had the most beautiful scent. Wasn't Ken thoughtful? A gesture like this said more than any declaration of undying love ever could. He wasn't usually the romantic type, but he was definitely improving.

After her bath, Michelle was still keyed up. Not in the mood for bed yet. This herbal remedy wasn't very effective, was it? Then she remembered that the day after the burglary in Shanowen Road, her mother had given her a sleeping pill she hadn't taken. Where had she put it? Yes, here it was in the cabinet over the sink. Should she take this after the wine?

It wasn't a strong pill, her mother had said . . . and she *did* want to crash out tonight. Lack of sleep was definitely making her edgy and depressed. Andrew's lesson wasn't until two o'clock the next day so she could have a long sleep in the morning.

She tied the belt on her bathrobe and put on her slippers. She'd bring the duvet downstairs, curl up on the couch and watch TV for a while.

He spied on her through the narrow gap in the folding doors. Would she ever fall asleep? She'd lain down and thrown a blanket or something over herself but she was still flicking the remote control. It must be nearly one o'clock and he'd been waiting for over two hours. He'd love a cigarette but that was out of the question.

Had she discovered the rose?

He'd got a real fright earlier when Ken Leavy had been about to come in here to the back room. Fortunately he'd changed his mind and gone into the kitchen with Michelle. That had been a bit scary, too.

What if Mr Ken Leavy had decided to spend the night? There were a few worrying moments before the front door slammed and was locked from the inside.

His methodical planning had paid off. Watching and waiting, timing. The timing was all-important but he'd always known that – it had been drummed into him from the time he was a child.

He'd mapped out this night in his mind for weeks but when it came down to it, no matter how carefully he'd worked it all out, he still had to depend on luck. And Lady Luck was on his side tonight.

Thoughtful of Ken Leavy to have left the key in his pocket. How many times had he watched Ken take it from that pocket on the left side of his jacket? Ken was a creature of habit – most people were.

The restaurant had been crowded, another piece of good fortune. Nobody had time to notice what he was up to, that's the one thing he'd learned from all this. People were too busy to see anything.

Michelle had passed within inches of him but she hadn't noticed him. And all the other times he'd followed her, she hadn't noticed him either. The annoying thing about Michelle was that she *didn't* notice.

Didn't listen.

When she'd been with him she hadn't listened, not really. Polite conversation, nods and smiles and pleasantries. But she hadn't heard anything, hadn't understood. He'd been dismissed.

She'd bloody well pay attention to him now.

He'd intended to wait till she'd fallen asleep and then follow her up to her bedroom, but this was better. Infinitely better. He wouldn't have to drag her downstairs.

She'd played right into his hands.

He could go in there now and overpower her. She'd never be able to match his strength, but he couldn't risk her screaming. The walls in these houses weren't that thick and the bloody neighbours next door would be in like a shot. He's seen them often enough peeping from behind the curtains.

It was a miracle he'd been able to sneak in here tonight without them spotting him. He'd deliberately worn a navy jacket, a replica of the one lover boy wore. He was about the same height too, and in the dark they'd never noticed the difference. If they had seen him, they'd taken him for Ken Leavy.

He'd been clever.

And he hadn't parked on the road tonight, either. Didn't want anyone to recognise his car – no trouble to park behind the house in the lane. It was a wonder more people didn't use the lane but lucky for him that they didn't. He'd already unlocked the kitchen door and unbolted the back gate. There'd be no difficulty getting her out the back way.

Pity about the cat.

Pretty little thing but it just wouldn't shut up. All that miaowing and caterwauling would have alerted the owners. He doubted if it had felt any pain, he'd despatched it quickly . . . the way he'd learnt to choke the chickens on his uncle's farm when he was a boy. A quick snap and the neck broke. No mess.

Michelle sighed softly and wriggled into a more comfortable position on the couch. The light from the coffee-table lamp beside her allowed him to watch her every movement. He should be able to tell from here when her eyes closed. Then he'd give her another hour or so until she was in a deep sleep. He'd waited months for this.

Another hour wouldn't make any difference.

She had to get upstairs. She couldn't sleep here, didn't want a crick in her neck like the last time. Come on, lazybones, up to bed. Swing your legs off the couch, stand up, move.

Michelle was too tired to move.

Jaded. The sleeping pill had kicked in.

The TV voices grew fainter and fainter, her eyelids grew heavier and heavier. Her breathing deepened. She felt around the couch for the remote control, pressed the red button and the screen flickered off.

She pulled up the duvet, snuggled into it and let her eyes close. A doze for a few minutes and then she'd have to go over and . . . plug . . . it . . . out.

He crept over to the couch, went down on his hunkers and put his ear close to her mouth.

In, out. In, out.

Her breath was cool on his face. Sleeping like a baby. A strand of her long blonde hair tickled his nose. She was so goddamned beautiful. He'd touch her face to see what happened.

He ran a finger very gently over her cheek.

Her eyelids fluttered.

Would he dare? He leaned forward and his lips brushed her forehead.

She stirred slightly but showed no sign of waking.

It was now or never. He stood up, bent over her and scooped his hands beneath the duvet, one under her knees, the other under her back.

Michelle moaned.

He lifted her and the duvet together. She was heavier than he'd figured, but not too heavy.

"Ken?" she mumbled sleepily. "Ken."

This was too awkward an angle for him to carry her. If he tripped with her now, it'd be a disaster. He'd have to chance it – he pushed her up in his arms and over his shoulder, like a sack of potatoes. To his amazement, she still didn't wake fully.

"Ken," she murmured.

She opened her eyes for a second but she couldn't see, it was pitch, pitch dark. Her eyes refused to stay open. She was floating, light, feathery. Ken was carrying her. He'd come back and he was putting her to bed. He was so good to her.

"Ken," she murmured again and then something cold and wet trickled down her face. "Ken, she grumbled, her voice getting slightly louder. "I'm – "

Darkness swamped her.

Why did it have to rain? He got the ends of the duvet and pushed them over her head as he struggled down the garden path.

"Stop trying to talk, Michelle," he hissed to the duvet. "Ssh, ssh, everything will be all right."

A louder groan.

If she kept at this, he'd have to shut her up.

"Put me down."

Michelle was afraid. Where was he taking her? Why was he so rough? She was being shoved and pushed.

"Ken, please. Put me down. I feel dizzy."

She writhed and squirmed and tried to break free from the grip of the strong arms which were holding her tightly, but her body wasn't her own, it didn't belong to her. It refused to do what she wanted.

Her arms were being tied behind her. He was hurting her.

Ken wouldn't hurt her.

This wasn't Ken.

"Stop, please stop." She mouthed the words but no sound came out. Now she was on her back on a hard seat. She smelled polish. Her arms hurt. She tried to wiggle the duvet off her face. She'd no strength, no strength at all.

A door slammed and a noise came from in front of her. Please, stop. Stop.

Another click and then a spurting, shuddering sound. Her body started to shake.

Please, oh please, what's happening?

For a fleeting moment her brain got into gear. Cyril

O'Connor. Cyril O'Connor. Cyril O'Connor had her . . . had her in his car.

The sound quietened down for a second, then got louder and hummed.

A car engine . . . yes, she'd been bundled into a car.

She tried to sit up but couldn't, her feet were tied too. Something rough and scratchy cut into her ankles. Rope. No, no, no. She drew in her breath and with all her might she screamed.

It wasn't a scream. It was barely a sigh, but it was enough to alarm him. He opened the back door of the car, got in and pulled the duvet off her face.

"I'm sorry but you asked for this, Michelle. You couldn't do as you were told, could you?"

He got a large handkerchief and tied it roughly around her mouth.

"That'll keep you quiet." He shoved her back on the seat, then he heaped the duvet on top of her, covering her completely.

"Just lie quietly. You'll be all right. We'll be there in half an hour. Less."

No movement from the back seat.

"All right, don't answer then. That's fine with me."

Michelle couldn't have answered if she'd wanted to.

She'd passed out.

Thirty-Seven

"Thanks, Sam. I haven't fully made up my mind yet, but I'm giving your offer very serious consideration. Yes, I need to discuss the idea with my daughter. I'll let you know by the weekend, OK? Bless you!"

Toni put down the phone and lit a cigarette. Ten-thirty. She stretched sleepily and grinned. She'd pulled it off. The interview had gone like a dream, she'd made an impression – known her facts, and she'd an excellent track record and references from the London company. She'd responded honestly, kept good eye contact and asked intelligent questions. She'd looked and sounded professional. They wanted someone with experience in publishing and her contacts in London would be a help, too. Toni was perfect for the job.

Six months' trial in a highly prestigious publishing firm in New York. Big salary, apartment in Manhattan, opportunities to travel. She'd be insane not to seize the chance.

How would Beth take it?

Toni got out of bed and pulled on her blue, silk kimono. She'd like her daughter to come with her – give them both a better chance to make a go of it away from Dublin.

It would be exciting. They'd each need a whole new wardrobe for New York. They could spend Saturday in Grafton Street and do the rounds of the shops. Beth would be thrilled to be let loose again in Oasis and Miss Selfridge.

Toni went into the *en suite* and ran a bath. She could hear Ken's objections. "Not possible, not remotely possible." The move would "interfere with Beth's schooling". She couldn't be "uprooted in the middle of a term".

But it was only for six months, Beth could always go to one of those grind schools next year for the Leaving and the experience of living in New York would be an education in itself. The company had assured Toni that they'd pull strings so that Beth could attend classes in a good high school.

Toni heard a key turn in the front door, came out to the landing and leaned over the banisters. "That you, darling? Sorry I missed you last night. Why are you back from school so early?"

Beth stood shivering in the middle of the hall. She was wearing black leather trousers and a skimpy white top, her long coat unbuttoned, her hair in a mess.

"Beth!" Toni hurried down the stairs. The bath would have to wait. "What happened to you?"

Beth started to sob, big heaving sobs.

"Honey, what's wrong?" Toni put her arm around her daughter and led her into the sitting-room, over to the sofa. "Sit down, Beth, tell me what's happened."

"It's Carmel." Beth blurted. "She's in the hospital, Mum. I was with her, I stayed all night. It was terrible, she was so sick." Beth fought for breath. "She went blue and her eyes rolled in her head. I though she was going to die, Mum. She nearly . . . died."

"Slow down, honey, slow down." Toni got a tissue from the sideboard and wiped her daugher's tears. "Now, as calmly as you can, tell me what happened."

Beth took another few deep breaths, then began again. "We were at a party in Stillorgan, a guy Wendy knows. Someone gave Carmel . . . something – "

"Drugs?"

"I don't know – "

"Beth! You'll *have* to tell me."

Beth nodded. "E. I'm not sure what happened exactly, she's often had it before . . . I mean she – "

"Go on," Toni said. "Carmel took an Ecstacy tablet, just the one?"

"Maybe t-two." Beth bit the tissue. "She'd had a few beers as well, I wasn't watching her, that's what's so terrible, Mum. I wasn't watching. I was in the . . . in another room when it happened."

How could she tell her mother that she was upstairs in bed smoking hash, with a boy whose name she couldn't now remember?

"Beth, what happened to Carmel? Tell me exactly."

"She fainted. At first they all thought she was messing but when Wendy realised she wasn't, she came looking for me. Everyone panicked. There was screaming and shouting and arguments. It was horrible."

Beth blew her nose in the scrunched-up tissue. Toni handed her a clean one. "And most of them scarpered, Mum. They didn't give a shit about her, just wanted to get the hell away before the cops arrived."

"Did the police arrive?" Toni asked, alarmed.

"No, no, not then but . . . the hospital had to call them. She'll be done, Mum, so will Paul, Wendy's boyfriend. They'll be done for possession."

"We'll worry about that later. Go on, tell me what happened. Did you go in the ambulance?"

"Paul, it was his house we were in, he phoned 999 and Wendy and I brought Carmel up to the toilet. We opened the window to get air for her and Wendy tried to force some milk down her throat. She puked up this black gunge and she was coughing and spluttering. It was a nightmare, Mum." Beth started to shake again. "A nightmare."

Toni stroked Beth's neck.

"When we got to the hospital, they pumped her stomach. They wouldn't let me into the room with her but I know that's what they did. Wendy said it had happened before to a friend of hers. There were doctors and nurses flying around, shouting and – "

"They were fighting for her life, Beth."

"She'll be all right, Mum, won't she?"

Toni hugged her.

"It started out as such a brilliant night. We were all having a great time and then, then . . . why did it have to happen to Carmel? Mrs Richardson, Mum. You should have seen Mrs Richardson in the hospital. She was . . . she nearly lost her reason. Had to be sedated. And Carmel's sister was there and her father was called back from Kerry in the middle of the night. He was on a golf holiday . . . " Beth's voice trailed off.

Toni helped her daughter off the couch. "Come on, young lady, up to bed for a sleep."

"No, Mum. There's no way I could sleep. I have to go back to the hospital."

"Later, sweetheart, I'll go back with you later. Right now you need a good long rest."

"This is not a good time, Mark." Toni held the front door half-open.

"Mrs Leavy, I want to see Beth." He knew he sounded aggressive and didn't mean to. "It's been over two weeks since I've heard from her and . . . I don't know what's going on."

Toni opened the door wider. "Come in." She showed him into the kitchen. "Coffee?" she asked coolly.

"No, thanks. I drove by the school this morning, hung around for over an hour, hoping to catch her on her way in but she never showed up." He brushed the hair back from his forehead. "When I asked Nikki Ross, a girl from her class, where Beth was, I was told she hadn't been in school for days. Is she sick?"

"No, she's not . . . sick."

Beth had been mitching, Toni realised. "Her friend Carmel Richardson, do you know her? Yes, well, Carmel was rushed to hospital last night. There was a party apparently and – "

"Jesus! Drugs?"

"Yes."

"I warned her." Mark gritted his teeth. "I warned her about the scene. I could see what that gang were like and I told her not to get involved. Carmel's a nice enough girl but she's very easily led. It's Wendy Friel who's the real problem."

"Wendy Friel? Yes, the party was in her boyfriend's house, I think that's what Beth said. I never heard of this Wendy before."

"Beth met up with her through Carmel. She's wild – quit school, found herself some dead-end job and a bedsit in town, hangs around with a bunch of no-hopers. For some reason, Beth thinks she's cool. I was afraid something like this would happen." Mark looked gloomy. "Mrs Leavy, what are we going to do about Beth?"

"She's going through a very rough patch . . . the divorce. She pretends she doesn't care but she's been avoiding me since her father and I told her about it. We tried to reassure her . . . "

"She's avoiding me, too." Mark went to the window

and stared out at the garden. "Do you know where she is now? Is she with Carmel?"

"No, she's here. I made her go to bed for a sleep. She's washed out. Mark, you said she hasn't been to school for days?" Toni lit a cigarette. "I didn't know that."

Mark said nothing. He could see Beth's mother was feeling guilty but he wasn't willing to be her confessor.

"I'd better phone the school," Toni said suddenly. "I haven't spoken to any of her teachers for years. Em, would you know . . . would you know if Mrs Rogers is still the principal?" She faltered. "I'd phone Ken but he's in London today and . . . stupid, isn't it? My not knowing who Beth's principal is."

More than stupid, Mark thought.

"Yes, Mrs Rogers is the head. Beth's form tutor is Ms Walsh, maybe you should contact her first." He turned back from the window and picked up his car keys from the table. "I'd better go. Mrs Leavy, would you please tell Beth I called and that I'm . . . anxious to see her."

"I will," she promised. "Mark, I'd like your opinion on something." She followed him out to the hall. "I'm thinking of going to the States for a few months, maybe longer if it works out. I'd like Beth to come with me and – "

Mark spun around. "Are you serious?"

"Yes. Why not?"

"Do you think this is a good time? If Beth's depressed and I think she is, Mrs Leavy, surely it wouldn't be right to unsettle her – "

"I think this is exactly the right time," Toni replied firmly. "What she needs is a change, a new start. A clean break from her friends . . . "

He looked hurt.

"Not you, I didn't mean you, Mark."

She probably did. "The States? It's a bit drastic"

"Beth's lost her granny, Mark, now she thinks she's lost her parents." Toni opened the hall door. "It's very difficult for her."

"Taking her away isn't going to make it easier," Mark insisted.

Toni would have loved to tell him to mind his own business but she'd asked for his opinion.

"All this talk of divorce," she went on, "it's depressing, and . . . do you know Beth's father wants to get married again?" Toni's eyes smarted but she fought back the tears.

"Mrs Leavy," he said, embarrassed, "I have to go. Would you tell Beth I called?"

He ran to the car, jumped in and drove off. The woman was incredible. Had she no thought for her daughter at all? Beth needed stability, routine. Anyone could see that. Whipping her off now to the States was the worst possible thing to do. He'd call up to Collins Avenue and see what Michelle made of all this.

Mark Patterson had annoyed her. Not a good idea to take Beth away, the nerve of him! What did he know? Unsettling her? Wasn't that the whole trouble, that she *was* unsettled? Her father was the one to blame for that.

He was the one who'd moved out, shirking his responsibilities at a time when his daughter needed him. And he was the one looking for a divorce, wanting to marry his mistress. If Beth was depressed, it was Ken's fault, not hers.

No, it would be the makings of her daughter to get away from this place. New York was vibrant, full of possibilities. A young girl like Beth, she'd have a ball there, meet new friends, spread her wings. Mark was nice, decent and it was obvious he cared deeply about Beth but he was too stodgy. A few weeks in America and Mark would be a thing of the past.

Toni would phone the school now and find out exactly what was going on. Why hadn't she been informed of Beth's absence? Discipline must be very lax. Wasn't it their responsibility to keep track of their students? What were they paid for? If Ken had a word to say about Beth's education, she had her ammunition now.

Toni, furious, picked up the receiver. Damn, she didn't know the number of the school. Had Ken noted it in the red address-book?

Yes, here it was neatly filed under S. Ken, methodical to the last. She idly flicked through the pages, doctor and dentist under D, Whitehall garda station under G and beside it, her old home phone number. G for Gwen or for granny? Ken had often phoned her mother, he'd been good at keeping in touch with the old lady. Out of curiosity she flicked to B.

Olive Bolger.

His girlfriend's *mother's* number. Olive – no "Mrs". It hinted at intimacy, closeness. Olive Bolger. Cosy, warm, familiar. And on the line directly underneath, Declan and Fiona Bolger. Jesus, all her bloody relations were in here.

Michelle's number? Yes, here it was, as expected, under M. She was tempted to phone her now and . . . what? Mark's phone number and address were pencilled in on the opposite page.

Ken had *no* listing for his wife on the T page. Just Terry Scott's number. Maybe she was under L for Leavy?

No, nothing.

W for wife or E for ex-wife? Toni laughed bitterly as she realised that she didn't appear in his little red book at all.

Thirty-Eight

Why wasn't she answering? Olive took a few steps back and looked up again at Michelle's bedroom window. Her daughter must have overslept – the curtains were still closed.

The O'Rourkes had a spare key. Olive slipped next door through a gap in the hedge and knocked. The neighbour, red-eyed and distraught-looking, opened the door.

"Sorry to disturb you, Mrs O'Rourke. I've been knocking for a few minutes and Michelle hasn't come down to the door. Did you see her go out this morning?"

Mrs O'Rourke wiped her hands on her apron in an agitated way. "No, I heard her telly on very late last night. Come to think of it, her alarm clock didn't go off this morning. She usually sets it for eight o'clock. I can hear it because her bedroom's next door to ours. Maybe she just decided to sleep in this morning?"

"I'm a bit worried. It's after one o'clock and she never

stays in bed this late. Could you let me have the spare key? I'd like to make sure she's all right."

"Of course, Mrs Bolger. I keep Michelle's key here in the drawer of the hall table. Step in for a minute."

"No, I won't come in, thanks. You've . . . I'm sure you're busy. Everything OK?" Olive took the key.

"Yes, yes, thanks." Mrs O'Rourke's face crumpled. "No, it's not, actually. I've been crying all morning . . . it's Billy, you see. He's . . . dead." She gulped hard.

"Your cat? Oh, I am sorry, Mrs O'Rourke. He was a sweet little creature, friendly."

"Yes, a real pet. He was part of the family. The children will be devastated, especially Zoë. I don't know how I'm going to tell her when she gets in from school."

"Was he . . . knocked down by a car?" Olive asked gently.

"No, he was far too clever for that. He never goes near the road . . . he never *went* near . . . I'm not sure what happened." She took a packet of Rothman's from her pocket and lit one.

Olive was edgy, she wanted to check on Michelle.

"I went out to the garden this morning to call him." Mrs O'Rourke took a long drag on the cigarette. "He's usually waiting for me on the window ledge for his saucer of milk. There was no sign of him and I called and called." Her eyes brimmed and her voice trembled. "I went down the garden and peeped over Johnson's wall but he wasn't there. Then I remembered that he often went in for a nap under Michelle's bushes. And there he was, stretched out in the sunshine . . . . I knew there was something wrong from the way he was lying there – all limp. I called Dan and he climbed over the wall." The ash from her cigarette fell on the carpet but she didn't notice. "Dan lifted him up in his arms . . . Billy's neck was broken."

"Oh, Mrs O'Rourke. How awful."

"We don't know how it could have happened. Somebody must have . . . "

Olive squeezed the other woman's hand.

"Dan took him in the car to Dollymount . . . to bury him in the dunes. I swear, Mrs Bolger, a grown man and he howled like a baby. It's just that Billy's been with us for over ten years. He's a year older than Zoë. I mean he . . . he was."

"You'll have to get another cat for the children," Olive said and immediately regretted it. "Not yet, of course. It takes time to – "

"Here, look! Dan's back. He'll be in bits. I should have gone with him."

Dan O'Rourke got out of his car, nodded at Olive and brushed past his wife.

"Go after him," Olive whispered. "That can't have been easy." She smiled kindly at Mrs O'Rourke and nipped back through the hedge again.

Olive remembered the little black-and-white mongrel, Teddy, they'd had years before. They'd got it for Declan's eight birthday. Her son and the dog became inseparable. Declan was nineteen when Teddy had to be put down and, even at that age, he'd taken it very badly. They all had. Olive swore she'd never have another pet – it was too upsetting when they died.

She opened the door and stepped inside. "Michelle! Michelle! Are you up, love?"

As she bent down to pick up the post from the hall mat, Olive noticed a belt lying on the floor, just outside the sitting-room. Yellow towelling. It belonged to Michelle's bathrobe. Maybe her daughter was taking a bath?

"Michelle!"

Olive put the letters on the hall table and went upstairs. The bathroom door was wide open, no one there. A black slip was thrown carelessly on the lid of the laundry-basket. Not like Michelle to leave it there like that. She must have been in a hurry – normally she was very tidy. She went into her daughter's bedroom and opened the curtains. Michelle's good black dress lay crumpled on the floor and the duvet and pillow were gone from the bed.

"Michelle!"

Olive rushed downstairs to the sitting-room which was also in darkness. She drew back the drapes. The television was still plugged in. Michelle never went to bed without unplugging it, she was meticulous about things like that. There was an empty glass on the floor beside the couch and . . . Jesus, Mary and Joseph, there was Michelle's pillow . . . but where was the duvet?

"Michelle! Michelle, love, where are you?"

Olive ran out to the kitchen. The bottle of Bioforce they'd bought yesterday stood on the counter beside the sink. Olive examined it, it had been opened. How much had Michelle used? Maybe it hadn't agreed with her? Could she be at the doctor's or in the hospital? No, sure it was only a herbal remedy – it couldn't have done her any harm.

Olive turned and accidentally kicked something over, soaking her foot in the process. She looked down. What on earth was a saucer of milk doing on the floor? She grumbled to herself, put the saucer into the sink and took a J-cloth from the press to mop up. She dabbed at her foot, there was nothing worse than the smell of stale milk. Billy must have been in here. She remembered Michelle saying that the cat dropped in to her two or three times a week.

And Dan O'Rourke had found the cat, dead, in Michelle's garden. Olive's heart thumped as she walked slowly towards the kitchen door.

It wasn't locked!

Her hands shaking, Olive opened the door and went out to the garden. She stared at the shed.

"Michelle!" she called, softly this time. "Michelle!"

Could her daughter be in there?

She held her breath and cautiously approached the shed, stuck her face up to the grimy window and peered in. The motor-mower, the clippers, the spade and garden fork. The floor could do with a good sweeping. In its usual place in the corner, the wheelbarrow. Nothing unusual.

She turned around to go back to the house when, inches away from her feet, she spotted something pink and furry, peeping out of the long wet grass. Olive stooped and picked it up. A pink slipper. One of a pair she'd bought for Michelle only last month.

One pink slipper.

Where's the match, Olive thought frantically. Where's the match?

Andrew Watkins was in high spirits as he walked up his teacher's garden path. She'd be delighted with his progress today. He'd spent hours and hours on the Debussy and he knew he had it perfect – well, as near to perfection as he could manage. He reached the hall door and was about to ring, but found it open. He walked in.

"Ms Bolger?"

A draught blew up the hall from the kitchen. She must be out in the back garden.

"Ms Bolger?"

Should he wait here? Go into the sitting-room? Yes, he could get started. He'd play the Debussy right through, let her hear it without interruption. She'd be proud of him.

The piano! Oh, thank God. She'd kill Michelle for putting the heart crossways in her like this. How *could* she?

Playing the piano – as cool as you like – and her poor mother, out here in the garden, scouring around for clues in the grass, imagining all sorts of dire things?

Had Michelle not heard her calling?

Olive rushed back into the house. "Michelle!" she shouted crossly and charged into the sitting-room.

Sitting at the piano was a fresh-faced, impeccably-uniformed schoolboy, who looked startled as Olive loomed over him.

"H-hello," he stammered. "I'm here for my music lesson. I'm a few minutes early and I wasn't sure where to wait."

"Thanks for coming over here, Fiona. Isn't this awful? Us sitting here in Michelle's kitchen and she's . . . God knows where. I don't like it. There's something radically wrong, I can feel it. Every morning after breakfast Michelle phones me, but this morning – nothing."

Her daughter-in-law poured Olive a cup of tea. "Something could have come up suddenly and she'd no time to telephone. Have you tried Ken?"

"Yes," Olive said worriedly. "He's not in the hotel, I was speaking to his secretary. He's gone to London for the day and won't be back till late this evening."

"Maybe Michelle's gone with him?" Fiona suggested. "A last-minute decision."

"With her duvet?" Olive snapped. "Her duvet's missing, Fiona. You can't explain that away. And there's the business of the slipper. Why was her slipper out in the garden?" Olive stood up. "I'm not waiting a moment longer, I'm phoning the police. I'll ask for that nice Detective Lacey."

"Dec says we should wait for a while. She'll probably show up soon. We don't even know how long she's been missing for – "

"Now!" Olive said triumphantly. "You've just said it yourself. Missing. Michelle's *missing*, Fiona."

"I didn't mean – "

"It doesn't matter what you meant because I know what I know and Michelle would never – "

"Wait till Dec gets here, Olive."

Olive sat down again angrily. "I don't have to wait till my son arrives to tell me what to do, Fiona. I'm not a total imbecile." She glared at her daughter-in-law. "I'm her mother, I know what to do – phone the police, that's what. It's the only sensible – "

"There's the doorbell now, that'll be Dec."

Fiona hurried out to answer it. It wasn't Declan. A tall, very handsome dark-haired stranger stood on the doorstep.

"I'm here to see Michelle Bolger, she's expecting me," he explained. He smiled politely. "My name is Cyril O'Connor."

Thirty-Nine

Olive heard the unfamiliar voice. She edged over to the bay-window to see who was talking to her daughter-in-law on the front step. Hopefully not another piano pupil – she'd had a hard time trying to excuse Michelle's absence to Andrew Watkins. He wasn't one bit pleased to have missed a lesson.

Olive was all of a dither. In her heart, she knew something was terribly wrong but she'd no real evidence that anything bad had happened to Michelle and she didn't wish to cause unnecessary alarm – this shilly-shallying was getting them nowhere and Michelle could be in serious danger . . . she'd phone Detective Lacey.

She craned her neck against the glass but no matter how much she twisted and turned, she couldn't get a proper view of the doorstep from here. Then, just behind Michelle's rhododendron bush, she spied it . . . the dark green car.

That did it!

Olive sneaked out to the hall and listened at the half-open door. Cyril O'Connor, she heard him introduce himself. The well-spoken caller from the other day?

Hadn't Michelle said she didn't want anything to do with him? What was he doing here? Her daughter had instructed Olive to hang up if he ever phoned again, and here he was telling Fiona that Michelle was expecting him! She picked up the telephone receiver and dialled 999.

Olive peeped out again and saw him going down the garden path. She couldn't let him get away – not before the gardaí arrived. She dashed past Fiona and out the door. "You're looking for Michelle?" Olive shouted after him.

Cyril turned around. "Yes, I told her I'd call today."

"She's not here at the moment, but we're expecting her presently." Olive ignored his perplexed expression.

"I was told that – "

"Would you care to come in and wait?"

He glanced at his watch. "Em, no, I don't think so."

Olive had to get him inside. "Oh do, come in and wait for her. She's only gone to the local shop and she'd be disappointed if she missed you."

"Well, maybe . . . yes, OK, thanks."

What was her mother-in-law up to? Fiona nodded embarrassedly at the visitor as she ushered him into the sitting-room. "I'm sorry, I got it wrong. I thought Michelle had gone into the city. Sit down, Mr O'Connor, I'll make some tea."

"Don't go to any trouble," Cyril said politely. Who was this woman? The older one was Michelle's mother, he recognised her.

"It's no trouble. Won't be a minute."

When Fiona came out to the kitchen, Olive grabbed her. "It's him. It's him," she hissed at Fiona. "I've called the guards."

"What?" Fiona was totally bewildered. "It's who? Who is it?"

"His car," Olive explained impatiently. "I've seen that car parked up the road for weeks, he's been watching this house."

"Watching? Olive, are you sure?"

"Yes, yes, I told Michelle about it. The police should be here any minute. Detective Lacey wasn't on duty, so I just said there'd been a burglary. I could hardly explain all this over the phone. I'll go and keep him talking – you slip down to the gate and take down his registration number in case he tries to bolt."

"Olive, you're being very melodramatic. I don't like this."

"Do you think *I* do?" Olive pushed her to the door. "It'll be all right, the guards will be here in a minute," she whispered. "I'll keep him busy. When they ring the bell, you let them in and then . . . Oh, my God, Fiona. Where's Michelle?" Olive wrung her hands. "What has he done with her?"

"Are you sure about this, Olive? He seems nice to me. Very nice. I can't believe that he has anything to do with Michelle's – "

"Do what I say, Fiona." Olive was peppering.

"You could be dreadfully wrong and you can't go accusing . . . there could be a perfectly good explanation – "

"I'm telling you, that man has been trailing Michelle. I'm not wrong about the car. I'm handing him over to the police!"

"But you've no proof, have you? Michelle's not here, that's all. She could be anywhere, she could have gone – "

"No, she could not. My daughter wouldn't leave here in her dressing-gown – "

"But you don't know that she did and – "

"Fiona, shut up!" Olive shouted. "Michelle would not go out leaving the back door *unlocked*! She's very careful about things like that – always lecturing me. She's been abducted or . . . "

"Please, Olive – "

"Something awful's happened to her, Fiona, I can feel it, and then there's the poor little cat – "

"Mrs Bolger?" Cyril O'Connor came up behind her, a strained look on his face.

Olive recoiled and knocked against the kitchen table.

"I think I was talking to you on the phone the other day."

Olive's stare was icy. "I know who you are, Mr O'Connor." Dear Jesus, what was keeping the police?

"I'm sorry, I couldn't help overhearing." Cyril walked over to the sink. "Michelle's not here, is she?"

"What have you done with her?" Olive spat the words.

Cyril O'Connor's mouth dropped.

"Run to the gate, Fiona," Olive roared. "Quickly. Don't stand there gawking, get help!"

"Mrs Bolger – " Cyril moved towards her.

"Get away! Get away from me, you . . . you blackguard!"

"Olive, Olive, stop!" Fiona cried.

"Lock the door, Fiona, lock the back door and take the key or he'll get away!"

"Mrs Bolger, please don't be afraid." Cyril came closer.

"One more, one more step and I'll . . . "

Fiona snapped out of her stupor and turned the key in the kitchen door. "What's going on here," she screeched.

"It was you." Olive shook her fist threateningly. "You're the one who's been hanging around. Parking outside for weeks – I knew there was something suspicious about it. Where's Michelle?" Olive's eyes flashed. "What have you done with my daughter?"

"Please, there's no need to be afraid," Cyril said quietly. "I'm here to help."

"*Help?* Don't listen to him, Fiona. Go into the hall and ring the police again."

Fiona continued to bar the door. "I'm not moving."

"Please, ladies," he pleaded, "You don't have anything to fear from me. I called to see Michelle, to warn her – "

A banging on the front door.

Olive's heart skipped a beat. "That's the police!"

The three of them stood, transfixed.

Two more urgent raps, then the letter-box rattled. "Michelle! Michelle! Are you in there?"

"Who the bloody hell is that?" Fiona gasped.

"It's Mark," the voice shouted. "Is everything all right?"

"Let him in, Fiona." Olive's voice quivered. "He'll be able to help us."

Cyril O'Connor shook his head in disbelief. How could he make these people listen?

Fiona sidled past Cyril and ran to the hall door. She opened it a few inches and peered out. "Come in, Mark."

The boy stepped inside. Michelle's mother was standing by the kitchen door, fear written all over her face. The woman who'd let him in looked hysterical.

"Go down to her," Fiona pleaded. "Don't take your eyes off him."

"Off who?" Mark rushed down the hall.

A tall, dark man was standing rigidly against the kitchen sink.

"What's going on here?" Mark asked sternly. He looked warily at the stranger. "Who are you?"

"Cyril O'Connor. I'm a friend of Michelle's. These ladies mistakenly think – "

"A friend?" Olive repeated scornfully. "He is not. This man has been pestering Michelle." She took a deep breath. "And now he's kidnapped her."

"You have it all wrong, Mrs Bolger, listen to me. I tried to warn Michelle about –"

"How can you deny you've been snooping around,

when I've seen your car parked here on numerous occasions? You've been watching Michelle – "

"Yes, I have been but – "

"Mr O'Connor," Mark interrupted, "you admit you were *following* Michelle?"

"In a way . . . I just wanted to make sure she was all right. I was afraid – "

"No, Mr O'Connor, it was my daughter who was afraid. Living in fear for weeks, I now realise. You've hounded her relentlessly, shamelessly. You're nothing but a – "

"Harassment is a criminal offence," Mark butted in.

"Harassment? I swear, I'm not what you think."

"My daughter told me what she thought of you, Mr O'Connor. She didn't want anything to do with you, maybe that's why you've – "

"You're wrong, Mrs Bolger. Michelle was expecting me today – "

"Rubbish!" Olive shouted.

"If you'll just hear me out!" He looked imploringly at Mark. "Please let me tell you – "

"Tell your story to the police." Olive folded her arms across her chest. "I'm sure they'll be very interested."

Cyril O'Connor slumped. "Please, oh please, listen to me."

Something about him got to Mark. "Mrs Bolger, perhaps we should hear what he has to say . . . "

"*After* the police arrive," Fiona said as she returned to the kitchen. "I phoned again. The squad car's on its way."

"You have to listen to me. I think I may be able to explain – "

"I don't want your explanations," Olive snapped. "I just want to know what you've done with my daughter. Where is she?"

"I didn't have anything to do with it – believe me, but . . . I'm almost certain I know where Michelle is."

"Where?" Fiona shouted. "Where *is* she?"

"Ratoath," he said softly. "I can bring you there now. I implore you not to involve the police – it would finish my sister – "

"What do *we* care about that?" Olive was enraged.

" . . . The scandal of it would kill her. I know I can handle this without garda involvement, if you'd only trust me."

"Trust you?" Olive exclaimed. "Your sister has kidnapped Michelle and you expect us to *trust* you?"

"My sister's not responsible." Cyril coughed. "She's very delicate, that's why . . . could I have a drink of water?"

"When you've answered the question," Mark said gruffly. "Where is Michelle?"

"I thought I could prevent it but – " Cyril put his hand in his coat pocket.

"Stop!" Mark jumped at him.

"Don't be alarmed. It's just . . . " Cyril took out a handkercheif and mopped his brow. "Please, a drink of water."

Forty

Tiny red-and-blue lights flashed and danced in her brain. Michelle forced her eyes open. Pitch dark. She was lying on her side. Her head pounded. Her chest felt tight and her arms ached. Her eyes closed again.

Where am I? What is this place?

Her nose itched, she had to scratch it. Michelle struggled to sit up but she was firmly bound. Rope. A thick rope tied her wrists behind her back. She squirmed and writhed but the rope roughly chafed her skin.

Little by little she was coming to and little by little she became aware of her body as fragmented bits: head, chest, arms, hands. Her stomach, bloated and nauseous, her legs bent back at the knees, cutting off the circulation, and her feet, when she finally felt them, were as cold as ice. She wriggled her toes and the rope tightened.

She was trussed like a chicken.

A searing pain shot through her lower back as she tried to roll her body from side to side. She was lying on something hard and cold. A floor? Soft material tickled her ear. A pillow? Could a bed be this hard?

She twisted her head as her eyes adjusted to the darkness. With a huge effort, she swung her shoulders forward. She was on a level surface, a very hard surface – had to be a floor.

Her mouth was dry, her tongue thick, swollen. "Water," she pleaded weakly to the emptiness around her. "Water."

What's going on? How did I get here?

She tried to grasp at what had happened last night but, apart from brief terrifying flashes, the whole thing was a blur. Her heart beat faster and faster as panic gripped her.

She collapsed back and moaned softly. Then the tears sprang. She lay there sobbing hot, salty tears until sleep mercifully came again.

"Michelle! Michelle!" He untied her hands. "Time to wake up!"

She refused to open her eyes. His face was inches from hers, she could smell his breath.

"Michelle! Try to sit up, there's a good girl."

She lay stiff with fear.

"Come on, up we go." She felt the rope being

loosened from her ankles and then her legs being rubbed hard. "That's better. You have to stand up, Michelle, I'll help you."

She closed her eyes and prayed.

"Get up," he said, angrily. "You can't lie there any longer." He propped her up in a sitting position.

Now or never. She opened her eyes and stared into his face but her eyes misted over.

He gripped her arm cruelly. "Do you know me, Michelle?"

His features were hazy, indistinct but, oh yes, she knew him.

"That's it, that's the girl. Now, lean on me and we'll get you on your feet. Don't fight this, Michelle." He pinched her viciously. "Stand up!"

"I feel weak," she protested. "I can't."

He gripped her under the arms and dragged her along the floor to another room.

"This is my shower-room," he said gruffly. "Fix yourself up."

Mortified, Michelle realised she'd wet herself. Was there no end to this horror?

"I've left fresh clothes hanging on the back of the door. Put them on," he commanded as he shoved her into the room and locked the door behind her.

"I need a drink," Michelle called out to him.

"Later," he shouted back. "Get ready."

Ready for what?

Michelle groped her way to the mirror over the small sink. Her face was deathly pale and huge dark circles ringed her eyes. She rubbed her tender, torn wrists and examined the skin. Big, red weals and blisters glared angrily, some oozing. Her ankles, too, were lacerated.

She was still in her dressing-gown but it was muddy and torn and the belt was missing. She turned on the cold tap and drank heavily.

She stripped off her filthy nightdress and shivered in the cold, tiled room. She stepped into the shower. The water was icy, stinging. She couldn't stay under it.

He'd left a clean towel on the ledge. She wrapped it around her bruised body and its warm comfort almost made her cry.

A dress hung on a peg. A pale blue dress – she seen it somewhere before . . . Oh, God, . . . it was identical to – a replica of one she'd worn years ago for a school concert.

Gordon James had attended the concert with his wife . . . he'd hugged and kissed her after the show . . .

Michelle shivered.

She remembered it all now. *He* remembered, too, that was the really frightening thing. All these years later. He'd somehow remembered that dress and deliberately gone out to get one the very same . . .

This whole thing had been planned.

Why? What did he want with her? Michelle pulled the

dress on. She was revolted. Gordon James was controlling her, manipulating, commanding, calling the shots. She had to get away . . . but she'd no strength, no strength at all.

Michelle was close to tears again. She couldn't let him see how upset she was. She'd have to play it cool. She'd pretend to go along with him and then, when she got some energy back, she'd make a run for it. There had to be a way. There had to be.

He opened the door of the shower-room, a wooden tray in his hand. "You look lovely, Michelle. Exactly the same as you did that night. The dress is a perfect fit. I had it made especially. Do you like it?"

There was no need for Michelle to answer.

"Here's some chicken soup. Sorry, there's nothing fancy but I found this brown bread. I think it's fresh. I buttered some for you."

She turned away in disgust.

"Michelle, why won't you look at me?" He placed a mug of steaming soup in her hand.

"I can't. Why do I have to eat in here?"

"No eating in the music room," he said sternly. "You know better than that, Michelle."

"The music room?" She turned around and stared at him.

"Next door." He smiled. "Time for your lesson."

She sipped the soup, her heart thumping. She was

terrified but she was starving. Bizarre, wasn't it? She was sitting here with a monster, so how was she able to eat? How long since she'd eaten with Ken? The meal in Il Corvo seemed a lifetime ago. How long had she been here?

"What time is it?" she asked sullenly.

"It's two o'clock in the afternoon but time's irrelevant now."

"What afternoon?" she persisted.

"Wednesday. You slept for nearly twelve hours. I watched and waited and let you sleep."

"Wednesday? Andrew will be waiting for his lesson and I have to be at the school at five. I – "

"At the school?" he guffawed. "You're not going *any*where, my dear. I'd a rough time trying to get you here and here you're going to stay."

"Please – "

"You were in a heavy sleep, like a coma," he continued, matter-of-factly. "Sleeping bodies are a dead weight, do you know that?"

"Gordon . . . why have you brought me here?"

He laughed.

"Please tell me. Why?"

"You really don't know, do you?" His eyes narrowed.

"No, I don't."

"I wanted you here, that's why. I invited you but you wouldn't come."

"But . . . but you can't do that. You can't invite people and if they refuse, simply *take* them by force."

"Can't you?" He scoffed. "I did."

"But," she spluttered, "that's kidnapping."

"Yes, it is, isn't it?" He gloated. "That's exactly what I've done with you. It's really quite easy to kidnap someone, by the way. Of course you have to plan carefully. The timing's crucial."

Michelle continued to eat the soup and not look at him. She'd play for time. If she kept him talking, she might be able to figure out a way to escape. There was no window in here but . . . the other room?

She'd ask him questions, lots of questions. He was bragging now about how clever he was, how organised. How he'd fooled everyone, even Ruth.

"Where *is* Ruth?" she asked evenly.

"Away. Holidaying in Cornwall in her cousin's home." He fondled Michelle's knee in a lecherous way. "We're all alone here," he said with a sneer. "Decent of Ruth to fall in with my plans. I wouldn't mind, but she only decided to go at the last minute. The gods were smiling on me, Michelle."

She'd show no emotion, no surprise, no fear. That way, he mightn't realise how repelled she was. When he'd touched her a second ago, she'd almost screamed.

"It was you, all the time, Gordon, even in Vienna, wasn't it?"

"Yes, me all the time." He leered repulsively. "Meeting you like that in the café in Stephensplatz – it was fate, Michelle. I'd thought about you a lot over the years, wondered about you, considered the possibility of bumping into you somewhere in Dublin. Of course I was ostracised from the music set . . . "

She kept silent. Wouldn't respond.

"I was tempted to join you that first night in the restaurant – you looked so lonely, like a lost little waif . . . "

Still Michelle wouldn't reply.

" . . . but then I thought, no, better to remain aloof. You were suprised when the waiter told you your bill had been paid?" He poked her arm, tired of being ignored. "Answer me, Michelle."

"Yes, I was surprised. Very surprised."

"I thought I'd add a bit of mystery to it. Nothing like a bit of mystery." He laughed loudly.

She bit into the bread.

"Mmh, and then it sort of took off. Actually, when I think about it now, I have to admit it started off as a prank – I wanted a bit of fun."

"Fun," she said quietly. "Fun."

"Yes, but then you disappointed me, Michelle."

She continued to avoid his eyes. She couldn't let him see the deep loathing there. "Did I, Gordon?"

That's it, keep him talking. Pretend to be interested in what he has to say.

"Yes, you didn't pay any attention to me, Michelle. I don't like being ignored. It irritates me."

"Gordon, I – "

"So I had to up my campaign, didn't I?" He ran his finger down her thigh and she flinched but he was too engrossed in what he was saying to notice. "The notes were good, I thought. It was easy to follow you around without being noticed. I took great pains to keep a few paces behind you in the Figarohaus. Wonderful place, eh?"

Michelle bit her lip.

"The streets in Vienna were crowded, busy. Nobody paid much attention. In Dublin it was harder. I resorted more to the phone. Inventive, wasn't I?"

He laughed again, smugly.

"Your answering-service was a bit of a surprise, Michelle. I was afraid you might record the calls but it wouldn't have made any difference – I always telephoned from a call-box, they'd never have been able to trace me."

"Why did you do it, Gordon?" Through sheer willpower, Michelle kept her voice calm. She wanted to throw the hot soup into his face, to scald him, disfigure him. From the depth of her being, she hated him for the torture he'd put her through.

"Why did I do it?" He took her face in his hands and glared into her eyes. "Because I wanted to make you see how it *felt*, that's why!"

443

He was hurting her but she didn't let on. "How it felt?"

"Being out of control. Being manipulated." His eyes blazed with a hatred that terrified her. Michelle thought he might strike her.

"Day in and day out, not knowing what might happen next," he went on. His voice rasped. "I had to make you *feel* it, Michelle, feel the pain, the terror, the shame; constantly watching over your shoulder, afraid when the phone rang . . . not knowing who you could trust. And you never told anyone, did you? You didn't *trust* anyone enough to tell?"

She shook her head, fighting back the tears of anger and humiliation.

"That's it, you see. Now you understand what it's like to be left out in the cold, to be different, to be condemned, to be . . . alone."

"Gordon, why did you do this to *me*? I never hurt you."

"Didn't you? Here, come and see."

He grabbed her by the arm and pulled her from the shower-room into a narrow hallway. She drew in her breath, in shock. On a table was a photograph in a makeshift wooden holder.

"I dumped the silver frame, had to. Along with a cut-glass bowl and some other garbage."

A photo of a young girl in a blue dress, sitting at a grand piano.

Michelle, in a daze, picked it up. The last time she'd seen this, it had been in her mother's house.

"I needed it, you see. Wanted to have the dress exactly right." He opened a drawer in the table. "These belong to you, too."

She stared, horrified, at her silver and bronze medals.

"The police . . . they arrested two boys . . . but it was *you*! You broke into my mother's home and . . . "

"They arrested two boys, did they?" He laughed. "Must have picked up the stuff in the lane. They deserved anything they got."

"Why, Gordon? Why?"

He shrugged. "I wanted them as mementos because I played a part in your winning them. I taught you the organ for four years, Michelle. Some of the credit for your brilliance belonged to me. How could you have forgotten?"

She'd won the medals for *piano* but he was past listening, past reason.

"I know what a wonderful teacher you were, Gordon and – "

"And you had me fired for it? Not very grateful, Michelle. I wouldn't call it grateful."

"Fired?" She stepped back and started at him. "What do you mean?"

"Complaints, Michelle. Complaints. Little rumours, nudge, nudge, wink, wink. 'Gordon James put his hand under my skirt', 'Gordon James tried to kiss me', 'Gordon James touched my chest' . . . do you see, Michelle? Do you understand?"

Michelle shook her head in disbelief.

"A few words in the right ear – in this case the parish priest's – and boom! I'm expelled. Career over. Removed, ousted, banished forever. Job gone, house gone, wife gone – to all intents and purposes. Ruth never let me touch her after that. I was a condemned man, do you hear me?" he fumed. "A condemned man."

"But, Gordon, I . . . "

"I didn't lay a hand on you, did I, Michelle? Ever?"

"No, no, you . . . you were always kind to me."

Michelle began to shake. A young girl's face came to mind. A pretty auburn-haired girl who ran out of a lesson, crying, swearing that she'd never go back.

"I took an interest in you because you were talented, that's all. You weren't the same as the others. You were my special student. But they accused me of *interfering* with you. Those *concerned mothers* told the priest – "

"Gordon, Gordon, listen – "

His eyes glazed over. A line of spittle ran down his chin. "It meant nothing, just fun and games, and anyway they wanted it. Yes, they wanted it, enjoyed it . . . I'd never have hurt you, Michelle. You were different – at least I thought you were. That was my big mistake – I thought you were different."

"Oh, Gordon, if you'd – "

"Enough! Come on." He grabbed her hand and pulled her up. "I've plans for you!"

"Gordon, please. I don't feel well – "

He didn't listen, he kicked open the door on the left and dragged her along behind him.

The music room was long and dark, the curtains closed. There was a grand piano in one corner. Four white candles in a silver candelabra threw ghostly shadows on the wall.

He pushed her forward.

Spellbound, Michelle approached the piano where the music waited for her. Yes, yes, the book was there. Though her tears dimmed her vision, she knew what piece he'd chosen – Mozart's "Fantasia in D Minor".

"Your favourite," he whispered in her ear, pulling the piano stool out for her. "First you'll play this for me, Michelle. Then I'll perform for you."

"Please, I feel ill, Gordon. Really ill."

"You'll be the first to hear my concerto – I wrote it for you."

"Gordon – "

"Begin."

She was dizzy. In the candlelight, her fingers slipped

and fumbled on the notes. She bungled the second *arpeggio* completely.

She heard him sigh angrily. His shadow on the wall was huge, intimidating. In a minute the candles would blow out, she'd feel his hands on her neck . . .

Forty-One

"Under arrest?" Cyril O'Connor was dumbfounded. "I haven't done anything."

"Aiding and abetting in the abduction of Michelle Bolger – I wouldn't call that nothing," the tall detective said. "You'll be detained for further questioning."

"I've explained all that," Cyril protested. "I'm co-operating with you, willing to go with you. You can't arrest me."

Detective Bill Murphy stood up and shut the sitting-room door. He didn't want to subject the Bolgers to any more unpleasantness. "Listen, mate, you're in no position to be issuing orders here or demanding your rights. Even if what you say is true, your part in all this is highly suspect. You've admitted to watching this house and that constitutes harassment. *Comprende?* It's a serious offence, Mr O'Connor."

"I told you, I was trying to protect – "

"Leave the protection to us," the sandy-haired

detective growled. "That's our job." He jotted down details in his note-book. "Why didn't you come to us when you first realised what your brother-in-law was up to?"

"I couldn't be sure that – "

"We're wasting valuable time here," Murphy butted in. "We have the address. Let's go." He took Cyril by the arm. "You too, Mr O'Connor. You've agreed to escort us."

"Yes, yes, OK." Cyril shrugged off the detective's arm. "I'm not under arrest, am I?"

"Let's just say, you're helping us with our enquiries."

As the two detectives conducted Cyril down the front path, he noticed a net curtain being pulled back next door. A crowd had gathered on the other side of the street. The garda car was unmarked but some people could sniff out stories.

"Mind your head," Detective Fennessy said as he bundled Cyril into the back seat. "We don't want any mishaps, do we?"

Was he being smart? Cyril couldn't make out his tone.

"Up the North Road, is that the quickest way?" Fennessy asked.

"Yes, and turn left before we hit Ashbourne." Cyril sat back.

Pity the way it turned out but he'd done all he could. Ruth would just have to face the music. He smiled at his private joke. "Mind if I light a cigarette?"

Bill Murphy turned around in the front passenger seat. "Go right ahead. It's not against the law . . . yet!"

"They've gone." Olive breathed a sigh of relief. "Pour me a drink, Mark. What's going to happen now? Fiona, what's keeping Declan? It's over an hour since you rang."

"He was in Leixlip, Mam. The traffic must be bad. He'll be here soon."

"Do you think Michelle's all right?" Olive's voice rose hysterically.

Mark poured a whiskey each for the two women. "You heard what Cyril said – his brother-in-law wouldn't be capable of . . . he wouldn't be armed or anything like that, Mrs Bolger. Don't worry, the cops know what they're doing."

"Armed? Oh, holy God, I never even thought of that." Olive tugged at Fiona's sleeve. "When did they say they'd phone?"

"It's nearly over now, Olive. Michelle will be home soon, safe and sound." Fiona wished she believed that.

"There'll be other police there, as back-up. Isn't that what they usually do? They're highly trained, Mrs Bolger," Mark said. "Used to these situations."

"But if they go storming in there, they could make matters worse. He could become violent, turn on Michelle – God knows what!" Olive put her head in her hands and started to cry.

Fiona frowned at Mark. "Please don't upset yourself, Olive. I know you're afraid, but think about it. This

Gordon James, why would he hurt Michelle now? If he's been after her for months, he could have . . . why wait till now? I don't think he means her any harm – "

"You don't understand." Olive took off her glasses and rubbed her eyes. "Gordon James is . . . evil."

"Evil?" Fiona repeated.

"It's years since I heard a word about him but I'll never forget him . . . that look he had in his eyes. He was bad." Olive stared into her whiskey glass. "He took on little girls, some as young as six or seven, taught them brilliantly, encouraged them, built up a relationship slowly with them and then . . . corrupted them."

"A paedophile?" Mark exclaimed. "Cyril-bloody-O'Connor never mentioned that little fact." He clenched his hands. "I could kill him! Mrs Bolger, Gordon James taught Michelle, didn't he? Did – "

"No, no, he never touched Michelle, I'm sure of that. I found out about him before he got the chance. There was one little girl from Swords. She had beautiful red hair and a big open smile. I knew her mother quite well. One day the child ran down the steps from the gallery – "

Fiona was horrified. "This happened in the church?"

"Yes," Olive said grimly. "Her mother was waiting in the end pew and when she saw her daughter she knew . . . the little girl's eyes were dead . . . the mother recognised the look because . . . because she'd been abused herself as a child."

Fiona groaned.

"Then there were rumours of other incidents . . . "

"Was that child actually . . . raped?" Mark was horror-struck.

Olive nodded.

"But the police . . . ?" Fiona asked.

Olive shrugged her shoulders despondently. "None of the women wanted the children further traumatised so . . . the police were never told."

"That's scandalous," Mark said.

"Different times," Olive murmured. "The priest was informed and Gordon James was removed from the job . . . he never taught again."

"But Michelle . . . she liked learning the organ." Fiona was baffled. "She liked it, she told me."

Olive nodded. "He was kind to her. Gordon James never did anything until he had the child's complete trust. Michelle was always a little aloof – maybe that's what saved her."

"And the parents trusted him implicitly." Mark sighed. "They'd have worried about their kids talking to strangers, but it would never have crossed their minds that the music teacher they employed to . . . it's the sickest thing I've ever heard."

"Gordon James always admired Michelle but . . . he hates me," Olive said blankly.

"You! Why?" Fiona looked at Mark.

Olive took a small sip of the whiskey. "He blamed me for getting him fired, me and the other mothers. He threatened me at the time, told me that one day he'd have his revenge. He's certainly done that, hasn't he? He couldn't have picked a better way to get at me than . . . "

Mark came over to Olive and took her hands in his. "Mrs Bolger, the police will find Michelle and bring her home. She'll be OK, you'll see. Michelle will be back with us very soon. She'll be all right, you've got to believe that."

Olive nodded and tried to smile. "I'd like us to say a prayer together. Would you mind?"

Forty-Two

"That's the house. There, the one with the blue door." Cyril squatted down in the back of the garda car.

"You can't be seen from here," Bill Murphy said impatiently, "too many bushes. Where's this extension you told us about?"

"It's not an extension, it's a separate building at the far end of the back field, but you have to go through the garden to get to it."

"Is there a side entrance?" Detective Fennessy took in the front of the house at a glance.

"Yes, through the hedge. The gate there leads to the field. The trouble is – he'll be able to spot you if he looks out."

"He won't spot us, Mr O'Connor," Murphy explained. "*You*'re the one going in. We don't want to alarm him."

"Me?" Cyril was startled. "You want me to go in to him? He never lets us in there, me or my sister. His music room's strictly off limits."

"You say you're not living here any more?"

"No," Cyril said gruffly, "I moved out a while ago."

"Where do you live now?" Fennessy asked.

None of their damned business. "Rathmines," he answered irritably.

"Your sister is away at the moment but you have this?" Murphy held up the key Cyril had given to them.

"Yes, this is the family home. I always had a key."

"OK, we want to accomplish this with as little fuss as possible. You go to the music room, tell your brother-in-law there's an urgent phone call from his wife. You said he'd no phone in the music room, so he'll have to come to the house to take the call. We'll be waiting inside the house. Right?"

Cyril nodded. He was afraid.

Michelle heard the knocking. Gordon had tied her again, this time to a hard-backed chair. He was intent on his playing and didn't turn around, wasn't distracted at all by the loud banging at the door.

"Gordon. It's me, Cyril. You've got to come to the phone."

Gordon played on, crashing through bar after bar of strident sounds. The music was discordant, jarring. A harsh cacophony.

"Gordon, can you hear me? There's an . . . emergency. It's Ruth."

What did Gordon care? Ruth had nothing to do with

him now. This was too important. He was here with Michelle as planned.

"Gordon, Gordon. Open the door," Cyril yelled.

The playing became louder, the melody more disturbed.

"Gordon!" Michelle shouted. "Ruth wants you."

He slammed the piano keys. "No, no, no."

"Ruth wants you on the phone," Michelle repeated. "She doesn't like to be kept waiting, does she?"

Gordon froze.

"Go in and take the call," Michelle said, very calmly. "I'll wait here for you."

He turned slowly and stared at her. "This wasn't supposed to happen."

"Go on, Gordon. I'll be here, waiting."

He frowned. "But our concert. What about our concert?"

Michelle managed a smile. "When you get back."

"But it wasn't supposed to be like this." He stared fixedly at some spot on the wall. His voice had become faint. "Not like this."

She held her breath as he rose from the piano stool and walked to the door. She watched him take the key from his pocket. He was about to put it in the lock when he stopped.

Put the key in, she screamed inwardly, put the blasted key in the lock.

"Michelle, you'll be here when I get back?" There were tears in his eyes. "You promise?"

"Yes," she lied and turned away.

"I have to hear you play again. You play so beautifully. My special student, you were always my special student." He was muttering now. "Different from the others."

Go on, go on, open the door. Open the door.

He turned the key slowly and Cyril barged in. Gordon walked by him in a daze, barely noticed him at all.

Cyril ran to her and untied her hands. "Michelle, I'm sorry. I'm so sorry."

Forty-Three

Gordon James puffed and panted his way through the long grass of the back field. What was so urgent that his wife had to ring him from Cornwall? Could she not leave him in peace for a few days? He hadn't time for this . . . this interference. Infuriating. How often had he warned her that he wasn't to be disturbed from his work?

Gordon ran faster – he must get back to Michelle. Aagh, a stitch in his side – he'd have to take it more slowly. He wasn't fit for this. It was so infernally hot. He pulled at his tie to loosen it, but the more he tugged and yanked, the tighter it got. Damn! Damn! When he reached the garden gate, he grasped the iron rail and paused to catch his breath.

He'd organised this day very carefully, down to the last detail, he couldn't let it be botched like this. He wouldn't. He finally had Michelle Bolger where he wanted her – in the music room – where she belonged.

She'd always recognised his genius, it was fitting that she'd be the first to hear his concerto. Michelle was the only one who'd understand his work – he'd written his masterpiece for her.

Ruth had to ruin everything; a phone call and his plans were smashed. Bad bloody timing – leave it to Ruth.

Michelle had said she'd wait, though. They could go on with the concert when he got back. Maybe all wasn't lost? His breathing returned to normal. He mopped his forehead with a white handkerchief. It wasn't too late to retrieve the situation.

He'd take the call from his wife, sort out whatever was bothering her and go back to Michelle . . . but . . . what about Cyril?

What would Cyril make of this? He was with Michelle right now. What was he telling her?

Why did Cyril have to turn up and spoil everything? Blast him to hell. He was as bad as his sister – a nuisance. The bloody O'Connors with their small-minded attitudes, their lack of ambition, their mean-spirited possessiveness. Ruth had made him come out here to live in the back of beyond and settle in *their family* house. She'd hidden him away from the world.

They'd given him nothing but trouble all his life – stopped him from developing his true potential. Yes, Gordon saw it all clearly now. Ruth and her lunatic brother had stunted him, suppressed his creative flow, stultified him.

Not any more.

Gordon would think of some way to get rid of his brother-in-law but first things first. He'd deal with Ruth's call and then he'd go back to the music room and . . . what the . . . ? Was that a movement in his kitchen?

Gordon's heart raced. Fear thudded in his chest. A high-pitched ringing reverberated in his ears. He clasped the squashed handkerchief and again wiped the beads of sweat from his brow.

He suddenly knew: there was someone waiting for him in his house.

Swearing under his breath, he crouched behind the hedge and peered through the scraggly branches.

Cyril had tricked him. The slimy . . .

He'd . . . he'd get Cyril for this.

Gordon wormed his way along by the hedge, keeping low, out of sight. Then he saw it. A black car. Police!

What now? He heard loud panting, then realised it was himself – his own laboured breathing. Almighty God, what was happening to him? Hunted to ground like an animal.

Why were they persecuting him like this? It wasn't right. Why couldn't they leave him alone?

Think fast. Got to think fast. If he made a quick dash for it, he'd reach his car before they spotted him. He could drive towards the North. If he got a head start on the police he might get away. He *had* to get away.

And Michelle? His heart sank. He'd lost her . . . and it was all Cyril's fault. If it took to the end of his days he'd *get* Cyril for this.

The roar of an engine and the loud crunch of tyres on gravel sent the younger detective flying downstairs to the kitchen. "Bill, did you hear that?"

"Yes! Come on! The bastard's getting away."

The two men ran from the front of the house, charged down the garden path and jumped into the unmarked squad car.

Detective Fennessy strapped on his belt. "What about the girl?"

"There's an ambulance on its way."

Gordon's Volvo slammed into reverse, then skidded forward with another screech of tyres.

"Boot, it Fennessy!" Bill Murphy shouted. "Quick, before he gets to the main road."

Gordon's knuckles whitened as he gripped the steering wheel. His heart hammered in his chest, his legs shook. The tremors spread upward through his body. Stay calm, stay calm, he told himself. His body began to go limp. Get control, got to get control.

The pain started in his chest, a burning stab that winded him. Please, oh please, God. The pain spread across his body, then shot into his upper arm.

No.

His took his right hand off the steering wheel and clutched at his chest. The pain was excruciating.

The trees, the sky, the road all blurred and the light began to fade. Gordon James slumped over the wheel.

Darkness.

John Fennessy hit seventy-five as he careered down the road in a cloud of smoke.

"Shit! We're losing him, John! Faster! Faster!" Bill Murphy swore loudly. "Come on, come on, man! Watch the corner, watch it! Jaysus, that was close! What must he be doing? Eighty? Eighty-five? He's a maniac. Look at the way he's driving that car. Christ, look! He's all over the road. Watch it, Fennessy."

"I'm watching, I'm watching!" Fennessy roared back.

"No, no, slow down. Slow down. We won't make the bend."

"Jesus, Bill, he's lost it! He's heading straight for that tree!"

John Fennessy braked and Bill Murphy lunged forward in the passenger seat with the suddenness of the jolt, bashing his forehead on the windscreen.

The crash of metal hitting the tree-trunk was an ear-splitting explosion . . . the silence after it eerie.

The world had gone into slow motion. The two

detectives got out of the police car and cautiously made their approach.

It was a typical crash scene, Detective Fennessy thought, and he'd seen far too many like it.

The Volvo was rammed into a massive oak, the front buckled and mangled. Shards of glass lay shattered and splintered all over the road. Thick black smoke belched from the bonnet.

Forty-Four

Fiona handed her mother-in-law the phone. "It's the police."

Olive gripped the corner of the hall table to steady herself. She'd been waiting for this call for hours. Michelle's neighbours had been very kind, dropped in cakes, offered to cook but neither Fiona nor herself could eat a morsel. They'd been too overwrought. They'd sat in the kitchen and drank cup after cup of tea, while Fiona chain-smoked. Every time the phone rang, Fiona ran to answer it but it was Declan or Lynn or Mark on the other end. Olive's nerves were in shreds.

"Hello."

"Mrs Bolger, you can stop worrying. Michelle's safe."

Olive flopped onto the hall chair. "Safe?"

"Yes. She's in the Mater Hospital. They took her in the ambulance."

Hospital. Olive started to shake.

"She's still in casualty, they're doing tests."

"Is she . . . is she badly hurt?"

"No, no. She's fine. The tests are routine and – "

"Oh, please, tell me the truth – "

"Hold on a moment, please. Detective Lacey's just come into the station, he wants a word with you."

Olive tried to steady herself but she felt faint.

"Hello, Mrs Bolger?"

"Oh, Detective Lacey, you heard what happened? Dreadful, yes, desperate. I'm at my wits' end here."

"Michelle's grand. She really is. She's upset, of course but physically she's in good shape, I was told – just a few bruises."

"Bruises? What did that animal do to her?"

"He didn't hurt her, Mrs Bolger. The boys got there in time – but she's in shock and naturally they won't let her out till they do tests to make sure – "

"Make sure . . . did he . . . oh my God, did he . . . rape her?"

"Michelle wasn't molested, Mrs Bolger. Listen, don't worry. Detective Fennessy is at the hospital with a female officer. Michelle gave them a full statement. They've assured me she's all right. You can have a word with them, it will ease your mind."

"I want to see her."

"Of course. Have you anyone to drive you?"

"My daughter-in-law is here with me. She'll bring me."

"Fine."

"Detective Lacey . . . did they get him?"

"Yes . . . "

"He's locked up?" Olive asked apprehensively.

Detective Lacey paused. "Eh, unfortunately there was an accident – his car. Gordon James is dead."

Olive almost dropped the phone.

"It was very sudden," Detective Lacey added.

"Dead?"

"I'm afraid so. Detective Murphy thinks it might have been a heart attack but we won't know that until after the post mortem."

"A post mortem? I see, yes, yes, of course."

Fiona Bolger sat at the kitchen table, listening to every word her mother-in-law was saying on the phone. She lit a cigarette and puffed furiously. She'd have to ring home and tell Declan to mind the kids for another few hours while she went with Olive to the hospital. Or would he want to go in? Probably not, Declan couldn't abide hospitals. And Michelle wouldn't want him there fussing. Declan took after his mother – no, that wasn't true anymore. Olive had changed.

Fiona had seen a side to her mother-in-law today that a few weeks ago she wouldn't have dreamed possible. Olive had behaved like a trooper – making tea for the neighbours who called, keeping up her spirits, smiling and looking after everyone else. She had been amazing . . .

"Good enough for him, I've no sympathy for that man. He may not have been guilty of any crime but his behaviour was . . . yes, I agree, he has a lot to answer for. But . . . Michelle, she's definitely all right? You're sure? Thank the Lord. I won't be off my knees for months giving thanks to God for Michelle's safe return. And thanks very much to you, Detective Lacey."

"I didn't do anything, Mrs Bolger. It was down to Detectives Fennessy and Murphy in the end."

"Thank them for me. I'll write to them later. Bye, Detective Lacey. Thanks again."

Olive put down the receiver and went back to Fiona in the kitchen.

Fiona looked at her. "Well?"

"She's all right, he said. A few scrapes and bruises and she's in shock, of course, but she'll be . . . "

Olive burst out crying. Her body convulsed with sobbing. All day long she'd kept her emotions under control but now . . . a floodgate had been opened and she bawled unashamedly.

Fiona, the tears springing to her own eyes, ran and hugged her mother-in-law. "Oh, Olive," she cried, her voice choked up.

"The Mater Hospital. She's in Casualty." Olive dabbed at her eyes. "Nothing serious, Dave Lacey said, but they're doing tests. Sweet Jesus, Fiona, it's over. It's over."

"We'll go to the hospital as soon as you feel up to it."

"In a few minutes." Olive clenched the tissue. "I hate that place . . . it's where Joe died. It'll bring it all back."

"I know, Olive, I know, but Michelle's all right. Keep telling yourself that. Michelle's all right."

"He's dead." Olive rubbed her forehead wearily. "Gordon James is dead."

"I gathered that from what you were saying on the phone."

"He tried to escape, the police car must have given chase and . . . he crashed."

Fiona nodded gravely.

"They think he had a heart attack at the wheel," Olive went on, "there's going to be a post mortem. You don't think . . . you don't imagine that they brought him to the Mater, too? His body, I mean?" Olive frowned. "It's gruesome to think about it. They wouldn't do that, would they?"

"I doubt it. No, hardly."

What did it matter where they brought Gordon James? He was dead, no longer a danger to anyone. Fiona felt sorry for his wife. Cyril O'Connor had tried to save his sister from worry and hassle . . . and now this. How was the poor woman going to cope with it?

"Did you hear anything about Cyril O'Connor?" Fiona asked.

"The detective told me he was at the station, answering questions. They've sent to England for his sister."

"It must be hard on Cyril O'Connor, too." Fiona lit another cigarette.

MARY McCARTHY

"Him? What do we care about *him*? He knew what was going on, Fiona. He could have stopped it. Why didn't he come forward sooner? Why didn't he warn Michelle?"

"I thing he was trying to," Fiona said quietly. "Isn't that what he told us? He did try to contact her – "

"He didn't try hard enough," Olive retorted bitterly. "He should have gone to the police."

"He was thinking of his sister, he didn't want her upset – "

"Upset? He didn't want *her* upset? Fiona, can't you see the seriousness of all this? Michelle could have been . . . anything could have happened." Olive shuddered.

"You're right. Of course, you're right."

"Come on." Olive took her coat from the back of a chair. "I want to see Michelle."

"What about Ken?" Fiona reminded her. "He'll have to be told."

"Yes, he will. He's due back from London tonight. I don't know what time his flight is arriving. Would you ring his house in Griffith Avenue? The number's in Michelle's address book beside the phone. His . . . his wife is there, and his daughter. Beth will know the flight time."

"I'll do it straight away." Fiona smiled. "You've been very brave today, Olive."

Olive sniffed. "I'll go and give my face a wash. Don't want Michelle to see me like this."

* * *

Toni put the phone down. She went into the sitting-room where her daughter was listening to CDs with Mark.

Mark jumped up off the sofa. "Any news?"

"Yes. That was Fiona Bolger. Michelle's in the Mater." Toni saw the look of alarm on Mark's face. "She'll be fine, her sister-in-law said. They're letting her out tonight and they wouldn't do that if there was anything seriously wrong."

"Huh!" Mark wasn't convinced.

"No, they're very good in the Mater, Mark," Beth insisted. "They were brilliant with Carmel. The nurses were super." She turned to her mother. "Michelle's all right?"

"Apparently." Toni searched the coffee table for her lighter. "There was . . . there was a car accident. A fatality."

"A fatality?" Mark repeated, aghast.

"Yes. The man who abducted Michelle."

"Jesus!" Mark put his arm around Beth.

"About your father, Beth, his plane's coming in at ten, isn't it? That's what Fiona Bolger wanted to know. We'll have to meet him to . . . to break the news."

Beth nodded. "Mark will drive you to the airport, Mum, won't you, Mark?"

"Of course. Yes, of course."

Toni hesitated. "I think it might be better if you went, Beth. You and Mark will want to see Michelle, won't you?"

"Not tonight," Mark pointed out. "Not after something like this. Michelle might be sedated or – "

"That's true," Toni conceded, "but Ken will need you, Beth, for moral support, and . . . isn't Michelle a good friend of yours, Mark? I still think she might like to see you . . . "

"I doubt it. She must be worn out. You know I had a feeling all along that Michelle was being . . . "

"What?" Beth looked at him suspiciously. "Michelle was being what?"

Mark shrugged. "Nothing."

He wouldn't say a word. Anything Michelle had told him had been in confidence. It was *her* business and he'd keep it that way.

"It'd be better for me to stay out of it," Toni said. "Anyhow, I've things to organise here. I'm going to see about our plane tickets. I think I can phone and book them by Visa. Hope your passport's not out of date, Beth."

"No, I had it renewed last summer."

"Well, Mark, I presume you've heard about our decision?" Toni lit a cigarette and passed one to her daughter.

"Yes, Mrs Leavy. Beth's been filling me in." He wasn't

sure what to say. "I suppose the offer of six months in one of the world's most exciting cities is too tempting to turn down."

"Quite," Toni agreed. Was the boy being ironic? Perhaps not.

"OK, Beth. We'll go to meet your dad at the airport." Mark checked the time on his watch. "I'd better phone my father and explain why I'll be late home with the car." He smiled apologetically at Toni. "My father always worries when I'm driving."

"Does he?" Toni replied pleasantly.

Would they ever leave? Toni wanted to be alone to get her thoughts together. This whole day had been a strain from the moment Mark had arrived to tell them about Michelle.

"Mum, I won't say anything about New York to Dad. Not tonight."

"No, Beth, don't. He'll have quite enough to deal with. Thankfully, Michelle wasn't seriously hurt." Toni poured herself another glass of wine. "If you do get to see her, Mark, please tell her . . . please give her my best."

Mark went to make his telephone call.

"It's been a scary few days, hasn't it? Beth glanced over at her mother. "At least Carmel's home. That's one good bit of news. She got an awful fright . . . so did I, Mum."

"I know you did, sweetheart. Maybe you were a bit

out of your depth? I think getting away from that gang for a few months mightn't be any harm."

"No," Beth agreed. "I think we both need a change, Mum."

"Yes, darling. We do."

Toni had a sad look on her face. Not sad, exactly. Wistful, Beth decided. Yes, wistful.

Forty-Five

"We'll have to X-ray that wrist." The doctor pressed her arm gently. He noticed her flinch. "Does it hurt?"

"A little," Michelle admitted. "But it's not bad. It's sore rather than painful – you know, the skin is very tender."

"It's quite badly bruised but I don't think it's broken. Still the X-ray will tell us more. Now a few more questions to fill out for this form for the radiographer. What was the date of your last period?"

Her last period? Michelle had to think. She was on about day sixteen of the Pill, so, sixteen days ago . . .

"Roughly?" The doctor hurried her along.

He was a bit abrupt but then Casualty was full tonight, as it was most nights, and Michelle would probably not have got to see the doctor as quickly as she did, if it hadn't been for the police. Detective Fennessy had Michelle rushed through. After the detective had taken Michelle's statement, a policewoman had arrived to stay with her. The guards couldn't have been better or kinder.

"About three weeks ago," Michelle answered. "It was a light period and it only lasted for a day or two."

The doctor got impatient. He peered at the computer screen. "Ms Bolger, is there any possibility that you might be pregnant?"

"Pregnant?" she spluttered. "No, no, of course not. I'm on the pill and . . . "

"Not an absolute guarantee," the doctor said abruptly.

She gaped at him. "I don't think so, I – "

"Let's make sure, eh?" He called to a nurse who scurried over. "Gravindex test for this patient, please, nurse. And make it snappy. I'm off duty in ten minutes."

"How's the headache?" the policewoman asked.

"It's almost gone, thanks," Michelle murmured. "Is it OK if I phone my mother now?"

"You don't have to, I've been on to the station. Detective Lacey has been in touch with your mother. Your sister-in-law is driving her down to collect you. They should be here any minute."

"Thanks. Do you know, I'm still feeling a bit woozy?"

"Shock. You've had a terrible ordeal, Michelle – both physical and emotional. Are they going to X-ray that arm?"

Michelle shook her head. "I'm not sure . . . they've given me a urine test . . . there's a chance I might be . . . "

Michelle shifted on the hard chair. The policewoman sensed her embarassment.

Pregnant? It was impossible. Mind you . . . she'd forgotten to take the pill that one morning but she'd taken two the following day . . . the doctor had given her a funny look when she'd told her that him her last period had been very light . . . and it had only lasted a day and a half but she'd put that down to tension, to being nervous . . . and the vomiting? The nausea? The running to the loo?

Could she be? That pressing feeling she'd had recently in the pit of her stomach . . . pregnant?

A baby?

Michelle felt numbed, almost dazed. Every now and again she nodded at the policewoman but she was too mesmerised to keep up a conversation.

A man was rushed through on a stretcher, screaming and yelling in pain. Despite herself, Michelle looked. The man was covered in blood.

"A stabbing," the policewoman explained as she glanced at her watch. "Nine-fifteen. It'll all be starting soon – the fights, the drunks, the motor accidents and then double trouble at pub closing time. You'd pity them here working in Casualty, wouldn't you?"

"Mmh," Michelle murmured.

The nurse arrived back and beckoned her into the cubicle again.

The doctor looked at her kindly. "How do you feel about that, then?"

"Sorry?"

"No X-ray for you tonight. We can't risk it. It could damage the baby."

Michelle stared blankly. "I can't believe it!"

"Your symptoms would have indicated – "

"I know, I know, but I thought . . . I thought it was tension. I've been . . . under a lot of pressure."

The doctor nodded.

"I'd no idea – it never occurred to me. I hadn't a clue . . . I can't believe it! You're positive?"

"You're the one who's positive!" He smiled.

There was a long crack in the ceiling. Michelle gazed up at it. It ran downwards at an angle and then branched off into two parts – like the river Ganges.

. . . She was sitting at the kitchen table in Shanowen Road, with her tracing paper, pencilling in the map of the river Ganges for her homework. Her father stood behind her, encouraging her. "Take your time, Michelle. You can do it." She was about ten years of age . . .

"Ms Bolger?" The doctor stood up. "I see this news is a bit of a shock for you – "

Michelle's eyes filled with tears.

The doctor glanced at his notes again. "Because you're unclear about your dates, we haven't determined how far you're gone but I'd hazard a guess at six to seven weeks. You'll need to see an obstretician. We can arrange – "

"No," Michelle said hurriedly, pulling herself out of her reverie. "I can do that myself. I'll go to my own GP first and . . . I simply can't believe it. I'm going to have a baby!"

The doctor added something to his notes. "It'll take a while for the idea to sink in. This probably wasn't the ideal time to hear something like this – you've had a hell of a day . . . but you're a strong woman, Ms Bolger. Very strong."

Michelle sat there, shaking.

A baby! She had a baby inside her!

"I'm sorry if the news is upsetting for you – "

"Upsetting?"

He had it all wrong.

"It's not upsetting, doctor. It's . . . "

"Good, that's good. You're feeling all right about it, then?"

Michelle started to laugh. "All right? Oh, doctor, I'm too gobsmacked to be sure how I feel but I . . . I think this may be the best news I've ever had in my life!"

* * *

Michelle sat in the waiting-room, her mind a maelstrom of thoughts, ideas, plans. One minute she felt like laughing, the next, weeping. It was a major miracle that she'd managed to stay in control. She wanted to jump off the seat and scream the news at everyone.

I'm pregnant. I'm pregnant. I'm going to have a baby. Ken and I are going to have a baby.

"You OK?" The policewoman asked.

"Michelle!" A cry from the far side of the room as Olive Bolger came flying over to her daughter. "Oh,

Michelle! I prayed to every saint and I prayed to your dad and . . . "

"Hi, Mam!" Michelle hugged her. She nodded over her mother's shoulder at Fiona. "It's good to see you!"

"Jesus, Michelle!" Fiona cried. "Is that all you can say?"

Olive shook hands with the policewoman. "Thanks for looking after my daughter so well. Is it OK if we take her home now?"

"Sure is! Bye, Michelle. Pity we had to meet in such terrible circumstances. Good luck with . . . everything."

Michelle linked her mother and Fiona. Then she remembered. She had to know. "Sergeant Nolan!" She called the policewoman back. "What . . . what have they done with him? What will happen to Gordon James?"

The policewoman gave Michelle's mother a warning look. "All taken care of, don't worry."

"But you'll want me for evidence . . . I'll have to make another statement, won't I? There'll be a court case?"

"That's another day's work, Michelle." Olive nodded at the policewoman. "Tonight you're coming home to rest."

"Your mother's right," Sergeant Nolan agreed. "You're not to think any more about it tonight. It's easy for me to say that, I know, but you'll have to rest. Try to get a good night's sleep."

"She will," Olive said emphatically. "I'll see to it that she does."

The policewoman smiled her goodbye and left.

"Now, Michelle," her mother said determinedly. "Back home and we'll forget all about this."

"But Mam – "

"No buts, Michelle. You'll have to put this behind you – it was a horrible thing to have happened but I think that talking about it will only prolong the horror."

"Mam, I want to talk about it, I have to."

Olive looked thoughtful. "Yes, maybe you do. Fiona and I will be there for you, we'll help you to work it through. You might need counselling, love."

Michelle paused at the exit door. "Yes, I think I might."

"I'll stay with you tonight of course and – "

"Mam, as far as I know Ken . . . Ken's staying, that's if he gets home from London and – how am I going to explain all this to him?" she said despairingly.

"You won't have to." Fiona held the heavy door open. "Ken's daughter and her boyfriend have gone to meet him at the airport, Michelle."

"Mark? Oh, I'm glad, that's good. I don't want Ken to get more of a shock than he's going to get when I tell him about . . . "

Michelle stopped. Ken had to be the first to hear her news. Her good news . . . her bloody *great* news!

"What are you beaming at, Michelle?" Olive asked as they came down the steps from the main door of the hospital.

"Just happy to see you, Mam! Grateful to be alive." She threw her arms up in the air. "Oh, it's started to rain.

I love the feel of the rain on my face!" She turned and grinned at them both. "Isn't it good to be alive?"

"I hope she's not concussed," Olive whispered to Fiona. "They should have kept her in for observation. It's a disgrace the way they throw you out of hospitals nowadays. No beds. Cutbacks. If your leg was hanging off, it wouldn't make any difference . . . "

Forty-Six

"I was frightened, Ken." Michelle curled up in an armchair in her sitting-room, sipping the cocoa he'd made. "So frightened." She stared at the folding doors. "Imagine – he was hiding behind those doors for hours – waiting for me to drop off to sleep!"

"If I'd only gone in there. I was going to go in and check the windows." He shook his head downheartedly. "Why didn't I?"

"How were you to know?" Michelle felt the headache coming back. "Gordon James really meant to harm me. It's horrible to think that anyone could hate me so much – "

"I don't think he hated you, Mich. In his twisted mind, which emotions were real?"

"He had no grip on reality. If you heard the things he said!"

Ken settled the rug around her knees. "I dread to think what might have happened if the police hadn't arrived when they did."

"He'd built up this fantasy in his head, saw me as . . . I don't know, a sort of nemesis."

"He was obsessed."

"Yes, he was – it was some kind of fixation. Gordon James was a complete eccentric, deep down I always knew that – even when I was his student. He wanted to play his concerto for me, did I tell you that? I was his private audience. He'd this bizarre notion of us playing together in that room and then . . . I haven't figured it all out yet, but neither had he." Michelle paused. "That's the really weird thing – I don't think he had a clue what he was going to do with me . . . "

"I'm glad we didn't get the chance to find out!"

"He wanted me to know how he felt, that's what he said."

"To know how *he* felt?!"

"Isolated. Cut off. Ken, I *did* feel it – "

"You're not isolated, Mich. You have people who love you, care for you."

Michelle wasn't listening. She was still locked up in the torment. "He'd carried this picture of me around in his head for years. He was very bitter about being dropped from the music scene and – "

"Bitter about being dropped?" Ken became enraged. "He deserved prison. He was a paedophile, Mich. He should have been locked up years ago."

"Yes, I know. But Ken, he wasn't well . . . didn't understand he'd done anything wrong, couldn't accept the damage he'd done to those girls. He'd convinced himself that he was the innocent party. He'd got used to blaming others for his own mistakes."

"Mistakes? Crimes, you mean."

"Yes, Gordon was a criminal," Michelle reluctantly admitted. "He'd have been appalled by that description of himself. When he spoke about teaching he got carried away. Enthralled. That's the sad thing – he was a brilliant teacher. Some part of me still believes that he did genuinely care about his pupils."

"He'd a sick way of showing it." Ken was disgusted.

"For years he'd harboured all these feelings of resentment and malice and revenge. The bitterness was gnawing away at him. Then he met me by accident in Vienna – it sparked off the whole crazy thing . . . and now he's dead." Michelle's lower lip trembled. "They didn't tell me that at the hospital. I thought he was . . . in custody."

"You'd had enough of a shock by then. They left it to me to tell you." Ken kissed her forehead. "This is the best end, you know that, Mich?"

She nodded. "Maybe."

"There's no maybe about it. When I think of what he put you through – what he put your mother through . . . "

"I'm home now, I'm fine. It's not a nice thing to say but his death *is* a release for me – no loose ends. It's a conclusion. A closure. It will be for Ruth James as well. She could never have faced a trial. Ken, do you think the police will be able to keep it quiet?"

"They'll do their best, Mich, for the sake of all concerned."

"If the papers get hold of it – "

"We'll set your mother on them," he joked. "Mich, I'm not putting this off for another minute. I know there's something else you've been dying to tell me but – no, don't interrupt, I've practised this speech all the way home on the plane and I have to get it said now before I lose my nerve."

"Ken – "

"No, just bear with me for a sec." He held her hands in his. "I love you. I want to be with you. I want us to live together. We ought to be together all the time, not like this . . . I think we should be married. There, I've said it."

"I agree," she murmured.

"There's no point in . . . *what*? What did you say?"

"I agree," Michelle repeated, smiling.

"You agree? That we should get married?"

"Mmh, absolutely. It's high time."

"You're serious?" He stood up and took his packet of Major from the mantelpiece. "I thought you were going to throw a fit. I – "

"You were right about everything, Ken. I see things differently now. When I was captured – there's no other way of saying it – I was held prisoner – when I was lying there, all tied up, alone and afraid, I started to think about my life, about you and Mam and my pupils . . . about what was really important to me."

"Your life flashed before you?" he teased.

"You know, in a way it did. I thought I might . . . I thought he might really hurt me, Ken."

He sat down by her and put his arm around her.

"He was demented, driven. There was something wild about his eyes . . . there was no knowing what he'd do. I prayed. I prayed but I didn't ask God for help. Instead I decided I'd give thanks. Me! I'm not normally one for prayer, but I sat there and thanked God for my life, my family, my friends, my career – sounds daft, I know. Gordon James was at the piano playing this over-the-top, macabre nonsense and I was tied to a chair, praying!"

Ken kissed her forehead.

"At one point I thought I'd landed slap bang in the middle of my dream – you know that horrible dream? But it was worse than any nightmare. When Cyril O'Connor rushed in, I started to scream and bawl like a child. You don't know how you're going to react until something happens . . . I never knew I could pray so hard."

"And me, Mich? Did you thank God for me?"

"Especially for you. I swore that if I got away, that if I came out of it all right . . . I'd propose to you. You're the most important part of my life, Ken. I don't think we should lose any more time."

"Do you have any idea how happy you've made me?"

"If it's half as happy as you make me, Ken, we'll be OK."

They sat there for a while, arms around one another, each locked in private thoughts. The silence between them was warm, intimate.

"Mich, what's this other bit of news you were bursting to tell me earlier?"

"The best wine till last!" She stared into the fire. "I thought Mam and Fiona would never leave."

"Well?" He tickled her. "What is it?"

"Ken . . . remember you said you'd love a second chance – "

"Now I'm going to get one."

"In more ways than one . . . "

"What are you saying, Mich?"

"I'm trying to break it to you gently that you're going to get a second chance at being a dad . . . "

"Being a dad? I don't – you mean you're . . . you're not? Michelle, are you?" He jumped up from the arm of the chair. "*Are* you?"

"Pregnant. Yes."

He stood there in front of her fireplace, a big grin all over his face. "Mich."

"A couple of weeks, they think, but I'll have to go to Doctor Cassidy to get myself checked – he can refer me on to a gynaecologist. My God, Ken, when you think about it – when you think of what might have happened. I might have lost – "

"Don't, don't. Ssh." He rushed to her and held her close.

"Gordon James was rough, very rough with me – I

could have lost the baby and I didn't even *know* I was pregnant."

Silent tears coursed down her cheeks.

"You didn't lose our baby, Mich, you hung on." He stroked her hair. "I love you so much. So very much."

"We'll be all right, won't we?" she whispered into his neck.

"Don't doubt it, even for a second. I'm going to mind you, take care of you." He drew back and looked into her eyes. "If you'll let me."

"I will, Ken. I want to be minded. I'm tired of being on my own."

"Mich," he said softly, "you'll never be on your own again."

* * *

Michelle slowly opened her eyes. Her mother stood by the bed, staring down at her.

"What time is it, Mam?"

"Just after nine o'clock. I made Ken an early breakfast. He's gone into work for a few hours." Olive sat down at the edge of the bed. "How are you, love?"

"I'm fine. How are you?"

"I'll survive! Looking at you lying there, Michelle, I was struck by . . . you reminded me of your dad, you're so like him." Olive Bolger sighed softly. "You were sleeping very peacefully, a radiant expression on your face."

"Radiant?" Michelle stretched and smiled. She spread her hands on her slightly rounded belly. "I was having a dream, Mam. I didn't want to wake, it was a wonderful, light-hearted dream. Pity life couldn't be like that."

Olive chuckled. "From now on, I think it might."

"Ooh, I feel so lazy." Michelle stretched again. "Sluggish."

"That'll get worse as the weeks go by, all part of the condition."

"Terrific!"

"But in the last few days, Michelle, you get this sudden burst of energy. It's amazing." Olive took her hand. "You know how pleased I am about the baby, Michelle. But," she hesitated, "how do you feel about it? Really feel about it?"

"Mam, I'm wondering if I can ever trust my feelings again. For years I'd convinced myself that I didn't want children. I genuinely believed it but . . . when the doctor told me – I was overjoyed. This enormous feeling of . . . relief, yes, it *was* a kind of relief, came over me. I felt suddenly liberated – that this was supposed to happen – that this was the way it was meant to be."

Olive nodded.

"I hadn't planned for it or thought of it at all and then, out of the blue, this baby comes along." Michelle chortled. "And I'm ecstatic about it. I really am. It's as if the *baby* chose to be born. Ken's and my baby, a tiny human being born out of our love – silly and sentimental, amn't I? I used to be cynical, Mam. I secretly thought that people who were engrossed in their children – I didn't understand."

"You don't," Olive said, "till you have your own."

"Having this baby . . . it just feels right."

"It is right. I'm so happy for you both. I can't wait for your baby to be born. I'm going to spoil him rotten."

"Or her."

Olive nodded. "Or her. What time is Ken coming back to bring you house-hunting? Are you sure you're up to it"

"About one o'clock, he said. Yes, yes, I'm up to it. He has his eye on a house in Howth. I'm not fussy about where we live, once we're together."

"You've finally come to your senses! Both of you! New beginnings, Michelle."

"Ken calls them second chances. Mam, I wonder how Beth will take the news . . . the baby, I mean."

"She'll handle it, Michelle. In time she'll come around. She's busy living her life – "

"That's what Ken says."

"Breakfast." Olive stood up. "You have a lie in this morning and I'll bring you up some tea and toast."

She watched her mother go to the door. "Mam," she called her back. "Lashings of butter. I'm starving."

"Understandable, you're eating for two now. Michelle . . . how about a couple of slices of bacon and some grilled tomatoes?"

"Sounds delicious." Michelle grinned. "Absolutely delicious!"

She laid her head back down on the pillow and

massaged her tummy again. "Hello baby! That was your gran. She's going to feed the two of us up for the next few months. By the time you're ready to pop out, you'll be big and chubby with a double chin and dimples."

Michelle turned towards the wall. An overwhelming desire to sleep again overcame her. She lay staring at the picture of her father on the wall. It was taken in the Garden of Remembrance about two years before he died. He was sitting on a bench, a newspaper draped over his knees. It was the day of her music exam, Grade V. She'd been very nervous and he'd gone with her to the academy, to give her moral support. Afterwards they'd gone to Wynn's Hotel for their lunch.

Michelle's eyes closed . . .

Coda

. . . She stood at the French window, looking out at the garden. It was late spring and the apple-trees buds were beginning to bloom, their pink and white flowers already opening up to the April sun.

She moved over to the piano, sat down and began to play. The lively rhythm of the Chopin mazurka lifted her spirits. The door behind her opened but she didn't turn around or stop playing. The footsteps behind her were light and quick, oddly familiar.

"Michelle!" he whispered. "Michelle!"

A gentle breeze from the open door fanned the pages of the music book. He approached to hold them open for her.

"I'm so proud of you, Michelle." He gently squeezed her shoulder. "I'll always watch over you."

Michelle searched his warm dark eyes and found peace. He lightly kissed her cheek, his touch tender, comforting. Then he moved away from the piano. Her

the keys, the melody
om.
her father had gone.

open window. Ken was
ball with a small curly-
ching them and waved,
ked to him. The little boy
Come on, Daddy! Kick it
" . . .

softly. The dream had
Changed . . . and nothing

Published by Poolbeg

REMEMBER ME

by

Mary McCarthy

Sheila is haunted by her past and the baby she gave up for adoption. She devotes her life to her skin care business, Natural Woman. Will success, affluence and fame compensate for the loss of Karen, her daughter?

Rita, Sheila's mother is a misguided woman whose interference could wreck her children's lives.

Caroline is married to Sheila's brother, Sean. Their relationship is threatened by his jealousy.

Mary, Sheila's friend has her own share of trauma. Will her marriage survive an affair and an abortion?

Karen is an ambitious journalist. She resents having been adopted. She is determined to find and confront her natural mother. But she wants to find her father too.

Donald settles back in Ireland after twenty years abroad, teaching. How will he react to the news that he fathered a child years before?

Remember Me is a story about love, loss, hope, family and ambition. It is, above all, the celebration of one woman's courage in the face of adversity.

ISBN 1-85371-610-3